The Women of Magnolia

Magnolia

by Marlene Mitchell

To Mae —
my pleasure
thanks
Marlene Mitchell.

a BlackWyrm book
Louisville, Kentucky

THE WOMEN OF MAGNOLIA

A BlackWyrm Book
BlackWyrm Publishing
10307 Chimney Ridge Ct, Louisville, KY 40299

Printed in the United States of America.

ISBN: 978-0-9827149-5-9
LCCN: 2010938671
Cover art by Marlene Mitchell

Second edition: October 2010
Third edition: October 2012

To my pal, Lydia Fisher Anderson.

I have known 'Fish' for almost forty years. We have shared the best of times and the worst of times together. She makes me laugh and she has always been there for me. She has encouraged my passion for writing even when I doubted myself. I can never thank her enough for just being 'My friend.'

Evan and Mary Elizabeth: The Beginning

Life is hard. No matter you be rich or poor, life can be hard. Some days it ain't worth gettin' out of da bed, but ya jest get yourself up and put one foot in front of da other.

Nona

Evan Vine sat astride his sorrel stallion and surveyed the workers in the nearby field. Their heads, covered in straw hats and bandanas, popped up and down like bobbers in a river of green. Running between rows of flourishing cotton plants, barefoot children kicked up dust, turning their skin to mocha. The elders chided the little ones and then once again bent low, picking the cotton tufts from the foliage.

Evan's horse raised his back leg and shied in an attempt to repel the insects buzzing around his tail. Evan clicked his teeth and the sorrel turned and carefully stepped between the ruts in the narrow corridors leading toward the road. Once on the packed mud, the horse knew his way home. Evan heard the voices of the Negroes rising in unison as they sang a spiritual hymn. It helped to pass their time as they performed their backbreaking work from dawn until dusk.

As the field disappeared from view, Evan relaxed and enjoyed the remainder of the ride. It was his duty to visit the fields at least once a day; a duty that he did not relish.

Chapter One

Evan Vine was heir to the plantation known as Vine Manor. When his parents wed, their combined wealth created a dynasty unequal to any other in Mississippi. Evan had every luxury a man of opulence could ever want, except the desire to own a plantation. After graduating college, Evan's family was shocked and disappointed that Evan would forfeit his future and choose to live in Europe rather than to follow in the family tradition.

He had no interest in rice or cotton or any other aspect of plantation life. He cared little for the social graces that were befitting a young man of his station in life. His outward appearance of arrogance kept people at bay. Evan was a self-imposed loner—a cover for the fact that he was painfully shy. As a small boy he had been afflicted with stuttering. It was difficult for him to make conversation and at times his father's booming voice would tell him, "Speak up boy!" This caused him to be even more withdrawn. Long after the affliction disappeared, his soft voice still prompted his father to admonish him by telling him to speak up. As an adult he worried that someday he may open his mouth and be unable to pronounce even the simplest of words. The relationship between Evan and his father was, at best, strained.

When still in school, Evan was forced to spend summers at Vine Manor. Being in the company of his father's friends was quite boring to him. Evan had never been interested in small talk and cared little for the constant debate of political and slave issues that always seemed to be the topics of discussion among the plantation owners. He despised his family's ceremonial dinners that lasted for hours. Rather than dress in formal attire and eat cold food, he preferred to eat alone, in his bedroom suite on the second floor, with a good book as his companion. He was also uncomfortable around women, finding most of them to be flighty, boring and only interested in their status in society.

Evan realized that he would never be comfortable living at Vine Manor.

After graduation, his dislike for plantation life made his decision to live abroad much easier. Evan settled in France. Living away made his life much simpler. Evan could walk down the cobbled streets of France, a book under his arm, and become anonymous in the crowd, something that was impossible to do in Mississippi. The Vine family, under constant scrutiny, was a favorite subject of gossip. Evan now had the freedom to pursue the three things he enjoyed most in life: reading, hunting, and procuring formulas for making fine wines and cordials.

In the winters, Evan stayed in Paris. He would visit the museums and peruse the shelves in the vast libraries. He found volumes of reading material, and devoured them each evening in his small apartment.

With the first hint of spring he was off to a small village called Marlenhiem in the Alsace region of France. Joining a few men who had become his acquaintances, he would spend his mornings hunting game and his afternoons stomping across the vast vineyards where a variety of grapes were grown. Evan enjoyed five peaceful years away from home.

Sitting in the dining room in the lodge, Evan conversed with his fellow hunters while they waited for the cooks to dish up the grouse hens the men had shot that day. Still wearing his hunting boots, he enjoyed a meal of game hen lathered with butter, roasted over an open pit, and served with soft bread and a bottle of Pinot Noir. It was during his meal that a courier was ushered into the room. The courier excused himself for the interruption and handed Evan a leather pouch sealed with a familiar wax stamp.

As Evan read the letter, a frown covered his face. He folded the paper and stuck it into his pocket.

"Bad news?" someone at his table asked.

"No sorrier than I," Evan replied.

Paul Dunn, the bearer of bad news was not only the business manager for Evan's father, but was also his father's good friend. Paul had lived at Vine Manor since Evan was a small boy. Evan was also close to Paul. Paul had more patience than Evan's father and had helped him with his studies when Evan was home during the summer.

Paul informed Evan in his letter that Evan's father had died suddenly and that his mother's health was also failing. She had become slightly irrational and he could no longer depend on her to make any kind of business decisions. The burden of running Vine Manor alone was too much for Paul to handle.

Evan was thrown into an impossible situation. He did not want to leave France, but he also knew that as the only son it was his duty to tend to his mother. He was unprepared and irritable at the thought of being the master of Vine Manor. He knew that any suggestion to his mother to sell the property would be met with shrieks of despair. There was nothing he could do. It was time for him to assume his duties.

Chapter Two

On the day Evan returned to Vine Manor he was met with smiles and bows from the house staff. They were glad to see him. Evan knew from Paul's letters that his mother, Rebecca, with her fragile bones, was now confined to her bed or a rolling chair, which made her even more disagreeable. She still insisted on presiding over the house staff. Rebecca carried a carved hickory stick in her chair and wielded it with little mercy. A piece of china out of place or a dinner fork with even a tinge of oxidation would bring the wrath of the stick.

Evan walked up the long winding staircase to his mother's room. He opened the door and slowly peered inside. His mother sat in her bed reading. She looked up from book, her glasses falling into her lap. "Well, it's about time you came home. Come closer to me."

Evan grinned. "Are you going to whack me with your stick?" he asked.

"Of course not. I want you to kiss my cheek. I cannot believe you have finally decided to give up that nonsense of staying in Europe." As he bent down to kiss her, he noticed her gnarled fingers were now devoid of all jewelry.

"How are you, mother? You look as beautiful as ever." He knew this remark would go to the core of her vanity.

"Oh, posh, don't lie. The five years you have been gone have not been kind to me. This damnable bone condition has left me a cripple and now I find that my only son prefers some foreign land to being home where he belongs."

"I didn't come all this way to listen to you complain, mother. I came home to take care of you. I am so very sorry about father. If I had known he was ill, I would have come home immediately."

Her face broke into a smile. "That's wonderful. I cannot tell you how happy it makes me that you have come back to stay.

Now, carry me downstairs and put me in my chair. We have so much to talk about. Your hair is thinning. You need to rub some chamomile on it before bed."

Evan gathered her up in his arms and carried her down the stairs. Her arms wrapped around his neck, she whispered into his ear, "Your father was not ill. He had been away for the night. When he came home, he was quite intoxicated. While he was trying to remove his trousers, he fell and hit his head on the bedpost. Paul helped me put him in bed. He died from his head wounds. I surely couldn't write that in a letter. Who knows who reads our posts."

Almost immediately after Evan's arrival at Vine Manor, he began to receive invitations to dinners and social gatherings. He politely refused them all under the guise of the overwhelming burden of tasks he needed to accomplish. Most landowners would like nothing better than for their daughters to marry into a family that possessed such wealth. Evan decided he would turn most of the mail over to Paul. He was better suited to make such decisions.

Evan was grateful for Paul's assistance since he knew every aspect of the complex daily life at Vine Manor. Paul was a stern man who ran the estate with a firm hand and was swift to deal with those who did not follow his orders.

A few weeks after Evan's arrival at Vine Manor, Paul made the suggestion to him that it was time to acquire several slaves to attend to his personal needs. "We all have our personal Negroes to attend to our needs. I have Mott and Evilly, and Ceria has been at your mother's beck and call for years. You must train them well and they can be a valuable asset to you," Paul said. "You should have a few slaves that will be loyal and trustworthy." These two words were not usually used to describe the Negroes.

Slaves were something that Evan had always taken for granted. He knew that the Negroes were a commodity used by all of the plantation owners for all manual labor. He paid little attention to them.

"Fine. Select a couple that you think would be suitable to my needs and have them report to me," Evan said as he looked over the stack of papers on his desk.

"No, it doesn't work that way, Evan. I cannot pick anyone that is already in our possession. They are quite loyal to each other and nothing said by you would be sacred. We will go into town tomorrow and you can choose several that you feel would be compatible to your taste."

Evan insisted he would trust Paul's judgment, but Paul refused. To actually pick out particular slaves made Evan feel uneasy. He had been away from the whole slave institution for over five years. Even before he had left for Europe, Evan had never been involved in selecting slaves. That was his father's forte.

Paul repeated to Evan that loyal slaves could provide a wealth of information as to what was going on in the plantation. They could help quell uprisings and also let their masters know when a flight for freedom was planned. He also suggested that Evan pick a man and a woman. The woman would attend to his clothing, food and the cleaning of his private chambers; the man would act as his valet and personal driver. He was also to make sure that Evan's horses were kept in the best of condition. Except for his parents and Paul, Evan's personal slaves would know more about him than anyone else and must be reminded to keep their mouths quiet.

Sitting on front-row chairs at the slave auction, Evan and Paul watched the parade of Negroes led from the long narrow buildings to the block where they were sold. It was almost a circus event, which seemed quite distasteful to Evan. Prospective buyers milled around in groups, talking and laughing while venders hawked their wares off carts that lined the street.

Evan felt he must make a decision before he died of heat stroke from baking in the hot sun or die of asphyxiation from the putrid smell emanating from the holding cages.

A young woman being led to the block drew his attention. She was small, with a straight back and a body that appeared to be void of seeping sores. She did not hang her head, but looked straight ahead as the auctioneer started the bidding. The roster of sales stated that her name was Nona. She was approximately twenty-five years of age, a good worker, with no apparent health problems. Paul seemed surprised at Evan's pick. The woman was younger than most personal servants and seemed to have a bit of arrogance about her. Evan nodded, putting in a handsome bid for the woman. As she exited the sale block, the next slave was put on the block. He was small in stature, but his eyes were

clear. Nona let out a low moan when she saw him. Evan watched
her as she turned to look at the man and he put his fingers to his
lips. Evan knew they were somehow connected. Yes, the roster
stated that he was indeed Nona's husband. When Evan opted to
buy this man, Paul was once again surprised, saying that the
man looked rather frail, yet Evan proceeded with the sale. Nona
and Jasper knew better than to touch each other as they stood
on the sidelines, but the joy in their eyes was enough to know
that they belonged together. They were put in the wagon with
the other slaves purchased that day and headed toward Vine
Manor.

Later that evening, Evan summoned Nona and Jasper to his
quarters. They stood in front of his desk and waited for him to
speak.

"I've purchased the two of you for a special reason. I am in
need of assistance in my personal business. I am uncomfortable
with people coming and going in my private living quarters."
Pointing at Nona, he asked, not really expecting an answer,
"Have you ever stolen anything?"

"Yes suh, I have. I stole some beet tops dat be thrown out for
da pigs."

Evan was surprised at her candid answer. "And you, Jasper,
do you have any experience with horses?"

Jasper grinned, showing gaps in between his teeth. "Yes suh,
I be real good with horses. I kin take real good care of dem. And
I be handy too; I kin fix anything."

Evan sat on the edge of the desk reading from the paper Paul
Dunn had given him as suggestions for training and keeping
personal servants. "As my personal assistants, you will live in
the quarters behind the kitchen. You will be available to me
whenever I need you. I expect my clothing to be kept clean and
in order and my food should always be warm—not hot, not cold. I
also want you to remain quiet unless you are spoken to."
Pointing to Jasper, he continued, "My horses are to be kept in
top-notch condition and my hunting dogs free of ticks and
mange. Is that clear?"

Almost in a state of shock, they both slowly nodded. "I also
would like to be apprised of anything going on with the other
slaves."

Before he could continue, Nona took a small step forward.
"Ya jest might as well send me and Jasper to da field to work.

We don't tell on nobody. It ain't our business." Jasper's eyes widened, knowing that Nona's tongue would surely bring them punishment.

Evan frowned. "I'll accept that for the time being. Now go downstairs and have the cook find you some proper clothing... and please, go outside and bathe as soon as possible." For a moment they stood motionless. Evan waved his hand. "Go. That is all for now." Evan gave a sigh of relief. He had made it through the first session of his new position with some sense of authority.

The idea that they were still together was all that mattered to Nona and Jasper. Many couples were split up when a buyer only wanted one of them. Nona had heard of women who had killed themselves rather than be alone, and of men who had run off trying to find their wives, only to end up dead.

To Nona, Evan Vine seemed like a nice enough man. He did not appear to have a violent temper like some of her past masters. She would keep everything clean and neat at all times, yet she wouldn't touch his desk. Nona would see that his clothes were kept free of lint and hair from the horses. She would also deliver his meals in a timely manner and never disturb Master Evan when he was reading or eating. She would learn to walk on cat paws.

After a few days, Nona found herself with more free time than she ever had in her life. When her duties for Master Evan were finished, she would go outside to the kitchen to see if she could help with the cooking. Preparing meals was one duty she always enjoyed. The women would immediately stop talking. It was the same all over the house. She was not welcome into the inner circle of the house slaves. She knew that they were jealous of her position and also afraid that anything they might say would be repeated to Master Evan. Her constant assurance to them did no good. She was pushed, tripped, doused with flour, and spattered with red sauce.

"We be needin' ta go talk to him together," Nona said to Jasper as they sat at the same wooden table in their room. "I be gettin' real tired of da others snubbin' me and doing bad things to me."

"Why yah want to start sumthin', Nona? Why can't ya jest leave it be? For dah first time we got to have a little rest and ya want to spoil it. Jest leaves it alone," Jasper said in an irritated voice.

Nona couldn't leave it alone and after another week of being treated badly by the other kitchen women, she quietly walked up the stairs carrying Master Evan's dinner tray. She sat it on his teacart. He was reading and didn't bother to look up. Nona fidgeted with her apron, twisting it round in her hands. Evan glanced over at her. "Yes," he said.

"I be wonderin' if I could ask a question?" she said.

"What is bothering you, Nona?"

"Somes of da others don't like me being here one bit and dey are resentful. I don't want to be startin' no trouble in yer house but dey be a real mean bunch." She was almost mumbling.

"It was my choice to pick a couple that I could trust and who would be with me for a long time. I do not like change. It is no one's business who I choose for any position on the plantation. If they give you any more trouble, you come to me and I will take care of them or you can just go about your business. In time it will work itself out."

"Yes suh," she said and scrambled out the door. In the hallway, she leaned against the wall and let the tears come down her face. He said he wanted them to be here for a long time. She and Jasper could stay together and maybe even have a family.

Chapter Three

Twice weekly, Evan would sit with Paul in the study to carry out the business of running Vine Manor. Paul would produce a mountain of paperwork for Evan to review. There were countless lists of supplies that needed to be procured, expenses for recent purchases, invoices that needed to be paid, and the distribution of the ever-increasing wealth that had been added to the coffer. As Evan had requested, Paul would then open the posts that had arrived and review them. Most he could answer, but occasionally Paul would place a few letters in front of Evan.

With his glasses pulled down on his nose, Paul leaned back in his chair and read the letter that was written on handmade vellum. He flicked the corner of the paper and handed it to Evan. "Here, I think you may want to respond to this. It's from Alston Handmaker. He was one of your father's business associates. He wants to pay you a visit."

"And why would that need my attention? I don't know the man and I doubt if my mother would remember him."

"Oh, yes, she will remember him. He always gave her compliments that made her blush. Every time he came to Vine Manor, he expressed interest in purchasing this property. He is living in Charlestown. Alston is a shrewd businessman, Evan. With your mother's health deteriorating, I think you might want to see him," Paul answered.

"Invite him for a visit," Evan said as he stood up. "That is enough for today. I need to get some air. My head is too full of business matters."

"By the way," Paul interjected, "He's bringing his wife and her niece from England. They are in the States on holiday." Evan was already in the foyer. He was ready for an afternoon of hunting.

Rebecca Vine sat opposite her son at the dining room table. She had insisted that at least twice weekly he share his dinner meal with her. It was a small concession that he agreed to since his arrival home. "I understand that we are indeed going to have visitors for a time."

"Yes, we are, mother, but I'm sure you won't remember the Handmakers. They haven't been here in years."

"My body may be failing, Evan, but my mind isn't. I want to plan a formal dinner while they are here. It will be the first since your poor father's untimely death," Rebecca said, giving Evan a soulful look. "I know you don't believe me, but I do remember the Handmakers. As I recall, your father had a fancy for Mrs. Handmaker."

Evan rolled his eyes. "Yes, mother, we're having visitors. Most of the time, Mr. Handmaker and I will be touring the plantation. It will be your obligation to entertain Mrs. Handmaker and her niece while they are here. They are only going to be here for a few weeks before they go on to New Orleans, so please do not invite the whole county to our house. Am I making myself clear, mother? If you want to plan a formal dinner, I will not object, but please, try to keep it small."

"Yes, dear," she replied, smiling.

In her bedchamber later that evening, Rebecca had Ceria push her chair up to her writing table. In her frail and almost illegible penmanship Rebecca began to compose a list of guests and supplies that would be needed for the upcoming festivities at Vine Manor.

In the weeks before the Handmakers' arrival, Rebecca was in a dither, barking orders at everyone who came into her view. She wanted the chandeliers in the foyer and the ballroom to sparkle. Every piece of crystal and silver in the house had to be cleaned and put on display. Rebecca spent hours with the cooks preparing menus and lists of food supplies that needed to be procured. Everything had to be perfect. Rebecca Vine was ready to entertain guests once again.

When the day finally arrived, Evan managed to stay out of his mother's way until early afternoon. Jasper had been sent ahead to meet the Handmakers' coaches. Rebecca insisted that everyone be properly dressed and at the front door when they arrived.

After returning from a morning hunt, Evan bathed and readied himself. Putting on a white shirt and buttoned collar, he opened the chiffonnier and pulled out a brown waistcoat.

"I be thinkin' yer tweed one would look real nice on you, today, Massa Evans," Nona said, as she put away his shaving kit, her back to him.

He hesitated for a moment, holding up the jacket. "Yes, I think you're right, Nona. I will wear this tweed one. Thank you."

Nona stood for a moment, holding the jacket over her arm. He had said, "Thank you." It was a well-known fact that Negroes need not be thanked. They were property.

An hour passed before Jasper returned home and told Evan that the coaches were just a few miles away. Evan poured himself a glass of brandy and drank it in one gulp. He smiled to himself. Perhaps he should give one to his mother. He entered the foyer, which was elegantly appointed in white magnolias and red roses. Rebecca sat in her rolling chair. She used a a silk shawl to cover her legs. A line of white-gloved valets and women servants dressed in their company attire stood behind Rebecca and Evan. The soldiers were now in place, ready for review.

Alston Handmaker escorted his wife up the marble steps of Vine Manor. The valet opened the door and bowed as they entered.

"Ah, Mrs. Vine, how nice to see you." He took both of Rebecca's hands in his. "You look as lovely as ever. You remember my wife, Amelia," he said, turning to the portly woman, who was red-faced and dusty from the trip.

"Oh, do go on, Alston. I am getting older as we speak and, yes, I remember your wife. I remember her quite well." A smile crossed Rebecca's lips at the sight of this rotund woman standing in front of her. "I do not think you have ever met my son, Evan," she said, waving her lace handkerchief toward Evan.

"No, I have never had the pleasure," Alston replied.

Evan shook Alston's hand. Alston looked anxiously toward the still-open door. "It's my niece. She was right behind Amelia and then she stopped to look at the roses. She should be here in a moment."

Mary Elizabeth Cates made a somewhat unconventional entrance. "Oh, my goodness, the garden is just elegant. I love roses," she said. "I must remove this bonnet immediately, my head is baking." As she removed her hat, auburn ringlets escaped from beneath the brim and landed on her forehead. "Oh, excuse me. I'm sure proper introductions have already taken place." She extended her hand to Rebecca and then to Evan.

Evan could see the look of annoyance on his mother's face. "Perhaps you and your niece would like to go upstairs to your rooms and freshen up, Mrs. Handmaker," Evan said. "A short rest will help you cool from the heat. I will have Nona bring you a glass of lemonade made with cold spring water to revive you." Evan tried to ease the moment, not really believing that his mother was at a loss for words.

"That sounds lovely. I am parched." Mary Elizabeth followed behind Nona as Amelia huffed up the stairs.

Alston waited until they were out of hearing range before he spoke. "You must forgive my niece. She is quite an ambitious young lady. Sometimes she forgets her manners, but I assure you she means no disrespect to you, Rebecca. She will thank you later for allowing her to stay in your lovely home."

In the first few days of their visit, Alston and Evan spent most of the daylight hours riding around the property and going over documents concerning Vine Manor. Evan had sworn Alston to secrecy as to the real reason for his visit. Evan had told his mother that the Handmakers were at Vine Manor for a purely social visit. He had forgotten how clever his mother really was.

After a long day in the fields with Alston, Evan returned home to prepare himself for the evening festivities. Nona had already laid out his clothes and he grimaced at the sight of the eveningwear. "Tonight my mother plans to shine, Nona. Let's all hope for the best. She has been looking forward to this dinner all week." He sat down and pulled off his hunting boots. "Have Amelia and her niece been enjoying their visit?" he asked Nona.

"I know dat Mizz Handmaker be doin' fine. You jest keep food in front of her and she be real happy. I ain't too sure bout Mizz Mary. Her auntie musta given it to her bad about da day dey got here and her makin' dem wait by da door, cause Mizz Mary don' say nothin' now. She be eatin' her dinner in her room. Dat be a real shame. A pretty girl like dat sittin here all alone. Maybe you could take her out of dis house and let her get away from your mother and dat Mizz Amelia. Dat is if ya want to," Nona said, meekly.

"I suppose I could do that," Evan responded. "Yes, I think that's a good idea."

Chapter Four

Dinner was served promptly at six in the summer months. Rebecca liked to enjoy her meals without the heat from candles. For her first formal dinner in over a year, she chose to serve her four-course meal on the china given to her by Andrew Jackson. Rebecca had taken the liberty of inviting fifteen guests in order to make an even twenty people at her elegantly appointed table.

As the guests arrived, they were escorted onto the balcony where Negroes in white jackets waved large bamboo fans in an attempt to cool the patrons. Perhaps it was the heat that made everyone seem so subdued or the actuality that some of Rebecca's visitors were weary from months of dinner invitations, yet fearful to refuse an invitation from the matriarch of Vine Manor.

The women seemed uncomfortable even in their sheerest summer dresses, and most of the men declined Evan's invite to share a brandy and cigar in the library before dinner in lieu of standing outside in the evening air.

When the clock in the foyer chimed six melodic strokes, Rebecca nodded to the servant standing at the dining room door. The doors were opened. Amelia took Alston's arm and started the procession to dinner.

At ten past six, there were nineteen chairs occupied. The chair to the left of Evan was empty. "You did tell Mary Elizabeth that dinner was served at six, Amelia?" Rebecca asked, frowning.

"Yes, of course, Rebecca. I tapped on her door when I prepared to come downstairs and she said she would be just a moment."

Small conversation spoken in low tones filled the room. The lone chair had become a symbol of defiance that was not tolerated by Rebecca. She picked up the small silver bell next to her napkin and gave it a brisk shake. Servants entered the room with tureens of soup, which were then ladled into the delicate bowls.

Alston was so ill at ease that perspiration beads formed on his forehead and upper lip. He ran his fingers around his shirt collar. "I'm sorry, Rebecca, I have no idea what is keeping that girl." He fretfully looked toward the door, waiting once again for Mary Elizabeth to make her appearance.

In between spoonfuls of soup, Amelia addressed Rebecca. "Mary Elizabeth is a fine pianist. Perhaps after dinner she will play for us."

It was at that moment Mary Elizabeth entered the dining room. "I am so very sorry to keep everyone waiting," she said, breathlessly. "I lost all track of time. Please forgive me." She rounded the table and took her place next to Evan, under the glaring eye of Alston and Amelia.

"You didn't keep us waiting, dear," Rebecca said, "As you can see, we have already begun our meal without your presence."

Mary Elizabeth lowered her head and whispered to Evan, "I'm in trouble again."

Evan could not help but be amused. She looked too lovely to be in trouble. Her face was framed with curls entwined in small white flowers and the green satin of her dress matched the color of her eyes. Yet he noticed that her hand shook as she tried to catch the small bits of vegetables on her spoon. After a few bites, she gently laid her spoon on her napkin and stood up. "You will have to excuse me, but I am not feeling well." Pushing back her chair, she bolted from the room. Amelia continued to eat her soup while the rest of the dinner guests waited for someone to speak.

It was Rebecca who broke the silence. "Evan, find Nona. Have her look after Mary Elizabeth. I would like to finish this meal sometime tonight." Her tone was stern and Evan knew that she was quite disturbed with the way this evening was progressing. In the past, Rebecca had always been in complete command of her formal affairs. Interruptions were not appreciated.

Nona had already found Mary Elizabeth by the time Evan reached the top of the stairs. Nona had taken her to the balcony outside the upstairs library. Mary Elizabeth was leaning against the railing with a pained look on her face.

"Are you all right?" he asked.

"I can't breathe," she said holding her abdomen. "It is this dress. I have not worn it in months and I must have gained a few pounds. All I did in Charlestown was eat. I was late for dinner because I could not find any of my evening gowns that would fit me. Nona helped me squeeze into this one, but when I sat down at the table, I could feel the seams giving way. If I would have raised my hand I am sure the whole dress would split apart. Right now, it is cutting me in two."

Evan began to laugh aloud. Something he hadn't done in a long time. "I'm sorry, Mary Elizabeth, I am not laughing at you. It's just the whole situation. If you knew how I hate formal dinners, you would understand, but I have never had the courage to depart as quickly as you did just now. I think it would be a good idea if you pretended to be ill to save what little grace you have left with my mother. Tomorrow I will tell her that a bit of fresh air will be good for you and I will arrange for a carriage to take us away from the house for a while."

"That would be just lovely, but after tonight I do not know if I will ever be allowed out of this house for the rest of our visit. If you will excuse me now, I should go to my room before someone discovers my secret. I will see you tomorrow." As she brushed past him, Evan heard the distinct sound of something ripping.

Evan returned to the dining room and explained that Mary Elizabeth was not feeling well and that she sent her apologies. His mother feigned concern, "Oh, the poor dear! I will have Ceria fix her some Chamomile tea." She was not fooling Evan.

After Rebecca bid goodnight to her neighbors, and the Handmakers had gone to their bedchamber, she sent Ceria to retrieve Evan. She wanted to see him at once. Still in her evening gown, Rebecca sat by the window removing her jewelry. When Evan entered she screamed at him. "That girl is incorrigible! First she leaves me standing at my door while she smells roses and tonight she embarrasses me in front of my guests."

"I have no idea why you're yelling at me mother, but I do believe that Mary Elizabeth was not feeling well tonight. Better be sick somewhere other than at your table, don't your agree?"

"Nonsense! No one gets sick at my dinner parties. Surely she could have at least made it through the meal before leaving."

Evan grinned. "Mother, if she would have stayed at the table, I think you would have really been angry." He could only imagine Mary Elizabeth's dress ripping from her body as she reached for a roll. "Goodnight, mother. Sleep well."

"Evan Vine, you do not leave my presence while I am still upset."

"Why am I the target of your anger, mother? I had nothing to do with this evening."

"Maybe not this evening, but I am sure you had something to do with the Handmaker's visit. Why did they find it necessary to bring Mary Elizabeth with them? Surely it was because they knew what a distraction she is."

"It had nothing to do with you, mother. The Handmakers thought it would be nice to show Mary Elizabeth some of the countryside before she returned to England. They expected it to be a pleasant trip. She is just different from the women you are accustom to, mother. She is unique and not at all like the uninteresting women you paraded into this house before I left for Europe. Goodnight, mother."

Evan went to his quarters and closed his door. He rarely had trouble falling asleep, but tonight he had something on his mind; it was not the business dealings with Alston. it was Mary Elizabeth. He was looking forward to spending time with her. What would they talk about? He was not known for being a great conversationalist.

In the morning, Evan made sure that the carriage was wiped dry of the morning dew. He had the cook prepare a basket of fruit and cheese and he had taken the liberty of selecting a light wine from the cellar.

Evan heard Mary Elizabeth laughing as she came out of the door. He was glad she was in good spirits. He took her hand and helped her into the carriage as Nona positioned herself in the buck seat. After everyone was seated, Jasper gently flicked the reins and the horses headed down the narrow lane leading to the road.

"I've been looking forward to this since last night," she said in her lilting voice. The soft morning breeze still held the coolness in its hands as an occasional droplet of dew fell from the Acacia trees onto the leather surrey.

Once the house was out of sight, Mary Elizabeth removed her bonnet and laid it on her lap much to Evan's surprise. "I really dislike hats," she said. "In England, the weather is so cool you are always told to wear them to protect your ears. My ears are fine. I love to feel the air on the top of my head."

She was not like any woman Evan had ever met. She was so unpretentious and unconcerned about the stray auburn ringlets that were wafting onto her neck.

Evan pointed out the Parrish plantation far off in the distance and also an occasional rabbit or squirrel that was inquisitive about this sudden intrusion into their habitat. Evan did not have to worry about a lull in the conversation. Mary Elizabeth's enthusiasm and questions kept the silence away.

As the sun began to erase the shadows from the road, Evan pulled the carriage into a small clearing. "I thought perhaps you would enjoy having lunch here. There is a stream just beyond the grove of trees."

"That would be wonderful. I just wanted to thank you, Evan, for your kindness last evening. I am sure your mother will never forgive me," she remarked as she removed her gloves. She motioned to Jasper and Nona. "Come, it is time for lunch. I'm sure you two must be hungry."

Nona shook her head. "You go on, Mizz Mary. I got sumthin' right here for us ta eat." Nona and Jasper had never been invited to eat with Evan and the shock of it caught him off guard.

"Ah, yes, Mary, they will be just fine. Now come with me and I will show you the stream." Evan nodded to Nona, which was her signal to spread the cloth and set out the basket.

Mary Elizabeth ran her fingers over the small, smooth pebbles she had picked up from the ground. She looked out at the clear water bubbling over the rocks. Tears glazed over her eyes as she stared down at the stream. "I don't fit in, Evan. No matter what I do, it seems I always find some way to turn things into a disaster. I thought today would be different, but I seemed to have embarrassed you in front of them," she said, nodding her head toward Nona and Jasper who were sitting next to the wagon. Tears now ran down her face. "I am sure the Handmakers cannot wait for me to return to England. I have caused them quite a bit of humiliation. I seem to always say the wrong things." Evan removed his handkerchief from his pocket and handed it to her.

Mary Elizabeth wiped her eyes and folded the handkerchief in half. "As a child I was constantly chastised for wanting to play outside with my brothers. I wanted to run and laugh and have fun. My mother always told me that it was improper behavior for a young lady. I had to stay inside and practice the piano or do needlework. It didn't change much as I grew older. The boys were off having fun times. I have never enjoyed the events that were chosen for me; stuffy luncheons with stiff women and cucumber sandwiches." She made a face, in distaste. "I'm British, and I hate tea! I detest sitting in a stifling parlor in a straight-backed chair, talking about nothing." She began to toss the pebbles into the water. "I would much rather curl up with a good book or enjoy the outdoors without a bonnet." They both laughed. "My mother said the kind of books I enjoy reading are scandalous. She wanted me to read poetry and the classics. I love a good story about the sea." She stopped talking and looked at Evan. "Oh, my goodness, I've forgotten my place, again."

"I have never fit in either, Mary Elizabeth. We are two of a sort. I don't believe my father was ever proud of me. I suppose because I did not chase women and get drunk on a regular basis I was not considered much of a man. I too hate formal dinners and stiff collars. I do not enjoy small talk about nothing and I would rather be out of doors than with my mother who constantly picks at me. I have a library full of books and you are welcome to read any you choose." Embarrassed by his words to her, he pulled the bottle of wine and glasses from the basket. "I don't know if bringing this along was proper, but I do believe we would both enjoy a glass now."

Sitting on the blanket, she held up her glass and he filled it. It was as if a huge weight had been lifted from both their shoulders and for the first time in months, she truly felt she was with someone who understood her.

She had no idea he felt the same way. They talked for hours while the ants took charge of the fruit and cheese.

Jasper came around the wagon and stood with his hat in his hand. "Massa Vine, I hates ta bother you, but it be nye on ta aftanoon. We best be getting' back to dah house."

Mary Elizabeth gathered up the dishes and put them in the basket and folded the cloth. "I just want you to know this has been one of the most enjoyable days I have had in a very long time. Who would have known that I would have to cross the ocean to find someone to talk to?"

Evan took her arm and helped her into the carriage. "Thank you for the compliment and thank you for making my day pleasant, too."

Paul pondered on the question for a moment. "Well, she speaks without thinking, she lets her imagination rule her emotions and if I were twenty years younger I might be a contender for her affections."

Evan smiled. "Thank you, Paul."

"You're welcome, Evan. Now do you think you can get your head out of the clouds long enough to get some work finished around here?" Paul retorted.

"I'll try, Paul, but it may be difficult," Evan replied.

The next three weeks passed too quickly for Evan. In between his business dealings with Alston and the social events planned by his mother, he spent the rest of his time with Mary Elizabeth. They would walk in the garden or share thoughts about a book they both had read. She never ceased to amaze him as she showed him how to make a whistle out of a blade of grass or the proper way to skip a rock. He tried to avoid looking at her while they shared dinner with guests. She had a habit of using her fan to cover up funny faces she made that were for only him to see. To keep from grinning he had to look away. Evan now looked forward to the evening meals knowing she would be sitting across from him.

On their last Friday night together, Evan and Mary Elizabeth sat on the balcony enjoying the breeze from an impending rainstorm.

"Doesn't that feel lovely, Evan? I can smell the rain in the air. Of course, by tomorrow my hair will be a mass of frizz and I will have to cover it with a cap."

Evan smiled. She always had a way of breaking the silence and making him smile. Tonight he wanted to be a little more serious. Evan stood up and walked to the railing of the balcony. "We only have a few more days before you leave. I have something that has been on my mind but I have no right to say this to you, Mary Elizabeth. I know you are young and much too energetic to even consider having feelings for someone like me, but—" Before he could finish his sentence she was in his arms.

"Evan, please, don't say another word. You can tell me I am too young, or that we have not known each other long enough, or even that we are not the same nationality, but it won't change anything. Just tell me you love me so that I know I am not making a fool of myself again."

"I love you Mary Elizabeth," he said, looking into her eyes.

"You mean more to me than you can ever imagine." Evan kissed her forehead and held her close until the rain began to fall and sent them running into the house.

Chapter Five

Mary Elizabeth decided to take Evan's advice and make some attempt to appease his mother, yet her new demeanor was not fooling Rebecca. Rebecca missed nothing that went on at Vine Manor. She had noticed a change in her son. For a long time she had considered him a reclusive bore, and now he had become more attentive to her and seemed to smile more than he ever had. She was well aware that he was falling in love with Mary Elizabeth.

Amelia Handmaker had recently told Rebecca that Mary Elizabeth's parents had only consented to a two-month stay and then she must return to England. After all, she was twenty-four years old. It was time she married and started a family. Amelia said that Mary Elizabeth had a bad habit of chasing off most of her suitors in the past with her tenacity and unbridled opinions.

Rebecca knew that Evan had never even expressed an interest in marriage, but if she could overlook Mary Elizabeth's unconventional ways, it could possibly change Evan's mind regarding the sale of Vine Manor. Rebecca was no fool. She knew that Alston Handmaker was here to make a bid for Vine Manor. If Rebecca could keep Mary Elizabeth at Vine Manor, Evan would have to reconsider selling the home Rebecca loved.

Mary Elizabeth wheeled Rebecca's chair into the conservatory and placed a shawl over her shoulders. "Here, Mrs. Vine. I don't want you to catch a chill," she said. Sitting across from Rebecca, Mary Elizabeth folded her hands in her lap.

"Come now, I cannot believe you are at a loss for words. Tell me something interesting," Rebecca said.

"What is it you would like me to say? We really have never had a real conversation. I suppose it is because I seem to always be causing you grief."

Rebecca put her head back and laughed. "My dear, you have no idea what grief is. Now tell me, what is the attraction you have for my boring son?"

"Oh, my goodness, Mrs. Vine. Evan is not boring at all. He is kind and gentle and he knows, oh so much about history. He has a sense of humor if you can draw it out of him and sometimes we just laugh at the silliest things." Mary Elizabeth did not realize that Rebecca was now smiling.

"Do you love him?" Rebecca asked.

Mary Elizabeth stood up and walked around the back of her chair. "I suppose in some ways, I do. No! Not in some ways. In every way. I do love him. Does that make you angry, Mrs. Vine?"

"Not at all. I love him, too," Rebecca answered.

The servants brought the trunks down from the garret and placed them in the Handmakers bedchamber. They also deposited two chests in Mary Elizabeth's room. The next day the maids would begin to carefully pack the clothing and accessories of the guests for the journey to the train depot in Biloxi. From there, Mary Elizabeth would be going home to England.

Rebecca's farewell dinner party for the Handmakers was given on the last Saturday in July.

After the wine was poured, Alston tapped the rim of his glass with his butter knife. "I would like to make a toast to my gracious hosts for allowing us to spend this past month at Vine Manor. It has been a most enjoyable visit. Rebecca, you and Evan have treated us with nothing but kindness and we want to thank you."

Amelia nodded in agreement. "Yes, thank you. It will be quite sad to leave here on Monday. I'm sure Mary Elizabeth would like to thank you, also," she said.

Mary Elizabeth sat with her hands folded in her lap. "Yes, I do want to thank Evan and Rebecca and I do not want to go home. I want to stay here," she said in a barely audible voice, without looking up.

"I'm sorry, Dear. I must have misunderstood you," Alston uttered. "I thought you said you wanted to remain here."

Mary Elizabeth stood up and turned toward Evan. "I said thank you, but what I really want to say is that I have decided not to return to England. I would like to remain here at Vine Manor. Unless Mrs. Vine refuses to let me stay."

Evan stood up. "Please sit, Mary Elizabeth. It is my duty to handle this."

Evan addressed the Handmakers. "In the past few weeks

Mary Elizabeth and I have become very close and I wish to start courting her with serious intentions of marrying her. I know this is sudden, but we both feel the same way and I do not wish for her to leave."

Alston's face reddened. "I do not think this is a proper time to discuss this, Mary Elizabeth. We will talk about this in private... later. Now lets enjoy this lovely meal." His fork clinked heavily on his plate.

Evan pushed his chair back and went to his mother's side. Bending down, so that his face was equal with hers, he took her hand, "Mother, please tell Mary Elizabeth that she can stay. You surely know that I need her here with me."

Rebecca searched his face. If she said no, would he tell her that he would then accompany Mary Elizabeth to England? Pretending to be upset, she said, "Let her stay, Alston. I will make sure that the proper rules of courting are followed and nothing will be planned without my consideration."

Amelia raised her hand to her head, and let out a loud sigh. With that, she fainted, falling from her chair onto the floor, catching the table cover on her bracelet. The next few minutes seem to create an accumulation of confusion, with wine glasses falling and startled guests backing away from the table. Alston and several servants tried to lift Amelia to her seat with no luck. Rather than be jostled, she sat up and leaned against the wall. Someone had dampened a napkin and placed it on her forehead. She closed her eyes again. How could she ever tell her sister that she had left her unwed daughter in the house of the man she intended to marry?

Evan and Mary Elizabeth had accomplished what they had planned to do. And so had Rebecca. They were going to stay together and, for now, Vine Manor would be safe.

On her return to Charlestown, Amelia Handmaker immediately sent a post to her sister, Margaret Cates, informing her of Mary Elizabeth's decision to stay in America. She explained to Margaret that the Vines were extremely wealthy and Mary Elizabeth seemed happier than she had ever seen her. Amelia begged her sister's forgiveness.

A month later, Rebecca Vine received a lengthy letter from Margaret Cates. Margaret said she was saddened by her daughter's decision to stay at Vine Manor. She was dismayed that Mary Elizabeth was going to marry a man that they had never met. Margaret wrote that she and her husband would not attend the wedding or send her dowry since they did not approve of the union. Rebecca showed the letter to Mary Elizabeth and Evan.

"Oh, pooh. My mother would use any excuse not to have to spend money on a trip to visit me. She is probably happy as a clam that I am not coming back and she does not have to give away any of her money. I don't care if my parents wish to keep every penny to themselves. I would rather live in a hut than go back to England."

Evan smiled. "My dear, I don't think you will ever have to worry about that."

Chapter Six

The temptation to be together was growing stronger every day for Mary Elizabeth and Evan. When they were able to slip away by themselves for a few minutes, they rushed into each other's arms. Holding her tightly, his lips pressed against her cheek, he murmured, "To hell with a spring wedding, let's get married before the holidays! I cannot wait to take you to my bed."

Evan's ensuing wedding had broken all tradition and protocol in the Mississippi aristocracy. No one would get married with only a two-month notice and especially since Evan's intended had not even been introduced into their society. The speculations ran rampant. Perhaps Rebecca Vine was ill or Evan was planning to sell the property. And of course, everyone knew that Mary Elizabeth was coming into the Vine family without a dowry. Even worse, perhaps Mary Elizabeth was with child. To keep the wolves at bay, Evan and Mary Elizabeth decided to marry in the parish church with only a few friends in attendance.

Three weeks before their marriage Evan informed Mary Elizabeth that he had to leave Vine Manor for a business trip and would return in four days. "Where are you going?" she asked, surprised at his announcement.

"It's just business. Something I must take care of before the wedding."

"I'm a bit nervous about being alone in the house with your mother for that length of time. Can you make it three days?"

Evan laughed. "I will be back to you as soon as possible. I hate the thought of not being with you every single day, but this is really important. Try to find things to do so that you will not have to spend too much time with mother. Tell her you have additional fittings on your dress or you're not feeling well. I would hate to find out that you two have been at it again when I get home." He pulled her into his arms and kissed her. "Everything will be just fine, you will see."

On the first morning after Evan's departure, Mary Elizabeth was summoned to Rebecca's bedchamber. Mary Elizabeth wondered what she had done to deserve such an early morning call.

Rebecca was sitting up in bed when Mary Elizabeth opened the door. She hesitated for a minute. Rebecca waved her gnarled hand. "Come in, come in. Just don't stand there. You're letting in a draft. Here," she said, pointing to the chair next to her bed. "Sit here. I had Ceria prepare us breakfast. You can eat while I talk. Now, I don't want you to say a word until I am finished speaking. Now about this trip Evan has so suddenly taken. I know what it is all about. Evan has gone off to Lott's Point to buy you a house as a wedding present. It is a magnificent structure called Magnolia. It belongs to a friend of ours and Evan visited there several times in his younger days. Evan said that you miss the ocean. This house sits less than a mile from the sea. Why you like the salty air is beyond me, but he wants you to have Magnolia."

Mary Elizabeth stared at Rebecca, for once actually speechless.

Rebecca continued, "The reason I am telling you this and spoiling his surprise is I know that once you are married Evan will want to whisk you away to Magnolia for God knows how long. I am not well. My physician tells me that my heart is growing weaker each day and that I will probably not live much longer. Even though, what does he know? I want to see my son married, but I do not wish to die while he is away on his honeymoon. You must convince him to stay here at Vine Manor after your marriage until my death. Then you can go off and do whatever you like." There was silence in the room. Mary Elizabeth sat with her head down, staring into her lap. "Well, say something. I am sure you must have something to say about what I have just told you," Rebecca said.

Mary Elizabeth stood up and leaned over the bed. She lightly put her arms around Rebecca's frail shoulders and kissed her on her wrinkled cheek. "I am so sorry, Rebecca. I will do whatever you say." When she stood, the tears lay on the brim of her eyes. "I had no idea you were so ill and I know sometimes I have made your life miserable, but you must know how much I love

Evan...and you."

"Good," Rebecca uttered. "Then we must practice your response so that when he tells you about Magnolia you will be surprised. Let me see your most startled look."

Mary Elizabeth jumped back and put her hands over her mouth and then threw her arms in the air. "How is that?" she asked. For the first time since her arrival the two women laughed together.

"Too much! Mary Elizabeth, you look as if you have just seen a ghost."

When Evan returned from Lott's Point, Mary Elizabeth met him at the door. She was anxious, knowing she had to deceive him about his surprise, but Rebecca had sworn her to secrecy. Surely her allegiance should be to Evan and someday she would tell him. Right now, though she wanted to make sure that she and Evan stayed at Vine Manor.

After dinner with his mother and Mary Elizabeth, Evan decided it was time to reveal his secret. Sitting in the parlor, Evan poured a glass of wine for each of the women. "My business was in a place called Lott's Point. It is on the Mississippi coast. I went there to purchase you a wedding present. It's a fine estate called Magnolia. My plan is to take you there as soon as we are married."

Mary Elizabeth threw her arms around his neck. It was almost impossible to look him in the face. "Thank you, my sweet, Evan. What a surprise." She winked at Rebecca who was sitting behind Evan.

"The problem is, Mary Elizabeth, I will be unable to take you there for a few months. There were some repairs that needed attending to and most of the furniture needs to be replaced. I thought since we could not use it right away, I would give you the pleasure of picking out new furnishings. I am still very disappointed. I was looking forward to spending time alone with you at Magnolia very soon."

"Please, don't be. It is just going to be wonderful. Besides, I think it would be nice to spend the holidays here at Vine Manor with your mother. We can go to Magnolia in the spring. Now come, I want you to tell me all about it." Mary Elizabeth took his arm and escorted him out of the parlor.

"My goodness. What has happened to you since I left? I thought you wanted to get away from my mother as soon as possible. Has she threatened you?" he said after they had left the parlor.

"Don't be silly, Evan. I'm fine," she said, hugging him. "Your mother and I have come to an agreement on several things and even had a few laughs together."

"Hmm...that is unusual, but I am glad," Evan replied.

Chapter Seven

Mary Elizabeth became Mrs. Evan Vine in a small but elegant ceremony at St. Stephens Church. Rebecca had invited a few neighbors and some of Evan's business associates. Rebecca purposely excluded the members of her society that had raised their eyebrows on the lack of etiquette shown by Evan and Mary Elizabeth for getting married without the proper interlude.

Dressed in a cream-colored, satin gown made especially for her, Mary Elizabeth was the picture of happiness. After a sumptuous dinner and too many glasses of wine, Mary Elizabeth and Evan slipped away from the reception and into their private quarters.

Since Mary Elizabeth had honored her wishes to remain at Vine Manor, Rebecca agreed to stay a week at the home of Mr. and Mrs. Parrish to give them the necessary privacy to adjust to becoming husband and wife. A time well spent.

On their first night together as man and wife, timidity overcame them both as they scrambled into bed and under the covers. Their first attempt at a union was awkward and left them both breathless and silent. "I'm sorry, Mary Elizabeth. I am really not very accomplished at this," Evan said. "Please forgive me if I hurt you."

Mary Elizabeth propped herself up on one elbow, pulling the covers over her bare breasts. "I do believe we have the right idea, Evan. We just need more practice." In the next week they practiced the majority of the time. They stayed in their bedchamber, surfacing occasionally to raid the kitchen or get a bit of fresh air. The house servants shook their heads and grinned as they heard the array of sounds coming from the upstairs rooms as they passed by the door.

When Rebecca returned to Vine Manor her first question to Mary Elizabeth was, "Well, am I going to be a grandmother in nine months?"

As Mary Elizabeth's face reddened, Evan remarked, "Mother, please!"

Evan tried to concentrate on his duties, but he was anxious to take his new wife to Magnolia. He continued to make trips between Vine Manor and Magnolia to check on the progress of the renovations and the delivery of the furnishings that were coming from Europe.

It was on one of those trips that Evan had his first encounter with August Lott. Just hours after Evan arrived at Magnolia, August appeared on his front porch. He was a ruddy-faced man with bushy brows and thinning hair. After introducing himself to Evan, August wasted no time in telling Evan that the town of Lott's Point was named after his grandfather. Almost every building in the town was built and owned by the Lott family. Evan had no idea where the conversation was going and politely interrupted August.

"I am sorry to cut this conversation short, Mr. Lott, but I am expecting a wagon of supplies to arrive at any moment and I must go prepare a space for them in the house."

"Then let me get right to the point, Mr. Vine. When I purchased the property adjoining yours, I was told that I would be the first one in line to acquire this parcel of land, also. My business is expanding and I need another access to the river. I know as a businessman you understand my predicament. I had no idea that the property had been sold." He stopped and gave Evan a false smile. "I know of your family, Mr. Vine. With the wealth your family possesses you can surely find another place suitable for you and your wife. I will be glad to pay you a fair price for Magnolia."

"Thank you for the offer, but I have already started renovation and this house was exactly what I had been looking for. I am afraid I must decline your proposal."

August Lott's face no longer held a smile. His hands closed into fists. "I don't believe I have made myself clear. I *need* this property. Name your price, Mr. Vine."

"And I don't believe you heard me the first time so I will repeat myself. This property is not for sale. I bid you good day, Mr. Lott." Evan turned and entered the house, leaving August standing on the porch.

Even though Mary Elizabeth was anxious to see the new house, she enjoyed her new role as wife of Evan Vine. Rebecca seemed to be getting weaker and stayed in her bed most of the time. Mary Elizabeth would sit with her. Rebecca initiated Mary Elizabeth into the duties of running a house. "Paul Dunn will be here to help you Mary Elizabeth. He is a champion when it comes to taking charge of situations, but I am sure he would appreciate your help with the household matters. We have a lovely house staff and they should give you very little difficulty." She stopped for a moment, watching Mary Elizabeth writing down her every word. "My dear, I think you will do well as mistress of this house."

Mary Elizabeth's eyes widened. "Oh, Rebecca, I would never try to take your place. I just want to be of as much help as possible."

Rebecca patted her hand. "My son made an excellent choice when he chose you for his wife. I must rest now, please close the door when you leave."

While Evan was away on one of his trips to Magnolia, Rebecca took a turn for the worse. Dr. Wilcox was called to the house. His report to Mary Elizabeth and Paul Dunn was grim. Rebecca's heartbeat had slowed to an almost inaudible sound. He could hear fluid rattling on her lungs. Mary Elizabeth sent a rider to tell Evan to come home quickly. She prayed that Evan would return home before his mother passed.

Sitting by Rebecca's bed in the dimly lit room, Mary Elizabeth heard the sound of horses coming across the cobble stones. Before she could make it to the hallway, Evan was bounding up the steps. Mary Elizabeth flew into his arms. "Oh, Evan, she is so weak. I am very worried about her."

Evan knelt next to his mother's bed and took her small hand in his. Rebecca opened her eyes. "About time you got home. Quit running off to Magnolia and stay here and take care of your wife. She misses you," she whispered.

"Even when you are ill you have enough breath to chastise me, you mean old lady," Evan said. A wry smile crossed her lips.

Rebecca died two days later with the ones she loved by her bedside.

The house was draped in black, but the sky was clear blue the day Rebecca was put to rest in the family cemetery. At the end of the service the mourners began to dissipate, heading back to Vine Manor for a reception in Rebecca's honor.

Rebecca's loyal servants moved in closer to her grave. Even

though she would never admit it, Rebecca was fond of the song *Swing Low Sweet Chariot*. Much to the dismay of some of the attendants, the Negroes broke into the song as a lasting memory to a kind, sharp-tongued woman whom they loved. Mary Elizabeth stood next to Evan, holding his arm tightly. The queasiness she felt in her stomach was not only her grief, but also the actuality that she was pregnant.

"I am going to miss her," Evan said as they rode back to the house in the carriage. "We never had a real close relationship, but she always intervened when my father berated me. These last few years have made me appreciate her and I know she loved me, too."

Mary Elizabeth waited a few weeks until she was sure of her condition before telling Evan. Preparing for bed, she sat at her vanity brushing her hair. Evan came up behind her and put his hand on her shoulders. "You are so beautiful and lately you seem to have a glow about you."

"That is because I do believe I am with child," she said. "I know that this is a very sad time for both of us and I wish your mother could have been here to see her first grandchild. But, good time or not, it has happened."

He was caught completely off guard. "Are you sure? Perhaps it's just your nerves and I know you haven't been eating very well the last couple of days."

"I can't eat, Evan. It makes me feel even worse. Are you not pleased with the idea of being a father?"

"I suppose I have been so happy and in love with you that I never gave it much thought." He took her into his arms. "Of course, I'm happy."

After Mary Elizabeth had gone to bed, Evan sat in a chair by the window. He wondered if he was really happy about the pregnancy. There had been little time for just the two of them to enjoy each other and now there would be a baby. Evan had no doubt that Mary Elizabeth would be a wonderful mother.

Three months after Rebecca's death, the black coverings were removed from the furniture and life at Vine Manor continued on. Mary Elizabeth was now very sure she was pregnant. Nona was overjoyed at the idea of having a new baby in the house. Even Paul Dunn expressed congratulations, saying he looked forward to the event.

Mary Elizabeth seemed more attentive to her husband than

ever. Evan wondered if she had sensed his trepidation about the baby and wanted to reassure him of her love. When Evan asked her, Mary Elizabeth laughed. "My dearest husband, you will always be first in my heart. Our child is just an added bonus to the love we feel for each other." If Evan had any doubts about her love for him, they were quickly put to rest.

Chapter Eight

As she arose from bed on a rainy Sunday morning, the sharp pains in her stomach made Mary Elizabeth double over. She called for Nona to help her. She knew something was terribly wrong. When the blood appeared on the bed cover, Mary Elizabeth let out a moan.

Just a little over three months into her pregnancy, Mary Elizabeth now lay in bed recovering from a miscarriage that left her weak and in tears. Evan comforted her the best he could, knowing she was devastated at the loss of their unborn child.

"I wanted so desperately to have a child and now it's all over." She buried her face in her hands. "What if I can never conceive again, Evan?"

"With or without children, I will still love you forever. But I know we will have lots of children. This time it was just not to be. You must take time to rest and get your strength back. In a few months we'll go to Magnolia." He sat in the chair next to her as she napped in a restless sleep. Nothing could ever make him stop loving her.

With Paul's blessings and a promise to take care of Vine Manor during Evan's absence, plans were made for their trip to Magnolia.

In February, Evan had a new barouche delivered. It was made of fine Italian leather to keep out the cold wind and to provide space for the luggage they were taking to Magnolia. Wrapped in a fur-lined blanket, Mary Elizabeth snuggled next to her husband. Wanting to have as much privacy as possible, she had decided to take only Jasper and Nona with them. The small staff at Magnolia would be more than adequate to take care of their needs. They would stop at a wayside inn before evenfall and continue their journey in the morning. Mary Elizabeth had recovered her strength and was eager to see this home that she had heard so much about from Evan.

After a two-day trip they arrived late the next afternoon just as the sun dipped below the shoreline.

"You keep telling me we are very near the house. Why can't I see it?" Mary Elizabeth asked, peering out the window of the coach.

"Be patient, we are almost there," Evan replied. "Look just beyond that grove of cypress and you will see the roof line." Evan's description of the house had been exact. An elegant front garden and manicured lawn framed a white clapboard house made of tidewater cypress. Evan had the portico extended to surround three sides of the house with stone steps encased in white newel posts that led to the front door. It gave the house a warm and inviting feeling. Balconies with rails made from ornate metal extended from each rounded window on the second and third floors. Evan had conceived the idea of putting a master bedroom suite on the first floor along with a birthing room next to it. When Mary Elizabeth was with child, she could spend her days as she wished, not confined to an upstairs chamber. Outside of the house Evan had the gardeners plant pink rose bushes and a white magnolia tree.

As Evan followed Mary Elizabeth through each room and watched the look of awe on her face, he could not stop grinning. He had planned everything just for her. Remembering each detail that she had mentioned in off-handed conversations about her home in England, he tried to duplicate her memories. Elegant Haviland china filled the dining room sideboards. Irish lace throws covered the backs of brocade chairs in the parlor. Evan had a black lacquered piano made especially for his new wife. It was just like the one she told him she had as a child. She was motionless for a moment. "Oh, Evan, I love it!" She sat down and ran her fingers across the smooth white keys, a melodic sound filling the room.

Climbing the stairs into the garret on the third floor, he pulled her to the window, "Someday we will have to use these rooms for all of our children. You can bring them to this window and tell them about your home far across the sea."

"This house is so beautiful and what you have done with it is amazing. There are not enough words to tell you what this means to me." That night, for the first time since the loss of their child, they came together in the bed covered in soft eider and dressed in English linens.

Mary Elizabeth blossomed during their stay at Magnolia. She and Evan would walk on the beach collecting shells to give to Nona. When the weather allowed, they would spend their evenings on the veranda listening to the sounds of the tree frogs and night birds. At other times she would sit at the piano and play for him. Her cheeks glowed from the unsullied air and her appetite returned to normal.

Nona made pies from the jars of fruit in the pantry and cooked fresh seafood that Jasper caught in his wooden traps. Life was good and even though Mary Elizabeth seemed content, occasionally, Evan could see a far away look in her eyes and he knew she was thinking about the child that would never be. His heart ached for her. Why was his grief only for her and not the unborn child? Was he emotionless when it came to another person coming into their lives? Perhaps he could not conceive of the idea of loving a child as much as he loved her.

Chapter Nine

In early April, a courier delivered a letter from Paul Dunn to Evan. The planting season was not going smoothly. Several Negroes had tried to escape from the plantation. When the overseers and their posse confronted the men, a fight broke out and one of the slaves was fatally shot. An insurgence was rapidly approaching and Paul wanted Evan to return to Vine Manor as soon as possible. Trying to quell Mary Elizabeth's fears when he told her she must remain at Magnolia while he attended to matters at home was not easy. After continued questioning, and knowing she would find out eventually, Evan told her the reason she had to stay behind. He wanted her to be safe until things calmed down at the plantation.

"These matters can usually be resolved quickly if they are caught early. Left to fester for very long we could have quite a mess on our hands. I don't want you to have to take sides against the house staff. Even though they love you, Mary Elizabeth, you are still the wife of their Master. It would best for you to stay here with Nona and Jasper."

"Why, why did they shoot the man? Surely, he was unarmed. I just don't understand this whole concept of slavery. It is hard for me to imagine that you actually own those people and then have the right to shoot them."

"My Christian beliefs tell me it is wrong, Mary Elizabeth, but you must realize that the Negroes are an inferior race and incapable of ever being our equal. We are providing them with a way of life that is quite suitable for them. Left on their own they would surely perish. Someday it may all change, but for now, I have to make sure that no one else gets hurt. I need to go to Vine Manor and talk to the Negroes. Usually these things can be halted without too much damage, but I insist you stay here." He was adamant about his decision.

"You are my husband and I will obey you, but this is not the last discussion we are going to have on this subject." She watched as he drove away and immediately regretted her harsh words to him. What if something happened to Evan? She would never forgive herself.

It took almost two months for conditions to return to normal at Vine Manor. After the shooting of one of the slaves, the planters refused to work. They sat in the fields while the overseers fired guns over their heads to frighten them, but they still would not move. Fights broke out and more of the Negroes fled from the plantation. When Paul had the Negroes food rations cut they begrudgingly began sowing the cottonseeds into the ground, but at a very slow pace.

Shrouded by darkness, some of the workers crept into the out buildings and set fires in the barns and tool sheds. The situation was not improving. The Negroes had taken to consuming large amounts of corn liquor in the evenings. Almost every night a fight broke out in the camps and injuries were common.

Evan knew that the only way to rectify the matter was to try and make peace with those that he knew could influence the others. Evan had been extremely lucky with his workers. Several incidents had happened in the past, but they were rectified with little interruption in the work. This was by far the most serious.

Evan arranged for several men from each field to meet with him. He situated himself on a platform built in the back of the house, searching the faces of the men who stood in the yard.

"We will have a very slim harvest this year," he said in a stern voice. "We are months behind and our plants are only a fourth as tall as they should be. If the weather holds we may be able to salvage our crop. I know you think that I am indifferent in regard to the loss of one of your kind, but I am not. What is happening now is unacceptable. Property is being destroyed and tempers are flaring. It is only a matter of time before someone else is killed and this time it will be at the hands of one of your own."

"I will make sure that each family who agrees to go back to work at full pace today will receive an extra allowance of food for the winter and two blankets. I will also give the wife of the man who was killed extra compensation. If you do not accept my terms, I will have no other recourse than to make arrangements for some of you to be sold down the river on the first of the month. I cannot continue to operate my plantation with slaves who do not wish to work. I will give you a few minutes to think over my offer. I will also assure you that no man, woman or child living on my land will ever be killed again unless they have harmed another." Evan stopped for a moment and surveyed the faces in the crowd.

A white-haired man, holding his hat in his hand, stepped forward. "Massa Vine, if ya keep ta yer word, I be back workin' in dah mown."

"I will," Evan replied.

Someone standing near the back yelled out, "Ya be givin' yer word ta a slave, that don mean nuttin'."

"I'm not my father, or like any of your former owners. I am Evan Vine, master of Vine Manor and a man of my word. I will expect to see you all in the field in the morning."

Paul Dunn was speechless when he heard about Evan's promise to the slaves. "You are insane. Not only have you undermined my authority with the workers, but also when the rest of this community hears about what you have just done they will be outraged. The more you give these coloreds, the more they will want and pretty soon, none of us will be able to afford to keep them working. They need to be handled with a strict hand and not mollycoddled. I know how Mary Elizabeth feels about the slaves and I think she is starting to influence your better judgment."

Evan slammed his hand down on the desk, "Enough! Try it my way for once, Paul. It may work. If it doesn't, what have we lost except a few extra barrels of seed corn and some cheap woolen blankets? I know I do not have as much experience with handling the slaves as you, but that doesn't mean I am stupid. And don't ever mention my wife's name in any of our business dealings. Her opinion does not sway me one way or another."

Paul was taken aback by Evan's disapproval. He could not believe that the once quiet man who had no interest in Vine Manor was now making concessions to the Negroes. "I suppose your new demeanor means you have decided not to sell this property?" Paul asked.

"Not right away. Perhaps in a year or two. Please accept my apology for yelling at you, Paul."

Paul nodded, "Apology accepted, if you accept mine." He extended his hand to Evan.

After Paul had left the study, Evan sat down and tried to

compose himself. Perhaps Mary Elizabeth's words did sway him. He wanted her home. Every three days a messenger would arrive from Magnolia with a letter from her. She told him how much she missed him and could not wait to be with him. Did he make allowances to the slaves so that she could join him or was he really concerned about their welfare?

With the planters once again working in the fields and the threat of disharmony eased, Evan felt it was now safe for Mary Elizabeth to return to Vine Manor. He would go to Magnolia and escort her home.

When Evan arrived at Magnolia, Mary Elizabeth covered his face with kisses and held him tightly and blurted out her news. She was now again with child, a result of their earlier time together in Magnolia. "Please, Evan, do not spoil this for me. I know you worry, but I am fine. I am weeks past the point where I miscarried before."

"Your physician said we should wait. It was my lust for you that brought this about. I want you to take to your bed and stay there until the doctor can make sure that everything is progressing as it should."

"Oh, fiddle, if you insist, I will, but I want you there beside me."

At night while she slept, Evan lay awake staring through the window at the half-moon light. He tried to imagine what it would be like to be a father, to have children that would suckle at her breast and take the time he shared with her. He wondered if keeping the plantation would take him away from her for long periods of time and whether or not the luster between them would fade away. If he sold Vine Manor it would give them more time together and a financial cushion that should last quite a few years, but then what? With many children who had to be provided for, the lavish lifestyle he had grown accustomed to might change. His mind was full of what-ifs tonight.

Chapter Ten

Mary Elizabeth sat with Nona in the sewing room. Her swollen feet rested on the ottoman while her needlework lay on her stomach. "Look at me, Nona, I look as though I have swallowed a watermelon. This child has kicked my insides raw and I know it has to be close to the time of his birth. I surely wish Dr. Mallard could have been more specific about my due date. He said it could be anytime within the next few weeks."

"You jest be patient, Mizz Mary, dey comes when it be time. Dis baby sure be havin some nice things ta wear. You be a real fine sewer." She held up the laced trimmed gown that Mary Elizabeth was working on.

Mary Elizabeth struggled to sit up in the chair. Her eyes widened as she clutched her stomach. "I do believe it may be today, Nona." Water soaked her robe and puddled on the floor."

Nona and Ceria helped her to the birthing room and Paul Dunn sent a rider to get Dr. Mallard. Nona called to Jasper to ride out to the field where Evan was hunting and bring him home. The house staff was excited. They all loved Mary Elizabeth. This kind and gentlewoman made living at Vine Manor more enjoyable for everyone.

By early evening, Mary Elizabeth was in full labor. Nona stood by her bedside, putting wet compresses on her head, while Dr. Mallard sterilized his instruments. He was becoming concerned that the fetus inside of Mary Elizabeth's small frame was extremely large and may cause complications. Mary Elizabeth continually asked for Evan.

Riding into the south field, Jasper passed the word that Evan was needed at home immediately. When Jasper finally spied Evan riding across the field he began calling to him. "You come fast, Massa Evans. Mizzes Mary is havin' da baby."

When Evan arrived at Vine Manor, he flew up the stairs and into her room, still dressed in his riding clothes and mud-covered boots. Mary Elizabeth smiled at him and took his hand. Her body once again arched as a pain ripped through her body. Biting into her lip, she squeezed his hand so tightly he felt as though his fingers would burst. He could not imagine her pain. Kissing her on the cheek, he nodded to Dr. Mallard to step outside with him.

"Why is it taking so long? Is there anything wrong?" he asked.

"Mary Elizabeth has really only been in labor for a few hours, Evan. She is handling it quite well. These things take time. I am trying to keep the room as free of infections as I possibly can. You should bathe and change into clean clothing. I will let you visit with her in a while. I suggest you prepare yourself for a long night. A glass of cordial may do you well." He patted Evan on the back and returned to his patient.

Evan handed Nona his jacket just as Jasper came into his bedchamber carrying a tray. "I dun brung ya some of yer best brandy, Massa Vine. Dis be a real happy time."

Evan took the glass and swallowed the purple liquid in one gulp. "This may be a happy time for me, Jasper, but right now my wife is lying next door in excruciating pain and I cannot do a thing to help her."

"Dis be women's duty, Massa Vine," Nona said. "I seed women havin' babies in da fields and den walkin' dah long way ta dar house. Somes have dem easy, somes hard, but dey comes out either way. We jest got ta pray fer Mizz Mary and da baby. She's bein' real brave, not even lettin out one holler." Nona turned away before Evan could see the concerned look on her face.

By morning, Mary Elizabeth was exhausted and weak from a night of non-stop labor. The infant had turned itself sideways and Dr. Mallard's attempts to right it had failed. When Nona came out of the room carrying a large bundle of bed linens covered in blood, Evan jumped up from the hall chair that had become his post. "What is that? Is she all right?" Nona nodded and kept on walking.

Evan knocked on the door. "I want to see my wife. I have to know that she is all right," he said to Dr. Mallard.

"You may sit with her for a few moments and then I want her to rest. I have given her a whiff of ether to relax her."

With her face flushed and covered in perspiration, Mary

Elizabeth's eyes opened for a moment and she mouthed the words, "I love you. Our baby will be here soon."

Dr. Mallard insisted Evan leave the room in an effort to keep Mary Elizabeth as relaxed as possible. With Evan around, Mary Elizabeth tried to hide her pain. Evan took his position in the hall chair and waited as the darkness faded into the light of the second morning. His eyes heavy from lack of sleep, he was startled when he heard a strange wailing sound. The baby had been born. Evan bounded to his feet and opened the door. Dr. Mallard stood holding the baby, cleaning fluid from its mouth as it loudly protested. "Please, go out, Evan. I'll let you see your wife in just a moment."

Evan reluctantly closed the door and stood in the hallway with Ceria and Jasper. The minutes ticked away as Evan stood outside the now quiet room. When the door opened again, Dr. Mallard's frame prevented Evan from entering, but Evan pushed him aside and rushed to his wife's bed. Dr. Mallard put his hand on Evan's back. "I am so sorry, Evan. I could not save her. By the time the baby was ready to be born Mary Elizabeth's strength was depleted and she had lost too much blood. She died peacefully under the ether."

Evan wasn't listening. He knelt by Mary Elizabeth's bed. Her auburn curls still damp from the arduous experience, framed her face. His mind was rushing. *What is wrong with her - she is not moving? Open your eyes, my darling.* He took her hand, which was still warm and put it to his cheek. He pulled her into his arms, her head going limp and falling onto his shoulder. Suddenly a mournful cry escaped from his throat. A cry heard throughout the house. "No, no, no." He sat by her bed until her body began to cool. He could not leave her.

Nona had taken the baby to the nursery and called for someone to bring her boiled goat's milk in a suckling bottle. She swaddled her tightly and rocked her back and forth in the chair that Evan had purchased for Mary Elizabeth. Tears ran down Nona's face. "Ya gonna be jest fine, baby girl. Yer momma gave up her life for ya, but ya gots a good daddy."

Dr. Mallard was still in the study when Evan came downstairs. "Why did you let my wife die? Why?" Evan cried. He could not be consoled.

"I am truly sorry, Evan. I did everything I could to save Mary Elizabeth. She put up a valiant battle to save her child. Please except my profound condolences." As he turned to leave Evan stepped in front of him.

"You did not do everything you could! You let her die; yet you managed to save the baby. You should have saved my wife instead of the child."

Dr. Mallard's jaw twitched. "It is not for me to say who lives or dies. I did my best to save them both. In time you will regret that remark. You have a daughter upstairs that needs you. Go take care of her!"

The mood at Vine Manor was somber. The draperies were kept closed and all decorations in the house were covered in dark purple. The house staff wore black outfits and were told to be as quiet as possible, although at times, some could be heard weeping. Evan sat beside a closed casket that rested on a bronze lift in the parlor. He remembered little about the visitors who came to pay their respects. Evan remained next to the casket for two days until the procession to the cemetery began. He was not aware of the ceremony, only that his beloved Mary Elizabeth was gone forever.

On the evening of the funeral, Nona dressed the baby in the gown that Mary Elizabeth had made for her and took her into Evan's bedchamber. He sat staring out the window. "Massa Vine, I got yer baby here. Would ya like to see her? Ya ain't looked at her yet."

He spoke without turning around. "Take her away, Nona. I have no need to see her."

"Dah baby needs a name, Massa Vine, what does ya want to call dah baby?"

"You name her, Nona. I don't care."

"Massa Vine, I jest want to say one thing ta ya. Life be hard. No matter ya be rich or poor, life be hard. Some days it ain't worth gettin' out of da bed, but ya jest get yerself up and put one foot in front of dah other. Dis baby gonna need ya." Evan continued to stare out the window. Nona left the room.

Nona sat in the nursery, rocking the sleeping baby. "I be gonna call ya Hallie. That be my mammy's name." She looked into the green eyes of the child lying in her arms. "Yes, I gonna call you Hallie."

Part Two:
Father and Child

*"Hallie? Heaven forbid, what kind of name is that? I do
believe we should find something more suitable. I don't
imagine that you know or even care that at this moment
your child is shoeless and dressed like a Negro waif.*
Margaret Cates

After the death of Mary Elizabeth, Evan suffered an unending
depression. He was a shell of his former self, leaving Paul Dunn
to run the plantation. Their conversations were short and Paul
was not sure he could continue his thankless job. One
conversation involved Magnolia. Paul had inquired what Evan
wished to do with it. "Do you want me to sell it, Evan?"

"No... close it up, board up the windows and bar the gate. I
want you to appoint a company nearby to keep it in good
condition. I will decide what to do with it later." Paul knew that
selling the home would be the best idea, yet he also knew that
continuing this conversation would be fruitless, so he abided by
Evan's wishes.

Evan made little attempt to form a bond with Hallie. He had
instructed Nona that she was to be in complete charge of the child
and he would be the one to decide when he wished to see her.
Occasionally, with empty eyes, he would look into her room or
watch her as Nona played with her. That was as far as his
relationship with his daughter progressed.

Capturing the love of everyone at Vine Manor was easy for
Hallie. With her endearing smile and love of life she scampered
from room to room. Even Paul Dunn could not escape her
engaging ways. Holding her on his lap, he would watch as she
scribbled on his desk pad. It was only when Hallie entered a

space occupied by Evan, that her mood changed and the unwelcome feeling would have her running off to somewhere she felt love.

On the second anniversary of Mary Elizabeth's death, Evan strode up the hill to the family cemetery. He sat down on the marble bench next to the angel that now guarded her grave. He cried until there were no more tears left.

To Paul's relief, the next day Evan announced that he was ready to take over his duties and run the plantation. They spent days pouring over the accumulation of paperwork that had been stacked in Evan's study. Evan attacked it with a vengeance. Work seemed to be the salvation that would pull him back from the depths of his despondency.

He began to make trips to the cotton fields to oversee the progress of the growing season. At times he would spend days away from home, living in the small work cabins located on the property. He spent his free time hunting game. Other times, he would go off to the shipyards to arrange for exporting the cotton. His presence in the house diminished. Sometimes Nona would find him sleeping in a chair in his office, his bed unmade from the night before. He became ingrained in every aspect of running the plantation. When he commanded that the overseers of the slave compounds make improvements and ease the workload of the older slaves, they grumbled, but were not given any choice other than to quit their jobs. Evan was honoring the memory of his wife who never understood slavery. He could no longer change what happened to her, but he could push it into the corner of his mind and try to go on. Yet, all the while, there was still a small auburn-haired girl with green eyes who ran through the hallways of Vine Manor with Nona close behind her.

Chapter Eleven

Hallie reached into the muddy water, her four-year-old hands wrapped around the body of a crayfish. "Is this a good one, Nona?" she asked, holding up the squirming creature.

"It be fine. Put it in da bucket, baby." Hallie dropped it into the pail with a resounding splash. "I think we gots enuf. Let's go home." Helping the shoeless Hallie up the bank, Nona took her hand and led her across a field of green grass.

Nona had taken on the task of raising Hallie with no qualms. She had loved Mary Elizabeth and had no doubt that she would feel the same about her child. Unable to bear her own children, perhaps Nona's pain would be eased with her new charge.

At that very moment, Margaret Cates was descending from a carriage in front of Vine Manor. She paused for a moment; her jaw dropping as she looked at the child coming across the yard. The child bore a striking resemblance to her own daughter when she was young, except no child of hers would ever be seen barefoot and muddy.

Margaret entered the foyer unannounced. "Take me to Evan Vine, this instant," she said to the first servant she encountered. Scurrying ahead of her, the girl went up the winding staircase and pointed to Evan's suite. Before the servant could knock, Margaret pushed her aside and opened the door. Evan gave a startled look at the woman dressed in traveling clothes standing before him. He was not accustomed to visitors, especially those that were unannounced. "Yes?" he asked, rising from his chair.

"Yes! Is that all you have to say is, yes? Do you know who I am? I am Margaret Cates! I am Mary Elizabeth's mother. I have been traveling for over a month now to this dastardly place to find out what in heaven's name has happened to my only grandchild. And what do I find when I arrive? I find her in the yard, shoeless, holding the hand of a niggah woman. Can you explain yourself to me, Evan Vine?"

Evan threw the book and his glasses on the desk. "I don't know why I owe you an explanation, madam. Since this is our very first encounter and you seem to want to come at me like a tigress, perhaps you can give me an explanation as to why it has taken you this long to make your first appearance in my house."

"I'll tell you why. The situation has never been in our favor since we allowed Mary Elizabeth to come to the states. After she married you, which of course, was without the consent of either her father or I, she kept her letters short and far apart. I assumed that she had found what she wanted and we were no longer her concern. When I received a letter from Mr. Dunn telling me that my daughter had passed away, I was despondent beyond compare. There was no mention in the letter in regard to the baby. I assumed it had died along with my blessed daughter. It wasn't until recently that Amelia Handmaker informed me that I did indeed have a granddaughter. I would have come sooner, but my husband was ill and also recently passed away. Does that answer your questions, Mr. Vine?"

Evan's tone softened. "Please accept my sympathy for the loss of your husband. I am sure it was an oversight that Paul failed to mention the child. We were all in such a grievous state that no one was really thinking clearly. I don't believe I received any letters from you after Mary Elizabeth's death. Perhaps they were lost."

Margaret Cates pulled the pins from her hat and removed it. "Now, let's not waste time. Four years is long enough. Let us talk about the child—" she interrupted her sentence, "What is her name?"

"It's Hallie."

"Hallie! Heaven forbid, what kind of name is that? I do believe we should find something more suitable. And as I was saying, let's not waste time. I think she should return to England with me. I am sure Mary Elizabeth would have preferred that her daughter be reared with some degree of dignity. I will be here for the next several months. We will talk again. Please have one of your servants show me to my quarters." She whirled around and was gone.

They did talk again and again, each of their conversations ended in raised voices. At one point Margaret threatening to take Evan into court to gain custody of Hallie. Evan, adamantly refusing to even consider Hallie leaving America.

"Why are you fighting so hard to keep her here?" Paul asked Evan after one of Evan's heated bouts with the woman he now called a hellion. "You know that Margaret would give her a good education and some formal training. I'm sure it would be better than keeping Hallie in the confines of Vine Manor and for you to continue to ignore her."

"She is my child," Evan replied in a harsh tone.

Paul crossed his arms over his chest. "Here I go again, opening my mouth where I shouldn't, but if you love Hallie, own up to it. Step up and do what is best for her. Either give her the attention she deserves or send her away. I know when you look at her you still blame her for Mary Elizabeth's death. That is so far from the truth. Blame yourself or Mary Elizabeth for getting pregnant, but don't blame Hallie. She is just a small child and what she needs more than an education or stiff dresses is the love of her father. Mary Elizabeth would turn in her grave if she could see how you are treating her little one. She would have loved that child as much as she loved you. Is that what scares you? Have you seen what happens when Hallie gets near Margaret Cates? She pulls back and shakes all over. Do what is right, Evan, make a decision." He pointed his finger in Evan's face. "And then live with it!"

Evan stared at Paul. He suddenly felt ashamed. Paul was right. He did blame Hallie's difficult birth for Mary Elizabeth's death. Sending her away would be the worst thing he could ever do to the memory of his beloved wife. It wouldn't be easy to endear himself to this child that he had almost completely ignored for four years, but he had to make every effort. Tomorrow, he would make arrangements for Margaret Cates to return to England without his daughter.

A week later, against her wishes, Evan helped Margaret into a carriage and Jasper drove her to the rail station. Margaret informed Evan that he would hear from her again. This was not the end of her bid for her granddaughter.

A few nights later, Evan opened the door to Hallie's room and quietly walked to her bedside. She lay there with her eyes open. "Hello, I thought you would be asleep by now." She gave him a shy grin. "Hallie, do you know who I am?"

Burying her head in her pillow, with barely a whisper she answered, "My father."

"Do you know what that means?" She shrugged, pushing a wispy curl from her forehead. "Well, my little girl, I guess we will learn together." He bent and kissed her forehead. *Oh, God, how he missed Mary Elizabeth. When he thought of his beloved wife, he knew he had to do the right thing. He had to become a father to a child he barely knew.*

School was now in session. Evan was the student and Hallie the teacher. He found it was not easy to concentrate as she ran around his office singing or taking things from his desk. He preferred not to listen to her tantrums when it was time for a bath or bed. On the nights that he let her dine with him, he endured spilt milk and gravy droplets on the white tablecloth. When his patience wore thin, he would call Nona to retrieve her. Hallie would throw her arms around this black woman and cover her face with kisses, telling Nona in her soft voice that she loved her. That, Evan found a little disconcerting, but what had he expected? Nona had been Hallie's caretaker for all the time he ignored her. He knew that they had formed a bond that would always be there. What was wrong with him? He wondered at times if he would ever learn to love this child. Perhaps a part of him was missing, or disconnected since the death of his wife. Mary Elizabeth would have taught him how to love Hallie. It was his fault that he let so much time pass before he made the decision to involve himself in Hallie's life. Yet, he soon realized that Hallie's response to him was unconditional. She did not expect an apology or special compensation for his past behavior; she now just wanted his undivided attention—all of it, all of the time. He could not believe how much of him she now commanded since she had been accepted into his life. Hallie asked a million questions: Where was he going? When would he be back? What was he doing? Her most often asked question was, "Why?"

When the weather was suitable, Evan would take Hallie for rides in the carriage. Hallie would sing Negro spirituals she had learned from Nona. He laughed as she rolled her eyes and threw back her head while she sang the mournful songs. Sitting in the open fields, she taught him how to make a necklace out of clover and make golly dolls out of reed grass. They were a mismatched pair but each small step made the distance between them seem less and less until one day while sitting in the afternoon sun, she touched his hand and said, "I love you."

Before he even thought, the words, "I love you, too," slipped from his mouth.

In the evenings after her dinner and bath, Nona would bring Hallie to Evan. He would read to her. At first Hallie sat in the chair next to him; in time, when the stories became more interesting to her, she climbed on his lap and turned the pages. While she pretended to read, he would rest his chin on her head and smell the scent of lilac soap. When he felt her small body go limp and could hear her rhythmic breathing, he carried his sleeping child to her bed. He would kiss her forehead and quietly close the door.

Evan now had another person to worry about, to protect, and to love. Even though his faith had been sorely shaken when Mary Elizabeth died, it was now his duty to make sure he gave her daughter the best life possible. In some ways he was now looking forward to the journey.

Chapter Twelve

"When is my father coming home?" Hallie asked. She followed the raindrops as they made crooked paths down the windowpane.

"He should be home tomorrow," Paul Dunn replied, rubbing his head. "Do you not have anything to keep you busy? Where is Nona?"

"She is cleaning the study and I am bored. I have nothing to do."

Paul knew it was going to be impossible to get any of his work done unless he found something to occupy her time. She had interrupted him every ten minutes, making him lose track of his addition. "Come here, Hallie. Sit down at the desk. I will teach you how to print your name." Hallie sat down and reached across the desk.

"No," Paul said, "You cannot use my pen. You need to use a pencil." Paul's afternoon turned into a lesson in letters. Paul would have a talk with Evan when he returned.

"It's time, Evan. You need to hire a governess for Hallie," Paul said. "She is seven and more than ready to start her studies. After all, what does she have to keep her busy living in a house with two men and a Negro nanny? She runs through the hall screaming and she keeps the house staff frustrated with the countless messes she makes in the kitchen. Before you object again, think about it."

Evan knew that Paul was right. She needed the attention of someone who could teach her how to behave as a young lady and start her scholastic studies. "You're right, Paul. How do I go about finding someone who is suitable to take over the major part of my daughter's life?"

"There are several good agencies I can contact in regard to hiring a companion for Hallie. I will make sure that whoever I hire is a capable person and has plenty of energy," Paul said with a sigh of relief.

It took three months before Evan and Paul found someone whom they felt was proficient and amiable enough to become a part of their household. Evan wanted to make sure he chose the right person for the post of caring for his daughter.

"Hallie, I have someone I want you to meet," Evan said, as he escorted a young woman toward her. Hallie had been dressed in a blue silk dress and sent to sit in a chair in the parlor. Nona told her it was a special day for her, but for some reason Hallie did not feel excited. Nona had a sad look in her eye.

The woman bent down in front of Hallie, touching her small fingers. "Hello, Hallie, I am glad to meet you." Hallie did not look up. If she looked into the face of this woman with the pure white hands her life would surely change forever.

The woman's name was Camille Dugan. She was from a middle-class family whose expectations for their daughter far surpassed their wealth. They believed that with her education, she could surely attract someone of position or wealth. After working as a schoolteacher in a quiet community in Georgia for over five years, Camille decided it was time to move on. She registered with a placement agency and now, only two months later, found herself in a palatial estate owned by one of the wealthiest men in Mississippi. Her pay was almost triple what she was making as a teacher, plus she now had very few expenses. She would do whatever was required of her to keep this arrangement. Camille was not an unappealing woman, but with her hair pulled back in a severe bun, and with her drab clothing, she was not particularly attractive.

Evan had set down a definite set of rules. Camille was by no means to strike Hallie, but any misbehavior should be reported to him. He expected Camille to teach her all the necessary skills for a proper young lady. He did not express an interest in Camille becoming Hallie's friend or nanny. Camille got the impression that Evan was almost afraid of her presence, fearing it would diminish his importance in Hallie's life.

Camille was a likeable person. It wasn't long before Hallie preferred spending time with her, rather than sitting quietly while Evan did paperwork or in following Nona around when her father was away on business. Hallie consumed the daily tasks that Camille set for her. Before long, the boisterous child who was prone to tantrums was almost unnoticeable in the house.

She spent the good daylight hours with Camille. Their time together often overflowed into the dinner hours when the two of them would eat together in the study, sometimes laughing, then getting suddenly quiet if Evan, Paul, or Nona ventured near the door. Evan knew the arrangement was much better for Hallie, yet on the days that he was home, and Hallie was not around, he missed her presence. Nona also felt a void in her life when Hallie announced she was old enough to bathe herself and she preferred that Camille do her hair.

When it came to Evan or Paul, Camille kept her distance. Her involvement in the family life was bland. Camille seemed to prefer not being a part of any of the activities in the house. After all, she told Paul, she was a paid employee and not a relative. Paul reminded her that he was also an employee, but felt that he was also an extension of the Vines. Her reply was that with his tenure he surely was entitled to be included.

Evan tapped his pencil on the desk, staring out the window. "Will you please stop, Evan?" Paul asked in an irritated voice. "I cannot concentrate with your constant racket. What is on your mind?"

"I've been wondering why Miss Dugan refuses to dine with Hallie and me or even sit with us in the parlor. It just seems odd to me since she and Hallie are so close. She gives me reports on Hallie's progress whenever I ask her, but never has anything else to say. Hallie is very fond of her. Surely Camille has some redeeming qualities that we also could enjoy."

"Perhaps that is what she was instructed to do when she took this position. She just wants to keep her proper place. This employment is very important to her. Besides, living with a single, middle-aged man may not be the most suitable arrangement if she were to become too friendly with you."

"Oh, nonsense, Paul! I have no intimate interest in Miss Dugan. I had only one wife and I shall never take another."

"Yes, I know. In fact, if Mary Elizabeth hadn't come along, you may have turned into an old curmudgeon like me. Let it be, Evan. Hallie is fine. That was your main concern. I will tell Nona to keep her ears open, just to ease your mind."

Paul continued to shuffle through the stack of letters on his desk. "By the way, Evan, I keep getting letters from a man named August Lott. He says he is still interested in buying Magnolia. This man is quite relentless. I have a stack of correspondence from him. Do you wish me to respond to his letters?"

"He is one persistent man. Just throw them away, Paul. I have no time to worry about him."

Chapter Thirteen

As the years passed, Evan accepted Camille's demeanor and concentrated on the business of running one of the most profitable plantations in Mississippi. He watched his daughter grow into a lovely young woman who was gentle and kind. Camille had indeed fulfilled her duty.

Camille Dugan remained at Vine Manor for eight years. Her relationship with Evan improved to some extent. She was always polite, but still kept her distance. She would leave Vine Manor for three weeks during the Christmas holidays and another three weeks in the summer to spend time with her family. Camille spoke little about them, and Evan assumed that they were not a very close unit.

When Hallie was fifteen years old, Camille suggested to Evan that it might be good for Hallie to study abroad. She would be more than happy to accompany her. Camille believed that Hallie would benefit immensely from actually experiencing the European culture they had studied for the past year.

Still waiting for two weeks for an answer to her request, it was Hallie who came to him. "I need to learn to think for myself, Father. Please let me go. I will miss you terribly, but when I return I will know so much more about the world. My mother was from England. I can visit Grandmother Cates and meet some of my other relatives. Don't you agree that it would be a good idea, father?" Evan smiled. He knew he could not win this argument.

When the weather was warm enough for sea travel, Evan accompanied his daughter and her entourage to New York for her voyage across the sea. She would study in England for six months and then travel throughout the British Isles. He was nervous. He worried about the dangers of the ocean voyage and the reality that he would not see her for a long time. Inclement weather and disease on the ships were always a concern of every traveler. He would miss their evening meals together and her joviality in the house. She kissed him goodbye and told him she would write at least once a week. Evan watched as she boarded the ship. The lump in his throat grew larger as the vessel disappeared into the huge expanse of water.

Hallie's letters came on a regular basis, each one filled with pages of news about her new school and lodgings. She shared a tiny room with Camille, but she loved every minute of being abroad. Evan sent her money on a regular basis, occasionally receiving a request from Camille for additional funds, due to unexpected expenses.

Near the end of Hallie's stay in England, Paul came to Evan with some disturbing news. It seems that he was having a problem with some of his financial records. He had reviewed some of his old ledgers to check on the cost of the hitches used on the carriages. He needed to reorder them and could not remember the original cost. When he checked the price he could not believe what he saw. Someone had meticulously changed the figures so that it appeared that he had paid more for them than the actual cost. When he posted a letter to the company they responded saying they had received a check for an excess amount and had returned it to his financial institution. Paul's inquiry to the bank showed that over the course of five years quite a few refunds had been posted to the Vine account and then withdrawn from the bank in the form of a draft picked up by a young lady, who showed her credentials as being an employee of Mr. Vine. On one occasion she had talked to the bank president and said that Mr. Vine preferred that he not notify Paul Dunn of the oversights, since he did not want to embarrass Mr. Dunn due to his advancing age and poor eyesight.

After Paul's discovery, he worked for weeks, going over each ledger book. The balances carried forward on some of the pages had been changed and with the huge amount of accounts he paid monthly, he hadn't noticed the small differences. Other incidents began to surface in Paul's mind. It seemed strange that Camille was always available when the postal carrier came. And then there were times when the downstairs maids complained of missing pieces of silver. Small things, several forks or a butter dish were reported to Paul. He assumed that one of the slaves had taken them or had been misplaced. He now recalled a hefty invoice from the clothier who made Hallie's gowns. When he asked Hallie about it, she said she only ordered two dresses. She was thirteen at the time and may have forgotten what she actually bought. This again proved to be an erroneous charge. Hallie had indeed only purchased two dresses.

Paul was physically ill when he took the information he had gathered to Evan. How could he have let this happen? It seemed that Camille Dugan had waged a silent campaign against Vine Manor to increase her coffer. Paul laid the list of missing items, that had grown to two pages, on Evan's desk along with the stack of papers he had poured over for the last several weeks. His eyes were rimmed with red and his hands shook as he sat in the chair facing Evan. "I cannot believe this is really true. Miss Dugan has been stealing from you for the last five years. She was quite brilliant. She never took a large amount, just enough so that it would not be noticed. I am prepared to reimburse every cent she has taken, Evan. I am so sorry. It is my entire fault. You trusted me to take care of your finances and I let that woman steal right under my nose. I will also regrettably give up my position here. When Camille returns from England with your daughter, I plan to have her arrested the minute she steps off the ship."

Evan leaned back in the chair. "First, I do not wish for you to leave, and second, I don't expect you to pay back the money she stole. I myself have sent her funds while she has been in England that I am sure Hallie never asked for. When she was living in this house I gave her money for special books and art supplies that she said would be beneficial for Hallie. I am sure my daughter never saw those, either. Camille told me not to mention it to you since you gave her ample money and she did not want you to think she was spending it foolishly. It looks as if we have both been duped, Paul. I don't want to make any rash moves that may upset Hallie. Let's sleep on this for a few days. They are not due back for several months. I haven't heard from Hallie lately, but I know that by now, she and Camille are traveling through Wales and Ireland. We have time to make a suitable plan."

The following week he received a lengthy letter from Hallie.

My Dearest Father,

I am writing to you from Brighton. I have been staying with Grandmother Cates for the past few weeks and I am quite miserable. Camille has left me here alone and I desperately wish to book passage home as soon as possible. A month ago she and I arranged to travel by train through Ireland and Wales. Two weeks into our trip Camille said she was not feeling well and so we returned to England. That is when Camille suggested we visit with Grandmother Cates for a few weeks and then make another attempt at traveling south. Our arrival took Grandmother Cates by surprise and she was not at all happy to see us, much less give us lodgings in her house. She was quite shocked that Camille and I were traveling unaccompanied by a male companion and because of that reason she agreed to let us stay. I do not like my grandmother at all. She is nosey, mean and had nothing good to say about you, our home, or our country. She is stingy with her food and only keeps the fireplaces burning during the days. The nights are miserable and cold. She has complained bitterly about the added expense I am costing her, even though I have given her money. I know that she does not need the money, since the house is very palatial and she wears a collection of fine jewelry. She talks about my mother continually and when I asked her why she did not come to see her, she told me it was none of my concern and that I was an insolent child. Now for the most dreadful part, father, just days after arriving here, Camille told me that she had relatives living just a few miles away. She said she wanted to visit them and I was surprised since Camille had never mentioned having relatives in England. She said it would give me time alone to spend with my grandmother. For two weeks I had to spend time alone with the shrew.

When Camille returned from her visit to her relatives, she told me she was going to stay in

*England and had taken a position as a governess
for a family in London. Camille said that since I
am almost sixteen, I should not need her very much
longer and this opportunity would be very good for
her. The family would pay excellent wages for her
services. I begged her to come home with me, but
she stood fast on her plan. She said she loved me,
but that it was time for me to let go and continue
on with my life.*

*Then to my surprise, when I awoke the next
morning, she had packed her things and left
during the night, without leaving me so much as a
scribble. Grandmother Cates said that a carriage
came to the house well after twelve. Of course,
grandmother never woke me when the carriage
came. She was quite disturbed by Camille's
departure and it has given her fuel enough to
chastise me further. She has even remarked that it
may be just as well for me to stay with her and
learn how to be a true lady. I cannot and will not
do that, Father.*

*Camille has taken all of my available funds
with her. Please, make arrangements for me to
come home as soon as possible. I miss Camille
terribly and still do not understand why she left
me. Patiently awaiting your response.*

Your loving daughter,
Hallie Vine

"We need to arrange for Hallie's passage home as soon as
possible," Evan told Paul after reading the letter. "I'll go to New
York to meet her to make sure she gets home safely."

"I've come to the conclusion that I am not going to tell Hallie
about what Camille has done. The money is of no consequence
and if I tell her, she will be devastated. She truly cared for
Camille and I don't think it will be of any advantage for her to
know this. What that woman has done by leaving Hallie alone
with her grandmother has been harsh enough. I am sure Camille
probably isn't in England. Leaving Hallie there was just another
part of her cunning plan. If I were to try and find her it would
probably take more money than she has taken from me. It is a

shame. I would have gladly given her money if she had asked for it. Hallie loved her and she was a good teacher. I do believe that despite what she has done, Camille did care for Hallie. Unfortunately she cared more for money. Let's make a pact, Paul. Hallie is never to know about this. Do we agree?"

"Yes, I agree," Paul answered.

Chapter Fourteen

Evan stood on the pier waiting for the *American Empress* to dock. It was hours before the ship was properly moored and passengers were able to disembark. Hallie was the first off. She ran down the ramp in a very unladylike fashion and into the arms of her father. She buried her head in his chest, unable to speak. Tears streamed down her face as she continued to hug him. Finally pulling herself away, she wiped her eyes with her handkerchief. "Oh, Father, I am so happy, so awfully happy to see you. I have been awake since dawn watching the horizon for a sign of land." Taking his arm, she pulled him toward the line of waiting carriages. "Which one is ours? I want to get away from the sight of the ocean as soon as possible."

"Please, wait, Hallie. We need to collect your luggage."

The driver maneuvered the horses onto the cobbled street, lined with the impressive New York skyline. "I'm sorry your trip was not as expected, Hallie. I really wanted you to enjoy your stay in England."

"The first part of our visit was fine. I loved the school and Camille really seemed to be enjoying her free time. It was only when we got to Grandmother Cates that everything changed. I am still so very grieved about Camille's departure. She had made remarks in the past about leaving when I turned sixteen, but I guess I never took her seriously. I think about her often." Hallie hesitated for a moment, on the verge of tears. "For the voyage home I was assigned to share a cabin with an elderly woman who stayed a pale shade of green for the entire sailing. At a moment's notice she would become violently ill, which sent me fleeing from the cabin," Hallie said, making a face.

"Perhaps in a small way I can make it up to you. I thought since you will be sixteen in less than a week, that you might enjoy spending some time in New York. We can take in a few shows and go shopping. They have some excellent shops in this city," Evan said, trying to ease the pain of his daughter's year abroad.

"One or two days would be fine, but then I would love to go home. I miss Vine Manor. It seems like I have been gone forever."

"It seems that way to me, too, Hallie."

Two days later they boarded a train to Mississippi.

Hallie was home at last. Once inside the house, she let out a gleeful shriek as she looked upon the entire house staff, dressed in their Sunday uniforms, waiting for her in the foyer. They smiled and greeted her. The house servants were actually glad that she was home. Nona stepped forward, "I sure be missin' you, Mizz Hallie. You be gone much too long."

"Oh, Nona, I have missed you so very much." Hallie hugged her before running off through the house, just as she did when she was a small child. "Where is Paul? I want to see him." She lifted her skirt and danced up the steps.

Nona called after her. "Mr. Paul be in da bed. He be ailing for a couple of days."

Hallie stopped halfway up the stairs and turned around. "Oh, I didn't know. Father, you must check on him at once. Perhaps we should call the doctor."

Nona shook her head. "Mr. Paul, he said he don want no doctor. He said he jest needed to rest, but he ain't eatin but jest a bite."

Evan frowned. He had never known Paul to stay in bed. Even when he was not feeling well, he would drag himself into his office and complain the whole day. Evan knew that Paul's demeanor had changed after the incident with Camille, and Paul seemed to doubt himself more often when doing the weekly ledgers. Evan thought it would pass in time and that being left alone for a while would help Paul to regain his normal composure.

"I'll look in on him right away," Evan said, passing his daughter on the steps.

Paul's room was dark. He lay on his side with his eyes closed. Evan touched him gently on the shoulder. "Paul, it's me, Evan."

Paul opened his eyes slightly and looked up, trying to focus in the dim light. "Evan, I'm glad you're home." His voice seemed weak and raspy. He talked in short sentences, breathing deeply. "Seems I've caught myself a dandy of a chest cold. I needed to take a few days to let it pass. I am feeling better everyday. By tomorrow, I should be my old self. I was hoping to be completely well before you returned home. How was your trip?"

"Fine. I am going to let you rest. I'll see you in the morning." He touched Paul's shoulder again. Paul did not reply. His eyes were already closed.

Evan tried to hide his concern for Paul, but Hallie could tell something was wrong. "Is Paul going to be okay?"

"I will send Jasper for the doctor in the morning and I'm sure with the proper medication he will be fine."

It took a few weeks for Paul to recover from his bout with pneumonia. It left him quite thin and with little energy. Evan was overwhelmed with work, but he knew that Paul was not capable of helping him. When Paul announced to Evan that this might be a good time to hire someone to help him, Evan was truly concerned.

"After all," Paul had said, "I am nearing my seventieth birthday and I should have retired long ago. I will contact some of the universities and make arrangements for you to interview candidates that will fit your needs. They always have bright young men whom I am sure are full of energy and ready to start their careers, just as I was when I came here over forty-five years ago."

Since his ordeal with Camille's theft, Paul seemed apprehensive about making any major decisions in regard to the plantation's finances. Evan knew that it would be up to him to choose Paul's successor. When Evan announced to Hallie that he had to leave awhile, she stomped her foot.

"My birthday is in three days. Surely, you'll be here for my birthday or maybe I can go with you on your trip?"

"It is not really a pleasure trip, Hallie. I promise I will not leave until after your birthday. I have something that may keep you busy while I am away. We will talk about it at your birthday dinner." Before she could protest, he gave her that look that meant the conversation was over. It was time for him to cross that last hurdle in his life—a place called Magnolia.

On her sixteenth birthday, Hallie and Evan ate dinner together in the dining room. Evan requested that the best china and silver be used for the occasion. Nona had the cook bake Hallie a white cake surrounded by roses picked from the garden. Evan placed a crystal wine glass at Hallie's place. He stood when she entered wearing a blue dress she had bought in England. Her hair was layered with ribbons atop her head, and for a moment, Evan felt as if he were looking into the eyes of Mary Elizabeth. He took her hand and pulled her chair away from the table. "I cannot tell you how lovely you look tonight. Your mother would be so very proud." Hallie smiled as he poured a bit of wine into each glass. "A toast to you, my dear. You have managed to make it to your sixteenth year without an illness, a broken bone, or a broken heart. That will come soon enough. Paul would have liked to spend this special day with you, but he is not feeling well and has taken to his bed once again."

"I have two birthday presents for you, Hallie. One was small enough to wrap, the other much too large." In the velvet box on the table was a gold heart-shaped locket on a slender chain, which Evan placed around her neck. She opened it. Inside was a picture of her mother.

Hallie rose from the table and kissed his cheek. "Thank you, Father! It's beautiful and I dare say enough of a birthday present. I will cherish it forever."

"And now for your second present. After much deliberation I have decided to give you a summer home at the seashore. It is the same house I gave to your mother as a wedding present. She loved that house and we spent many happy times there. After her death, I closed up the house and haven't been there since. At one time I considered selling it, but something kept me from it and now I know why. I think it will make you as happy as it made her." Evan could hardly talk. Just the thoughts of going to Magnolia made him choke back tears.

Hallie hung on every word, as Evan continued with his story. Evan told her about the property just above the edge of the ocean, a wondrous place called Magnolia where the soft ocean breeze wrapped its arms around willow trees that dripped with Spanish moss. The house was open and airy with large rooms and white pine floors. "Your mother loved Magnolia. She could not get enough of it. If you would like to go there while I am away on business, I will send a messenger to tell the staff to prepare the house for you; otherwise, you can wait for my return from my trip and I will accompany you there. The house is yours to do with as you see fit. You can buy new furniture if you wish, or keep what is there. You can do whatever you want, but please don't remove the piano in the parlor."

"I should wait until your return to go there but I know how long your business trips can take and you have filled me with too much wonder to wait until you return. I would like to rest for a week or so and then go to Magnolia. This is a lot for me to take in at once, Father. Why have you never mentioned this place before now?"

"We will talk about Magnolia at length when I return, but right now I think it would be a good idea if we both readied ourselves for our destinations. I am going to send Nona and Jasper with you. They both know a lot about Magnolia. You can question them, if you like."

Chapter Fifteen

"There you are. You gave me a scare! I have searched half the house for you," Evan said as he stepped onto the terrace.

Paul slowly turned his head. "What did you think, that I had died and been buried before you returned? I would not give you the pleasure of not attending my funeral. You are back a lot sooner than I expected. No luck in your hunt for my replacement?" Paul asked in a raspy voice. "You must forgive my appearance. I have been ailing again and a bath at this time is just too much for me to muster."

Evan was indeed surprised at Paul's appearance. Paul was always dressed meticulously. Today he sat in rumpled clothing, with stubbly growth on his face. Evan decided to leave his questions about Paul's health until later. He was not anxious to hear the bad news.

"Actually, I had much better luck than I expected. I hired two young men," Evan said, sitting down in the chair next to Paul's desk.

Paul gave a wry grin, "I see. It takes two people to replace me. I should be flattered."

"No one could ever fill your shoes, but these two will surely try. I think a little competition might help them to try and accomplish the business of running this place. They are quite different in mannerism, but both are very ambitious and energetic. Besides, I don't intend to spend all of my time doing paperwork. Still, I do believe it may take them both to replace you."

"And where do you plan on housing these two young men? Surely they aren't going to stay in the main house. You have a young daughter who lives here, remember?"

"I hadn't really thought about it, but I presume you are right. It is not as if we haven't caused our share of scandal in this community. I understand that once again my neighbors are frowning on my behavior. Letting Hallie return from England without an escort and then sending her off to Magnolia with just her Negro slaves still has tongues wagging. I never have done anything conventional, have I, Paul? I suppose I shall have to convert some of the back buildings into suitable living quarters for our two prospects."

"Well, are you going to tell me about them, or should I just remain envious of the fact that they are young and energetic?" Paul asked.

Evan sat down next to Paul and looked into his thinning face. "Phillip Thixton is from Baton Rouge. He has degrees in accounting and financial management. He is articulate and precise in everything he does. I spent several days with him and I could find no fault with his credentials or his abilities. His family owns a financial institution, yet they seem to struggle to live a quite nice lifestyle. I suppose overspending is one of their main problems. Although he had considered taking a position with his father, my offer tempted him. I have no doubt that someday he will be quite wealthy."

"James Simmons is also an accountant and I found him to be a man full of ideas that may or may not work, but he is dedicated to his goals and I feel he will be a great asset to us. Unlike Phillip, James enjoys fieldwork."

What Evan was not telling Paul was that James loved to read and hunt and was not really the type that enjoyed being chained to a desk every day. Just as Evan had surpassed his own expectation when he was thrown into running the plantation after his father's death, James had chosen a profession that would please his parents and had excelled in it. James was honest with Evan, telling him that he planned to work very hard for a few years and then take another path in life. Evan liked his candor.

"What are the ages of these men, Evan?" Paul asked.

"Phillip is twenty-five and James, twenty-four. Much too old for Hallie if that is what you are thinking. I can see that look on your face."

"I really hadn't given it a thought, but I do believe you were eleven years older than Mary Elizabeth. So, I guess there is no cause to think Hallie would be the least bit interested in either of these young men," Paul said sarcastically, a demeanor he excelled in. "When she returns home, I am sure she will just ignore the fact that two young men have been added to our staff."

"Good grief, Paul. There are rooms in this house that have never been used, but if you like, I will make Hallie stay at Magnolia until the living quarters for Phillip and James are finished. I can also build an office for them and put a stone wall around it." Evan was returning the barb.

"Is that to keep Hallie out or the men in?" Paul shot back.

Evan grinned, tapping the envelope he held in his hand on the corner of the desk. "Perhaps both. I have a letter from Hallie that just came today. I will let you know how soon I need to worry." He settled back in his chair to read the letter from his daughter.

> *My Dearest Father,*
>
> *I am truly in love with Magnolia and I should be angry with you for not telling me about this place sooner. It is glorious. Nona and I have opened every portal in the house daily to let in the breeze. We had all the linens washed and hung outside to dry. The cook, her name is Meta, makes delicious meals from the fresh seafood that Jasper catches for us.*
>
> *Please don't be upset but I have been eating in the kitchen with Nona and Jasper. I do not like dining alone and it gives us time to talk about Magnolia and my mother. I know how much you loved her and I am sad that I never got a chance to meet her. Nona and I found a few photographs of hers in the garret and I now have them in my room. She was beautiful, father, and I know now why you felt such a loss when she died. I will not talk further on the subject, lest I should upset you.*
>
> *Nona and I went into town and bought lilac bushes to plant along the front of the house, and blue hyacinths to put in the walk planters. The interior of the house is lovely. The furniture is in excellent condition and I understand from Nona that you selected most of it. You have wonderful taste, father.*
>
> *Jasper has taken us to the beach several times*

and I find it so relaxing. I do wish I did not have to wear a bonnet, but Nona said the sun is not good for my fair skin.

When are you planning on joining me? I am sure your business dealings are over and I would love it if you would come as soon as possible. The magnolia trees are in full bloom, but I cannot force myself to pick them. They look so grand on the trees. I look forward to spending many happy times with you at Magnolia.

Your loving daughter, Hallie Vine

"I shall answer her letter today, Paul. She seems happy at Magnolia. I think I can stave her off for a little while longer. I just don't know if I am ready to go there."

Paul's first meeting with Phillip and James took place two days later. After giving them time to rest from the journey, the new arrivals were shown into the library by a manservant. Paul and Evan were already present in the room. The valet poured brandy into crystal goblets and served the four men. Paul took the glass and raised it into the air. "A toast to my new protégées"

Phillip stood. "Excuse me sir, please do not take this as an offense, but I do not consider myself a protégée. I already have quite a bit of knowledge about financial matters and I am ready to start my duties as soon as possible."

"Ah, yes, that is what I like—confidence!" Paul said. "Well then, young man, if you wish to have a position adding up columns of figures, I suggest you go home and get a job in a four-walled office. What Evan and I expect from you far exceeds those boundaries and the knowledge you might *think* you possess in regard to running a plantation. You see, for every bushel of wealth, we have half-a-bushel of woe to go along with it. We must be prepared at all times for the unexpected, which in our case, is usually expected. Are you following me?"

James interjected. "Perhaps Phillip is, but I am completely lost."

Paul smiled. "A good place to start. Your instruction will be in perseverance at best. You must learn to handle yourself in the face of adversity. At times there are problems with the slave community that, if not handled swiftly and with proper caution, can cause quite a bit of unrest."

"We must produce enough cotton and crops to meet our expenses and hopefully make a profit. We have over three hundred mouths to feed on this plantation. In the spring, it may rain for weeks; in the summer it may not rain at all, making the ground so hard you cannot even drive a nail into it." Paul stopped a moment to catch his breath. "We must deal with yellow fever, malaria and dysentery that can take half our workers at one time. If, and when, we get the cotton in the warehouses, we wrestle with mold in the bins and vermin that come to rob us during the night. And through all of this, exact and detailed records must be kept on everything from needles bought for sewing to the timbers used to make fences. So if you thought this was going to be an easy job, you're wrong. That is why Evan pays his employees more than most. Do you wish me to go on?"

James shook his head, not really knowing how to answer to such a grandiose oration on plantation life.

Phillip was the first to speak. He turned to Evan who had remained silent while Paul spoke. "My extreme apologies to you, Mr. Vine." Then turning to Paul, "And to you too, Mr. Dunn. I will give you one-hundred percent of myself." He extended his hand to Evan.

Paul continued, "Now if you will excuse us, we need to talk in private and give you time to think over what you are getting yourself into. If you are still interested in the position in the morning, I will tell you all the good things that living at Vine Manor can provide you. I assure you, it will be a short list," giving James and Phillip their cue to leave. "We will see you at six in the morning. Get a good nights sleep."

James and Phillip bid their hosts goodnight and left the room.

"If that speech didn't scare them away, it did a good job of making me want to leave," Evan said.

"Which one do you think will leave before the week is out? My bet is on Phillip. I do not believe he will appreciate mud on his boots or sores on his ass from checking the fields all day," Paul remarked.

Paul was wrong. At the end of the week both Phillip and James were still at Vine Manor.

Chapter Sixteen

On the second week of their employment, Paul was not feeling well, which gave Evan a chance to take Phillip and James on an extended tour of the plantation. "I cannot cover everything. I own close to a thousand acres. Not all of the fields are in cotton at the same time. Some lay fallow to regain their growth potential, but I can show you a sample of what we do every day. I need not even go into what it takes to operate the house and gardens. Paul has done an excellent job of giving out detailed instructions to everyone involved in the running of those areas. He will show you those ledgers when he is feeling better."

By noon they had surveyed the main warehouses and observed the detailed process of loading the wagons that would be taken to the docks for shipping. Evan took them through the vast stables that contained everything from elegant barouches to one-horse surreys. Rows of stalls filled with fine riding horses, trotters, and field horses. The stable alone was a huge operation, with three Negro blacksmiths working long hours to forge the shoes and tackle needed.

Later in the day they rode through mud paths lined with rows of slave cabins and then on to the north field.

Half way through their journey into the field, Evan stopped when he heard the screams of the Negro women. Turning on his seat, he could see the blur of white cotton dresses running through the waist-high plants, the women's arms flailing in the air. Evan put his horse to a gallop and caught up with the overseer who was standing at the side of the road. "What is going on?" Evan asked as he brought the horse to a stop, with Phillip and James close behind him.

The burly man scratched the side of his sweat-stained shirt. "Ain't nothing for you to worry about, Mr. Vine. One of them slave kids wandered off. They can't find 'em. I'll get 'em back to work real soon, Mr. Vine, don't you worry."

James stood up in the stirrups and surveyed the scene in front of him. The women were now crying and calling out the name of the child over and over. "Isn't anyone going to help them?" James asked.

The field overseer growled. "They know better than to bring them youngins out to the field and let em run loose. I keep telling them to keep an eye on them little chillin'."

To Evans surprise, James pulled his horse to the left and headed across the field, the cotton plants yielding to the hooves of his horse as he trotted up and down the rows searching the ground. At the edge of the field, he turned into a grove of trees lining the riverbank. He saw the child standing alone, looking into the water with tears running down his face. The boy turned when he saw the horse coming near him. James was afraid the boy was going to run. With one fell swoop of his hand he gathered up the child and put him astride the horse. James carried him back to the mother who was on her knees in the soft dirt, praying to the Lord to return her son. James lifted him into the air and set him down. Rocking him softly back and forth, she mouthed the words, "Thank you." He nodded and rejoined his party.

"I'm real sorry, Mr. Vine," the overseer said. "Didn't expect your party to get into this mess."

James prodded his horse forward, causing the man to stumble backward to keep from falling. "Sorry for what, you bastard? You don't lose slaves, whether they are five or fifty. At the end of the day you account for all your charges and if a child is missing you find him, do you hear?"

The overseer's eyes narrowed. He looked from Evan to James, not knowing what to say to this man half his age who he had never seen before.

"Take care of your workers or you will be replaced," Evan said in a stern voice. He then turned and rode away. James knew he was in trouble.

When they reached the stables, Evan dismounted and came toward James, smacking his riding crop on the side of his pant leg, "You, Mr. Simmons, have overstepped your boundaries and compromised my authority. It will never happen again. Do you understand?"

"Yes sir," James replied, relieved that he was not fired or hit by the leather strap.

Evan handed the reins to the stable boy and headed toward the open door. He turned toward James. "Don't go soft on me. I understand your concern for the child, but don't go soft on me."

Phillip followed behind Evan, "You will not last out the week, James." Phillip said. "With your attitude, he may let you go today." Phillip was enjoying making James squirm.

Phillip was also wrong.

With Paul's health failing, he was impatient with the progress James and Phillip were making. He found countless mistakes in their calculations and admonished them daily. "I cannot tell you how important it is to keep accurate records. Our taxes are based on our profit and we must make sure that we can document all of our expenses. You two have only three weeks more in which to be competent enough to take over the management duties of Vine Manor."

James gave him a puzzled look. "And, why the three-week deadline, Paul? Are you leaving?"

"No—I am going to die. I may go sooner, but I think I can last at least three weeks," Paul responded.

Phillip stood up, removing his glasses and placing them on the desk. "That is ridiculous. No man knows exactly when he is going to die. I know your condition is deteriorating, but to say that—"

Paul did not let him finish. "I said I am going to be gone in three weeks. Now, let us get back to work." Paul knew his health was failing and each day spent with the two men was excruciating. His back ached terribly and at times he felt as if his throat was going to close shut. He knew his time was limited. Giving himself three weeks was a gift to himself.

Just one day short of three weeks, Paul collapsed in his office.

Evan sent word to Hallie that Paul was gravely ill and if she wished to see him alive she should come home at once. It took her only three days to return to Vine Manor. Upon arrival she went immediately to Paul's bedchamber. Her eyes narrowed as she tried to adjust to the dim light in the room. Quietly, she crossed the floor and stood next to his bed. He stirred for a moment, "My goodness, I must be closer to death than I thought if Evan has sent for you," he murmured.

"You're not even close. I was homesick. How are you feeling?

Is there anything I can do for you?" Hallie asked.

Paul smiled. "Too many questions. Go downstairs and retrieve a decanter of brandy and two glasses. The doctor said I should avoid alcohol; it is bad for my health. Try to make some sense out of that gibberish. Now go, before we are interrupted."

Hallie hugged the railing of the stairs as she stealthily made her way down the stairs and into the parlor. Opening the sideboard, she took a carafe of brandy and two glasses off the silver tray inside the door.

She was startled when Nona came up behind her. "What you doing, Mizz Hallie?"

"Nothing. I was just looking for father." She held the glasses and bottle behind her back. Sliding sideways, she stepped into the hall and hurried up the stairs. Nona took her apron and dusted the two rings from the tray and rearranged the rest of the decanters in the cabinet.

"I almost got caught," Hallie said breathlessly as sat down next to Paul's bed.

"Pour the brandy. I want to make a toast," Paul said. Hallie poured a few inches into each glass and handed one to Paul. His hand shaking, he raised his glass.

"Here is to my past—or should I say passing—and your future." He downed half the brandy, while Hallie only touched the liquid to her lips.

"Ah, the nectar of the gods. It takes the edge off of pain." Paul finished off his glass of brandy. "Now, my dear, Hallie. I want you to take care of your father, he will be lonely without me. He probably will not show much emotion, but I know he will be sad when I die. I have a few regrets and I am not afraid of dying, but it will be much easier if I know that Evan and you will have a good life. The hard times will come and pass. They will leave you stronger, Hallie." His voice was now barely audible. "Please don't wear black for more than a week. You look so much better in blue."

"This all sounds so final. I dare say you will be up on your feet in a day or two," Hallie said, taking the glass from his trembling hand.

Paul had closed his eyes. She ran her hand across his cheek. "I love you, Paul Dunn." He raised his fingers from the cover and touched her cheek.

Paul died the next day, with Evan and Hallie at his bedside.

Lightnings flashed across the murky sky as the funeral procession marched up the hill to the cemetery. The Negroes followed behind the family and friends that had come to pay their respects to Paul Dunn. With everyone in place, the priest held his hand on his bible page to mark his place as the cloth of his robe flapped like a full-mast ship. "I will make this very short, lest we all be drenched." His voice was lost in between the growling claps of thunder. Another bolt of lightning zigzagged across the sky as the clouds opened and the rain began to pummel the crowd. Women trying to hold their umbrellas open and gentlemen holding down their hats ran for the carriages coming up the hill to retrieve them.

Phillip slid across the seat of the coach to make room for James. The drivers tried to steady their teams in the sheets of rain while they waited for the carriage of Evan and Hallie to pull onto the road.

"I want Paul's office," Phillip stated.

"Well, aren't you a mourning bastard. You could at least wait until he is buried or better still, until his personal affects are removed from his desk," James said, surprised at Phillip's candid remark.

"I am not grieving for Paul Dunn. He has taught me well, but I did not consider him my friend and I knew him just a short time. It's time for us to meet with Evan and get on with the business of running this plantation. Soon the keys will be turned over to at least one of us," Phillip said.

Inside the first coach, Evan took Hallie's hand. "Thank you for coming home. It meant a lot to Paul and also to me. I will sorely miss him."

"And so will I," Hallie said. "Father, please stay well. I really don't know what I would do if something happened to you." Hallie wrapped her arm through his and held on tight.

Part Three: Hallie and James – 1846

"Take your pick...you can choose anything in this room," James said, as he swiveled around in his chair. Hallie murmured, "I choose you."

Hallie Vine

Why hadn't he noticed her before now? James knew Evan had a daughter, but little was said about her. How old was she—fourteen, fifteen? Whatever her age, she was beautiful. He was formally introduced to her before Paul Dunn's funeral. Dressed in black with her hair tucked under her bonnet, she looked plain and demure. Tonight Hallie stepped into the dining room in blue silk, with sprigs of white flowers tucked into her hair. She was anything but plain or demure.

Chapter Seventeen

The gentlemen stood as she entered. "I believe you all know my daughter, Hallie Vine," Evan said, as the server pulled out her chair. Hallie nodded and everyone took to their seats. Phillip and James sat across from Hallie, while John Blake sat next to her. John Blake was Evan's financier and had been to Vine Manor many times in the past few months.

Hallie felt uncomfortable under the stares of both young men. She lowered her head, the silence broken by John Blake. "I do believe you are prettier every time I see you, Miss Vine. How old are you now, fifteen?"

"No sir, I am sixteen. Actually, sixteen and a half." She regretted her comment. Camille had told her that a lady never reveals her age. Yet tonight she wanted to be considered a young lady, not a child.

Evan's astute insight immediately picked up the attraction that both young men seemed to have for Hallie. He had not intended for Hallie to even consider taking a suitor at her age. He should have listened to Paul's advice and kept Phillip and James away from her. Evan glanced at his daughter. She was easy to look at. With the natural curl of her hair and soft features she reminded him of Mary Elizabeth. Evan would have to talk with Nona about Hallie's choice of clothing. He did not like the cut of her dress. It was much too revealing.

Evan nodded to the server. The dinner had begun. "I would like to compliment my new assistants on their handling of my affairs. I am quite pleased. I know that stepping into Paul's shoes has not been easy. I still cannot figure out how Paul was able to fit everything into his schedule. With everything there is to do around here, I am sure the duties of managing the internal affairs of this house are quite cumbersome. I am considering hiring a housekeeper to take care of the staff and inventories. That would give you gentlemen more time to spend on the more important matters."

"Excuse me for interrupting you, Father," Hallie said. "I would be more than happy to take care of some of the household duties. I know I am not old enough to attend to the staff, but I could take care of the inventories and menus."

"You sure you are ready to have the discipline to take on the organization and record keeping? It is a daunting assignment. Are you sure you have the demeanor to handle the task?" Evan asked. "Surely, Hallie, you must be joking."

Evan was immediately regretful of his last remark, knowing by Hallie's face that he had embarrassed her.

"I have never been asked to assume any of the duties, but I feel sure I am quite old enough and have enough education to handle the responsibilities. My goodness! How hard can it actually be?" Hallie replied.

"I do believe it may be an excellent idea, Mr. Vine," Phillip interjected. "After all, she is the lady of the house." He smiled at Hallie.

"Then it is done. Phillip can help you with the inventory lists that Paul had compiled. You can start your initiation process tomorrow." Evan turned his attention to the men at the table and Hallie was left to finish her meal in silence.

The following day, Hallie met with Phillip after the breakfast hour. She sat next to Phillip at the table in the library while he opened the ledgers all written in Paul Dunn's perfect script.

"These are what you need to prepare your orders. Some things take longer to arrive here, so make sure that you do not let the stock deplete. Paul has notations in here as to the amount that should be kept on hand at all times. I am sure you will have no problem," Phillip said. He placed his hand over Hallie's. She promptly pulled her hand away.

"We will meet once a week to discuss the orders. Perhaps we can have dinner together on those days," Phillip said smiling.

Hallie stood up. "If I have any questions, I will let you know, Phillip." She couldn't wait to leave his office. There was something about Phillip's demeanor that made her very uncomfortable.

The following week, Evan sent Phillip to the shipyard to make sure that the cotton bales were properly counted and loaded on the ships; Evan and James were going on an overnight trip to the south field. It was time to make the annual count of field workers.

Riding out in the early morning, James and Evan crossed the creek while mist still hugged the ground. It was Evan who broke the silence. "What do you think of my daughter, James?" he asked.

"I don't think of her at all, Mr. Vine," James replied, knowing that was far from the truth.

"Ah, I see. That was a very good answer. I have an uneasy feeling that perhaps Phillip might want to court her. He makes every opportunity he can to see her and is always telling me how nice she is to him. I suppose it is only natural. Hallie is a very appealing young woman. Knowing how precise Phillip is in everything he does, I am afraid that he would treat marriage as just another business venture."

James did not respond. He was bewildered at the conversation and remained silent as Evan continued.

"I miss having these talks with Paul. He always had a way of easing my mind in most situations. I can tell by your silence that you are concerned about saying the wrong thing."

Evan decided to change the subject. "What about your parents, James? You never speak of them. Phillip has told me more than I need to know about his family."

"They were good parents, but there were too many children. Some died before I was born, but there were still too many. My mother never had much time to give us individual attention and my parents spent little time together. When I marry I only want a few children, so that my wife and I can have time for just the two of us."

"I think that is quite honorable, James," Evan said, finding a renewed interest in the young man by his side.

On their return from the field, James and Evan entered the house to find Hallie wearing a bandana on her head, her faced smudged with black soot. She carried a straw broom in her hand.

Hallie was surprised to see them. "I had no idea you would be home so soon."

"Hallie, what in heaven's name is going on? Why are you dressed like that?" Evan asked in a surprised tone.

"Well, you see, Nona and I opened the windows in the parlor. The room seemed so stuffy. What I didn't know is that a raccoon had chewed a hole in the wire around the chicken pen last night and the chickens are now running loose. When I went back into the parlor to close the window there was a chicken walking around the room. It had made quite a mess. I tried to shoo it out the window, but it flew into the fire pit and came out covered with ashes. Now ashes are everywhere! I was trying to help clean up the mess before you got home."

Evan could not help from grinning. "Where is the bird?"

Hallie held up the broom. "I hit it a little too hard. We are having roast chicken for dinner."

The evening meal was filled with mirth, while Hallie retold her story. James and Evan laughed at the thought of her chasing the quite tasty hen with her broom.

"I must have looked a sight," Hallie said, "with all that soot on me."

"I thought you looked very charming," James said, without thinking. "Ah, what I meant is, you always look nice," he fumbled for something more to say hoping Evan had not heard his comment.

"Never mind, James," Evan said curtly. "We quite understand. Now let's at least pay homage to the bird that gave us all a good laugh." Holding up his glass, he made a toast.

Chapter Eighteen

A month later, Hallie threw herself across the bed and buried her head into her pillow. "I cannot do this, Nona. I have made a mess of another supply list. I am sure that we do not have enough flour to last the week, much less until the end of the month and somehow I have misplaced a whole set of bed linens."

"Dat don' have to be a big problem. We kin make more vegetables and less bread. I kin have the cooks make puddins, stead of cakes for dessert. Lessen ya want to tell Massa Vine what ya did."

Hallie sat up. "No! If I have to, I will lie. I will tell them that the flour was filled with weevils and we had to throw half of it away."

Nona folded the clean linens piled on the floor. "Massa Paul used to open dah barrels as soon as dey come, he make shu dey be free of dah bugs before dah driver left."

"All right, so I just didn't bother to check what we had on hand before I placed my order. It is no use trying to pretend that I am doing a good job when I am messing everything up. Oh, fiddle, I might as well tell father. He is too smart to fool. I might as well face him now and get it over with," Hallie said.

Hallie waited until after dinner and made sure that her father seemed to be in a good mood before approaching him with her bad news. He stood in front of the mantel smoking his cigar and drinking his after-dinner brandy.

Hallie plopped down on the settee and folded her arms across her chest. "I am sorry, father. I failed you miserably. Perhaps I am too young," Hallie said, choking back tears.

"You are not too young, Hallie. I was the one who thrust these duties on you without ever thinking that you needed more instruction. It was always a mother's duty to teach her daughters the proper way to run a household. Paul always took care of it and I suppose most of the servants followed his instructions to the letter. I assume most were afraid of him. Without their help, it is a big task." He touched her hand. "I will ride to the Parrish house tomorrow and see if Mrs. Parrish can spare a few days to help you organize this monstrous duty." Evan reached into the box of andirons sitting near the fire. He pulled out a polished wooden stick. "This belonged to your grandmother. It will be your authority."

Hallie laughed and held up the stick. "Maybe I should pop myself on the head first."

With Mrs. Parrish's help, Hallie began to relax and fall into the routine of her duties.

"You see dear, it is really not that difficult. You just have to allot time each day to make sure you get everything completed," she said as she stood in front of the linen closet with her pad and pencil in hand. "Just one day can throw you completely off schedule. You must make sure the kitchen workers know that you mean business. They may try to sabotage your authority from time to time."

"I can't thank you enough, Mrs. Parrish. I wish I could return the favor."

"Hallie, there is something you can do for me. My granddaughter, Evalinn Parrish, is coming to stay with me. I would love it if you would come visit when she arrives. It would make it so much easier on her if she had someone younger to spend time with. It may keep her from getting homesick. She thinks she is coming here to help me, but really her mother is trying to make it easier on her. She is a very unhappy girl right now." Mrs. Parrish did not elaborate so Hallie did not question why Evalinn was unhappy at home.

"I shall be more than happy to do it. I really would like to have a friend myself," Hallie answered.

On the day Evalinn came to the Parrish house, Mrs. Parrish sent a messenger to tell Hallie that her granddaughter had arrived. Evan and Hallie were invited to dinner the next evening. Hallie was anxious to meet Evalinn.

They shared a love of books and gardening and both loved needlepoint. They both liked to gossip about men, although neither one was well versed on the subject of courting. Evalinn and Hallie bonded instantly, even though Evalinn was four years older than Hallie.

"A social life is very important, Hallie," Evalinn said as she threaded her needle. Hallie and Evalinn had spent all day in the sewing room mending lace trims. "I have been to many cotillions and we have had four weddings in our home, but I have yet to find a suitor. Perhaps I will have better luck in Mississippi. I suppose if I were nicer looking like you it wouldn't be as much of a problem."

"Thank you for the compliment, Evalinn, but there is nothing wrong with your looks," Hallie replied.

Hallie was being kind. Evalinn was quite heavy around her girth. She had problems with her complexion at an early age, leaving pocked marks on her cheeks and forehead. Evalinn took little care with her appearance preferring to pull her black hair away from her face and into a tight bun. Not an attractive style for a girl her age.

"I've only been to one formal ball and Paul Dunn escorted me to that one. Father says he wants me to wait until I am at least eighteen before I even think about dating," Hallie groaned. "That is a whole year away."

Evalinn enjoyed spending time at Vine Manor. She followed Hallie around while Hallie did her daily inventory of the household supplies. She hoped of getting a glimpse of either James or Phillip. Evalinn was elated when she found that Hallie had two young men living on the plantation but it seemed that both men were very good at keeping out of sight whenever Evalinn was present in the house. Her loud laughter and constant chatter kept them at bay.

"I do swear, Hallie, I can't imagine how nice it must be to have not one, but two young men living right here on the property. I would find myself distracted all of the time," Evalinn said as she fanned herself. "Do you think they are about right now?" she asked, looking up and down the hall. Perhaps they would like to take us for a carriage ride."

"They are busy working, Evalinn. I am not allowed to disturb them." Evalinn sighed. A visit would be quite a bit more pleasant if the gentlemen were around.

A few months later, when Evalinn went home for her younger sister's wedding, Hallie found that she missed Evalinn's company. James and Phillip were both relieved that they could now roam the house freely without being detained by Evalinn and her constant prattle, yet Hallie was lonely without her.

With her house duties completed and Evalinn still out of

town, Hallie found herself with idle hours. Selecting a book from the library shelf, she ambled into the garden. Walking along the path she caught sight of James standing at his office window. She waved to him as she walked closer to the open window. "It is much too nice a day to stay inside. I would love to go for a carriage ride and pick some wildflowers for the house vases."

"I have tons of paperwork to do, Hallie," James remarked.

"Oh fiddle, you can do it later."

James had been tempted. Perhaps for just an hour and then he would return to his work. He threw his leg over the sill and climbed out the window. He made a grand gesture with his hand. "Lead the way, Madam."

James followed Hallie to the back of the house. Pulling Jasper away from his garden weeding, they went into the stable and waited while he readied the carriage.

With Jasper driving, Hallie gave directions. Jasper had no idea where he was going when she directed him to drive through the creek bed beyond the open field.

"Here, stop here, Jasper," Hallie said as they neared a bluff choked with overgrowth. Hallie stepped down from the carriage before James could help her and began walking into the thicket.

"Miss Vine, do you think this is a good idea? The grass is very high," James said.

"Jasper, light a couple of lanterns." Hallie called back to him as she neared the entrance to the cave.

Jasper shook his head. He had no idea what she was up to, but when he saw her disappear behind the curtain of leaves, he was not totally in favor of going any further. With shrill-pitched cries and a flutter of wings, a family of bats swooped low from their sleeping den. Jasper ducked and covered his head with his hands. "Oh, Lawdy, please, Massa James, don make me go in dar! I be afraid, real afraid, dem is devil bats. Dey put dah devil in ya," he said, dropping the lanterns to the ground.

James picked up the lanterns. "You stay here and watch the carriage. I need to see what she is doing." Stepping inside, he held the lanterns high and called her name. She did not answer. He called again. "This is not funny, Hallie. You best come out. It is far too dark in here to play games."

Hallie jumped down from the ledge where she was standing and touched him on the shoulder. James stumbled backward, falling onto the damp floor.

"I'm sorry if I scared you," she said, laughing.

James stood up, brushing off the seat of his pants. "Jasper is right, this cave will put the devil in you. You scared the blazes out of me. Seems to me you've been here before." He sat down on the ledge next to her as she took the lantern and began lighting the rest of the lamps. Their illumination cast a yellow glow along the wall.

"This is a secret place where only special people are invited. My father and I were the only ones who knew about it, that is, until now. My father brought me here when I was just a child. You must swear to me that you will keep my secret. I am sure father would be upset if he knew I brought you here," Hallie said.

"But why? There must be a hundred caves like this along the river bluff. The Indians used to live in them years ago. What makes this one so special?"

"Don't spoil it for me, James. It is special because I only share it with people who mean something to me. Father and I would sit on this ledge and make shadow puppets on the wall. We would talk about wonderful things, like my mother and fairies and Nona's chocolate cake. It was a grand time!" Suddenly quiet, Hallie turned her back to James as she ran her hand across the smooth wall.

"My father said I was to keep my distance from you and Phillip. It is easy with Phillip. I cannot stand his smug condescending attitude toward me. He makes me shiver when he talks to me like a child. You, on the other hand, make me feel grown up, and I like that. Look," Hallie said, pointing to the top of the cave where beautiful stalactites held fast to the ceiling. "Aren't they just gorgeous. They are millions of years old. Did you know that, James?"

He wanted to reach out and take her hand, instead he uttered, "We had better go. Jasper will think we have been swallowed by the cave monsters," James said.

Jasper was also sworn to secrecy on the way home. "If you tell anyone where we were, those bats may come after you," Hallie said, laughing. She knew Jasper would never tell.

James glanced at her as they rode back to the house. *She was really quite beautiful, but so unpredictable.*

Chapter Nineteen

Another year had passed since James and Phillip had taken on the responsibility of running Vine Manor. With winter quickly approaching the quilts were brought down from the garret and the wool rugs once again covered the floors.

Everyone in the house seemed to be bearing their silent angst. It was as if a heavy fog had separated the geese from the vee. Evan had taken a fall from his horse and was quite irritable. He was suffering from excruciating back pain, which made it impossible to make the long ride to the far fields. James insisted on going in Evan's place, which made Hallie irritable, since she did not see him for days on end. With James away, Phillip was ill tempered with the increased amount of work he had to accomplish each day.

Phillip also wrestled with his own lifestyle. He knew that it was time for him to make some changes. He had conceded on his bid to court Hallie and had no viable prospects of his own. Hallie would have been a feather in his cap, but it was obvious to everyone that she was not interested in him as a suitor.

Phillip did not want to grow old sitting at a desk in Vine Manor as Paul Dunn had. If by chance, Hallie and James did marry, would James fire him? He and James seemed to disagree on many business issues, but Evan knew that Phillip was sharp when it came to figures. Evan also knew that Hallie was not fond of Phillip, which pleased him a great deal.

In almost three years at Vine Manor, Phillip had not been able to save money. His parents' constant demands for him to send funds home had left little for his own use. Their only hope was that Phillip or one of his five sisters would marry into a wealthy family. They could not present their daughters into high society without Phillip's financial help. Even though it was distasteful to him, he was considering the idea of courting Evalinn Parrish. Phillip did not like plump women, especially

one who seemed to prattle on and on. At least Evalinn was not a
shrew and of course she was heir to a large part of the Parrish
estate. Phillip knew that it would take little coaxing to get her
interested in him. She was a desperate woman. He could be
comfortable and quite happy living at the Parrish plantation
house. She was expected at Vine Manor that afternoon. He
would begin his campaign to win her.

Sitting in front of the hearth, drinking warm milk with
Hallie, Evalinn was bursting with news, "I wanted to tell you
that I do believe Phillip is starting to show an interest in me,
Hallie. Today when I arrived, he took my hand and told me that
I looked lovely." She giggled, putting her hand to her mouth. "He
wanted to know if he could come to the Parrish House to visit
with me on Sunday. I am so excited! You never talk much of
Phillip. What do you really think of him, Hallie?"

"He looks like a chicken," Hallie said, putting her hands on
her hips. She began to bob her head in and out. "A tall, lanky
chicken."

"Oh, Hallie, you are so funny. Look at me. I surely am no
prize. I am much too abundant for someone my age—most men
prefer shapely women. My teeth are quite crooked and my hips
as wide as the hearth."

"Nona says women with wide hips have an easier time
birthing babies," Hallie said.

Evalinn let out a loud, honking laugh, "Then I should have
no trouble at all! What do you think it is like, you know, being
with a man, Hallie? Does the thought scare you?" Evalinn asked.

"Sometimes when I am with James, I would like to be very
close to him and I don't even think about being scared, but at
night when I am alone, I do wonder. Nona told me that if your
husband is gentle and patient, a powerful feeling will come over
you when you are together. She said most women don't
experience it, but if you do, you are going to remember it forever.
I wish that Camille were still here. I know she would explain it
all to me."

Evalinn giggled again. "I can't believe we are talking about
this. Let's make a pact. Whoever marries first must tell the
other what it is like. I must be going or I will miss supper."
Evalinn rose from her chair and hugged Hallie. "You are my very
dearest friend."

After Evalinn left, Hallie went to Phillip's office and knocked on the door.

"Well, this is a surprise! And to what do I owe the honor of your presence?" Phillip asked, as he escorted her into his office.

"I have a question. Are you *really* interested in Evalinn Parrish? She thinks that you want to court her. Is that true? You have never mentioned her in this house except to make remarks about her appearance or demeanor. Evalinn said you have paid an unusual amount of attention to her today and she is quite thrilled. Are you playing games, Phillip? Evalinn has tender feelings."

Phillip turned away, his hand tightening around his pen. "She had no right to tell you that at such an early stage, but, yes, I am thinking about seeing her socially."

"You didn't answer my question, Phillip. Do you have real feelings for her?"

Phillip was annoyed. "Stop reading your romance novels, Hallie. Evalinn and I could become compatible. Any feelings I have for her will increase in time. She is lucky that I am even interested in her. I am sure she has not had many suitors, if any. If you must know, I plan to marry her, Hallie—that is, unless you are still available."

Hallie turned and started toward the door. Phillip took her arm firmly in his hand and stopped her. "I don't think it would be wise of you to tell Evalinn of our conversation. It would be a shame if Evalinn had to make a choice between her good friend and me. I guess you know who she would choose. Besides if you are truly her friend you would want her to be happy."

Hallie pulled her arm away, "Leave her alone." She left before she lost her dignity and slapped his face.

Much to Hallie's dismay, Phillip Thixton began courting Evalinn Parrish a few weeks later. In less than six months, he asked for her hand in marriage. Even though Hallie tried to give her friend subtle hints, Evalinn's head was spinning. The entire Parrish family was ecstatic at the prospect of her marriage. No one wanted to let too much time elapse lest Phillip should change his mind.

After an elaborate wedding at the Parrish plantation and a honeymoon in Paris, Evalinn returned to Mississippi and to the inquisitive ears of her best friend. Evalinn did not keep her word to Hallie. She refused to talk about her consummation with Phillip. Hanging her head, she told Hallie that it would be disrespectful to her husband to talk about private matters.

Phillip continued to work at Vine Manor, telling Evan that he would not desert him until a replacement was found. Phillip knew that as soon as Evalinn became pregnant his fate would be sealed. It would be the Parrish's first great-grandchild and he would never have to work again. The attention that they lavished on him would be trice-fold if a child were born.

As each week passed, Hallie saw less and less of Evalinn. She always seemed to have some reason why she could not visit. Hallie knew that Phillip was keeping them apart. When she mentioned this to her father or James, they both said she was probably taking time to adjust to her new life as a married woman. Only Nona agreed with her.

Chapter Twenty

Hallie stood in front of her mirror while Nona fastened the buttons on the back of her dress. Tonight she would attend a reception at the home of John Blake. She had been looking forward to this evening, until James begged off, saying he was not feeling well. Her father would now be her escort.

"I just don't understand James," Hallie said. "I try to look my best whenever I am around him. I listen to his every word and pretend to be interested when he talks about business, but he still seems so distant."

"I think he be half fraid of yer father and half fraid of you," Nona said as she continued to button the dress.

"Me! Why would he be afraid of me?"

"Mister James be a shy man. He be 'fraid if he says dah wrong thing, ya be turnin yer back on him. If ya want him, ya gots tah go get him."

Hallie laughed. "Is that what you did to Jasper?"

"Sho 'nuf. If I waited til he come'd to me, I still be waitin'. Dar, ya all buttoned up."

"Thank you, Nona," Hallie said. She kissed Nona affectionately on the cheek.

Hallie's campaign to make James take an interest in her began with furtive glances, compliments, hands touching accidentally and dance cards filled in four places with James' name.

Even though Hallie felt they were drawing closer together, the words were never spoken, until today. "I'm bored," Hallie said as she ran her fingers across the shelves of books in back of James' desk. "I thought I would come in here and get something to read from your wall of books. I have read almost all of the books in my father's library."

"Take your pick," James said as he swiveled around in his chair. "You can have anything in this room you like."

Hallie murmured, "I choose you."

"When are we going to stop pretending that we don't care about each other?" James asked, touching her hand. "I'm in love with you, Hallie."

"James Simmons, do you know how long I have waited for you to say those words?" Hallie said. "It has been so incredibly long that I was sure you did not have feelings for me and I would have made a terrible presumption. I know it was very unladylike for me to have approached you, but I don't care. The next time you have something to say to me, please don't wait so long."

He took her into his arms and kissed her. It was a soft, moist kiss, his tongue playing on her upper lip. "I'll say it again. I love you, Hallie Vine."

Hallie pulled her head back. "I love you, too, James. And I love kissing. Let's do it again."

"You had better go before someone finds us here in a very precarious position."

Hallie giggled and released him, "Yes, that would be unfortunate."

"Do I have your permission to ask your father if I may court you?" James asked.

"Oh, I can't wait. Let's do it right now. He is in the parlor," Hallie said, pulling James toward the door.

Evan was not surprised. He had seen the looks exchanged between them and had known it was only a matter of time before they succumbed to each other. Evan approved of James. He would be a nice match for Hallie. Evan was amazed that it had taken this long for them to confess their feelings for each other. It would be difficult to keep them apart.

Evan was not ready to let go of his daughter, but he remembered the love he had shared with Mary Elizabeth. James was patient and kind and very much in love with his daughter.

Evan tried to stay out of the way as the plans for the wedding commenced. A steady stream of merchants descended on the house to help Hallie with her decisions for her wedding day. Samples of material, crystal and ornate decorations covered the dining room and parlor. Evan wished Paul could have lived long enough to be present at the wedding. He missed his old friend.

Evalinn sat on the couch in Hallie's sitting room. "What do you think of this one?" Hallie asked as she held a white headpiece up in front of Evalinn. "I like the pearls, but it is rather heavy."

Evalinn shrugged. "It's nice, I guess."

"What is wrong with you, Evalinn? You seem so distant lately. Is everything all right?"

"Everything is fine," she snapped back. "I've just been tired lately. I have to go home now. Phillip will be waiting for me." She hurriedly left the room.

Hallie turned to Nona who was folding samples of linen napkins. "Did I do something to hurt Evalinn's feelings? She doesn't seem at all interested in my wedding. Evalinn has been so testy lately."

"Jest livin' wid dat Mistah Phillip would be nuf to make anybody crabby," Nona replied.

Strains of organ music filled the church, which was exquisitely decorated in white roses and gold candles. Hallie stood at the back of the church holding tightly to her father's arm. After much decision Hallie chose to wear the same dress her mother had worn on her wedding day. It fit her perfectly.

As the music signaled it was time, Hallie turned to her father, "I love James, but you will always be my first love." She kissed his cheek as Evan tried to hide his tears.

James smiled as the most beautiful woman in the world to him came forward to be his wife.

After the ceremony, Hallie hugged Evalinn. Hallie kissed her on the cheek and told her she loved her. Evalinn broke into tears, saying that she would pray for Hallie. Hallie was not sure what she meant. Evalinn had just told her a few days before the wedding that she was pregnant. Hallie was overjoyed for her, but Evalinn just smiled and thanked her.

That evening after everyone had left, Nona prepared the wedding chamber for the newlyweds to share. Just as Rebecca had done when he married, Evan left the house for a few days. He would stay in one of the smaller houses on the property until James and Hallie left for Magnolia to spend their honeymoon.

"Of course, but I've been told that if you are patient and gentle with me, I will experience a powerful feeling. Is that true?"

On the fourth morning Hallie awoke to find her husband dressed and standing before the mirror combing his hair. "Where are you going?" she asked.

Her arms hugged his neck and she pulled him close. James' hands moved across her body and up the hem of her nightdress. Her eyes widened, and she stiffened. "Relax, Hallie. I am not going to hurt you," James whispered. As he continued to stroke her, she tried to lie still, but her body moved up and down in a rhythmic sway. She closed her eyes, making little humming noises, feeling the warmth inside her release and now she understood about the powerful feeling. It took James only moments to undress.

Living with her new husband at Magnolia was a glorious time for Hallie. James had nothing to divert his attention from her. There was no work to be done. Just a time to relax and become accustommed to each other. James found that Hallie liked to sleep late, while he was an early riser. She preferred to eat a late supper, while he enjoyed an earlier meal. They both loved the beach and spent hours sitting under a canopy reading and munching on snacks prepared by the cook.

James loved Magnolia as much as Hallie. He knew that Evan must have adored Mary Elizabeth very much to prepare such a grand house for her.

When Hallie and James returned from their three-month stay in Magnolia, she was glowing with the news that she was almost certain that she was expecting her first child. She couldn't wait to tell Evalinn. Mrs. Parrish met her at the door. "Evalinn is in bed, Hallie. She took a terrible fall down these very steps," she said, pointing to the spiral of stairs in the foyer. "The doctor said he feels her baby sustained no harm, but we are terribly worried. I am sure she will be glad to see you."

Evalinn lay in the bed, a white cloth resting on her face. When Hallie entered, she propped herself up on one elbow. The sleeve of her gown fell away revealing a bracelet of bruises on her wrist. Her right eye was blackened and her cheek swollen even with the bridge of her nose. Hallie gave her a gentle hug. "Oh, Evalinn, I am so sorry to hear about your accident. How did it happen?"

Evalinn groaned as she shifted her position, the bed creaking under her weight. "It was so stupid. It was dark and I was going down the back stairs to the kitchen and my heel caught on the corner of my dress and I took a hard tumble. I have no broken bones, and the baby is still moving."

Hallie stiffened. "But, your grandmother said you fell down the staircase in the foyer?"

"Oh...yes, it was the foyer. I fell..." tears began to flow down her face as Evalinn let out a moan. She dabbed her tears, but she winced when her hands touched the wounds.

Hallie took her hand. "Evalinn, please—tell me what happened. Tell me the truth."

Evalinn sobbed, her hands gripping the covers. "Phillip is sleeping with the colored women. He goes each night to the slave quarters and comes home smelling of his own fluids. He has hit me before, but never this badly, Hallie. He had been drinking and he called me a fat beast not worthy of his attention. He pushed me and I called him a bad name and he knocked me to the floor and punched my face. I should not have called him a blasphemous name."

"Oh, Evalinn, please don't tell me you are blaming yourself for the way Phillip is treating you. He should never lay a hand on you and if he is sleeping with the coloreds, you need to tell your grandparents. Tell them right now and have him thrown off this property. I will make sure that my father releases him from his duties today." Hallie stomped her foot. "He is a bastard!"

"No! No, Hallie, please! My grandparents adore him. I have made comments to my grandmother before about Phillip, but she always seems to turn it around and blame me. My grandmother says I should be a better wife. They will not believe me and even if they did, my grandparents will still side with him. If your father fires him, we will have no money for our personal use."

"I cannot sit by and do nothing while that bastard is beating you up. Let me think on it for a few days. I promise I will say nothing without talking to you first."

"How was your honeymoon?" Evalinn asked as she dabbed at her face.

Hallie smiled. "It was fine. I am almost positive I am going to have a baby."

"I'm happy for you," Evalinn murmured staring down at her hands.

Hallie kissed Evalinn's cheek. "I'm going to go now and let you get some rest. Promise me you will send for me if you need me."

Evalinn grasped Hallie's hand, not wanting to let go. "Thank you, Hallie. You are a dear friend."

Hallie bounded out of the carriage and ran up the stairs to

Vine Manor. She entered the house throwing her hat and gloves on the foyer table, she slammed open the doors to the parlor. Evan and James looked up in surprise. The room was thick with cigar smoke and the two men sipped their brandy.

"Well, don't break the door down, Hallie," her father said. "We were just talking about you. Do you have news for me?"

"Yes, I do!" Hallie replied. "Phillip is beating Evalinn. He has blackened her eyes and bruised her arms. She tells me this is not the first time either. Just a few weeks ago he kicked her in the stomach. Oh, I hate that man! You must do something right away."

Evan shook his head. "That is sad news. I will surely let him know that we are aware of his behavior, but I cannot intervene in his marriage, Hallie."

"But, father, what if it were James abusing me?"

"That is completely different. James would be shot the moment I found out. Evalinn will have to tell her grandparents what is going on and let them handle it."

"I will talk to him in the morning, Hallie. When I am through with him, he will know that his actions are intolerable," James added.

"Evalinn is my best friend and she is scared out of her wits. I am going to find some way to protect her, even if it means shooting that no-good bastard myself." She whirled around and left the room, leaving the two men stunned at her outburst.

The next morning when Phillip arrived for work James confronted him. Phillip denied the charges leveled against him, saying that Evalinn was having bouts of frenzy since she became pregnant. He professed his love to his wife and said he was shocked that Evalinn would say such a thing. Phillip said that Evalinn had been in a state of confusion since her fall and everyone in the house was concerned. He said that he was not the kind of man that would hit his wife, especially one that was carrying his child. Evan and James had no choice, but to drop the matter.

Hallie had a different plan. "It will work. I know it will work, Nona. All you have to do is tell one field woman about the rumor you heard about Phillip. I know within days it will get back to the Parrish household. Maybe then, Mrs. Parrish will take notice of what is going on beneath her very eyes."

"But, Mizz Hallie, whose I gonna tell? I don't want me or ya gettin ourselves in trouble with Massa Vine."

"Surely, Nona, you must know someone out there who loves to gossip. By the time it travels 'round, no one will even remember where it started. Please do this for me."

Nona rolled her eyes. "For you, I'll do it."

Nona made a trip to the Parrish house with the guise of visiting a young servant who had just given birth. Hallie prepared a basket with a new blanket and some muffins for the new mother. Once inside the slave camp, it didn't take Nona long to get the women talking. The rumor circulated for over a week before Mr. Parrish gained word of it. He thundered in to Phillip's office and confronted him with the information. Phillip once again denied the bad behavior. He convinced Mr. Parrish that the servants did not like him and had started the ugly rumor to discredit him. Mr. Parrish relented, saying that was a possibility.

Aware that if he were to abuse Evalinn again, he would be in a dilemma, for the next few months Phillip begrudgingly treated her with a little more kindness.

James repeatedly asked Hallie if she had anything to do with the start of the rumor. Her answer always responded the same way, "What rumor?"

As Hallie's pregnancy progressed, Evalinn also grew weary from the weight she had gained. She spent most of her time in bed, ordering the servants to bring her food. Eating seemed to be her only enjoyment in life. She was plagued by the notion that Phillip was not well. He appeared to be losing weight and his complexion had turned a pale shade of gray. When a rash began to appear on Phillip's hands and feet, Evalinn's worst fear was confirmed. He had syphilis, just as her brother had when he returned from his tour of duty in the army.

When he first discovered the papules on his penis, Phillip consulted Doctor Wilcox and began treatment. He had begged off work, telling Evan that he needed to be close to his wife since her fall. The day Evalinn confronted Phillip he lay down on the bed and sobbed. He pleaded for her forgiveness. He promised that when he returned to health, he would be a faithful and dutiful husband and father. Evalinn knew that Phillip was extremely frightened at the thought of dying, but she did not believe his pitiful pleas.

Hallie paid almost daily visits to Evalinn. On this day

Evalinn seemed unusually agitated. "I need to tell you something, Hallie, and I am only telling you this because I want you to know that if something happens to me, I want you to take my baby out of this house right away." Hallie did not know what to say. Evalinn was drained of every emotion inside of her. "Do you promise me, Hallie? Please, take my baby back to Virginia for my mother to rear. My grandparents are much too old to take on a new baby. I came here to help them, and I have been nothing but a burden."

Hallie nodded her head, "I promise." Her hands instinctively went to her stomach. Her little one was safe inside.

Three months had passed and it was now time for Evalinn to give birth. The morning sun brought beams of light through the bedroom window and across the face of Evalinn Thixton, who writhed in pain. Her hands wrapped around the bedposts as she pushed her massive weight against the midwife who was helping to deliver her baby. "Take it out! Take it out!" she screamed. Streams of blood and urine soaked the bedding. Two housemaids stood nearby, their hands holding white cloths, waiting to take the baby. Exhausted, Evalinn gave one last push and the midwife gently pulled a shriveled baby boy from her womb. "What is it?" Evalinn asked.

"It's a boy," the midwife replied. Turning it over, she began to rub his back. The small blue body went limp in her hands. She quickly cut the cord and took the baby from the room. In the nursery, she laid him on the table and breathed into his mouth. It was no use. He had been dead for some time. She wrapped him in a blanket and went back to the birthing room. News of the stillborn baby was soon heard throughout the house as Evalinn screamed, "No! No!" over and over again. Phillip, who now lay in the next room, too weak to stand, felt a pang of grief at hearing his wife's shrieks.

Sometime during the night, Evalinn struggled from her bed. She took the gun Phillip kept in the nightstand and went to his room. Standing next to his bed, her voice cracked as she softly called his name. His eyes opened. "It is all your fault. You killed my baby." She pointed the gun at his chest.

"What are you doing?" he gasped. "Give me that gun!"

"I am sending you to hell!" Putting a pillow over her hand to muffle the sound, she pulled the trigger.

They found her in the morning. The room was bathed in blood. It was spattered on the bed and the walls, and pooled on the floor where Evalinn lay, barely breathing. She was carried back to her room and put to bed. Repeating over and over again that she wanted to see her baby, the doctor ordered a strong dose of sedatives to calm her nerves.

Hallie and James, along with Evan attended the funerals of Phillip and the child, who was named, John. It was two weeks before Hallie was allowed to see Evalinn. Hallie was told that when Evalinn heard the gun go off, she made it as far as Phillip's bed. Evalinn had collapsed when she saw what had happened and hemorrhaged from getting out of her bed so soon. The doctor assured everyone that she was going to recover. The consensus was that when Phillip found out about the death of the baby, he had shot himself. No one had any idea that Evalinn had killed him. It was difficult for Evalinn to remember what happened. She had blurred images of Phillip's face rushing through her head.

Hallie put the vase of spring flowers on the bedside table and sat down next to Evalinn, who was positioned next to the window, a blanket covering her legs. "I love this time of year. Don't you, Hallie? Everything is about ready to bloom again. It's funny how everything dies in the winter and then comes back again in the spring. Isn't that strange? It seems that once the flowers die, they should be gone forever." She stopped. Turning her head, she looked at Hallie. "I killed him, you know. I killed him, just as he killed my baby. I thought he was going to die from the syphilis and I wanted to see him suffer, but then Doctor Wilcox said he was actually improving. He is dead now, so that is all that matters. They wanted to bury John in the same casket with Phillip, but I said no. Phillip might have dragged poor baby John down when the devil came to get him. I am glad I was too weak to go to the funeral. I would have spit on his grave." Evalinn gave a high-pitched laugh, her head hitting against the back of the chair. "When I am well enough to travel, you and I will go to Magnolia. I will have my baby at Magnolia." She grabbed for Hallie's hand. "Here, touch my stomach. Can you feel him moving? You are my best friend ever. Perhaps when you get married, you will have a baby, too."

Hallie pulled back, stunned at the notion that Evalinn thought she was still pregnant.

Hallie reached over and kissed Evalinn on her cheek. "You need to rest. I will visit you again, soon." Evalinn was not listening. She was looking out the window and humming softly to herself.

Hallie cried when she told James about Evalinn. " Poor Evalinn has lost all of her senses. Mrs. Parrish says that Evalinn insists that she killed Phillip, but they know she didn't. They have reserved a place for her in a sanitarium not far from her parent's home in Virginia. The doctor says she is having delusions from the loss of her husband and baby and is not really living in this world right now."

"Please, Hallie, I know this is all so upsetting to you, but Evalinn needs to go away to get well. You need to take care of yourself right now," James said.

On the day that Evalinn was to be taken to the sanitarium, Hallie arrived early at the Parrish house. Her body, heavy with the weight of her own child that would be born very soon, Hallie helped Evalinn into a simple blue dress. In the past weeks, Evalinn had taken to pulling out strands of her hair, twining it around her fingers until it lay in her hand. Hallie carefully brushed across her head, trying to cover the bare patches. Evalinn had been quiet all morning. Hallie chatted on about anything she could think of that would not upset her friend.

"I'm going to miss you, Hallie," Evalinn said. "I know I will probably never be back."

Hallie sucked in her breath and tried to keep calm. "Nonsense, as soon as you are well you can come back and visit me." She hugged her friend's shoulders.

When Mrs. Parrish said that the attendants were ready to leave, Hallie accompanied Evalinn down the stairs to the waiting coach. Evalinn stopped for a moment on the porch and looked back at her grandparents. "I don't blame you for your decision. I know you are doing the best for me. Please take care of Phillip and little John. " She took Hallie's hand. "Hallie, now that James is dead you must marry someone who will give up their life for you."

As the coach pulled away, Hallie mouthed the words, "James is not dead," knowing that Evalinn was once again confused. Mrs. Parrish broke into sobs and held tight to her husband. Hallie knew she would never see Evalinn again.

Chapter Twenty-One

Another summer, another fall, another winter and now it was spring. The pale green buds of yesterday have burst into saucers of sweet-smelling blooms, while others lay asleep in their cradles of satin leaves. Hallie stood beneath the tree in the front yard of Vine Manor and filled her lungs with the fragrance. As she reached to pick a single magnolia blossom, a trickle of warm water ran down her legs. It was time once again.

Within two years, Hallie gave birth to two daughters, Mary Elizabeth and Lydia Vine.

On the birth of her second child, Dr. Wilcox said the words she did not want to hear. "Hallie, I suggest that you not have any more children. Both of your deliveries were quite worrisome for me. This time the bleeding was excessive. Remember what happened to your mother. You have two precious gifts. Don't tempt fate."

James entered the room with Mary Elizabeth in her arm. She held out her hands wanting her mother to hold her. James smiled at the small infant cradled in Hallie's arms. Hallie patted the bed and Mary snuggled next to her mother. "She doesn't understand; she is just a baby herself. Look, Mary Elizabeth, you have a new baby sister."

She shook her head no and held onto her mother.

"I heard what the doctor said, Hallie. We're now a family of four. Four and no more."

"But, I wanted to give you a son, James. Maybe in a few years, we can try again."

"I don't want a son if it means losing you. We have two healthy daughters and you're still here with me. Two children are all I ever wanted." His eyes clouded and he lay down next to his wife. "I was very scared this time and so was your father. I don't want you to go through that again."

Hallie leaned over and whispered into his ear. "Do you mean

you will never, ever make love to me again?"

"Now, that I did not say," James answered.

With the blessing of two healthy grandchildren, Evan handed the deed to Vine Manor over to James and Hallie. Even though James objected vehemently, Evan would not change his mind. Vine Manor and Magnolia now belonged to James and Hallie.

Chapter Twenty-Two

Strands of invisible seasons are woven together to form a blanket of memories. The sleeping earth turned its head to the sun, greeting each new season, each new year.

Arms that reached out to catch her baby's first step now reached out to hug her children going off on their first summer vacation without her. Toys were traded for books and youth traded for adolescence. They were two daughters that were truly loved by their parents.

Fifteen years had gone by since James and Hallie married. The lust that once clouded their vision had been replaced with knowing looks and tender caresses. Time had given them the ability to form a union that was complete. They knew each other's weaknesses and relied on each other's strengths.

James was the adhesive that held the family together and Hallie was now far removed from the headstrong girl who threw herself on the bed and announced that she was too young to be responsible for the house at Vine Manor. She was now Mistress of both Vine Manor and Magnolia, managing a staff of over forty—and doing it quite well. Hallie considered her first priority to be her husband and children; the children that she adored and coddled now made her realize what she had missed as a child by not having a mother. When James accused her of being over-possessive, she assured him that, "unlike boys, girls need special attention." When Nona complained that the children were being wild and unruly, Hallie would tell her that girls needed to have as much fun as boys. They were her constant companions and except for Nona, she was in complete charge of their care. She loved to bathe them and brush their hair and read to them at night. The words, "I love you, momma," became the melting spot in her heart. Those three words could erase a day's worth of misbehavior.

When the children were asleep for the night, Hallie would

turn her full attention to her husband. She would listen to him talk about his day and try to soothe him with her softness. She would also tell him about her encounters with the ladies of the Mississippi social set. While she lay close to James, she would repeat some of the terrible things the ladies said.

"James do you realize that most of the wives agree that they are not entitled to an opinion on anything other than the house or the children? Their husbands are not interested in their wives' input. It is ridiculous! You always listen to me. And do you believe that they talk about the men who keep mistresses or see prostitutes, some even talked about their husbands sleeping with the Negro women. You would never do that to me, would you James?"

As much as he assured her that he was nothing like those men or had any intention of ever leaving her, she fretted about the constant talk from the women. "I would just die if I knew you were sleeping with someone else. They talk about the disease some of them had to endure. It is just terrible. Remember what happened to Evalinn? Please tell me you will always be faithful to me, James."

James would put his hand over her mouth and give her his constant promise. "I don't know how else to tell you, Hallie. I love you and I will always be faithful to you and you alone."

Together, they endured years when the crops were in abundance; other seasons when the cotton shriveled on the plants from lack of rain or attacks of flea-hoppers were so fierce that you could not go outside for fear that they would tangle in their hair. When bouts of yellow fever and cholera plagued the plantations, Hallie spent her days tending to those that were sick or dying. Exhausted from the long days in the heat, she would scream at anyone in earshot that the animals on the plantation were treated more humanly than the slaves.

They spent summers at Magnolia, where the girls would run barefoot on the beach, watching as the neverending flow of water unearthed the ocean's gifts and pirouetted them onto the beach. Nona would carry an empty pail to collect their treasures as she avoided the waves snatching at her toes.

Many nights at Magnolia, James and Hallie snuggled in the porch swing. They were still very much in love: James feeling blessed every day that he had a wife like Hallie and she feeling blessed everyday that she had a husband like James. Just as

Hallie had heard stories about the husbands who wandered, he had heard stories about the wives, harpies who wanted to do nothing but spend money and attend lavish affairs. The overbearing women admonished the servants at every turn and spent their days planning their next move to make their husbands' lives miserable. One of their favorite ploys was to fill the house with relatives who came for over-extended stays.

Not Hallie. She enjoyed spending time with her family, watching her children grow from infancy into young ladies. In many ways she was like her father. As she grew older, she had little concern for fashionable gowns and jewelry. She told James that she had given that up when she realized how foolish it was to keep chiffoniers overstuffed with clothing and wall safes full of baubles she seldom wore. Her father may not have been around much when she was growing up, but somehow she had managed to attain a good degree of common sense. She chose her friends with caution and would rather stay home with James than go to a gala. It gave her great pride to be able to help him solve his problems. Concern for her family was her driving force.

Chapter Twenty-Three

Although Evan preferred to remain at Vine Manor while
Hallie and her family spent time at Magnolia, he was very much
a part of the family. Hallie's relationship with her father had
come full circle. She was now the one admonishing him for not
eating properly or staying up too late reading. She had taken to
choosing his clothing and making sure he wore a warm jacket
when he left the house. Although Hallie worried about her
father's health, he assured her that other than the damnable
pain in his back, he was a good as ever. Evan was devoted to
Hallie and her family. Nothing gave him more pleasure than
seeing the love they all shared, with him included in the mix.

Evan devoted most of his time to hunting, reading, and his
passion for making brandy and wine. He had kept the recipes he
had acquired when he was in Europe and read every book he
could find on the subject. He and Jasper would peruse over the
list of ingredients needed to make good wine.

Several years previous when he announced that he had
bought winemaking equipment and was having a cellar dug in
the rear of the house, James and Hallie were not surprised. His
animation and attention to detail convinced them that this
might be something that would keep him interested in life.
When his back pain left him immobile at times, Hallie could see
the depression settling on him. When his eyes tired of reading,
he would stand at the window or roam the house. It was only
when the grape vines that he had imported from Italy had
arrived that he seemed renewed. Carefully unpacking the fragile
plants, Evan and Jasper carried them to the newly tilled
orchard. Jasper knew about soil. He walked around the field,
picking up handfuls of the black soil and holding it to his nose.
Finding the right spot he would kneel on the ground and plant
the tender shoots.

Much to Hallie's surprise, the following year, two wagons

filled with young cherry trees arrived from Washington. Evan and Jasper were proud of their vineyard and small stand of fruit trees.

When the first grapes appeared on the gnarled branches woven around lines of wire, Evan brought them into the house and laid the shiny green fruit in a china bowl. He and Jasper beamed as everyone made over the single bunch of grapes. The sideboard in the dining room was soon filled with crystal decanters holding the treasures of his endeavors.

Evan was sometimes amazed at the knowledge Jasper possessed. He was an illiterate black man, but his common sense gave Evan solutions to many of his problems when they assembled the vats and presses for the winemaking.

The relationship between the two men had reached a point far beyond slave and master. When Evan suggested to Jasper that it might be time for him to give him and Nona their papers to make them freedmen, Jasper just shook his head. "Where'd we be going, Massa Vine. Dis be our life and we is happy wid it. Before we comes here, we be cold, beat, and starved. If we leave, we be cold, beat, and starved agin. Dis be just fine as it is. Yer a good man, Massa Vine." The matter was never brought up again.

Evan spent a good deal of his time reading. When Mary and Lydia were small, he would put them on his knee and read to them just as he had done with Hallie, but when the weather was cool and his back eased a little, he still enjoyed a morning of hunting. He took pleasure in providing fresh game for the evening meal. Hallie insisted that Jasper go with her father on the hunts, but sometimes Evan preferred going alone. He would slip out without notice.

On an early October morning, Evan put on his field boots and leather gloves. He retrieved his rifle from the gun closet and set out across the open expanse of grass behind the stables. The mist was still hanging low over the fields. It was a good day to hunt.

Hallie sat at the table in the conservatory watching Lydia and Nona pick roses to put in the vases throughout the house. "Have you seen my father today, Nona?" she asked, sipping her tea. Even though it was not unusual for Evan to stay upstairs until afternoon, he had promised Hallie that he would have lunch with her today.

"No ma'am. He ain't been in his room all day. He didn't eat

no breakfast. Da food was cold on da plate. I guess he be out huntin'."

"That's strange, he should be back by now. Please go ask Jasper to look for him." She rose from her chair and walked to the wall of windows. He was always home from hunting by this time of day.

After lunch, an afternoon piano lesson for both girls took up a few more hours of Hallie's day. It wasn't until she was putting the sheet music away that she realized she still hadn't seen her father. She looked at her watch. It was almost three o'clock. She wished James were home. He had gone to Natchez and wouldn't be home until morning. Hallie called to Nona. "Tell Jasper to take a wagon to the back field and see if he can find my father. Something is wrong—I know it is. Father should have been back hours ago." The words were barely out of her mouth when Jasper came through the door holding his hat in his hands. "I be real sorry Mizz Hallie. I looked all back yonder. I called his name. I didn't find him. It be gettin' dark. We need to get some lanterns and go look some more." Hallie could see the concern on Jasper's face. "Massa Vine always hunts by da creek. I looked up and down and back agin."

Jasper assembled a party of men from the field. Armed with lanterns, they spread out across the fields as far as the bluffs. Hallie, wrapped in a shawl, stood on the porch watching the yellow glow, like giant fireflies, pop up in the fields. The men calling out her father's name. Mary and Lydia had both gone to bed in tears, worried about their grandfather, even though Hallie had assured them that he would be fine. She now knew he was not fine. Her father was somewhere out there in the darkness. The night stalkers with their keen eyes would be padding through the fields, their noses to the ground, looking for prey.

Near dawn, Nona found Hallie asleep on the settee in the parlor. She gently touched her shoulder. Hallie's body jerked and she bolted upright. "Have they found him? Is he okay?"

Nona shook her head. "Dey ain't found him yet. Dey went all da way to da creek bed and back."

"Oh, my God! I think I know where he might be! Nona, get some blankets and come with me." Hallie opened the front door and ran outside calling Jasper's name. He came from behind the house, his eyes red from lack of sleep. "I be still lookin', Mizz

Simmons."

"Jasper, get a wagon quick. Bring it around back. Go!" she screamed.

Jasper took off in a trot as Nona appeared in the doorway, her arms filled with blankets. With the two women settled in the wagon, Jasper waited for directions from Hallie.

"Drive across the south field, stay in the middle and don't take the road. When you get to the creek bed, follow it down to the first outcrop," Hallie said, almost breathless. Holding onto the buckboard, she pointed to where Jasper should turn. "There, Jasper. Over there, by those vines. Stop there." Hallie jumped down, and ran toward the overgrowth. Pulling back the curtain of leaves, she called her father's name. "Jasper, Nona, come quick! Bring the blankets."

"Oh, Lawdy, I remember dis now. We be goin' into dat hole in da ground," Jasper said. He took Nona's arm and hurried her along.

Hallie was already inside. A small yellow flame coming from an almost empty lantern guided her to her father. He was lying on his side next to the lamp. His arms were cradled under his head and his body shivered from the cold ground. Hallie dropped to her knees and motioned to Nona, who came toward her with the blankets draped over her head for fear of the bats. She handed them to Hallie. Hallie covered him up and put her hand on his face. His eyes were closed. She called his name but he did not answer. Putting her face on his chest, she listened for even the slightest breath. "He is still alive. He is breathing! We have to get him out of here."

"He be bleedin'. See, der on dah ground by his side," Jasper said. Pulling back the blanket, Hallie gasped. The left side of his leather jacket had been ripped away and blood was seeping out. "Quickly! Help me get him to the wagon."

Who knows where they got the strength to carry him, but the three of them picked him up off of the ground and carried him to the wagon as if he were as light as a feather. Hallie put his head on her lap while Nona pressed her hand into the side of the blanket that was now stained with blood. Evan opened his eyes and looked up at his daughter. "Hallie," he murmured.

"Father, please don't talk. Save your strength," she said, holding him closer.

"Stupid mistake... fell... gun went off. I knew you would find me. I love you." His voice came in short pants. He closed his eyes again.

Hallie could hear the screams as some of the house servants rushed to the wagon. "Someone go for the doctor! Please, hurry!"

Evan was carried up the steps and into his bedroom. He was still unconscious. While some of the servants undressed him and covered his wound with white cloths, Hallie stood motionless. It was Nona who pulled her away. "You got to get out of dem bloody clothes, Mizz Hallie. Your girls see you like dat, dey will faint dead away. We gonna keep him safe 'til the doctor gets here."

Hallie didn't remember being taken from the room or being helped out of her clothes and the blood rinsed off her. She sat by his bed, staring at his ashen face as they waited for the doctor to arrive. She watched as the servants took turns putting pressure on the wound, the only thing they knew to do to stop the bleeding until the doctor arrived.

"It is a very deep wound, Hallie. I'm sure it has damaged his liver or kidneys," Dr. Wilcox said, after he finished examining Evan. "I have managed to stop the bleeding for now. We just have to wait and see. I have given him something for pain."

When James arrived home a few hours later, Hallie fell into his arms. "It's Father, he..." wracked with sobs, she could not continue. James held her close until she was able to speak.

Evan Vine lingered for two more days before he succumbed to the fury of his wounds. He was sixty-seven years old.

Unlike Paul, who had never professed any particular religion, Evan considered himself a devout Catholic. He attended mass at least twice a month, taking Lydia and Mary with him. It had been years since Hallie had been in St. Stephen's Church. Today the pews were filled to capacity, with people standing in the rear of the church to hear the mass for Evan Vine.

It had been a long week, with the house filled with guests and relatives. Hallie felt as though she had no time to grieve for her father. She would have to do that later, in private. Today she must give her father a proper funeral and put him to rest next to her mother. Once the procession had left the church and the coffin put on the wagon, Hallie went back into the church to retrieve a bouquet of white roses for the grave. As she stood looking up at the stained glass windows, she closed her eyes and said a small prayer, asking God to take care of her father.

Three months after Evan died, Hallie once again needed soothing. Mary Elizabeth and Lydia were going to Atlanta for a few weeks to spend time with the Handmakers' grandchildren. Hallie was worried about the trip and insisted that extra attendants were assigned to the coach. This would be the first time she would be separated from them for more than a few days and she tried not to show her concern as she helped them choose outfits to take with them. The death of their grandfather had been hard on them. James felt it would be a good idea for them to get away from home for the summer.

Although Hallie felt somewhat confident that Mary would do well away from home, she worried about Lydia. At thirteen, Lydia was full of life and not one to sit for too long in one place. She was bored with most adult conversations and Hallie knew that the Handmakers loved to entertain and have dinner guests. Hallie repeatedly reminded Lydia that she must behave and sit quietly during dinner, that she must not squirm in her chair, a habit Lydia had learned from her mother when the conversation was not to her liking.

When their carriage pulled away from the house, Hallie burst into tears. She stood on the porch until it was no longer in view. "I can't believe I am actually letting them go. Three weeks is such a long time."

James put his arm around his wife. "They will be fine. They need a change. Except for Magnolia, they haven't been away from home. They need to learn to rely on each other instead of only you."

While the girls were away, Hallie decided she would use the time to repay some of the kindness shown to her after her father's death. She arranged for several dinner parties to be held at Vine Manor. She soon realized that she was not ready for social events. She still missed her father and was silently distressing over the absence of her daughters.

"Can we not have one dinner party without someone bringing up the subject of slavery and war? As soon as you gentlemen have a chance to excuse yourself from the table you huddle in groups. I saw those northern newspapers being passed around," Hallie said, as she prepared for bed. "The people writing that nonsense don't even know us. Why do they present us as decadent, cruel, money-hungry people who care nothing for our workers?"

James sat on the stool unlacing his boots. "They are always quick to point out every injustice they can find to prove their point. Reporters are always taking interviews with Negroes who had fled from our plantations and they show pictures of slaves being hung for what they say was nothing more than talking back. It is a hard time for everyone to accept."

James was like most of the southerners who were agonizing over their own moral issues when it came to the slaves. If they were to free the slaves where would they go? Chaos would reign and the economy would collapse. Disgruntled slaves would take to violence and everyone's life would be in jeopardy. As it were, slaves were disappearing from the plantations each month at an alarming rate and to replace them cost close to a thousand dollars each. More and more plantation owners were leaving half of their fields fallow. Given time, the system would collapse on its own, but the northern states felt an urgency to change things now.

"I have an idea," Hallie said, as she pulled back the covers. "Do you have enough energy left in you to listen to my plan?" James nodded and lay back on the bed. "I was thinking that maybe it would be a good idea to leave this place. Parcel the land out to those workers who want to stay and sell the rest. We could move to Magnolia. We don't need this big house and all this property. All it does is cause us headaches. There would be plenty of money from the sale of Vine Manor and you could open a law or accounting practice in Lott's Point. Since father is gone, the house just doesn't mean the same to me."

"If the government can come to a reasonable plan for everyone it would be a great idea, but right now we couldn't even give this land away. There is too much uncertainty. Besides, it is our home and our children's legacy. Is it right for someone to come and just take it away from us?" He took her hand. "Please don't be afraid, Hallie. I will never let anything happen to you and our daughters."

She put her head on this chest. "I am afraid, so afraid, James."

When the girls returned from their stay with the Handmakers, Mary was ready to continue her studies in English and History. Lydia, as usual, was resistant. She would rather pound away on the piano for hours, driving her parents out of the parlor. "Is she really a good pianist or am I tone deaf?"

James asked as he escaped to the balcony.

Hallie smiled. "She is very good, it's just that Lydia cannot do anything in moderation. She hasn't learned that louder is not better. Her teacher says she is doing quite well."

James smiled. "He is probably saying that so she will stop taking lessons."

At almost fourteen, Mary was quite the young lady. She was polite, unobtrusive, and agreeable. Lydia was none of those things. She was boisterous, inquisitive, and always asking, "Why?" Yet it was Lydia who would throw her arms around her parents and openly express her love while Mary was more likely to give her mother a peck on the cheek. Hallie enjoyed both of them immensely, whether it was reading with Mary or playing games with Lydia in the conservatory.

The girls barely tolerated each other, Mary screamed when Lydia poked her as they passed in the hall or Lydia found that Mary had used her hairbrush. It was only when storms struck at night and the thunder rumbled through the house that you could find them in the same bed. Awakened by the storm, Hallie would open the bedroom door and look in on her two girls wrapped in each other arms, with Mary's blond hair entwined with the auburn tresses of her sister. Hallie loved them both so much. She had decided they would have to stave off any more trips until they were much older.

Chapter Twenty-Four

Rain, rivulets of rain running off the roof into barrels. Rain, overflowing the water troughs, bubbling in the roads. Rain, washing layers of red clay off the backs of the plow horses and filling the creeks she could hear but not see. Rain was falling from the sky like the tears from Hallie's eyes as she openly grieved for her father.

As Hallie cleaned out his office, she uncovered a flood of memories. Pictures of the two of them together, books he had read to her, and a small handkerchief that had belonged to her mother. Putting it all into a teakwood chest, she stood by the window, watching the patterns of water run across the glass.

Out in the field, an overseer sat on his horse in his sodden coat. He cursed to himself as his foot slipped from the stirrup, shifting his body sideways. Righting himself, he prodded the horse further under the still lifeless branches of a tree. Rain was also dripping off the hat brims and noses of the workers as they used their hands to dig trenches around the rows of cotton plants. The rain that they would pray for in the summer was drowning the tender roots of the plants this spring.

Then the message came. Call the workers in. The battle was over. The rain had won.

He cupped his hands around his mouth and called out, "We're done for the day. Pass it on." As the short message was passed from row to row, the workers stood up, mired into the sinking pools they had just made with their cold and aching feet. They slowly walked to the end of the row and waited for the wagons. There would be no comfort in their quarters. The leaking roofs and sodden firewood would leave them shivering in the dark with not even a cup of boiled water to keep them warm.

James stood with his hands on the mantel, turning his cheek as the heat warmed his face. "It's over, Hallie. If it doesn't stop raining by tomorrow, the entire crop will be lost. I have never seen so damn much rain," he said as he kicked a log further into the fire, sending up a shower of sparks.

"The Negroes need dry wood," Hallie said, as she continued her needlework.

"What? I'm talking about our future and you're talking about wood. What brought that up?"

"Their cabins are freezing and all of the wood outside is unusable. You need to load some wagons with wood and take it to them."

"So, if I take them dry wood, what are we supposed to use?"

Hallie knew it was not a good time to discuss wood, but it had to be done, and quickly, before those huddled together would all die from the chills. "We do not need to keep fires going in all these rooms. We can sleep here, on the first floor. We have plenty of wood, James, and when the weather dries we can have more cut. Besides, it is not going to rain forever."

James sighed. He knew she was right. The slaves should not be punished for the wrath of nature. "I'll tend to it."

As the morning light filtered into the room, Hallie shivered and pulled the covers up to her neck. The fire had gone out long ago. James was still not home. Perhaps she was wrong to send him out last night. She rose from the bed and wrapped a blanket around her nightdress. Silently descending the steps, she bounded across the cold marble floor in the foyer and peered into the parlor. James was asleep on the sofa. His muddy boots lay on the floor. He must have been exhausted and dropped himself on the first available spot. Hallie took the blanket from around her shoulders and covered him. She opened the grate and put two logs into the still smoldering embers. Blowing into the hearth, Hallie accidentally flooded the room with smoke. Standing up, she coughed and waved her hands at the fire, as if by some magic the blaze would start and the smoke would disappear like the girl behind the curtain.

"What are you doing?" James asked, as he sat up and rubbed his eyes.

Hallie jumped. "You startled me. I didn't mean to wake you. I was just trying to build a fire."

"Come here. You can keep me warm," James said, pulling her down on top of him on the narrow couch. "I will have to teach you the proper way to make a fire." He kissed her face, leaving smudges of mud on her cheeks.

He did not want to tell her that more than a third of the workers had taken their families and most of the mules and left the plantation. The new plants lay buried in mud and even the overseers had given up the battle. After giving James their resignations, most of them were leaving. They were going home to their families. There would be no crop this year. He would have the rest of the workers plant garden crops. They would need corn and wheat for the winter. Even the orchard and grapevines that Evan had coveted succumbed to the cold spring and the torrents of rain. James wished that the crops were the worst of his worries. They weren't.

Talk of abolishing slavery was no longer just idle conversation, but looming on the horizon. The news that Mississippi had seceded from the union was the turning of the tide. Surely it would never come to bloodshed between fellow countrymen, yet James had decided over six months prior that he would not sit idle and let his family be put in jeopardy. He hoped that what he had done was enough. It was now a waiting game to see who made the first move and if the bleating lamb would become the roar of the lion.

Later that morning, James called Hallie and the girls into the parlor and shut the door. "Please sit down. News has come over the wire that the new confederate states and our northern aggressors are now at war." Hallie gasped, her hands covering her mouth. Mary grabbed Lydia's hand. James continued, "The war is going to touch everyone, whether we are rich, poor, young, old, black or white. No one is going to be immune to the devastation that Mr. Lincoln and his armies will bring to our lands. I have made a plan that I need to discuss with you." He stopped for a moment, wondering if maybe he should have talked to Hallie alone, but he knew that his children needed to know what was in their future. "I have been sending money to my brother, Stuart, in St. Louis for the past several months. Stuart and his wife Ellen have graciously agreed to let the three of you come stay with them until this situation is over. I will rest easier knowing my family is safe."

Hallie stood up, "I have no intention of leaving my home, especially not without you. How could you even consider such a move without consulting me first? The war is far away from us right now. It will be long over before it reaches Mississippi."

"We have no way of knowing what is going to happen, Hallie.

I hope you are right, but either way it is going to affect our lives. You can stay here and pretend that nothing is happening, but I cannot do that. I am your husband and the father of these children. It is my duty to protect you the best way I know how. I am standing firm on my decision. The three of you are going to St. Louis by train as soon as I can arrange passage. Soon you will not be able to leave, so we must plan your trip quickly. Soon the railroads will be used only to transport troops and supplies."

Lydia stood up, tears running down her face, "But what about Jasper and Nona and the rest of the people?"

"I offered to send Nona and Jasper further up north with some funds and their papers, but they said no. They are staying here. Jasper and I have been taking provisions to the cave as often as we can slip away from the other workers. I have told the workers that if any of them want to leave, I will give them their papers and a few dollars. If they want to stay on the land, they can. I cannot guarantee anyone's safety if the northern forces move into our territory."

"And you, James, what are you going to do? Stay here and try to run this place by yourself? You know the housekeepers will leave and so will most of the field hands. We are a family," Hallie said.

"I've given this issue a great deal of thought, Hallie. I already know that you will not agree with me but I cannot in good conscience sit by and watch my countrymen fall by the wayside while I do nothing. Our rights are being trampled on. We must all fight for the same cause. I will enlist in the army."

Hallie leapt from her chair, "No! No, I don't want that to happen! Please, James, for all of us, stay here or we can all go to Magnolia together."

His voice was softer now. "I can't. I have no idea how safe it would be at Magnolia either, although I am sure August Lott will protect his precious town at all cost. The process of packing up what we can will begin early tomorrow morning. I have secured a warehouse in Ohio for our personal possessions. We have only a day or two before it will be impossible for that to happen, too." James did not tell Hallie that stories of untold horror against the southern plantation women were beginning to surface. "Do not argue with me, Hallie. My mind is made up. Please, Hallie, don't make this any more difficult than it already is."

There was no sleep in the Simmons' house that night. Hallie did not give in easily. "There are so many younger men who can take up arms. Why you?" she asked.

"The army will need people with my credentials. Most of the poor souls who will be fighting don't own a decent pair of shoes, much less know how to read or write. They are fighting for our cause, Hallie. I have to go where I can be of the most assistance."

"I'll never forgive you if you get injured or killed in this stupid war, James Simmons."

James hugged her. "Yes, you will, because you love me, but don't worry, I fully intend to come back to you in one piece."

In the first light of morning, Hallie and Nona called the house servants into the foyer. Hallie stood on the steps commanding their full attention. "We are going to remove a lot of things from the house today, things that we will need when everything returns to normal. Mary, Lydia and I have lists of what needs to be packed into the crates and cloth bags. We can only take what will fit into the two wagons outside, so please, pack everything as tightly as you can."

Within hours the dining room and parlor were devoid of many of the things that had been in the house for nearly a hundred years. Crystal and china were carefully packed in straw, while paintings were wrapped in quilts. Kitchen pots were filled with the silverware and stored inside small trunks. Mirrors were wrapped in the Aubusson and Savonnerie rugs. Bibles and books were wrapped and placed in every vacant crevice of the buckboards. By sunset the wagons were packed and covered in canvas. James paid the drivers, and the teams of horses pulled their full load slowly away from the house.

"You all did a very good job," James said to the women now resting in the dining room. "Nona, I am proud of you. You kept everyone from panic. I know they are all confused and not sure what is going on. Tomorrow I will tell them."

Hallie stood up and stretched, putting her hands in the small of her back. She groaned. "I wouldn't care if all of those belongings fell into the river if it meant we could all stay here together." James was silent. He had no words left to convince her of the urgency of the situation.

Saying goodbye at the train station was almost more than Hallie could bear. It was as if the lights were going out in her life. Holding tightly to his hand, she could not bring herself to leave him. In over fifteen years of marriage they had never been apart for more than a few days. He was a part of her heart, a heart that now felt as though it was breaking. She knew he felt the same way as he tried to comfort her and assure her that the war would not last long and they would soon be together again. Tears running down their faces, Lydia and Mary hugged their father and then boarded the train. Hallie lingered for a moment. "Please take care of yourself, James. I will write you every day. I love you."

"I love you, too, Hallie," he said, his voice choking back his tears. He took her arm and helped her up the train steps. Smoke poured from the steam engines. The train slowly lurched forward, each turn of the wheels taking Hallie further and further away from her beloved husband.

Chapter Twenty-Five

Two days later, Hallie and her daughters had reached their destination. Waiting on the platform of the train station, Hallie saw a tall gentleman holding up a sign that had the name Simmons written on it. Walking toward him, Hallie extended her hand. "Hello, you must be Stuart."

Stuart was a quiet man, ten years older than James, and almost as handsome. He greeted Hallie with kindness and expressed his concern for James.

Ellen, Stuart's wife, hugged Hallie and the girls, telling them how glad she was to finally meet relatives. "I do believe that it would be best for all of us to dispense with formalities. After all, we are family. Heavens, we should have met long ago."

Hallie was relieved that their first meeting was so amiable. With everyone settled inside the coach, Ellen began to point out landmarks on the route to their home. "I know this is going to be a completely different lifestyle for you, Hallie. Stuart says your plantation home is enormous. And I know you must be very sad right now. To leave your husband and your home—that just has to be terrible. Exactly how large is your home in Mississippi?" Ellen asked.

Lydia leaned forward in her seat. "We have twenty-two rooms in our house and over two hundred workers in our fields," she said with enthusiasm, much to the chagrin of Hallie.

"I do believe you call them slaves, don't you dear? We have only five servants in our home, but they are paid every week. We don't own them. We had a few more, but this silly old war has devastated the economy of our city. It has just ruined the river trade." Without taking a breath, she changed subjects. Ellen pointed out into the street. "This is Grand Avenue. We have a horse-drawn trolley here and quite a lot of fashionable stores." While Ellen continued to prattle on, Hallie pondered on her remark about the slaves. James had told her that both Stuart and Ellen were southern sympathizers. She did not get that impression at this moment.

The Simmons House on Shaw Avenue was one of twenty homes squeezed into an area the size of the great lawn at Vine Manor. Just a few feet off the sidewalk, an iron gate led directly to the front steps. The coach pulled into a passageway leading to the rear of the house and the team of horses came to a halt under the carriage house. Everyone paraded up the narrow walk to the small porch and entered through the back door.

Once inside, Ellen removed her hat and gloves while Hallie and her daughters stood in the crowded foyer, not knowing which way to go.

"I hope you are comfortable here, Hallie. I will just give you a short tour. We have six rooms here on the first floor," Ellen said, pointing to the right. "Over here is the formal parlor, the library, and the sitting room. Across the hall are the dayroom, the dining room, and the kitchen. I just had it all redone last year. Now upstairs on the second floor we have four bedrooms, but I have taken the liberty to give you and your daughters the whole third floor. Come, follow me. I think you will be quite comfortable in your lodgings."

The hallway narrowed as they marched up the corkscrew stairs and entered a rather small bedroom. "You see, Hallie, you can have your own room and the girls can share the larger bedroom across the hall. Oh, there is a very nice water closet on this floor, but to bathe you will have to use the one on the second floor." Ellen motioned around the room with her hand. "This furniture is all new and look over here, Hallie, I have a writing desk for you. I know you will be anxious to write to your dear husband. Now I will have your luggage brought up and you can change and rest. Dinner is at six." Ellen turned and left the room.

Lydia threw herself down on the bed. "I do believe she is the most long-winded woman I have ever met. I felt like I was on a museum tour. I have never entered anyone's house by the rear door. That was unusual."

Hallie berated her, "Please, Lydia, we are accepting their hospitality. Don't make things more uncomfortable than they already are," Hallie said. "In the future let us keep the subject of slavery out of our conversations."

Lydia stood up and twirled around. "But, mother, relatives

never stay on the third floor. Relatives stay on the second floor. It is going to be so warm up here—and crowded."

"Stop complaining," Mary said. "Think of father. Who knows what is going to happen to him once the war comes into Mississippi. We should be glad that we are safe."

In the next few weeks, Ellen filled the house with family and friends. A constant stream of dinner guests arrived almost nightly. It seemed that being southern was now of interest. Hallie was asked numerous questions: "What was life like in Mississippi? What about her husband?" Some were even so bold as to ask about her finances. These questions she did not answer. She was the center of curiosity. It made her very uncomfortable. Behind cupped hands or fluttering fans, the women visitors talked about the wealthy southern woman who owned slaves and now may lose everything because of the war. "Tsk, tsk, what a shame," they would lament.

Ellen's two oldest granddaughters, who seemed to be constant visitors in the house, agreed to escort Mary and Lydia around the town. They strolled in Shaw's Botanical Garden, lunched at outdoor tearooms, and visited the museums. Lydia seemed to ingrain herself to her new surroundings with little adjustment, while Mary remained quiet and withdrawn. She preferred reading in her uncle's library. Mary, like her mother, missed her father terribly. She was homesick and constantly worried about what may happen to him. Each day the newspaper spread the tale of new battles and more loss of life in the south.

Hallie tried to fit into Ellen's lifestyle, but the fast pace and constant activities did not give her much time to herself. The breakfast dishes were taken away before the last bit of coffee was consumed. No one lingered to talk or simply enjoy the morning. After Stuart went off to his office at the bank, Ellen busied herself with making menus and barking orders at the household staff. Each day after lunch Ellen would commandeer Hallie through the shops along Grand Avenue. Ellen was an avid shopper and seemed to be a welcome customer in most of the stores. The shopping was usually followed by visits to friends, an afternoon that Hallie would have preferred to eliminate.

When Hallie told Ellen that it was not necessary to go shopping every day on her account, Ellen screwed up her face and remarked that this was her regular routine and she thought that Hallie would enjoy it rather than staying at home each day.

Hallie always felt the urgency to return to her room and write to James. She tried to keep her letters light and optimistic. She did not want him to think that she was too miserable or too happy, either. She wrote that she missed him dearly and could not wait to return home. She did not want to tell him that Mary was having problems adjusting to her new lifestyle or that Lydia was now saying that she much preferred city life to that of the plantation. Hallie told James that Stuart was a man of few words, but seemed very kind. Hallie wrote little about Ellen.

It seemed to Hallie that Ellen spent little time with her own husband, even though she expressed her concern for James, a man she had never met. On evenings when guests were not present, Stuart would seclude himself in his library. Usually he would find Mary there and they would sit side by side and read in silence or discuss a book they had both read. Stuart enjoyed talking to someone that could discuss history or literature without bringing up the subject of fashion or gossip about the neighbors.

Ellen's two oldest daughters and their families were present in the house every weekend. Although Ellen and Stuart had five children, Ellen seldom mentioned her two younger daughters or her son. She told Hallie that they lived away and she seldom saw them or heard from them.

Chapter Twenty-Six

There were lies, fabrications, and omissions written to comfort, to reassure, to ease the pain of separation – words carefully scripted on parchment stationary that seemed to come less and less as the war continued. What were Hallie and James not telling each other?

James said that the post was only being picked up once a week because of the destruction to the rail tracks and the embargo on the steamships, but he would continue to write in hopes that she was getting his mail. That was the truth.

James never told Hallie in his letters that a good number of the field hands had left Vine Manor taking with them all of the livestock and two wagons. Nona and Jasper were still helping James move supplies to the cave even though Nona was not at all pleased with the idea of staying there. He wrote that the house was intact and they had plenty of provisions. That was not the truth.

Hallie remained patient, but sometimes it was wearisome to be in this environment. She did not tell James that as much as she tried to stay out of the way and not disrupt Ellen's life, there were still times when she felt like an intruder. That was the truth.

She failed to mention the innuendos directed at her by Ellen that made her feel uncomfortable. There were remarks made about the amount of food needed to feed three additional people and the workload put on her laundress and cleaning women. Ellen would then rescind her comments with a smile or a pat on the hand. Hallie wrote that everything at the Simmons house was just fine, a definite untruth.

When Hallie decided to hire a woman to do laundry for her own family and also a lady to come in once a week to clean the upstairs rooms, Ellen protested, saying there was no need. Hallie said that was the least she could do. She wanted to pay for her and her daughter's expenses. Hallie had no idea how much she was really paying for. In her letters, Hallie mentioned none of this to James.

What James didn't say in his letters was that he was alarmed by the boldness of the slaves and had taken extra precautions to keep them from storming the house. The downstairs shutters were kept closed at all times and the doors bolted. He would escort the cooks from the summer kitchen into the house. Most of the house servants were nervous and afraid of the unknown. When a wagon came through with two white men aboard making statements that they could assure the Negroes safety, most of the servants decided to leave. James begged them to stay. He had heard about scams that were being played on the coloreds to get them away from the plantations and then sell them to sweatshop owners further north. By the end of the first year, there were only thirteen field hands and three house servants left, aside from Nona and Jasper. Hallie knew none of this.

James' last letter from Mississippi came to Hallie in the summer of 1862. He had enlisted in the army. He was assigned to Fourth Mississippi Infantry and was to report to the regiment in Grenada as soon as possible. He said he was truly sorry that he had to leave their home unattended, but he was needed elsewhere. He had no idea that two days after he left Vine Manor, the house was totally stripped of everything that could be carried away by a band of marauding Negroes who also convinced more of the workers to go with them. Knowing that their lives were now in danger, the few remaining servants gathered their meager belongings and were escorted by Jasper to the cave. The displaced group consisted of Nona, Jasper, a young boy named Asia, old May and Noah, and the house valet. Everyone else was gone.

As the months passed, the tension in the Stuart house began to simmer. Ellen's demeanor towards Hallie changed. Mary remarked to her mother several times that she did not think the marriage between Stuart and Ellen was a happy one. Ellen's materialistic ways and her constant bickering with Stuart occasionally prompted Stuart to confide in Mary while they sat together in the library. Offhanded remarks hinted to Mary that Ellen was spending an excessive amount of money, much more than he could afford. Mary asked if their being there had caused additional financial strain and he replied that on the contrary, their money was a great deal of help. Mary could tell he had regretted their conversation.

Hallie also knew that the financial arrangement James had made with Stuart was falling apart. After she received a sizable bill from one of the boutiques Lydia was frequenting, Hallie questioned her daughter. Lydia claimed that Ellen's granddaughters made most of the charges. They told her that their grandmother said she would take care of them. At Mary's insistence, Hallie agreed it was time she found out exactly how much money she had left in the bank.

After a restless night, Hallie begged off on the days shopping trip with Ellen, telling her she did not feel well. Hallie waited until Ellen left the house. Then she quickly dressed and slipped out unnoticed. She rode the horse-drawn trolley the seven blocks to the bank. It was her first experience with public transportation.

Stuart was surprised to see her. He stood up as she was escorted into his small office in the rear of the building. "Please, Hallie, sit. This is a pleasant surprise."

"I wish I could say this was just an unexpected social call, but actually, Stuart, I have some questions I would like to ask you."

He seemed nervous as he pulled out a chair for her across from his desk. "What is it I can do for you?"

"I was wanting to know if you could give me an account of how much money I have left? James told me he sent an equitable amount, but I just want to make sure that my daughters and I are not becoming a financial burden on you. Your wife has made some remarks to the contrary."

The gentle smile left Stuart's face. "I knew this time would come and it would be my duty to tell you, but I had hoped this damnable war would have been long over by now." He stood up, "You see, Hallie, my wife has luxuriant tastes and unfortunately I cannot always satisfy them. She insisted on having the third floor completely refurbished before you arrived. She used your money to buy everything in the rooms. It put a large dent in the money James had sent me. I had no choice but to use it for the furnishing. There was not enough money in my account to cover the charges. I thought she had learned her lesson, but I should know better. You see, Hallie, over the years, she has managed to alienate both of our younger daughters and our son because of the amounts of money she borrowed from them and never repaid. If I would have ever suggested a visit to you and James in Mississippi, she would have spent every dime we had on new wardrobes and coaches." Stuart rubbed his forehead, his hands trembling. "There is no money left in your account, Hallie. My wife has spent it all."

"What does that mean, Stuart? Do you mean we are now depending on you for our livelihood? Why didn't you tell me sooner? How dare Ellen take what was not hers to spend!"

"I wanted to tell you long before this, Hallie, but Ellen kept insisting that she would stop spending and reimburse your account. Of course, it was another fabrication I should not have believed. Ellen has no sense when it comes to money, especially that which is not hers. She wanted to impress you and make us out to be something we are not, and that is rich like you."

Hallie slowly stood up. "It seems that I am no longer rich, either. Let me ponder on this, Stuart. I will not mention our talk to Ellen." As she turned to leave, Hallie stopped, "I must say Stuart, I am disappointed that a man who is my husband's brother would let his wife lead him around by the tip of his nose and cause him to commit fraudulent acts by taking money out of this institution that does not belong to him. I believe that is a crime, isn't it, Stuart?"

Stuart's face grew pale. "I would hope that since we are relatives, Hallie, it won't be necessary for you to ponder on that issue."

That evening, Hallie told Mary and Lydia what had transpired that day. Lydia whined, "So you are saying we have no money for our expenses? Find father. Tell him to send us more."

Mary responded sharply, "You are becoming a spoiled brat, just like those you have made friends with, Lydia. There is no more money. Our father is fighting a war." Her voice softened, "What shall we do, mother? Live here on their charity?"

"No! I have made up my mind. We will move from this place as soon as we can find suitable lodgings. We will find employment and take care of ourselves until we can go home and join your father."

Lydia gasped, "Work! Are you saying we are going to work? What in heaven's name can we do?"

"Mary has enough education to tutor or teach in one of the private schools. I will look into a position at the library or any place I can find that will hire me, and you my dear, can stay home and keep house. Our days of being ladies of leisure are over," Hallie stated.

"I will not clean house mother and I will not cook. I don't know how," she murmured. Lydia put her hands on her hips and stomped her foot. "I am going downstairs and telling that sweet-talking shrew that we want our money. She can sell some of her stuff and give it back to us. We are not poor people, mother. Besides, she has not asked us to leave."

"I do not need her charity. Since we paid for this furniture, we will take it with us when we leave. That is a small compensation for what she is putting us through. Now, no one is to say anything until our plan is in place, do you understand, Lydia?"

A pout was her reply.

Mary was first to find work, teaching first grade at an Episcopalian girls' school. After quite a bit of searching, Hallie acquired a position at Shaw's Botanical Gardens. Her task was to write descriptions of the plants and trees for a periodical published by Mr. Shaw.

Between their two salaries Hallie was able to secure an upstairs apartment on Flora Avenue. It was small and drab, but all they could afford. When Hallie broke the news to Ellen that she was moving and that she knew her money had been spent, Ellen was distraught. She cried pitifully and told Hallie that it was not her intention, it had just happened. It was only then that Hallie informed Ellen that she was taking the furniture and accessories from their living quarters with them. Ellen screamed at Stuart that he must stop them from taking her possessions. She was convinced that the furniture belonged to her.

On the day that the movers came, Ellen threw herself on the stairs to prevent them from taking the furniture. Stuart bodily removed her. Never once did she apologize to Hallie for what she had done. It was Lydia who had the final words. "I would just love to smack you, Aunt Ellen, but my mother said I can't, but I would just love to smack you."

Ellen pretended to stumble backward as if she was swooning from the acrid remarks made by Lydia.

Hallie did not tell James that they had moved or that she

was working. Stuart agreed that any letters Hallie received at
the Shaw Avenue house would be immediately brought to her.
Her letters to James were still filled with her love and the
constant reminder that he need not worry about them. They
were doing just fine. The biggest untruth she had ever told
James.

After a month of sitting alone in the apartment, Lydia took a
position as a salesclerk in a dry goods store. The pay was
minimal and at first she was embarrassed to stand behind the
counter and wait on the same women who had come to the
Simmons house as guests. Yet, the additional money each week
helped to keep the fires burning in the apartment.

On a cold January evening after everyone had returned from
work, they sat in front of the fire eating bread and cheese. Hallie
put her arms around her two daughters. She kissed each one on
the cheek. "We are a formidable trio, not to be reckoned with."
They laughed and hugged each other.

"Honestly, mother, I never thought in my whole life that I
would be a sales clerk living in a two-room apartment in St.
Louis. I feel like now I can do most anything," Lydia said
proudly.

Mary smiled at her. "I do believe you're right, Lydia, but let's
hope this is the worst of it."

It was not the worst for Hallie. Her heart ached for her
husband. Her life was now measured in months and years away
from James, instead of weeks as they originally had hoped. She
continued to write each day, spending her change on postage to
put on letters that were never delivered.

Chapter Twenty-Seven

Mary and Lydia had blossomed in the almost five years they lived in St. Louis. No longer adolescents, but young women, they refused the advances of the northern men, telling their mother they would rather die than marry a Yankee. Mary kept busy with her students, but Lydia had difficulty being seventeen and still waiting to be invited to her first formal ball or to spend an afternoon with a gentleman caller. Her life was on hold. She prayed for the war to end and her father to come and retrieve them, but James was far away and fighting a war.

James's life had also changed dramatically in the last five years. After enlisting in the army, he was commissioned as a captain and temporary quartermaster of the post in Grenada. His duties included transporting troops and supplies. He watched as young men not even old enough to shave stood in line to enlist in the army, most not knowing how to spell their names. Young boys with no shoes and only a ragged coat to keep them warm came to give their lives for a cause they really didn't understand. The recruiters who visited the farms and small communities told them that it was their duty, and so they came to Grenada, Mississippi to join up. James held the post for almost three years. He watched as the war depleted the south of most its young men.

The fighting was intense as the northern troops conquered each mile of land as they moved deeper into the south. As each report of a battle lost by the south came across the wire, more men were called into the fray. When the last battalion left Grenada, James was told he would lead a company of men. There were no more men left to send. He wrote a letter to Hallie telling her it might be months before she heard from him again. It was a difficult letter to write.

James crisscrossed through Tennessee, Mississippi, Alabama, and Virginia. At times full companies of men were lost. He and his men would retreat until replacements were sent to the camp. Living in crowded tents with little to eat and no sanitation, the cold winters and wet springs added to the misery of the troops.

When there was no food at all and no weapons to fight with, they would sit huddled in some unknown field waiting for the enemy to capture them. To many, capture would be a relief from their misery. A chance to sit by a fire and dry their bones. Disease ran rampant among the troops, with bouts of dysentery wiping out hundreds of men in a week. Waiting to die, injured soldiers with gaping wounds were lined up on handmade stretchers. The pleadings of the injured to be killed rather than to suffer was sometimes anonymously granted and the troops would move on. In their living misery they had no options and most had no idea where they were. Even killing one's self was more than welcome, rather than an unknown death at the hands of their enemies. A continuous line of confrontations that dulled the senses persisted for the next two years.

The last battle James fought in the Civil War was at Sailor's Creek, Virginia in April of 1865. The Confederate army was cut off from all routes. James and his men knew it was over. No one would say the words lest they should just lie down and die on the pile of dead soldiers they now used for shields. The rich Virginia soil resembled red clay as the blood of their comrades mixed with the earth.

When the word came that their commander, General Richard Ewell, had surrendered, James told his men to lay down their arms. Numbed and despondent, James and his remaining troops sat in the field waiting for the northern troops to surround them.

With rifles trained on them, James and his men marched in a long line of bedraggled soldiers that plodded toward an encampment where they would be kept for the next two months. When the news came that General Lee had surrendered and the war was over, the Union forces were too weak to enforce their southern prisoners detainment. When the fence was torn down, the men simply walked away. Tearing off the remains of their ragged uniforms, their eyes showed nothing but emptiness as they now faced the daunting task of finding their way home.

In the four months it took James to return to Mississippi, he thought of his family often. It kept him sane and able to put one foot in front of the other as he and others walked the roads in the footsteps of those who had fallen before him. James had no idea how many men he had killed, how many fathers, and sons and husbands who had wives waiting for them to come home would never be there. He had no idea how many lives he had destroyed, but he didn't care. His own life had been reduced to misery. He wondered if the northern armies felt good about what they had done. He wondered if President Lincoln slept well at night. He had no idea that President Lincoln had already been shot.

At times a wagon would pass, giving him a ride for a day. Sleep would come with such necessity that even rain falling on his face would not wake him as he lay in the back on the creaking boards.

Nearing Mississippi, James searched the inhospitable fields for remnants of the war, which he would sell for a few pennies. Confederate Kepis, leather belts, broken swords, and occasionally a personal memento that some young soldier had carried into battle would buy him food to continue his journey. He felt like a ghoul robbing the dead, but these soldiers were gone, their flesh picked clean by the beetles and scavengers. He would say a brief prayer over their bones and bless them for letting him take their small possessions to help make it through one more day.

When James reached Mississippi, nothing was familiar. The landscape had turned into an odyssey of misshapen buildings, stripped fields, and burnt trees. Occasionally the sight of a house still standing would give him hope.

Ten miles from home, James rested on the side of the road. He looked across into a field of scarlet honeysuckle whose vines sent tendrils across the cold iron of a rusting cannon. James thought it a fitting funeral bough. The field was a land of spirits now. The air was devoid of sound. What happen to the thunder of war? Did it ripple into some unknown canyon, a constant reminder that a dying soldier who screamed when his world ended would never hear his own echo?

Resting for a few hours, James rose to his feet and started down the road. He was now on his own property. Property that once was covered with cotton and crops was stripped and barren. The fences were gone, torn down to be used as firewood, but most of the trees were still standing. It was almost dusk when he reached the place where his front gate once stood. Looking down the narrow corridor covered in weeds, James could make out the shape of a building. Tears came to his eyes. He wiped his face with his soiled hands. It was Vine Manor. His own home was still standing. James began to walk faster, the words, "Thank you Lord, thank you Lord," echoing in his head.

James walked up the front steps and onto the porch. His legs felt like rubber. He pushed on the door and it swung open, the hinges singing a rusty tune. It was too dark inside for him to see, but he knew this house from memory. Turning toward the parlor, he could feel the warmth of the room and see remnants of a fire in the hearth. Small embers still glowed red. Slowing his step, he listened. His heart beat faster. Someone was in the house! Putting his hand on his pistol, he jerked when a shuffling noise came from the rear of the room. With both hands on his firearm ready to squeeze the trigger he peered into the darkness. "Who's there? Show yourself or I will shoot!" he yelled.

"Don' shoot me, Mistah. I ain't got a gun. Don' shoot." James could barely see the shadowy outline of a thin black boy who stood with his hands in the air.

"Who are you? Are you alone?" James asked in a gruff voice.

"I be Asia. I be all alone."

James slowly lowered his gun. "What are you doing here, Asia? Do you know whose house this is?"

"Yes suh, I sure do. Dis house belongs tah Massa James Simmons. Massa James, he be away at da war."

James whole body relaxed. "I am James Simmons. I own this house."

Asia loped across the floor and stood before James. He wasn't more than fourteen or fifteen years old. "Massa James. You shu done scart me. You home. I shu be glad to meet ya. Old Jasper, he tol me all about ya." He pumped James's hand up and down.

"Thank God, Jasper is still alive. And Nona?"

"Yes suh, she still be alive. Dey be down at da cave right now. Me and old Jasper, take turns watchin' dah house. We be tryin' to keep dem soldiers away. Dey come by and sometimes dey stop and sometimes dey go on by. Dey ain't been here in some days."

"Is there anything at all left in the house?" James asked.

"No suh. Dey done stripped it to da bone, but dey never burnt it like somes of dah other houses."

"It is too dark to go to the cave tonight and I am much too weary. We will go in the morning." James lay down on the floor in front of the still warm hearth, the first time in months that he lay on anything but the earth. He ran his hand over the smooth wood. He was home at last. Asia laid down a few feet from him.

"Massa James, kin I tell you sumthin? Ya sure be smellin bad. Ya need a bath real bad. I gonna move ta the other side of dah room."

"I know that, Asia. I will wash in the creek first thing in the morning. Is there anyone else at the cave besides Nona and Jasper?"

"Dats all. They used ta be more, but some died and some left with dah soldiers. Dey never tell dem soldiers that we be in dah cave. Nobody likes stayin dar. It be dark and spooky, but it been savin' my life."

"I don't remember you, Asia. Were you here when I left?"

"No suh, I come here couply seasons ago. I walked a long time and when I fell down, old Jasper, he found me in dah road. He took me to dah cave. I woke up seeing dem walls and I thought I done passed on and I be in hell. Nona, she nursed me to good-as-new."

James was already asleep before Asia had stopped talking.

In the first light of dawn James arose and went outside to relieve himself. He looked around at what was left of the outside buildings and stables. Shards of boards and weathered pieces of leather lay on the ground. There was nothing else of the stables. The house was no longer white, but a soiled shade of gray. Creeping vines and Spanish moss covered most of the exterior as if to protect it from the enemy. Most of the railings were gone and the porch floor revealed the earth beneath it.

Inside, the house seemed almost eerie. Damp from the failing roof, the walls had buckled into odd shapes that protruded into each room. In the distance the faint sound of water dripping onto the warped floors could be heard.

It would be okay, James said to himself. It would be okay. Waking Asia, they started across the field.

At the creek, James removed his ragged clothes and walked into the water. Sitting down he now looked at his naked body for the first time. He was covered in sores and bites from the fleas and lice that infested the camps. His feet were a pale shade of purple with most of his toenails missing. The gentle flow of cold water was almost too painful to bear as it touched his flimsy skin. Slowly washing the filth from this body, he lay in the water and let the sun shine down on him.

Asia watched with amazement, wondering how this man could have ever been the master of Vine Manor. When he was finished bathing, James pulled on his pants, leaving the rest of his clothes lying in the water.

Asia let out a low whistle when he neared the cave, which was a signal that he and Jasper had devised. Stepping inside, James followed. It was Nona who saw him first. She was fanning a small fire in the far corner. She dropped to her knees and let out a scream that brought Jasper running to her. "Oh, lawdy, Massa James! Ya be home, Massa James," she cried, her arms flailing in the air. Jasper broke into a toothless grin and came toward James. "You be a sight, Massa James. We didn't know if we ever be seein' you agin'." He wrapped his arms around James.

Nona came forward with a blanket and gathered it around James. "Set yerself down here, Massa James. I got some broth. You need sumthin' to eat."

James sat down on a log that had been pulled into the cave. Holding the cup of warm broth in his shaking hands, he slowly put his lips to the rim. "I want to know what has happened since I have been away, but I need a day or two to rest and then we will talk." Nona nodded, resisting the urge to reach out and rock him in her arms.

He slept for almost two days. Rising to the smell of coffee, he went outside, shielding his eyes from the noonday sun. They wanted to know about the war. Jasper asked him questions he did not want to answer. He told them what he could, things that would not make his own stomach turn and only things that he cared to remember. They shook their heads and listened as his monotone voice sent him to places visited every night in his sleep. Places where he would rather not ever go again. Perhaps saying the words would take the memories from his mind and send them on the wind. When he was finished, he sat quietly for a few moments. "Now, tell me about what happened here?" he asked.

"It be okay for a long time after ya left, Massa James," Jasper said. "'Cept for the workers comin' and takin' everything from dah house, it be okay. Nobody came for a long time. It be real quiet 'round here. When ya left dey was pretty many of us still here. We was doin' okay. Me and Nona, we stayed in the house and kept our garden goin'. We tilled the ground and helped each other. We caught game and fish and ate good. I be thinkin that dey was all plannin' on stayin' here. Sometimes when we heard voices we hid, but they—dem blue-capped soldiers—dey rode on, bunches of dem, but dey don't come up here." He paused for a moment. "Den they comes agin. Dey comes up to dah house. Dem stupid niggahs, dey ran to dem soldiers like dem soldiers were here to save 'em. Dem soldiers ain't gonna saved dem. Dey took everything. Dey took all our vegetables and game and even dah shoes from dem other slaves. Dey stayed for weeks. They be laughin and eatin' everything and drinkin' corn licker. One of dem slave women and three mens were kilt by dem soldiers who were all lickered up. We be 'fraid to light a fire 'til we found we kin light one way back in dah cave and dah smoke don't come out."

Asia stood up. "And den I come here to dah house. Me and old Jasper, we likes ta poke fun at dem soldiers. Once we took a blanket and caught dem bats," he said, pointing to the cave. "When dem soldiers wuz sleepin' in dah house, we ducked by dah window and made real spook noises. Den we let dem bats go in dah window. Dem soldiers took off runnin'. Sums totin' der pants in der hands." Asia slapped his knee and laughed.

Jasper began to talk again. " Asia and me, we been finding some good timbers in dah river. We be pullin' it out of dah water and dryin' it out. Some ain't no good, but we gots 'nuf to fix dah steps goin' upstairs and some of dah floor in the kitchen. We be finding pots and all kinds of things comin down river. Some days we stay down by the bank all day. Most time we wait for you. Dats why we take turns goin' to the house. We wait for you."

"You have no idea what it means to me to be home. I want to thank you for all you've done. You are good people." James stood up and extended his hand to Jasper. Jasper hesitated for a minute, really not knowing what to do. James closed his hand over Jasper's. "Thank you."

James had come to the decision that the house and property were too much of an undertaking for him at the present time. He was still in poor health, with a constant cough and seeping lesions on his body. Nona prepared plasters and salves for his sores, but the lesions continued to spread over his skin. He spent his days resting near the cave or sitting by the river. He seldom talked and even though he ate whatever Nona fixed for him, he did not gain weight. Jasper hunted game and fished almost everyday. Nona would still go to the garden patch and dig up buried carrots and potatoes that were overlooked by the scavengers. There were also a few grapes left on the vine and blackberries growing under a tangle of weeds.

James said that when he was well enough they would travel to Magnolia. If the house was still livable, he would then send for Hallie and his children. Nona fretted over him constantly. She gathered fresh clover and dried it to make a mattress for him to sleep on. She mended his clothes the best she could and sewed tanned rabbit skins on his shoes. Nothing seemed to change his mood. He would often talk in halted sentences, sometimes not really making much sense. At night, in fitful sleep, his body would jerk and he would call out as if demons were after him.

"I be real worried about Massa James," Nona said to Jasper. "He just don' seem right in dah head. Maybe dat war done drove him crazy."

"He jest got to let it go, Nona. Maybe when Mizz Hallie comes, he be better. He needs sumthin' to take his mind off bad things."

Chapter Twenty-Eight

In the weeks to come James managed to find a carrier that would take the letter he had written to Hallie. He told her that he was home, but that there was so much unrest he did not want her to even think about coming to Vine Manor until some of the turmoil had settled. James told her he missed her terribly, but after all this time apart, a few more months may help to guarantee her safety. James really did not want Hallie to see him in such a sorry state.

Hallie got the letter three months later. She was overwhelmed with relief. She was also anxious to return home. Mary's position at the school had ended when the semester was over and Hallie had been let go from her employment. There was simply not enough money for her to be paid. The war had taken its toll on more than just soldiers.

Hallie had managed to save a few dollars knowing that when it was time to return home she would have to have enough money to pay for the passage back to Mississippi, but they were now having to use her savings for daily expenses. Hallie agreed to help the owner of the building keep the hallways and porches clean in exchange for part of the rent. Wielding a heavy mop she was now doing the work of a scullery maid.

After Hallie received James's letter, she and Mary went to the ticket office of one of the few steamboat lines that was once again traveling down river. She was crushed to discover that they did not have near enough money to book passage on a steamboat home, much less hire a carriage when they arrived in Mississippi.

"I don't understand why we are doing this, mother. Father clearly stated in his letter that he did not want us to come home until he said it was safe," Mary said.

"That letter was written over three months ago. Surely the conditions have improved. I cannot wait, Mary. I need to see your father."

That night, lying in bed, Hallie made a decision that grated against her very soul.

The following day, donning her best dress and hat, Hallie arrived on the doorstep of Ellen and Stuart Simmons at the dinner hour. The door was opened by a valet, who she breezed pass. Hallie opened the dining room door. Stuart scrambled to his feet, his napkin falling to the floor, while Ellen just sat with her mouth agape.

"I am sure that you are both more than surprised to see me, but I have come for a very important reason. I have received a letter from James that he is safe and is now at Vine Manor. My daughters and I are anxious to return home as soon as possible. I need one hundred and eighty dollars to complete the entire trip. We have no money. I wish for you to give me that amount." She folded her hands across her chest and waited for a reply.

"You have your nerve, Hallie Simmons, asking us for money after you stripped my house of its furniture. And, I will never forget how your daughter spoke to me. I am still offended."

"Oh, please, Ellen. You can use any excuse you like to relieve yourself of the guilt you must feel for using all my money, but the fact is I want to go home."

"I am so glad to hear that James is safe. I will be glad to help you, Hallie," Stuart said. "Please wait in the foyer and I will be right back." Ellen pushed her chair from the table and started to rise. Stuart stopped her short with a curt voice. "Sit down, Ellen! Stay right where you are!"

Stuart opened the door for Hallie and followed her into the hallway. He went up the stairs and returned a few minutes later with a wooden jewelry case. He presented it to Hallie. "You can take this to any jeweler you prefer and I am sure you will get more than enough money to take you home." He put the box in Hallie's hands. "I have worried about you for the last three years. I am so sorry for what Ellen did and so sorry that I did not make it right. Is there anyway you can accept my apology?"

"I don't think so, Stuart. You've had no idea what happened to us after we left your house. There is no excuse for you not coming to see us occasionally. I thought you would have been a kinder person than to turn your back on us. I will take these jewels and use the money so that I can return to the person who really knows how to care for the people he loves. James is your brother. I feel sorry for you, Stuart," Hallie said.

As she left the house she could hear the screams of Ellen Simmons after finding out that Stuart had given Hallie her jewels. Ellen stood at the window her fists clenched. Hallie waved to her and smiled as she passed by.

The jeweler peered through his loop at a diamond-encrusted pin. He carefully laid it on the purple cloth on the counter. "You have fine taste in jewelry, Mrs. Simmons. These are very lovely pieces. I am afraid the best I can do at this time is pay you four hundred dollars for the lot."

"Oh my—I was expecting more," Hallie said in a surprised voice.

"I know that, Mrs. Simmons, but unfortunately I have not been selling very much because of the war. Everyone is using their funds to get their lives back in order. You know, St. Louis suffered a great deal without our normal river traffic."

She wanted to tell him that he had no idea about suffering. Had he been away from his family for almost five years? Did he have to worry that someone he loved dearly may not come back to him? Instead, she softly said, "Yes, I will take the four hundred dollars." She wondered what Ellen would do if she knew that less than two miles from her house her jewelry was being sold for a pittance.

Her next stop was at the steamship office, where she booked passage. In two days the price had gone up. It now cost two hundred dollars for three fares. The boats captains insisted that guards equipped with rifles walk the decks in case of an attack by bands of marauders.

With or without James' permission, she was going home. Lydia and Mary packed their trunks as Hallie drafted her last letter to James from St. Louis. She simply stated that she refused to spend another winter away from him. With the weather getting cooler they had to come before the river froze in the shallow places making it impassable for the steamboats. She would be home in less than two months. James never got the letter.

When the boat finally arrived in Biloxi, Hallie and her daughters were tired, cold and hungry. Stale biscuits and lukewarm tea was all that was available on the boat. They slept on small cots with the wind blowing in through the cracks in the boards.

Once in Biloxi the situation was not much better. Anxious to hire a coach, Hallie began to realize that the new south was a dangerous place to travel. There was still a good amount of strife and unrest. She had heard stories while on the steamer that were difficult to believe. Seeing it firsthand, she knew the stories were true.

On the first day, Hallie stood in line with hundreds of other travelers trying to find a way to their homes. Whenever the wagon masters appeared on the porch of the coach office, the mob swarmed at them, holding up money and shouting out destinations. It was necessary for armed riders to escort the caravans of coaches across the rutted roads. With no luck in booking a coach, Hallie and the girls were forced to spend the night in an overcrowded, undesirable boarding house.

The next morning, Hallie arrived early and elbowed her way to the front of the throng of people. Hallie held up her money just as she had seen the men do the day before. The wagon master reached down and took the money from her hand. He pointed to a line of enclosed coaches that were now taking on passengers. The fee for them to travel would be fifty dollars each. Once again she was forced to pay the charge.

Huddled together, the weary group of travelers was addressed by the wagon master. "Now, listen to me and listen good. Keep them windows covered and if you're told to get down, then get down as low as you can. You women especially are in danger, so don't be gawking out the windows. We will stop only when I say so, so if you need to do your business, do it before we leave. Each one of you will be taken as close as we can get to your home. That's all I can guarantee. Now let's get moving."

Cramped six to a coach, with two men on horseback riding along side, the coaches began to move. It would be uncomfortable: her bones would ache and her stomach growl, but she did not care. Each turn of the wheel was taking her closer to home. Hallie was going to see her husband very soon.

At times, the temptation to see what was left of the towns would make someone in the coach pull the curtain back. Taking in the sight of a burned-out house or a field left in desolation gave them all cause to despair. It was much worse than they had expected.

On the third day, Hallie, Mary and Lydia, along with three trunks and two satchels, were left on the side of the road less than a mile from Vine Manor. Two of the men put the luggage in a secluded spot in a grove of trees. "Sorry about this ma'am but there ain't no way we kin get up that road. Lots of big branches block the way," one of the men said. He tipped his hat. "You all be careful now."

Hallie was almost giddy. Holding each of her daughters' hand, they moved as quickly as they could up the path that they had traveled so many times before. When they were within sight of the house they began to run.

It was Jasper who saw them first. Cupping his hands over his eyes he watched for a few moments and then, removing his hat, he began to wave to them. He shouted, "Massa James! Massa James! Come quick, it be Mizz Hallie and da girls. Come quick!"

Limping out onto the front porch, James stood in bewilderment, watching his family coming toward him.

Tears streaming down her face, her breath coming in short pants, Hallie stopped in front of him. As her arms went up to caress him for the first time in over five years, he backed away.

"Oh, God, Hallie, I can't believe it's you and my daughters. How did you get here?" He grabbed her hands and kissed them. "What are you doing here? How did you get here?" he asked again. Mary and Lydia were jumping up and down for their turn with their father. "My girls, my precious girls. Look at them! They are all grown." James began to sob, choking sobs that shook his body. "Please, let me see you all."

Hallie could not contain her shock at the sight of her husband. He was so thin. His eyes seemed hollow and dark. Some of his teeth were missing and patches of his hair were gone. But he was alive. "James, my dearest James. You don't know how glad we are to be here." She once again tried to put her arms around him, but he just took her hands in his.

Lydia and Mary rallied around their father. "I am so sorry I really can't greet you the way I would like to, but I have this condition, sores on my body. I will tell you all about it later," James said.

When Nona and Asia arrived, the crying started all over again. Hallie hugged Nona until she squealed to be let go. It was so much to take in. Everyone seemed to be talking at once.

"Oh, mother, look at our house," Lydia said, realizing that Vine Manor was now a shell of what it once was. Slowly stepping over the missing boards, Hallie made her way across the porch. She sat down on a rough bench that Jasper had made for Nona.

"It doesn't look too bad. I think it will be fine. I'm just glad to be here with my family."

They stayed on the porch and talked for hours, while Nona served cold water and berries. Hallie sat next to James, holding his hand, while Mary and Lydia stood behind him. They just wanted to touch him, to be as close to him as possible. They had no idea how painful their touch was to him. As the sun began to dip behind the oak trees, everyone realized how exhausted they were.

After Jasper and Asia retrieved the luggage, Nona prepared pallets on the parlor floor in front of the fireplace. Asia would sleep in the upstairs bedroom to alert them if he heard someone coming. Still confused about James' condition, Hallie lay down next to him and stared into his eyes. "I wish I could at least touch you," she said softly.

"You will, my love. Soon I will be better. Nona has been taking good care of me. Just give me a little more time." As she closed her eyes to sleep, James stared at her. He hadn't wanted her to see him like this. He wanted to be well before she came home. He worried that it was still not safe. *Hallie, my sweet Hallie, why didn't you wait 'til I sent for you,* he thought to himself.

Chapter Twenty-Nine

Kneeling on the soft earth, Lydia used a stick to dig up turnips buried beneath the earth. She dropped each muddy root into Mary's outstretched apron.

"Get away," she screamed, as a bumblebee circled her head. Striking out with the stick, she fell backward. She wiped her hands on her already soiled dress. "Look at me, Mary. I am so grimy and I smell. I can hardly stand my own foul odor." She plopped the stick up and down on the ground. "I hate this place. I hate those wretched creatures that ruined our lives and I hate that everything here is covered with filth. There isn't one place to stand or sit or sleep without feeling dirty. I want to go back to St. Louis. At least I would be able to take a bath and not have to run off to that smelly cave every time a stranger passes."

She stood up and stomped her foot. "Why are you so calm, Mary? You must hate this as much as I do. At least father could let us go stay at the Parrish house. They still have some furniture and a working pump."

"It is too dangerous for us there. Mr. and Mrs. Parrish are very old. I guess that is why the soldiers let them be, but now they are in as much danger as us. Besides, Lydia, have you really looked at our parents? Can't you see how they are suffering? They can't even touch each other and father seems to be getting thinner every day. Mother is doing the best she can. Don't be such a shrew."

"A shrew? I can't believe you called me that! Our lives have been torn apart as much as theirs. Did I think I would have to leave here and go to work? No. Did I think I would have to come back to Vine Manor and dig turnips? I am almost eighteen years old, Mary, and I spend most of my time scared to death of what will happen next." Tears welled up in her eyes. "Why did mother bring us back here? She should have waited."

Mary put her arms around her sister. "I know. I'm sorry I

called you a shrew. If we just keep our wits about us, Lydia, we can do this. I know that father still has investments and when we get some money, the house will be repaired and then we can send for our furniture. It will be all right."

"What about Magnolia? Father said he was going to try and find out if it was still standing. We could go there. At least we would have the ocean to bathe in."

"He is waiting for word from August Lott. So be patient, Lydia. It takes a long time to find out anything these days. Let's go. Mother will be worried about us."

And worry she did. Each time the girls left her sight, Hallie worried. Long talks with Nona and Jasper had filled her in on the time she was away. Each story or bit of information gave rise to a new feeling of anger. "Why, Nona, why? Why did they have to destroy our homes and our livelihood? We gave them what they wanted. We freed our workers. Why won't they just go away and leave us alone? James is so sick. He won't even let me come near him. I haven't been able to touch him since I got here. Please tell me what I can do to get my husband back, Nona. I feel so alienated from him right now. All I dreamed about while I was away was to wake up in the morning next to him. As soon as I fall asleep he moves away from me."

"He be afraid to touch you, Mizz Hallie. Dat rash done a poor job on his body. He be afraid dat layin' by you is a temptation he needs to let go right now. 'Sides, he don' want you ta see his body."

Nona prepared an ointment of coal ashes and pine tar. She added hickory bark that she had boiled and thickened and mixed it all together with rendered fat. "Dis be an ole fixin' for sores. It burns like dah fire, but it jest may help Massa James."

Hallie took the wooden bowl from her. "Here, let me do it, Nona. I will put it on him."

Nona looked at her in surprise. "Hmm, I jest don't know 'bout dat. He always takes dah salve, den he tell me to leave."

"James has to get used to me taking care of him, Nona. I plan on doing it for a long time." Taking the ointment and a piece of soft cloth from one of her petticoats, Hallie went into the parlor and closed the door. James was stacking wood for the night's fire. "Here, I want to put this salve on you. Nona said it will probably sting, but it may help you. Take your shirt off and I will put some on your back."

James spoke without turning around. "Please, Hallie, I can do it myself."

Hallie knelt down next to him. "James, I am your wife. Let me help you." She wanted to be strong, but it was too late, tears were already streaming down her face.

James slowly removed his shirt. His chest, back, and arms were covered in lesions and scaly red patches. "It was the fleas. In Virginia we had such an infestation in the camp that you could actually hear them. If you listen real closely they make a clicking sound. They covered my body and at night I had to put shreds of cloth in my ears to keep them from going inside my head and driving me crazy." His voice trailed off as Hallie ever so gently applied the ointment to his back and arms. The sores on his legs and groin were even worse, but Hallie managed to keep her composure as James bit his lip to keep from screaming in anguish from the fire that burned on his body.

With James in a weakened condition, it would be up to Hallie to start the healing process and piece their lives back together. In the days to follow, there would be small comments and pauses. Testing his reaction to the love she still felt for him, she would find a way to regain the intensity that made their union special. It would have to start by accepting her into the inner circle of his world of pain.

It had been raining a cold, biting rain for three days—rain that crept into their bones and made them shiver. Ripples of water ran down most of the walls in spite of the patchwork that had been done on the roof of the house. Everyone gathered in the parlor. Nona prepared turnips and potatoes in a boiling pot on the hearth, while Hallie read to the family from the Bible. A sharp rap on the door caught them off guard, startling everyone. James jumped to his feet and picked up his pistol. "Jasper come with me. The rest of you stay here." A few moments later James escorted a lone rider into the parlor. Shaking water from his hat, he stood in a circle of mud that dripped from his coat hem and boot tops. "This is Aaron," James said. "He has word for us from August Lott." Taking the leather pouch from the man, James motioned toward the fire. "Warm your hands. We have soup. I know you must be hungry." Aaron bobbed his head and mumbled "Thank you." Making tracks across the floor, he squatted down and held his hands to the fire. "Open it, father," Lydia said. "Please, hurry, open it." James slowly unfolded the letter and began to read.

> *James,*
>
> *Glad to hear that you made it through this disastrous ordeal. We at Lott's Point have been blessed. Although there were several battles at Pass Christian, the northern troops came out to the point only a few times. I, myself, supplied the soldiers with most everything in my stores to keep them from destroying our precious town. We have sustained some damage from over zealous soldiers, but nothing like I had expected. After I received your post, I took it upon myself to visit Magnolia. Without proper maintenance, Magnolia has taken on a somewhat disparaging appearance, but is still intact along with some of your belongings. I do believe that some of the troops stayed there, but they did not destroy everything. The town is beginning to show new signs of life with people returning to their homes and new residents coming. Unfortunately, quite a few of them are carpetbaggers from the northern states. They are here to dig deeper into our pockets for the last few dollars we have. They are buying up property at an alarming rate for mere pennies.*
>
> *I am grateful that you made it through this damnable war and that you are back in Mississippi. If you and your family feel it is detrimental to come here, I will be glad to purchase the property from you at an equitable price. It would be the best thing for you and your family. Please consider my offer.*
>
> *With fond regards,*
> *August Lott*

It was a joyous moment for all of them. Lydia and Mary danced around the room while Hallie and James hugged each other. They still had a home.

"My goodness that is a strange letter. August must have changed. He sounds almost too nice. Are you sure it is from him?" Hallie said.

Aaron, who was still by the fire, said in a low voice, "War changes everyone."

Sitting down to their meager bowl of soup, James began to ask Aaron questions. It was just good to have someone else to talk to. Aaron's home had been destroyed and his only son had been killed in the war. "I took this job as a courier because it just don't seem to matter much to me anymore. One place is as good as another. If you don't mind, I'll just grab my bedroll and find a room to rest my head." He stood up. "Thanks for the soup. It was real tasty."

Aaron stopped at the door. "By the way...if you decide to go to Lott's Point you got a stretch of road between here and Chapel Bridge that ain't too safe. A lot of the coloreds are livin down in them woods and I seen a couple of bands of renegades roaming around there. They like to catch travelers off guard and take everything they got, especially if you got women on your wagon. Once you get across the bridge where it's open land, you'll be okay. Pretty many travelers on that road."

He tipped his hat and disappeared from the room. He was gone in the morning when they awoke.

Chapter Thirty

The decision was made. They would go to Magnolia. They would sleep in real beds and buy tea and sugar and flour. They would wash their clothes and bathe in the porcelain tub filled with warm water. When the winter was over, they would decide what they wanted to do with Vine Manor. It was a time for celebration. The last scrape of salt pork was boiled with the remainder of the carrots and potatoes. After licking their bowls clean, they laughed and talked, then began to gather up their belongings. Jasper retrieved the two horses and the wagon that was kept hidden deep in the field, next to the cave. They would load up the cookware and blankets in the cave and then bring the wagon up to the house. It was Nona's comment that took Hallie by surprise.

"I guess dis be our last day together," Nona said in a sorrowful voice.

"What do you mean? Surely you are coming with us. I won't have it any other way. You are a part of our family, Nona. I won't leave without you again," Hallie exclaimed.

"We'd be more den grateful, Mizz Hallie, but we ain't expectin' ya to tote us along."

"Nonsense. Now get whatever it is you want to take and put it in the wagon."

"I jest be needin' my pots, dat's all I need. What about dah boy, kin he come too?"

"Yes, Asia is welcome, too. And you can tell him he can come out from behind the door. I know he is there." Asia stepped forward, a wide grin covering his face.

As Hallie stuffed her soiled dresses into her trunk, she turned her head. "Oh, look at this one, it's all torn and so rank, James. It smells just awful. When we get to Magnolia I can have new clothing made for the whole family. It will be so nice to have something soft and clean to wear. Let's get all new linens, too.

I'm sure that the ones we left behind are quite musty by now. You are so quiet, James. Are you sad to be leaving Vine Manor?"

"I suppose in some way I am." He took her into his arms and hugged her. "We will make it work, Hallie. We have each other and our daughters. Once we get to Magnolia I will petition for the sale of Vine Manor. I know it will be difficult to sell your home, but I promise, you will never have to make another sacrifice."

In the morning, James awoke early. Everything had been packed and the wagon was hidden away in the cave. Jasper had spent the night keeping the lanterns going so the horses would stay calm in the cave.

Hallie raised her head and yawned. "Where are you going?" she whispered.

"I want to go see Mr. and Mrs. Parrish before we leave. I am still worried about them. I am going to try and convince them to come with us. They are too old to stay the winter here without help. When I return, we will be on our way to a better life." He bent down and kissed her cheek. "I love you. I'll be back soon." She smiled and pulled the cover up over her shoulders.

James gave the low-whistle signal as he neared the cave. "Jasper, I'm taking Asia with me to see Mr. Parrish. Go to the house and make sure everyone is ready to go. I should be back in about three hours and then we will be on our way," James said as he put a halter on one of the horses.

"What it be like in Magnolia?" Asia asked.

"It's nice. You'll like it. We will probably have to do quite a bit to get it back to its former glory, but at least we will be safe there."

"Id be real nice ta be safe, Massa James. I would like dat," Asia said.

When they arrived at the Parrish house, James handed Asia the reins to his horse. "You watch the horses and the road. I'll be back shortly."

Thomas Parrish opened the door just an inch or two. When he saw James, a broad grin crossed his face. He toddled out the door, his frail legs almost unable to support his lean body. "James, how good to see you," he said in a raspy voice. "Please come in." James put his arm around Thomas and entered into another structure that had been scarred by the war. Like Vine Manor, the house was in disarray with most of the rooms missing those touches that had once made it elegant and special.

"I haven't much to offer you. I do have fresh water and two chairs. I am expecting a supply wagon any day now," Thomas said as he ushered James into the library. "This room is still the warmest in the house. I cannot convince Lilly to come down here to sleep. She still prefers her upstairs bedchamber. She is not well, James. These past years have taken their toll on both of us."

"My reason for being here is the same as my last visit. I want to ask that you and Lilly come with us, Thomas. We are leaving here today. I am taking my family to Lott's Point."

"I truly thank you for your offer, James, but my wife and I have decided to stay here. I have two women servants living in the house and a few workers still on the property. They have been a great help. Soon others will return and I may get help rebuilding in return for a parcel of my land. I have been here almost eighty-three years and I cannot and will not leave."

James nodded his head. "I understand, but I think it is going to be some time before the unrest stops, and I have to protect my family. I do wish you would change your mind." James had just finished his sentence when the door flew open and Asia came running into the parlor.

"It's dem bad men, dem shirkers, they be comin' dis way."

"Oh, God," Thomas moaned. "I have heard there was a band of villainous deserters roaming these roads, but that was over a week ago. Hurry! You have to go, James. You had enough depredations in the war. You don't need to face this."

"No! There is no way I am going to leave you to face them alone. Do you know how many there are, Asia?"

Asia held up six fingers. "They be 'bout dis many."

"Asia, take my horse. Ride to the house! Ride as fast as you can and tell Jasper to get everyone into the cave along with the wagon. Do not leave the cave until I return. Now go! They are not to linger for a minute. Tell Jasper to dig up the jars. He knows what I am talking about."

Asia never wasted a minute. With a burst of energy, he was out the door and prodding the horse to go faster.

Rushing back to the library, James yelled at Thomas. "The women. Tell the women to run and hide in the field. Quickly! We must go and get your wife into a safe place."

It was too late. The sound of horse hooves echoed through the empty front hall as the riders dismounted and kicked open the front door. The library door slammed open and the room was filled with the stench of the six men standing before James and Thomas.

They wore ill-fitting, confederate uniforms that were torn and dirty. One man, his hair pulled back and tied into a horsetail, wore a captain's hat. He carried two firearms in his belt and a long saber sheathed at his side. A crooked scar crossed his forehead and disappeared behind a leather patch that covered his left eye. He chewed on the stump of a sodden cigar. He stopped for a moment, looking around the room, and then spat on the floor.

"Well, lookee here, ain't this just fine. What we got here, some kinda meeting?"

He strode around the room, his one good eye not leaving James or Thomas.

The man pointed his cigar at James. "And who might you be?"

"Just a friend. I came from Natchez to check on Thomas."

The man threw the cigar down and stepped on it. "I didn't ask for no story. Tell me your name."

"My name is James Simmons. What is it you want? There is nothing left."

"You jest let me be the judge of that. We need food."

Thomas quivered. "I have a few bags of corn and there are some potatoes in the shed. That's all I have."

He turned to his men. "Go check outside," he said, pointing to the two nearest the door. Motioning to a few more of the men he continued, "Go upstairs. Take what you can."

"No!" Thomas said in a loud voice, stepping toward the man. "My wife is upstairs. She is very sick. Leave her be."

A loud commotion outside interrupted the men. Two men entered the house dragging the Negro women with them. Addressing the one-eyed man, one of the men said, "We found em hiding in the shed, Captain Roode." One of the men pulled the younger of the two women close to him and ran his hand down the front of her dress.

Roode put his arm around the neck of the older woman and yanked her backward by her hair. With his face just inches from hers, he held her trembling body and pointed to James. "Now you tell me, niggah, you tell me if this man lives around here."

Her eyes widened as his arm tightened around her chest. As she tried to nod, he tightened his grip. She let out a moan. "That be Massa James. He live at Vine Manor."

He let her drop to the floor. "Put em in the wagon," Roode said, as the two women continued to wail and scream.

"Now see what happens when you lie?" Roode said as he pulled his saber from its sheath. "I don't cotton to liars." He held the point of the sword to James's throat. A small trickle of blood ran down James's neck. "Go get the old lady," Roode growled.

Two of his men bounded up the stairs. Thomas heard his wife scream. When the men re-entered the library, one of them whispered something into Roode's ear. Roode grinned.

"Seems like your old woman done flung herself out the window. Yes sir, she hit the ground with a plop. Kill't herself, she did. Damn shame."

Thomas lunged at the man, his arms flaying in the air struck Roode in the chest. "You bastards! You savage bastards!"

One of the men stepped forward and caught the side of Thomas's head with the butt of his rifle. Thomas fell backward, blood spewing from his temple.

"Now, here, let me help you up," Roode said, smiling as he bent over Thomas. "You don't hit the captain, you hear."

Thomas reared up and spat in his face.

Roode drew his gun and fired point blank. The thunderous blast sent shards of flesh and bone against the wall. Thomas slumped forward in a pool of his own blood.

James clenched his fist, his ears deafened from the blast. He knew he had to remain calm. He had to give Asia time to get to Vine Manor and alert the family.

The marauders searched the house, gathering up whatever they could, and loaded it into the wagon. A gun barrel was pushed into James' back and he was shoved toward the door.

"Now, you and me are gonna take a little ride to your place. I know where it is. I seen that place before," Roode shouted out orders and then yelled to one of the riders, "Put him on a horse."

James could see the two women tied in the back of the wagon. Rocking back and forth, they continued to sob. They had no doubt about their fate.

Walking down the steps, Roode turned to his men. "Torch it." The fire was in full blaze by the time James and the band of dissenters were out the front gate. James silently hoped Asia had made it home by now. If not, perhaps seeing the red sky might alert Jasper.

Heading toward the road, Roode and his men did not know the short cut that James and Asia had taken to get to the Parrish house. James would lead them around the perimeter of Vine Manor, which would add more time to the journey. James knew that with or without him, Roode and his men would find a way to Vine Manor. Stalling them was the only salvation for his family.

The men laughed and joked as they rode behind James and Roode. They seemed to take great pleasure in the destruction and agony they were causing. Roode looked over at James.

"She at your house?"

"No. I just got back from the war a few weeks ago and she is still in England with her family." He had said it calmly, hoping this calloused man might believe him.

"Guess you're gonna tell me next that you ain't got no niggahs on your property. Well, we'll jest see about that, won't we? We was gonna pay you a visit later tonight. You jest got to see us a little earlier."

"Why are you doing this? What have we done to deserve this?" James asked, not knowing what reaction his question would bring.

Roode stood up in his saddle for a moment and then settled back down. "You look at me. You look at me real good. I got one eye missing and buckshot festering in my back. These men and me, we got the real short end of the stick. We was minding our own business. None of us wanted to be in your damned army, but they came and got us anyway. Dragged us right off our farms and put us in wagons. They told us we were now soldiers. Ha! That was a joke. We lost our women and our homes for nothing. I wasn't going to die to protect a bunch of niggahs and rich white asses like you. So a bunch of us just took off. Soldiers wearing the same uniform as us hunted us like coons. When they caught up with us they shot most of the men in the back or hung them from a tree. Now, we gonna take back what we deserve. Ain't no glory in being poor or dead." He kicked his horse and rode ahead of James.

Asia was riding in fear. He galloped through the field ignoring the small rocks and twigs that pelted his legs. Once at the house, he slid from the horse and ran inside screaming, "We gotta go to dah cave! Hurry! Dey be comin'. Dem bad mens is comin. Massa James say we gotta go!"

Jasper grabbed Asia by the front of the shirt. "You jest settle down, boy. What is it you tryin' to tell us?"

Hallie let out a scream. "Where is James? Why didn't he come with you?"

"He be at dah the Parrish house. Dem nasty men are dar. We gots tah go to dah cave. Massa James said we should stay dar 'til he come."

Jasper hurriedly hitched the horse to the wagon, ushering everyone aboard. Hallie held tightly to Lydia as the wagon bounced and shuddered through the field. At the entrance to the cave, Asia jumped down and pulled back the brush cover far enough for the horse and wagon to enter while Jasper swept away the wagon tracks and replaced the bramble in front of the cave opening.

They huddled in the wagon, afraid to light the lanterns. "I can't believe this is happening," Hallie said. "We were so close, so very close to leaving. What did they want?"

"They be wantin' anything dat dey kin find. Dey be real bad," Asia said, still shaking from the experience.

Lydia grabbed Nona's hand. "What is happening? Why won't they just leave us alone? I thought the war was over!"

Nona put her arm around Lydia. "The devil gets into des men. Dey wants us all dead. But yer daddy, he will take care of us."

They sat quiet in the cold. Their bodies shivering under blankets they pulled over their shoulders. They waited, listening for a sound, any sound to let them know that James was coming. They had no idea that James was now entering the yard of Vine Manor. His only hope was that Asia had made it home in time.

James sucked in his breath as he entered the house in front of Roode and his men. The house was quiet. Asia had succeeded in his mission.

The men spread out and starting searching the house one room at a time, returning with nothing. Roode sat down on the corner of the wooden table that Jasper had built in the parlor. He lit a cigar. "Looks to me you been working pretty hard on this house for somebody who has been here by himself. Don't seem to be too wet in here. You patch the roof all by yerself?"

He was a cunning man and James knew he was not easily

fooled. "I had help for a little while, but then they left. It was some migrants."

Roode got up and walked around the empty room, his footsteps echoing on the wooden floor. "Now let me get this right, you been here all alone for how long now? Don't answer that— I don't care." He pushed his foot into the fireplace. Squatting down, he ran his hand over the ashes. "Where are they, Simmons? Where is yer family?" Grabbing James by the front of the shirt, he asked again, "You'd be real smart to tell me where they are."

"Hey, Roode, look what I found," one of the men said, holding up a dress that Hallie had left on the bedroom floor.

Roode took the dress and held it up to his nose. Throwing it on the ground he grabbed James by the front of his shirt. "Where are they, Simmons? Where's yer family?"

"They're gone and safe from you, you cowardly bastard!" James barked at Roode.

Roode turned to one of his men. "Take him outside and tie him to a tree. Then bring me those niggah women. I'll deal with him later."

James stumbled down the steps between two of the men, struggling to keep his balance. One of the men pulled a rope from his belt and bound it tightly around James' hands. Pulling him close to the tree the rope dug into his neck, almost cutting off his breath.

James watched as the two women were dragged into the house crying. The sound of terror and laughter continued inside the house for hours. James listened helplessly to the woman's screams as he twisted his arms to loosen the twine tethering him to the tree.

Sometime later Roode emerged from the house. He had removed his jacket and pants. He stood in a filthy one-piece, scratching his stomach. Walking slowly down the steps he came towards James. "Now, it's time for you and me to have a little talk."

"Go to hell," James said.

"You ain't making things easy for me. Now I'm a patient man, but lessen you start talking pretty soon, you may not have a tongue to talk with. You gonna tell me where them women are?"

James did not answer. He should have been afraid, but a

kaleidoscope of faces of those he loved kept revolving in his mind. He had to protect his family.

Roode motioned to one of the men standing near him to hand him his pistol. Roode held it up to James's neck. "You ain't a scared of me are you?"

Chapter Thirty-One

By evening, Hallie was almost inconsolable. She wanted to leave the cave and look for James, but Mary held her back. They could hear the flutter of wings as the bats prepared to leave the cave for their evening forage. Occasionally droplets of icy water would fall from the ceiling and landing on their heads causing them to flinch. Huddled together, their weariness lulled them into a restless sleep.

Hallie awoke first. She groaned as she tried to straighten her body. Suddenly remembering what was happening, she stood up and jumped down from the wagon. *James, where are you? Please, please, just get here soon. Surely those men have left by now.*

She whispered to Jasper, who was leaning against the wagon asleep, his head tucked beneath his arms. "Jasper, it is morning. We have to go look for James."

Pulling back the vines, Hallie peered into the hazy mist. It was so quiet. She could not hear the killdeers running through the brush or the call of the morning doves. Where was James?

"You stay here, Mizz Hallie. Me and Asia will go look for Massa James," Jasper said.

It was too late: Hallie took off running across the open field. Propelled toward the house, she picked up her pace, her heart racing and fear filling her lungs. Something was terribly wrong. Though Asia and Jasper lagged behind, she hiked her skirt and ran faster. She fought through the brambles, whose burrs scratched her arms and legs. Asia caught up and stepped in front of her. Panting, he said, "Ya got tah stop. Dem men maybe still dar. Ya don't want dem to find us. Think about dem girls of yers." Hallie dropped to her knees, her breath coming in short pants. "Then go. I'll give you five minutes and then I'm coming after you."

There was no sign of movement as they crawled on hands and knees around the side of the house. They waited for a few minutes and then continued around to the front yard.

It was Jasper who saw him first.

With his knees bent, he stood with his head hanging down to his chin; his blue shirt was stained black with his own blood. Jasper slowly moved forward toward him. A sob choked in the old man's throat as he took his small knife from his pocket and cut the rope that held James to the tree. James' body buckled and fell to the ground. Jasper rolled him over. He removed his jacket and placed it over James.

Jasper did not see Hallie coming through the yard. "No!" she screamed, "No! No! No!" She fell on her knees next to her husband's lifeless body and threw back Jasper's jacket. Thrashing her head back and forth, Hallie moaned and called James' name over and over.

Mary was now just a few feet away from her. "Don't come any closer, Mary Elizabeth, you need not see this," Hallie cried out, but it was too late. Mary drew her breath at the first sight of her father; she turned and ran toward Lydia and Nona who were just entering the yard.

Nona knelt next to Hallie, draping her arms around her shoulders, "Dem bastard, I hate dem bastards. Dey got no right to do this."

Engulfed in grief, their hearts were filled with an unstoppable ache.

Hallie had no idea how long she sat next to her fallen husband, touching his face, smoothing his hair, and praying that it was all a bad dream. Nona stayed at her side.

Jasper leaned down. "You come, Mizz Hallie. You come over here and sit." He took Hallie's arm. As she stumbled to her feet, her eyes remained riveted on her husband.

Jasper led her to her daughters. Mary and Lydia sat under the oak tree, both of them sobbing uncontrollably. Hallie could not console them. She rocked back and forth so rapped in her own grief. "Why? Why? We were so close to being safe and having a new life together. Why?"

"Mizz Hallie, I hate dis, I hate dis more din ya know. I surely did like Massa James," Jasper said, holding tightly to his straw hat, "But, we gots to go real soon. We gots a long trip and them mens jest might come around agin. Massa James said sumthin happened to him, I waz to still take you to Magnolia. We needs to go."

"I am not leaving here until I bury my husband. I will not let him lay here and rot like some useless field animal."

"We don't got a shovel here; we got nothing to dig with," Asia said, his eyes darting around, afraid that they might be next to die.

"Then we'll dig with our hands. We will bury him here under this tree." She crawled around on all fours frantically looking for a soft place in the soil.

"Get up! Get up everyone! We have to bury my husband." Hallie clawed at the dirt.

"Mother, please, we can't do this. Let Jasper and Asia take him to the cave," Mary said, trying to stop the frenzy that was consuming her mother.

"No! I want him buried right out here in plain sight, so that everyone can see what those demons have done. He won't be hid away in that dark cave."

Jasper and Asia began to scoop out a hollow in the ground, while Lydia, Mary, and Nona searched for rocks. Hallie sat beside James' body, holding his hand to her mud-stained cheek.

After they dug a shallow grave, they gently laid James' body down to rest. Jasper began to push the dirt over him.

"Wait, just a moment, please," Hallie said. She reached beneath her skirt and tore a length of material from her petticoat. Brushing back his matted hair, she folded the cloth and laid it over his face. "Goodbye, my sweet husband."

Everyone helped place the stones on top of his body. Nona, Asia, and Jasper hummed a mournful hymn that would help send him on his way. Mary said a prayer and they all closed their eyes for a moment.

"We gots ta go, Mizz Hallie. It be getting nye on to noon," Jasper murmured.

Hallie stood up and smoothed her stained dress. She picked up the rope, still damp with his blood that had bound James to the tree. "Find me two sturdy branches. I want to make a cross for his grave."

With the cross in place, they walked silently toward the back of the house. "I want you to light it afire, Jasper," she said in a low voice. "I want Vine Manor to be burnt to the ground."

Jasper's eyes widened, "But, Mizz Hallie."

"If you won't do it, I will," she said. "I will go to the cave and get fluid and flint and burn it. I'll not have another intruder in this house!"

"I'll do it, Mizz Hallie, but first I gots ta git y'all back to dah cave."

Looking back at James's grave, they started slowly walking away.

"Did you hear that?" Lydia said, stopping. "I heard something." She stopped in the waist- tall grass. Someone is in this field."

Asia's eyes widened "Lawd, have mercy, are dey back?" His body trembled with fear.

"No," Lydia said, putting her hand to her lips, "Everyone be still. It sounds like someone crying." She crept forward a few feet and stopped again. This time she was sure. Slowly parting the tall weeds, she let out a scream. "Oh, no!"

Lying on the ground was a young black woman. She lay in a fetal position, her naked body covered in blood. Her eyes were swollen shut and her lips split down the middle. Her hair was pasted to her head with her own blood.

When Nona saw the girl, she squealed. "Dat be dah girl who worked for Mr. Parrish. Lydia pulled off her top shirt and covered the girl. "We have to get her to the wagon. Asia come here and pick her up."

"Me? I don't want to. She be all bloody," Asia said.

"Asia, dammit, pick her up right now!" Lydia screamed.

Asia came forward and scooped her into his arms. She moaned in pain as his hands touched her. He turned his face away from her.

Hallie stood with vacant eyes and watched as the girl was put into the back of the wagon. She had nothing to give. Her husband was dead and at this moment she wished she were too.

Asia laid the girl in the back of the wagon and Lydia gave her small sips of water. She winced as Lydia tried to wipe her face.

Once the wagon was out of the cave and onto the bumpy road, Jasper wondered how safe they were going to be on the open road. It was Asia that remembered at the last minute that James had told him about the jars. "You need to stop, Jasper. Massa James said I was tah tell ya to dig up dem jars. He said ya would know what he meant."

Jasper pulled the horse to a stop. "I shure do. Ya stay put; I be right back." He went back to the cave on foot. Jasper returned with a muddy burlap bag, which he placed under his feet in the wagon. "That waz good, Asia. You done a good thing by rememberin'."

With the wagon pulled into the yard of Vine Manor, Jasper took a lantern and poured the yellow liquid on the front porch. With one flick of his flint, a small flame followed the path of the oil into the house. In just a few minutes the flames licked through the windows as if waving farewell to them. No one was crying. Empty stares watched as a lifetime of memories erupted with the sound of breaking timbers and floors giving way.

Hallie's mind raced. She thought about Rebecca and Paul and her father, all buried on a hill in graves where the stones had been disseminated by horse hooves. Now, James lay in the cold ground with only a layer of rock to keep him safe. Vine Manor was the only thing given a civilized farewell.

They traveled only a few miles before Jasper pulled the wagon into a grove of trees that hid them from view. They dared not build a fire for fear of attracting nearby lurkers. Eating cold biscuits and drinking water seemed to be enough for everyone. Their thoughts were not on food. While Mary tried to comfort her mother, Lydia attended to the girl. The girl had fallen asleep, but held on to Lydia's hand with a tight grip. At times she would whimper and her whole body would tremble. Lydia could only imagine what she had been through. Everyone seemed to be in limbo, uncertain of what to do next.

Knowing that her mother was in no condition to take charge, Mary decided it was time for her to step in and take the situation into her own hands. Her mother was withdrawn into her own thoughts and cared little about anything right now. Someone had to get them to safety.

"Listen to me. I need everyone's attention. I have a plan," Mary announced. "It may help us get to Magnolia without being accosted. I read about it when I was in school." They listened while Mary told them what they would do in the morning.

"That be soundin' like a good idea," Jasper said. "We will tend to it, early morn."

Mary instructed Asia that, the next morning, he would lay on the board that Jasper had placed across the buckboard. "I ain't sure, Miss Mary. I sure don' like havin' to be on top of dat wagon. I be scared," Asia said, shaking his head.

"Listen to me, Asia. No one will bother you. It is the only way we can make it out of these woods and across Chapel Bridge. If we try just driving the wagon through, we may all be killed."

"You gonna do it, boy. You gonna do it for everyone, and dat is dat," Nona said grabbing Asia by the ear. "Now git some sleep. It gonna be a long night."

The women huddled together to keep warm in the wagon, while Jasper and Asia took turns keeping watch. Occasionally the silence of the night was broken by the sound of someone crying softly. No one questioned who it could be. They all had their moments of sorrow during that first long night without James.

In the morning, the young Negro girl struggled to sit up in the wagon, pulling a blanket around her still naked body. She looked around at everyone. "Where is I?" she asked softly.

Lydia explained how they found her. The memory of what had happened came flooding back to her. She rolled her head back and forth. "Dem men took Sue and me in dah house. Dey..." she stopped.

Lydia touched her arm. "Don't, please. Don't. We know what those bastards did. They killed our father, too."

"Dey kill't Sue. When dey was done with us, we lay on dah floor. I laid real still-like. Dey kicked me hard," she said, pointing to the wound in her side. "But I still lay real still. Dey be thinking I wuz dead. When dey left, I crawled over, but Sue, she be dead. Dey done stuffed a rag in her mouth. She choked." She put her hands on her stomach. "I be tore up real bad. I hurt."

Nona sat next to her. "You gonna be all right, baby. We gonna take care of you." She looked over at Hallie, who sat motionless on the side of the wagon. Nona wished there was something she could do something to ease her pain. "What be yer name, girl?" Nona asked.

"Mandy, I be called Mandy," she answered. "Massa and Mizz Parrish, are dey dead too?"

"I suppose so. We seed dah fire coming from der house."

Mandy nodded, and wrapped her arms around her own body. "I guessin' I be all alone now." She began to cry again.

While Nona tried to comfort Mandy and Hallie, Mary helped Jasper and Asia arranged the trunks on each side of the wagon, leaving an open space in the middle. "There is not much room for us to sit, but we will have to make do," she said.

Jumping off the back of the wagon, Mary walked along the bank of the stream to gather bunches of yellowweed. Pouring water from her drinking vessel onto the ground next to the wagon, she created a mud puddle. With Asia sitting in front of her, Mary spread the yellow powder from the weed across his face and hands. With the end of a small stick, Mary dotted Asia's yellow face with the mud, giving him the appearance of pustules on his skin.

With the five women seated in the cramped quarters, Jasper covered the wagon with the canvas wrap. He laid a plank across the back of the wagon and directed Asia to position himself on the board. He covered Asia's body with a blanket. Only his head and hands were visible.

With everything in place, Jasper pulled the wagon onto the road. It was a quiet trip for the first half of the day, with the exception of Asia complaining that his back hurt and that he had to relieve himself. Just as Jasper looked for a spot to pull the wagon off the road, his back stiffened.

He heard the sound of voices. A group of Negroes were camped just a few hundred feet away. One of the men stood up and started toward the wagon. Jasper let out a yell. "Pox! Don't come near, we got pox on dis wagon." The man stopped and peered at the wagon. The sight of Asia lying on the board sent him running. Within minutes the entire group of people had disappeared into the woods. Jasper grinned. Mary had made a good plan. He knew that encounters with strangers on this road were as welcome as stepping on a rattlesnake.

It was on the morning of the second day that a threat of danger once again raised its ugly head. There were four men, carrying weapons, looking for something to scavenge. When Jasper called out his warning words, they pulled their horses to a slow gate, but continued to come closer to the wagon.

"What you got in that wagon, niggah?" one of the men called out.

"I gots my son here. He gots dah pox. Ya better step aside," Jasper yelled again, attempting to be convincing.

A dark-hair fellow put his neckerchief over his nose and continued toward the wagon. "Bullshit," he said.

Jasper whispered to Mary. "They be comin', Mizz Mary. They ain't stoppin'."

Mary raised the corner of the cover, "Asia, you must moan.

Moan real loud. Make them think you are very sick. We have to get them away from the wagon."

Asia bolted straight up, his eyes widen and he let out a piercing scream.

The rider pulled the reins of his horse and veered to the side of the rode. He yelled to the other men. "Pox! They got pox on this wagon."

"Don't you be burying that niggah around here," one of the men shouted. "You just keep right on going."

Once the men were out of sight, Asia sat up again, rubbing his backside. "Damn, Mizz Mary, you done poked a hole in my heiney. What'd ya do dat for?'

Jasper couldn't help from grinning. "She sure did make ya yowl."

There were five encounters with intruders before they reached the Chapel Bridge. Each one ended with a scatter of people frightened at the thought of contracting pox. Jasper felt sorry for the families of blacks who begged him to let them ride with him, but he stuck to his story. He left them awaiting their fate on the side of the road. What else could he do? Jasper had women to protect. He had made a pact with James and he had to honor it. Just like James died to protect his family, Jasper was ready to do the same.

With the smell of salt air filling his lungs and the sound of the wagon wheels clattering across Chapel Bridge, Jasper told Asia he could sit in the front of the wagon with him. Asia brushed the mud from his face and removed the cover so the women could get some fresh air. They were only miles from Lott's Point. In just a few more hours they would be at Magnolia.

Part Four:
The Ladies

We consider ourselves courtesans. We tend to our gentlemen friends with the utmost of care. Our bodies are clean and free of disease. Please do not refer to us as whores.
Lola Passion

Narrow, unlit hallways littered with trash. Children running, mothers yelling, babies crying, the smell of cabbage cooking, strings of Irish profanity shouted out of windows, and cockroaches and rats skittering along the side rails. This was the verge to the apartment that Delores and Polly Gillian shared with their parents and seven siblings in the Five Point District of New York.

It was one of the worst slums in the country, with house fires and gang wars a constant threat. Poor immigrant families who had come to America with the hope of a better life lived in tiny apartments in decaying buildings.

The disappointment was evident at every turn. Beggars and prostitutes owned the street corners and the thieves who stole from the merchants lolled against the buildings waiting for the right moment to snatch someone's bag or wallet.

It was not a place for ladies.

Chapter Thirty-Two

Delores and Polly Gillian were the two eldest girls of nine children born to Irish immigrants whose hopes had been dashed on Ellis Island. Like so many others that had made the arduous trip across the ocean, disappointment set in quickly for the Gillian family. With no education, no money, and too many children, the immigrants were forced to endure the worst America had to offer.

In order to stave off the hunger and cold that were their constant companions, the young sisters were put to work in a textile factory ten blocks from their home.

Delores and Polly arrived at the mill at six in the morning and left at six at night every day of the week except Sunday. Aside from two fifteen-minute breaks, the girls worked at their machines, spinning wool into thread. Sitting on wooden benches with no backs, their arms and backs ached as they performed their monotonous tasks. The factory was a dimly lit place where they froze in the winter and sweltered in the summer heat.

After a full workday, Delores and Polly were required to help their mother with the younger children as she tried to prepare a meager meal for eleven people. Usually boiled potatoes and a small piece of bread would be all they were allowed. Before bed, Delores and Polly would clean the smaller children and lay them on their pallets. With just a few small lanterns to see by, the family was usually in bed very early. Delores would lay on the pallet she shared with three others, with hardly enough room to turn over.

Each night her prayers were the same. "Please, Lord, help me find a way to get out of this place. Don't make me spend another day here."

Her prayers went unanswered and after five years working in the factory, Delores vowed she would escape the drudgery one way or another. Her first attempt was to try and save a few pennies from her pay each week, but her father knew exactly what she made and took her entire pay envelope every Friday. He would then give them a dollar or two for lunches and anything else they required during the month. The girls needed to eat each day to keep up their strength so Delores tried to cut back, eating only one slice of bread for lunch, but Polly refused. After a month, Delores had only saved twenty cents.

Her second attempt worked somewhat better. On Saturdays, while she and Polly worked, their father would go to the pub. Spending most of the day there, swilling down the cheap ale, he would stagger home and fall into a drunken sleep. Delores would silently creep behind the blanket that separated her parents' bed from the children's pallets and ever so-slowly stick her hand into his pocket. Pulling out a few pennies or a nickel, she would stow it away in a pouch hidden under her pallet. He never missed the few cents she took, thinking he had spent it on ale.

On Sundays after church, all of the children were allowed two hours of free time. Delores would escape from the house and run across to the city park that separated the squalor of her street from the rest of the world. Delores would walk up and down the tree-lined streets of the shopping district, looking into the store windows that were filled with clothing and accessories she could only dream about. Stares from the shoppers reminded her that she did not belong on this side of town. Her worn gray dress and scuffed shoes were an offense against their finery. Depressed, she would return to the apartment and help her mother wash mounds of clothes that were hung on a maze of lines stretched between the apartment buildings.

Since Delores was the first-born, she had been allowed to go to school for a few years. Her father needed for her to learn to read and write so she could help him with his affairs. It was a known fact that the employers of illiterate immigrants were notorious for shorting their worker's pay.

Delores had loved school and was miserable when she was forced to leave after only three years. She was determined not to forget what she had learned in those precious years. At night she would take a small candle out to the rusted balcony and read books borrowed from the library.

Her favorite books were romance novels set in the southern states. She identified herself with the affluent lifestyle of the women in her books. She fancied herself living in Savannah and wearing a red, satin gown to a cotillion. The men would be handsome and courteous, not bloody browsers like those who worked at the mill. The gentlemen would smell of cologne and have clean fingernails and be nothing like the foul speaking, grimy men in Five Points. The men who abused their wives and children and smelled of swill and tobacco.

Delores knew that the only way to change her life was to run away from her home. It would not be too long before her father would expect her to marry. Her husband would add to the income of the family and her life would be as miserable as her mother's. At night, when Delores lay on her pallet, she would plan her escape. She would pack a small bag, take it to work with her and never come home again. She was afraid to make the move without Polly. It was dangerous for a woman to be traveling alone and she could not think of leaving Polly behind. She had no idea it would be Polly who made the decision so much easier.

One day after her work shift, Polly came to Delores in tears. She had been fired from her job. When she asked to be excused for a few minutes to relieve herself, the floor manager said no. After waiting for almost an hour, she was bent over with stomach cramps and she left her bench to go outside to the privy. When she returned, she was told she was fired and to come back on Saturday to collect her final pay. Polly knew that this meant a sure beating when she got home, plus finding another job away from her sister.

Delores comforted Polly. Delores told Polly of her dream to leave New York. Polly was scared of leaving, but even more afraid of the wrath of her father. Together they made a plan. Polly would have to pretend for two days that she was going to work so her father would not suspect anything. When they were given their pay envelopes on Saturday, they would not go home, but straight to the train station and buy tickets. Delores decided to leave a note on her bed pallet. It would simply read, "Polly and I have gone away. We are going out west to start a new life— Delores." She did not want to worry her mother. When their father discovered what they had done he would be furious and may even come looking for them. They would both be whipped and probably get no money at all from then on. They had to take the chance. They must make sure they left town before her father found someone to read the note to him and came looking for them.

Chapter Thirty-Three

Train number twenty-six, leaving New York, was heading south at 4 a.m. They would have to change trains twice before they reached Savannah, the city that Delores had chosen for their final destination. After purchasing two tickets, Delores returned to the waiting room where Polly had taken up residence.

"What are you doing? Why have you taken off your shoes?" Delores asked, seeing Polly with her stocking feet resting on the bench.

"If we are to spend the night here, I want to be comfortable. I have saved room for you on the bench."

"We have to leave here for a little while, Polly. Put your shoes back on. We cannot stay in the station. When we do not arrive home after work, I'm sure poppa will have figured something out. He will be looking for us. We need to find some place to spend a few hours and maybe get a bite to eat. Get your bag."

Polly smiled. She was always hungry. "Where is my bag?" she screamed, as she searched the bench next to her for the quilted satchel she had placed on the wooden plank to save a place for Delores. The bag was not there. She fell to her knees and searched under the bench. "Oh, no! Some feckin' gobshite has taken my bag. How could that be? I have never left this spot, not even for a moment."

"Did you lean over when you were removing your shoes? Someone probably leaned over the bench and just plucked it up," Delores said.

Polly broke into sobs. "Yes, but it was just for a short time to take them off. Whatever am I going to do? I had a change of clothes, my clean knickers and my hairbrush in my bag. Oh, blimey, my pay envelope was in there, too!" She put her hands to her face and wailed.

Delores knelt down in front of Polly and took her hands. "Don't cry. It will be okay. I still have a few dollars left. We will make it. Let's leave, Polly. People are staring at us."

Delores put her arm around her sister and led Polly down the shadowy street, looking for someplace to eat. She found a small restaurant and stepped inside. In the back of the room Delores found an empty table.

The meal of the evening was much too expensive. Delores ordered one bowl of soup and a small loaf of bread. When the tray was set on the table, Delores pushed the soup bowl to the middle of the table and broke the loaf in half. Polly took her part and began dipping pieces into the thick soup. Delores watched her, feeling sorry for her sister and wondering if she had done the right thing by taking Polly away from her family. Delores tore her bread in half and pushed it across the table. "I'm not really very hungry. Here, you take this."

While Polly concentrated on her food, Delores noticed two men sitting at a table across the aisle were watching them. They were dressed in linen suits with clean-shaven faces and shined shoes. One of the men tipped his hat. She had no idea why she did it, but she smiled at him. Yes, she thought, they were gentlemen, like the ones she admired in the books she had read.

"What are we to do now, Delores?" Polly asked, as she wiped the bowl clean with the last scrap of bread. I suppose we'd best go home." She began to sob again. "I am so sorry, Delores."

Delores reached across the table and took her hand. "Stop crying! What's done is done. I would rather die on the street than go home. You know we will be punished. We will be beaten and most likely you will get the worst of it for losing your pay envelope and clothes. Then we will be forced to get new jobs and we will once again be in the same situation. You go home if you want to Polly, but I have a ticket and I am bloody well going to use it."

Before Polly could answer her, one of the men who had been sitting at the table was standing next to them. "Please excuse my intrusion into your conversation but it is getting very late and I noticed that you ladies are unescorted. My friend and I would be honored to see you home to avoid any harm coming to you."

"Oh, we ain't going home," Polly said, " We are going to sleep in the train station tonight." Delores kicked her under the table.

"Ow, what's the bloody reason for that?" Polly asked, reaching down to rub her shin.

The man raised his eyebrow. "My, my, that does not seem like a very good idea. Sleeping in the train station can be very dangerous."

Polly rambled on. "You can say that again. Some bastard stole my bag and my pay envelope when my back was turned for a second and we don't have much money, but are going on the train in the morning."

Delores squeezed Polly's arm. "I'm sure this gentleman doesn't want to hear of our troubles." She was embarrassed by Polly's outburst.

"Perhaps my friend and I could buy you some dessert and coffee to fill the time. We can then take you to the train station."

"Oh, no, we are fine. Thank you," Delores said, glaring at Polly.

"I would sure like some cake and coffee. I'm still hungry," Polly said.

Delores put her head down. It was no use. Polly had won this battle.

The man nodded for the waitress and called his friend to the table. "May we sit?" he asked.

"Yes," Polly said, not looking at Delores, who had turned a pale shade of red.

He introduced himself as Randolph Carter; his companion was named Ben Jansen. Randolph ordered a whole butter cake and a pot of coffee. It was sweet cake, filled with cream: a taste that Delores and Polly had never shared. The men watched in amusement as Delores daintily ate her cake while Polly wolfed down two large pieces. Randolph said he and Ben were in New York on business and were pleased to spend some time with two such lovely ladies. Polly giggled. The sweet cream from the cake covered her upper lip.

Delores had never been in the company of a man before. She wanted to be on her best behavior. She was not allowed to have boyfriends. Her father would decide when it was time for her to marry. He would wait until he could find some bloke with a decent job and bring him to the house. If he didn't suit Delores, he would probably be pushed off on Polly. Polly was much more agreeable than Delores.

Leaning back in her chair, Polly let out a sigh. "Thank ye

kindly. That was quite toothsome. I be takin' the rest with me, if ye don't mind," she said, placing the cake platter in front of her.

"No, I don't mind. Please, be my guest." Randolph motioned for the waiter to the table and the half- cake was wrapped in white paper. Polly took it and placed it on her lap.

"If I might be so bold, may I suggest that we go to a nearby establishment and complete the evening with a nice pint of whiskey?" Ben said. "It would make your stay at the station a less uncomfortable. I hope I am not being too forward," he said. "A flagon of Jameson is a fine way to end the evening."

After a few awkward minutes and some prodding from Polly, Delores agreed to go with them. As they walked to the front of the restaurant, she liked the idea that perhaps the other patrons thought they were couples. She was conscious of the blue cotton dress she wore, which was not at all fitting for a woman who was out for the evening. Genteel women did not wear dresses made of cotton flannel.

At the counter by the restaurant door, Delores opened her small purse to pay for the soup and bread. Ben told her to put her money away. He said it would be his pleasure to pay for their meal. She was relieved. It gave her a few extra cents for the trip. She imagined they were very rich.

Two blocks away they entered the pub. Ben led them to a diminutive room in the rear of the building where women were allowed to have a glass of beer or wine. Ben ordered a bottle of Jameson and held out Delores's chair as she sat down. She had never tasted alcohol and knew it would be too bitter for her to drink. At first it took her breath away and the men laughed at her reaction. Taking just a sip at a time, the warm feeling inside her stomach somehow made the whiskey much more palatable. Polly giggled as she downed her glass of whiskey and Ben poured her another. When the bottle was empty, Randolph ordered a second and then a third. Polly was now leaning on Randolph and telling him that he smelled really good.

Delores didn't remember much about the carriage ride or walking into the hotel or being carried into a bedchamber. She remembered asking where Polly was and she was told she was asleep in the next room. Dizzy from the alcohol and unable to raise herself from the bed she must have fallen asleep. She awoke abruptly to find Benjamin on top of her naked body. He was sweating and pushing himself inside of her. She could feel the pain with each thrust. She screamed for him to stop and she began to whimper, but he continued. Delores laid there in total shock, knowing that he was performing a husband's duty on her. When he was finished he rolled over with his back to her. Afraid to move, the alcohol still swirling in her head, she closed her eyes.

In the morning, Ben was gone. The bedclothes were stained red with her blood and she felt pain as she stood up, yet her only concern was Polly. Where was she? Delores quickly dressed and looked around for her bag, her eyes widened. The man had left a dollar on the bedside table. She quickly dressed, collected her bag and headed for the door. Delores paused for a moment and then stepped back. She took the dollar and shoved it into her dress pocket.

When Delores opened the door, she found Polly sitting on the floor in the hallway. Her hair was disheveled and her shoes unlaced. She held her bag and the wrapped cake in her lap. Her eyes were red from crying and she continually wiped her nose.

"I did a really bad thing last night, Delores. I did a bloody bad thing last night. I let that man do things to me that ain't right. I was so blathered that I didn't have the strength to stop him. He was pantin' like a hunting dog that just chased a rabbit two miles. T'was really embarrassing, Delores. I just closed my eyes and prayed for it to be over." She began to cry again.

Delores sat down next to her. " I think we both had the same thing happen to us. Those men weren't gentlemen. They must have thought we were common brassers because I got paid."

Delores reached into her pocket and pulled out a dollar.

"Well, I don't remember everything, except I'm kind of sore in my private parts." Polly blubbered as she handed Delores two dollars. "That bloody bastard left this on the table and I took it."

Tears welled up in Delores' eyes. "I hate what happened. I wanted to protect you and look at the mess I got us in." With tears running down her face, she held tight to the money. "You must have been better than me. I only got one dollar."

Once on the train, they had time to think about what really happened to them. Polly cried and said they were now ruined women and the devil was in them. No one would ever want them. "We ain't decent women anymore. We been to bed with men and we ain't married."

"Don't think that a little blood on the bed sheet will ever turn a man away from you, Polly. I don't think those men would have cared what we were. They just wanted our bodies for their use. Being virgins was just an extra bonus for the bloody bastards," Delores sniped.

Delores vowed she and Polly would never let another man take advantage of them. They were too young to start their life in this manner. Delores remembered her mother's words: "You listen to me, girl. When a bloke pays ye a compliment he wants more than a thank ye. Keep your knickers on girl."

Chapter Thirty-Four

Arriving in Savannah gave Delores quite a let down. Once they left the train station she was disillusioned by the same squalor she had just come from in New York. There was the rich section of town with the large mansions and the poor section, with trash in the street and run-down tenements, and not much in between. They soon knew where they belonged.

After a few days of living in a cheap hotel, Delores and Polly found lodgings in a rooming house near Forsythe Park. They had two rooms on the third floor. The apartment was sparsely furnished and smelled of mildew. Children in dirty clothing played on the steps and ran through the hallways. Water was fetched from a pump in the rear of the apartment house and no one was allowed to have a fire in the hearth before six in the evening. It wasn't nice. It wasn't clean. But for the first time in their lives they were able to sleep two in a bed and not worry about a sibling wetting on them.

Delores knew they had to find work right away since their money was running low. After walking the streets for almost a week, she spied a *Help Wanted* sign in a small tailor shop window. Lying about her past work experience, Delores told the owner, Mr. Munson, that she had worked as a seamstress in New York. Though unsure of her qualifications, he was behind on his orders, so he hired her.

Delores now spent her workdays sewing sequins and pearls on the elegant dresses made for the society women of Savannah. At times, when Mr. Munson was not around, she would hold the dresses in front of her and look in the mirror. She vowed she would own dresses like these some day.

Polly decided she wanted nothing to do with sewing and after a few weeks she found work as a domestic in the house of Doctor and Mrs. Richard Finley. She was assigned to the second-floor bedrooms. She emptied chamber pots and scrubbed floors for just a few dollars a week. The one advantage to the job was that she was required to sit with the Finley's three children while they ate their lunch. They never cleaned their plates, which left plenty of food for Polly. These leftovers were delicious to her and made the distasteful parts of her job worthwhile. Mrs. Finley treated Polly as if she were a slave instead of a paid employee.

Dr. Finley had very little to say about the running of the house and seemed to be chastised quite often by Mrs. Finley as well.

Delores and Polly realized that they were barely making their expenses. At times, Polly would cry and say she wanted to go home. Delores would comfort her and tell her that very soon their lives would get better. An occasion to alter their positions came sooner than Delores imagined.

Mr. Munson and Delores had formed a good working relationship. He was a kind man and appreciated the long hours and hard work that Delores performed in the shop. He now trusted her to handle the patrons when he stepped out for a few minutes.

Today he needed Delores to deliver a dress to one of his customers. He had worked all night to finish it and the lady who had ordered it demanded that it be brought to her house early the next morning. Delores was given money for the coach ride and the dress was wrapped in a large white sheet.

Delores stared out the window as the coach meandered through the downtown streets of Savannah into an upscale neighborhood. The cobbled streets were lined with palatial, antebellum homes, each one more extensive than the next. The coach stopped in front of a large white home. Delores carefully carried the dress up the marble steps and dropped the brass knocker against the door.

A domestic opened the door and ushered her up the winding staircase and down a long carpeted hallway. She had never in her life been inside a house so beautiful. At the top of the stairs, a maid who opened the door to a lavish bedchamber met Delores. She gave her instructions to hang the dress on the chiffonier door and be sure to smooth out the creases or Mrs. Langston would be upset. Delores followed her orders. She hung the dress up on the hook and uncovered it. She hummed to herself as she creased the satin material between her fingers, layering it into folds.

"And who, may I ask, are you?" came a man's voice.

Startled, Delores quickly turned. "It isn't nice to sneak up on someone. You could have at least made a noise so I knew you were there."

Jerome Langston put his head back and laughed. "I had no idea that you did not hear me come in. I was not at all quiet. You must have been engrossed in your work. Please accept my apology. And once again, who are you?"

"My name is Delores Gillian and I work for Mr. Munson. He said the lady of the house wanted this dress right away. So I delivered it."

He stood with his arm braced against the door. "That was kind of you. My wife very rarely lets anyone into her bedroom, not even me," he said, laughing.

"It's plain red," she answered.

"And I suppose you say your eyes are just plain green?"

"Yes. Now if you will excuse me." She ducked under his arm and started down the steps.

"Wait!" he said. "I need to pay you for the dress."

She stopped near the front door. He removed his money clip from his pocket and peeled off several bills and handed them to her. "This is for the dress, and here is a little something for you." He held out a dollar bill.

"Oh, that is quite all right. I am just doing my job," Delores replied, wanting very much to take the money.

He opened her hand and put the dollar in it. "Take it. My wife will be most appreciative that the dress is here. I hope it may put her in a better mood."

Delores smiled at him, "Thank ye. Ye are very kind."

She was aware that he was watching her walk toward the carriage. She turned slightly, looking back toward the house and he smiled at her.

When she related the story to Polly later that night it all seemed so innocent, but somehow Delores knew that she would be seeing Mr. Langston again. He had that same look in his eye that the men they met at the train station had.

Two weeks later Mr. Langston came into the shop while Delores was busy with a customer. She saw him through the window, but when he entered the shop she pretended not to notice him. He talked to Mr. Munson for a few minutes and looked at the items in the display case. When the customer left the shop, he casually strode over to the table where Delores was now sorting out beads. He removed his hat. "Well, hello, it's good to see you again. My wife loved her dress and wanted me to thank you for delivering it to the house." Delores doubted that very much. He continued, "Her birthday is in a month and I would like to surprise her with a traveling outfit. She is going to Virginia to visit her parents for an extended period. Do you have some extra special buttons you can put on the jacket? Mr. Munson is making the outfit out of gray tweed."

"That will be up to Mr. Munson. He makes all of those decisions. I'm sure he will pick out something nice and I will attach them to the jacket." She returned to her sorting.

Mr. Langston fiddled with the brim of his hat. Unable to think of anything else to say, he bid her good day.

Delores knew he had come into the shop to see her. He had volunteered too much information for a man who was just ordering a suit. His wife would be out of town for several months and she was sure he wanted her to know that. She also knew that Mr. Munson had told her earlier in the week that they would be working on some new outfits for Mrs. Langston, including a traveling outfit. There was really no need for Mr. Langston to come to the shop. She was a lucky woman, that Mrs. Langston. She had a handsome husband and the money to travel at her will.

Chapter Thirty-Five

Delores lay awake in the dark room next to Polly. She was restless and warm and Polly was taking up most of the bed. "Polly, wake up, I need to talk to you," she said as she jostled Polly's shoulder.

Polly turned and opened her eyes. "Blimey, it still be dark out, Delores. I need to sleep."

"Just listen to me for just a few minutes. What would you say if you could do a job that would only take about an hour a day and you would make more money than you made in a week? Would you take it?"

Polly sat up. "Of course! What kind of eejit do ye think I am? Where can you get a job like that?"

"I have a gentleman who is interested in me and I think he is wanting favors from me. I know he would make it worth my while. He is very rich and handsome to boot."

Polly's eyes widened. "Do ye mean what I think you mean? Are ye talking about givin' bed favors to men? Are ye talking about whorin'? What is the bloody hell wrong with ye, Delores? We are not that kind of women. We were raised good Catholic girls. Just because we made one stupid mistake that don't make us bad women."

"I know that, Polly, but hear me out before ye say no. I have given this quite a bit of thought. We are still young and attractive and that is what most of the rich men are looking for. Their wives have too many children or have just become uninteresting to their husbands. These men are looking for something new and exciting. I think I can make it work to my advantage. I will not be just a common slapper, nor will I act like one. I will insist that he wear a sheath and I will only do what is comfortable for me. We are not getting anywhere, Polly. We need to make some money so we can move on. We are still counting pennies. I want to make dollars."

Delores sat up in bed and turned to Polly, who now had her pillow over her head. Grabbing the pillow, Delores said, "Will ye just listen to me for a minute? We could at least try it for a little while. I think just a couple of months will give us enough to move to better living quarters and get some new clothes. Wouldn't it be nice to walk into a bakery and buy a loaf of bread that isn't three days old? Do ye know that the one of the dresses I sew cost more than my whole year's wages? I am so tired of wearing the same rags every day. I would never force ye into something like this, but I do believe I am going to give it a try. How bad could it be? Could it hurt anymore than the needles I run through my fingers from sewing beads all day or the ache in my stomach from not eating proper food. I think not."

Polly would not agree to her idea. "Ye go do it, if ye must, but not me. No man is going to be staring at my diddies. One time in bed with a man was enough for me."

On Mr. Langston's next visit to the shop, Delores played into his hands. Batting her eyes, she asked him if his wife was still out of town. The conversation changed quickly. It took only a few minutes for him to arrange for a carriage to pick her up that evening and bring her to his house just to get her opinion on some clothing his wife would be wanting, of course. The evening turned into much more than that.

Delores's affair with Mr. Langston lasted three months. He then informed her that his wife was coming home and he needed to put Delores aside. She was ready to end the affair. He was becoming tighter with his money on each visit she made to his house. She had other men who were interested in her. It wouldn't take her long to entice another spider into her web.

After Mr. Langston, there was Mr. Jillion who was one of Mr. Munson's oldest customers. He just wanted someone to keep him company and share a meal or two with him. Delores was glad to accommodate him. It was an easy dollar to make.

Next was Mr. Hayes, who was a bit more challenging. She had to rub his feet with lotion and give him extra time to complete his act. She decided he was not really her favorite and called off seeing him after only three weeks.

She was now seeing Mr. Fields. He was a meticulously dressed and well-educated man, who found Delores' common ways charming at first. He also owned a carriage house in the rear of his property, which was a convenient meeting place.

Delores kept her job at the tailor shop and Mr. Munson was thrilled at the increase in business, as each new customer seemed to come in often to order clothing and accessories. It was the only way they had of communicating with Delores. Mr. Fields came in at least once a week, if it was just to buy a pair of cuffs or a collar.

Lying across the bed in Mr. Fields' carriage house, Delores watched as he dressed. "Did I do ye good, Mr. Fields?" she asked slipping back into her Irish brogue. "Ye seem quiet today."

"The word is 'you,' not 'ye,' Delores, I wish you would remember that. Everything is fine," he said, yet he seemed annoyed. "My wife is returning from Wellston in the morning and I will not be able to see you for a while."

Delores groaned. "Ye have been so nice to me, Mr. Fields, and now I have to find someone else again. Every time your wife returns from one of her visits, I am put out like the cat. I should tell her to stay away," she laughed.

"Let me give you some advice, Delores. You are pleasant to look at and you have a decent body, but you are a little rough around the edges and sometimes comments like the one you just made make me nervous. You consider yourself a courtesan, but a true courtesan keeps her mind to her business and never divulges anything about her gentlemen callers, especially to their wives. You are far from that standard. Also a good courtesan has her own residence where I would be free to visit and I wouldn't have to be sneaking you into my carriage house." He stood up and opened the door. "It is time for you to go," he said curtly.

She quickly finished dressing and took her money from the nightstand. As she passed him, she reached up to kiss his cheek. He turned his head. "If you want to make a lot more money, you have got to change a goodly amount of things about yourself. Right now you are just one step above a common whore and that is not what I am looking for when I choose a woman."

"You have hurt my feelings. I am not a common whore. Why do you mess with me if you think I'm common?"

"Because you are good in bed, something my wife is not," he said. "And I do like you, Delores. You always please me, but occasionally it would be nice to have a decent conversation with you about something other than bedroom talk. Let me ask you a question, can you read?"

"Yes, of course I can," she answered quite smugly.

"Wait just a moment," he said. Mr. Fields wrote an address on a piece of paper and handed it to Delores. "Go see this lady. Tell her I sent you. She can give you some good advice. After she is finished with you, I will expect one free night in your company."

Delores smiled. "I will, I promise."

The very next day, Delores dressed in a demure blue suit and hailed a horse-drawn cabby outside her building. She watched out the window as the carriage took her through a neighborhood she had never seen. Tucked away in a corner of the city, redbrick mansions dressed in magnificent ironwork and secret courtyards created an atmosphere of guarded privacy. They seemed to say that no one was allowed to enter without an invitation. The driver pulled up in front of one of these houses, a two-story house just off Pier Pointe Circle.

Delores dropped the gold-plated knocker onto the door and waited. A valet greeted her. No, she did not have an appointment. No, the lady of the house was not expecting her. No, she would not go away and come another day. Delores instructed the valet to tell the lady of the house that Mr. Fields had sent her.

"Very well, you may come in and I will see if Miss Diamond will see you." He left her standing in the foyer while he ascended the steps to the second floor. The house , draped in green velvet and gold, was elegant. Delores was awed by so much luxury. Looking up, Delores was showered by sprinkles of light dancing off the crystal chandelier. She had no idea that Miss Diamond had descended the steps until she heard the sound of a heeled shoe on the marble floor of the foyer.

Startled, she stepped backward, almost tripping over a porcelain umbrella stand. "Please excuse me, I was just..."

"Gawking, is that the word you are looking for? I am Chantal Diamond and who, may I ask, are you?"

Delores was suddenly at a loss for words. She inhaled the sweet smell of lilacs emanating from Miss Diamond, who wore a red silk robe, trimmed in white fur. Miss Diamond's ebony hair was pulled back in a cameo clip, revealing the alabaster skin of a woman who spent little time outdoors.

"My name is Delores Gillian and I am also a courtesan. Mr. Fenley said I should come here and you would give me some help."

With long polished nails, she beckoned Delores to follow her into the parlor. Sitting down on a pink couch, she crossed her legs revealing black stockings that ended at the top of her thigh. "Did he now? I haven't seen him in a few years." She contemplated her nails. "He was a lovely man, but I had problems fitting him into my schedule. You say you are a courtesan. That is quite interesting. I have never heard of you. Where is your place of business?"

Delores sat down. "I have none. I go to where I am called."

Chantal smiled. "Then you are a prostitute, is that correct?"

Delores looked down into her lap. "Yes, but that is not what I want to be. I want to be a classy lady who services gentlemen of her choice for a lot of money."

Chantal threw her head back and laughed. "Those are lofty goals. How old are you? How long have you been in the business?"

"I'm almost nineteen and it has been eight months."

"My dear, you have not even begun to realize what you are doing. So you have seen a couple of gentlemen. That only means you have a lovely face and you are young—two things in your favor, but in this business neither of those things will last long."

"Will ye be able to help me?" Delores asked.

"The use of the ye is very irritating to me, Delores. That is something used by low-class Irish immigrants. You may think it sounds charming, but it isn't. Get rid of it right now. You must refine your English. Real gentlemen know the difference between gutter girls and courtesans. Are you literate?" she asked, with no response from Delores. Chantal selected a rolled cigarette from a gold case on the table and lit it. "I am asking you if you can read and write," she said.

Delores smiled. "Yes, I can."

"That is in your favor. I would be glad to give you some advice, but not now. I am expecting a gentlemen caller at any moment. He likes me to be ready for him. His schedule is very demanding." Standing up, she smoothed her gown and escorted Delores to the door. "Come back on Friday morning around nine. Bring paper and pencil and twenty dollars. My services are not free."

Delores thanked her. As she was leaving, a handsome barouche arrived and a fine looking gentlemen stepped out and entered the courtyard of Chantal Diamond.

Once home, Delores rushed into the house to a waiting Polly. "Where have ye been? Did you bring supper? I am hungry."

"Please shush, Polly, I have exciting news. A woman named Chantal Diamond is going to teach me how to be a proper courtesan." She rambled on about Chantal's house and her clothes and the way she carried herself.

Polly was not interested. She wanted dinner. "A true courtesan, ye say. That's nice, but what about food?"

"It is not 'ye,' Polly. The word is 'you.' I need twenty dollars. I need all the money you have. I have to go buy some new clothes and perfume and bed linens."

Chapter Thirty-Six

Delores had a tablet full of notes after four visits with Chantal. She wrote down everything Chantal said. Chantal instructed her that correct English was very important. It showed good breeding. She also told Delores that keeping her hair and body clean at all times was important. Men also liked the smell of good perfume. Proper clothing was a major part of the whole scheme. Delores must have scanty undergarments and lots of sheer negligees. Under no circumstances should she present herself to a caller wearing knickers. Delores should pay attention to each man and what was his particular fancy. It was important to know her client's foibles. She must learn to be a good listener and sympathetic to the woes of her gentlemen callers. Chantal said it would be up to Delores to decide just what she wanted to do for money. It was always good to let the clients know in advance, so they did not expect something they were not going to get. It would keep her out of harm's way. In the moment of passion, men could also be violent if they did not get their way.

Lastly, Delores needed to have a place of respite where the men could come and forget about their work, their wives, and their children. It had to be a fitting room with clean linens and a small tray of liquor. Not too much, just enough for one or two drinks. A drunken client could become quite annoying.

On their last scheduled visit, Delores closed her tablet and placed it in her purse. "I have enjoyed our visits," Chantal said. "Besides, Mr. Fields and I had a very special relationship until his wife reined him in. He always gave me such wonderful presents. Gifts are a welcome benefit in this business. I prefer jewelry. If I don't like it, it can always be sold."

Delores leaned back in the satin chair. "Whew, I am exhausted. I just don't know if I can pull all of this together. Right now I do not have the right clothes or the right living conditions to assure a gentlemen caller will feel comfortable, especially since I share the only bedroom with my sister. Perhaps I have just been fooling myself. I will never be able to make the kind of money you make, Chantal. You must be very special."

Chantal smiled. "Let's just say I am not against diversity." She studied Delores's face. "I do not know why I am doing this, but I do believe you have what it takes to make this business a little more respectable. I know for sure you have the determination. That is the first step." Pulling out the drawer on her writing desk, Chantal retrieved a leather bound book. After writing out a bank draft she handed it to Delores. "This is just a loan, my dear. I expect it back within a few years. Don't disappoint me." She handed it to Delores.

"Oh, my, I can't accept this. It is more money than..."

Chantal dismissed her rebuttal with a wave of her hand. "Please, let's not go through these formalities. I am quite wealthy and it is only a loan. Find yourself decent living quarters and outfit yourself properly. I do believe you will do quite well. And now my dear, I have saved one of my best two secrets for last. Remember that the more time you take preparing for consummation with your gentleman clients; the less time they will take actually doing it. Secondly, do not see any one gentleman long enough for him to think that he is in love with you. If you begin to get that feeling, stop the relationship at once. Men professing love can cause you insurmountable problems. I have had enough dealings with irate wives whose husbands want a divorce to marry me. They can also become very jealous and keep your other clients away. Remember those two things and you will do well."

Standing at the door, on an impulse, Delores impulsively put her arms around Chantal and hugged her. To her surprise, Chantal took her face in her hands and kissed her full on the lips. "If you ever decide you are bored with men, come see me. I find you quite attractive." She ran her hand down Delores's arm. "One more thing, change your name."

Delores quickly made her exit, still feeling the sensation of Chantal's soft lips on hers.

Two months before Christmas, Delores surprised Polly by telling her that she had rented a cottage just off Victory Drive. It had two bedrooms and was much nicer than their present

apartment. She also told Polly that her name was now Lola
Passion. Polly could consider it her stage name, but from that
day forward Delores demanded that Polly call her Lola.

Lola, as she was now known, used part of the money Chantal
had loaned her to decorate her new bedroom in shades of blue
satin. She also found a seamstress who agreed to make a
wardrobe befitting a lady of her profession. Lola enrolled herself
in elocution classes and shopped for perfume and talcum.
Several weeks later, much to Mr. Munson's dismay, she quit her
job at the tailor shop.

Polly continued to question Lola about the money and
wanted to know where she had gotten it. Lola kept insisting it
was a gift from Mr. Munson. Polly did not believe her and the
bickering continued until in a weak moment, Lola told her that
it was a loan from Chantal.

"I can't believe ye took money from a bloody whore who
probably will come looking for ye wanting her money back twice
fold. All this just to keep ye from working and making a decent
day's wages."

"You are wrong, Polly Gillian, I am trying to make more than
a day's wages and not by working myself to death. If you want to
continue emptying privy pots and taking care of a rich man's
brats, you go right ahead. I shall make a lot more money in a
much easier way. And the word is 'you,' not 'ye.'"

Lola kept her visits with the gentlemen to herself. She
refused to answer any questions that Polly asked her. In the
beginning business was slow until Chantal was kind enough to
send Lola a few of her gentlemen customers.

At first Lola was overwhelmed by trying to pass herself off as
a lady. Talking in a softer, more sophisticated voice was the
hardest thing to do. She began to pay close attention to what
each man's secret desire was and she was always complimentary
about his sexual prowess. She also learned not to talk about any
of her other clients and to pretend that the one she was with was
the most important man in the world. Most of the men were
quite a bit older than her and they seemed enthralled to be with
such a young girl with copper hair and green eyes. Sometimes,
with a new customer, Lola would pretend that she was a virgin,
which usually garnered her a higher price. A bit of cherry juice
put into a snuffbox and kept under her pillow could accomplish
that quite easily.

Chapter Thirty-Seven

Another two years passed and Polly was still working for the Fenleys. She was becoming more and more inquisitive about what went on while she was away at work. The house was changing every month. New pieces of furniture and ornate lanterns arrived almost monthly. Tailored dresses sewn at one of the best shops in town were presents to Polly from Lola. The pantry was always filled with food, including truffles and sweets that Polly loved. Lola made sure that all of her callers were out of the house by the time Polly arrived home at seven.

Even though Polly still did not approve of Lola's profession, her complaints were less and less. Polly was reaping the benefits. She had thought about quitting her own job. The food was plentiful and there was always extra money in the sugar jar on the shelf in the kitchen. Polly knew that Lola would not be happy about supporting her. She would have to stay with the Fenleys until something better came along. She had no idea that an unexpected conflict at the Fenleys would thrust her into a new profession within the week.

It was early in the summer and the cool air filtering into Lola's bedroom made her task much easier. She had just poured oil into her hands and begun to massage the back of a rotund man lying on her bed when she heard the front door open. The door slammed shut and Lola heard noise in the parlor. Putting on her robe, she patted the man's back. "You just lie here and rest. I will return shortly." She closed her bedroom door behind her. "Why are you home?" she asked Polly, in a whisper.

"I have been fired from my job. That bitch, Mrs. Finley, fired me."

Lola put her fingers to her lips, "Be quiet." She tossed her head toward her door.

Polly continued in a loud voice, ignoring Lola's request. "One of Mrs. Fenley's brats kicked over a full chamber pot and the

Mistress expected me to clean it up. There was a disgusting stinking mess all over the floor and the brats were laughing. I told her I didn't mind emptying them, but I surely was not going to get down on my knees and clean it off the floor. She pulled my hair and hit my face real hard. I bloody well smacked her back. I knocked her a good one, right in the puss. She was holding her jaw and kept screaming at me to get out of her house. When I asked her for my pay, she just kept yelling at me. She refused to pay me for the four days I already worked this week and got her clammy butlers to take me out the door. Dammit! I want my money," Polly said, stomping her foot.

"Polly, please be quiet. Go away for another hour." Rifling through the desk, Lola pulled out a handful of coins and handed them to Polly. "Here, go to the bakery. I will come and get you soon."

"Bloody lovely! Now I am being ousted from my own house, too," Polly said as she stomped off.

Later that evening Lola listened while Polly told her the story over again. She felt sorry for her sister, but how could she conduct business with Polly home every day?

"I really would like to have my wages," Polly said, wiping her nose. I feel like calling the bloody law on her."

"I really don't think you should do that, Polly. I mean, I am really not in any position to be having the law coming around here."

Polly looked for another job for almost a month. Gossip travels faster in the wealthy community than the poor. Each time she applied for a job, she was shown to the door as soon as she gave her name. She was chastised for what she had done to "poor Mrs. Fenley."

After a particularly difficult day she returned home crying. "What am I to do, Lola? I know you must be tired of me living off you and I am tired of having to stay away from the house all day." Removing her shoes, she sat in front of the fire warming herself.

"I could get you work if you wanted it Polly," Lola said.

"How many times have I told you I am not going to bed with some bloke for money? I am not like you, Lola. I have poor English, I am overweight and I am scared out of my wits at the thought of doing anything so vile."

"I know you are, Polly, and I would never force you to do

anything that you did not want to do. I have a few gentlemen who just wish to spend time with a lady and will pay them. Right now I have a gentlemen who wants to pay me three dollars just to have tea with him for an hour."

"You're gone out of ye bloody head. That is more money than I make in a week working sixty hours."

"He has a peculiarity, Polly. He wants to wear my clothes while we have tea. Unfortunately, my clothes are too small for him."

Polly's eyes widened "What a mad plonker! He wants to wear your clothes? Why?"

"It is just his desire. Chantal said they are called cross-dressers and it is a fetish they have that gives them pleasure. He could fit into one of your outfits, Polly, and all you have to do is have tea with him. He even brings the teacakes."

"Will he wear my knickers, too?"

"Yes," Lola answered.

"And I don't have to touch his bloody body? Just have tea?" Polly mused. "This has to be one of the oddest things I have heard. If ye promise he won't sniff at me, I will do it. I will do it just this once."

On Thursday Polly was apprised of the preparation she needed to take for her guest. She was to lay a pair of knickers, a camisole, and a dress on her bed. She was to wait in the parlor with the door closed and he would join her there.

She was nervous as she made tea and set up the cart in the parlor. Filling up the new silver sugar bowl, she put linen napkins and a pitcher of milk on the tray. Her hands were perspiring and she continued to wipe them on her skirt.

Sitting with her hands folded in her lap, she passed the time by repeating the speech Lola had prepared for her. When he entered, she was to stand, smile and then take his hand and show him to the settee.

A slight knock on the door made her heart jump. As the door opened, Polly gasped. "Dr. Fenley! Blimey, it *is* Dr. Fenley and you are wearing my clothes."

Dr. Fenley was startled. He quickly entered the room and closed the door. "What are you doing here, Polly? I was to meet someone here!" He stumbled through the words, beads of sweat forming under the blonde wig he wore.

Polly fell back on the settee and kicked her feet in the air.

She grabbed her stomach and rolled with laughter. "Dr. Fenley, in my clothes. What a bloody shenanigan!" Finally getting her composure, she sat up. "I am the woman you were to meet. My sister is Lola Passion. She is a courtesan. Since your wife fired me, I have been reduced to this, seeing you in a dress." She covered her mouth with her hand, still snickering.

"I think I look quite well. It is good we are about the same size," he said, twirling around in front of the wall mirror. "I will excuse your behavior only because I find your clothes quite comfortable, and since we know each other, we can skip all the formalities. I have brought a chocolate truffle. My secret will never leave this room, do your understand, Polly? If it does, I will know who to look for and make sure you and your sister are forced to leave this town."

"Relax, Dr. Fenley. As long as you don't put your hands on me, everything will be fine. Now sit down and I will wet the tea. You have one hour."

His voice changed to a shrill high-pitched tone and he suddenly became embarrassingly effeminate. He fanned himself with her chapel fan and batted his eyes. At times Polly felt as though she was entertaining a girlfriend.

When the hour was up, Dr. Fenley stood up. "After getting over my initial embarrassment, I had a very good time, Polly. Perhaps we can do it again next week."

"Yes, I suppose that would be all right. I would like cream-filled éclairs next week."

"Fine. I will leave your clothing and money in your room. I would like some silk or satin undergarments next week."

"I expect six dollars on my nightstand. Three for today and three that your biddy wife still owes me for stiffen' me on my wages," Polly shot at him.

Later that evening she once again broke into laughter as she recounted the incident to Lola. "Holding up the six dollars," she danced around the room. "It was sure an easy way to make this much money. Three times what I made in a week for scrubbing his floors."

"I have other men who have requests that do not involve having sex with them. Are you interested?" Lola asked, timidly.

"Ye gads, Delores, don't say that word! Lordy, what other bloody things do they do, besides dressing up like women?"

"Oh, some just like to touch your shoes, or let you spank

them with a paddle, or—"

"You stop right now, Lola!" Polly said covering her ears with her hands. "That is disgusting." She hesitated for a moment and then asked, "How much do they pay for that sort of thing?"

Chapter Thirty-Eight

The life of a prostitute was much more satisfying to Polly than she could have ever imagined. She could sleep late in the morning and have more than enough food to eat. Along with Dr. Fenley's weekly visit, Lola had found her several good customers. Polly was no longer embarrassed to see men clomping around in her shoes or wearing make-up. With two good incomes Polly and Lola were finding it easier to relax and not worry about spending too much money. They would don their finery and go downtown in a private carriage to shop whenever the mood struck them, bringing home boxes filled with new clothes and accessories.

Lola wished that Polly would take more initiative with her customers. Polly preferred only the men who had fetishes that did not include the actual act of sex. Lola knew there might come a time when one of the men may take a notion to make Polly have sex with him. Polly would have to perform. Lola dreaded that day, even though she had repeatedly warned Polly that it might happen.

Since Polly was of no help to her with the household chores, Lola hired a cook and a housemaid. The added expense made it necessary to take on a few more clients. It was time to expand her business. She decided she needed to hire a few more ladies. That would mean moving to a larger home and charging more. Lola sometimes wished she could be like Chantel and live on her own. But it was her decision to bring Polly along when she left home and now it was her responsibility to take care of her. She would have to become the madam of a house. Her only worry would be to find women that could meet the needs of her customers. They would have to be special ladies.

"What do you mean? Why do we need more women in our house? We do okay. You're getting greedy, Lola," Polly said when Lola told her of the plan.

"It may be fine for you, Polly, but I am seeing too many clients a day and I am getting tired. I worry about getting pregnant with so much activity. A few more women would take the burden off me. I never want to be poor again, Polly. It could happen very easily you know. If I got sick or we had to quit our business for a while to keep the law away, we could be poor again. Do you remember what it was like, Polly, when we had very little to eat?"

The last sentence was enough to convince Polly that Lola was probably right. She never wanted to be without good food again.

Finding new women to work with them was not an easy task. Most upscale houses held on to their good women and were not especially happy when other madams courted their women. It could cause a nasty confrontation between madams.

Lola decided she would try to get information from her customers to assist in her hunt. Waiting for just the right time, usually after a good session, Lola would quiz the men about other women who they had seen. A few of the men volunteered enough information for her to take her search to the streets near Forsythe Park. She was given the name of a few women that might meet her needs.

The first woman Lola visited was named Ramona. She was a striking ebony-haired woman in her late twenties. Lola was impressed with her appearance. She had an allure about her that Lola felt would be very appealing to men. She had long legs and a good-sized chest, two things men liked. Given the proper clothing and a few lessons in demeanor, Lola was sure that Ramona would fare well in an upscale house. When Lola asked her about her background, Ramona was anxious to volunteer information in her broken English.

Ramona said that she and her husband had moved to California from Spain to find a better life. Her husband got a job working on the railroad and they moved from place to place with the rail workers. The work was arduous, but the money was good. Just three weeks after he started his job, her husband lost his footing while working on an overhead trestle and fell to his death on the rocks below. Ramona had no money and nowhere to go. She also did not speak English. In order to survive she became a camp follower. She moved with the workers across the United States. Living in a tattered tent and having sex with five or six men each night had taken its toll on her. When she arrived in Savannah, she spent three weeks in the city's charity hospital regaining her strength from months of improper nourishment and curing a bout of venereal disease.

After her release from the hospital she had to find work quickly. Prostitution was all she knew and with her looks, finding work in Savannah was easy.

Although she made a decent living in the brothel where she now worked, she had to give more than half her wages to the madam of the house. Lola assured her that would not be the case if she were to come live in her house. She would charge her only ten percent of what she made.

A visit to Chantal provided Lola with her second employee, a woman she had known for some years. Her name was Venus and although she considered herself a cut above most prostitutes, she would perform almost any act for money. Venus knew how to use her curvaceous body and long legs to attract men. Venus was from a family that could provide quite well for her, but she preferred her life, saying she really enjoyed her work.

Chantal said that since Lola was expanding her business there were times when someone like Venus could be an advantage. Even though she would be running an upscale house, the requests from some of the men were difficult at times. Lola had turned some of the men away because of their requests for unusual sex acts.

When Lola told Venus her proposal she was pleased to be included, even though Lola said that Ramona and Venus would have to refine their ways and lose the temptation to be bawdy. She impressed upon them that they had to dress properly and keep their bodies and hair clean.

They would never refer to themselves as prostitutes, but as courtesans. They were to stay free of disease and require their clients to wear sheaths. If a pregnancy should occur, it would be their obligation to take care of the matter in a timely way. The speech she had given the girls was the information that Chantal had given Lola when she went to repay the money she had borrowed from Chantal.

"I wish you luck, Lola," Chantal said. "I, myself, prefer to stay away from running a house. Being a madam will give you gray hair before you are thirty. Women are quite bitches, you know."

Lola agreed. "I would not do it, Chantal, were it not for my sister. She brings very little income into the house and so I have to support her as well as myself. I am hoping that having other women around will encourage her to be more involved. All she wants to do is lay in her bed eating sweets and looking at picture books."

Lola told her new girls that she was not interested in their personal lives and that they should keep their business to themselves. To Ramona and Venus it all seemed too good to be true and they were anxious to join Lola and Polly in this new venture. Venus could not believe that Lola, who was at least ten years younger than herself, had reached this degree of success.

The new residence Lola had chosen was located one mile outside the city limits of Savannah. It was tucked away behind a rock wall and a cluster of trees. A stone-paved driveway circled the entire house, which allowed the carriages to be driven to the back of the building and remain secret from the road. Each girl was given her own room, with two extra rooms to spare. Lola had no intention of hiring anyone else. With Polly and herself, two additional women would be perfect. It would provide her with a comfortable living and lessen her client list. Lola worried about Polly because her weight was blossoming at an alarming rate. Perhaps the new girls would take over some of her clients and still leave Polly to those clients that were a bit odd. The odd ones cared little about what the woman they visited looked like as long as they would play along with their games.

A week after Lola completed furnishing the house, the ladies arrived. When the carriage carrying Ramona and Venus arrived, Lola went outside to greet them.

The door of the carriage opened and she heard Venus yell in a loud voice, "Get out! Get the hell out, you little bitch!" A small girl came tumbling down the steps. She stood up and brushed off her dress.

"What is going on? Who is this girl?" Lola asked, already wondering if she had made a big mistake by bringing the women to her house.

Venus sputtered. "This little bitch hid in the luggage compartment of the coach. We had no idea she was with us until we were almost here. Her name is Angel and she is a street whore."

Lola stared at the small girl standing in front of her. She was childlike, her long blonde hair hung over her face as she twisted her soiled white dress in her hands. Venus shoved the girl, sending her tumbling forward falling to the ground. "Dirty little bitch."

Lola stepped forward and picked her up. "Why did you come with the girls? Surely you must know I have no place for you and you were not invited."

Angel crawled forward and took hold of Lola's legs. "Please, please, don't send me back! I would rather die than go back. I don't want to live on the street. I can keep up with the best of them," she said, pointing at Ramona and Venus. "I've been whore'n since I was twelve. Please don't send me back." Tears began to run down her face. "I overheard them talking about this place while they was waiting for the coach. Just give me a chance."

"For heaven's sakes, get up," Lola said. "Let's all go inside and we'll talk about this."

Ramona and Venus grumbled for a few minutes. Once inside, their demeanor changed. They marveled at the inside of the house. They had never worked in such a grand house. Ramona grabbed Lola's hand and pumped it up and down. "Thank you. I will be very happy here." They had forgotten all about Angel.

When the girls had gone to their rooms, Lola sat with Angel in the parlor. "How old are you?" Lola asked.

"I'm sixteen, ma'am," she replied.

"Why are you living on the streets? Do you not have a family?"

Angel shook her head. "No, just me. I'm all alone and homeless. I was working in Tybee's saloon, but I got fired for throwing beer on a man. It ain't easy to find a house that will take you in. You saw what happened between Venus and me. Other prostitutes are always jealous of me. Soon as I start making more money than them, they find some way to get me out. That has happened to me twice before."

Lola was amused by her candor. "How did you get started in this business?" was Lola's next question.

"My momma was a whore. She ran the upstairs rooms at a tavern. She tried to protect me, but a jealous man killed my momma. He wanted her all to himself. When she said no, he shot her. I have been on my own since I was twelve."

"I want you to get one thing straight, Missy. We, in this house, are not whores. We considered ourselves courtesans. We tend to our gentlemen friends with the utmost of care. Our bodies are clean and free of disease. Please do not refer to us as whores."

"Yes ma'am," Angel replied. "I know that the others are real mad at me for coming along. You just don't know what it was like. I have nowhere to go. I'm afraid I'm going to die every night. Please, please don't send me back."

"It is hard for me to realize that you are old enough to be in this business, but I was not much older than you when I started. I suppose I could hire you for a month or so and see how it works out. I promise you that no one here will mistreat you and if they do, they will answer to me."

Angel jumped up from the sofa and threw her arms around Lola. "Thank you. You will not be sorry. I promise you, you will not be sorry."

It took about a week before everything settled down in the house and the men started arriving. The girls marveled at the clientele and the gentlemen were more than pleased with them. Each girl began to pick up her regulars. It was much easier than not knowing who would appear when their bedroom door opened.

It would not be long before Lola realized that even though she was young and not at all educated, Angel was a professional when it came to men. She plied her trade like someone who had been at it for many years. She would greet the older gentlemen with her flaxen hair in braids and a white, high-necked nightgown. It gave her the appearance of being much younger than her sixteen years, which seem to arouse them. Younger men were treated like boyfriends that had come to court her. Her favorite words with them were, "Let's pretend." At other times, dressed in black satin with red rouge on her pouting lips, she could play the part of a sensuous siren.

Angel was able to make a considerable amount of money much to the chagrin of the others. Lola knew that the underlying jealousy between them stirred a competition that was good for business.

Ramona's steamy looks and broken English was an enticement few men could resist. She had a way of being in charge of her clients. They seemed to like her dominant stance. She had few complaints from her customers.

Lola never asked Venus about her customers. She knew that Venus gave most men much more than they expected. She knew how to use every inch of her skin to entice them into her web. She had a steady stream of men asking to see her.

Lola realized when it came to the sexual act she was probably the most benign. She serviced gentlemen caller's who liked to sit and talk with her before going to bed. She became a sounding board where the men could discuss their wives and family. She would comfort them and sometimes offer advice. At the age of twenty-eight, Lola felt quite matronly.

For the next few years, the money began to flow into the coffer and life moved like a well-oiled rocking chair. Lola had reached an agreement with the police chief of Savannah. An envelope was delivered to him each Friday, which kept him happy and away from her doors in a legal capacity. He came around twice a month to see Polly. He had a fixation for fat women. He would climb into Polly's lap and she would cuddle him like a small child. Other times he enjoyed looking at her while she lay naked on the bed. To keep from being embarrassed, Polly would eat while he watched her. When crumbs of food dropped onto her rolls of fat, it pleased him even more.

The house was now known as Castle Knoll. Lola liked the sound of it. She had seen the name in a book years before. It sounded like an elegant estate where you could find both solace and privacy. She had a fountain and a reflecting pool constructed that was surrounded by a formal garden complete with walking-paths. She felt it gave the house an air of dignity. The inside was decorated in cool colors of blues and whites. Lola avoided the garish gold and reds used in other bordellos. She wanted her residence to be decorated tastefully and reflect the kind of service her gentlemen callers would receive there.

Lola was now free to shop in the most expensive boutiques in Savannah. She had money to spend and she spent it. Once home, she would store the treasures she had bought that day in ornate hatboxes stacked in the corner of her room.

Chapter Thirty-Nine

When the talk of secession and war began to surface, Lola became concerned. She vacillated between staying in Savannah or moving North. It would be difficult to leave, but talks with her clients did not make her feel comfortable staying at Castle Knoll.

The women in the house agreed that they would all stay together, knowing that now was not a time to be on your own. Lola decided she would stay at Castle Knoll as long as possible. She was not anxious to leave, but she became increasingly nervous when news of a battle was received. She had no desire to be trapped inside the boundaries of the war. Lola was worried that the encroachment of the Northern soldiers would not be a healthy situation for them. Even though her clients hated to see her leave, they understood. Most agreed that left alone, the women would be at the mercy of the troops, both North and South.

In February 1862, Fort Pulaski, at the mouth of the Savannah River, was fired upon. The sound of the cannons rumbling across the fields and the black clouds of smoke from the fires was enough to convince Lola it was time to leave. She closed up the house and hired two large carriages to take the women and herself to safer ground. She had sold off most of the furniture and accessories that were too cumbersome to move. Her heart was heavy the day she left Castle Knoll. She had been so proud of her achievement and now it was left to be stripped of all its splendor.

For the next few years the five women traveled through Ohio and Michigan, living a modest life for women who had enjoyed extravagance in the past. They were often forced to stay in rooming houses or hotels that would accommodate them. The women soon learned that the feeling about prostitutes was not as acceptable in the Midwest as they were in the South. Lola refused to live in the red-light districts or slums. Most towns were not receptive to have a bordello in their vicinity and forced the women to leave. The local law enforcement in most of the places wanted much more than they could afford to let them conduct their business. Without their protection, the girls would surely end up in jail quite frequently.

The customers they now served did not care about Southern gentlemen principles and many times the girls, including Lola, were mistreated. Venus suffered several broken fingers and multiple bruises when she refused the advances of a drunken customer.

Polly had become depressed now that she was forced to perform sexual favors just like the other women. She could no longer be selective about the callers she would see. A heated argument between Lola and her convinced Polly she had no other choice. Lola gave her an ultimatum. Either do it all or leave the house. Polly had nowhere to go and she knew that Lola was under a good deal of pressure.

In Savannah, most of the women saw three or four men a day. Now, they were seeing three times that many for half the money. After a particularly bad night with a customer, Angel told Lola she was afraid of what was happening to the men since they were all concerned about war and seemed to take their vengeance out on the girls. Lola selected Angel's customers carefully. The war was taking its toll on everyone and Lola was afraid Angel might be the next one to be injured. Angry men made angry customers.

After three unsettling years, Lola and the women chose Pittsburgh as their new destination. They hoped that living in a larger city might improve business. Lola leased a two-story Victorian house in an upper class neighborhood. Her plan was once again to attract wealthy clients. It was a lavish house filled with ornate woodwork and spacious rooms. Everyone seemed to breath a sigh of relief when they were settled into their new surroundings.

Within a few months her plan had come to fruition. A steady stream of northern gentlemen now entered and left by the side door of her home. With piano music playing in the parlor and valets serving fine wines and cheese, the women once again donned their best dresses and paraded themselves in front of prospective customers.

Polly was not happy. Since her weight had ballooned to

almost three hundred pounds, Lola had cut back on her food intake. She wanted desserts and candy, which Lola refused to give her. "I am trying to keep you alive until this stupid war ends and we can go back to Castle Knoll. At the rate you are going, there won't be a carriage large enough to carry you. None of the gentlemen we are seeing are interested in you. You have got to carry your share of the burden." Lola had no idea that along with many other buildings in Savannah, Castle Knoll was no more than a pile of cinders.

After almost a year of profit, Venus announced to Lola that she was pregnant. She was distraught and wanted the pregnancy over with as soon as possible. She had taken prepared potions and quinine pills, but nothing had worked to end the pregnancy. It did not take Lola long to locate a mid-wife who also performed abortions. The mid-wife arrived at the house the next day. Venus knew the procedure. This was her third abortion.

The midwife gave Venus a glass of water in which she had mixed a packet of white powder. As she waited for the medication to take effect, the woman opened her bag and laid a white towel on the table. She told Lola she needed a pallet of cloths to put under Venus. Ramona slipped the folded sheets under Venus's naked body. The medication Venus was given appeared to have relaxed her.

Opening her bag again, the midwife took out a steel rod and a roll of cotton stripping. Wiping the rod with alcohol, she waited a few minutes more. Lola felt a bit queasy and decided to leave the room. There were a few minutes of silence and then Venus let out a piercing scream that was heard throughout the house. Lola rushed back into the room. Blood ran down Venus's thighs as she drew her legs to her chest and moaned.

The woman wiped the blood from the rod and placed it back in her bag. "I packed her real good, but you need to change the dressing when it gets soaked. She's bleeding heavy now, but it should stop in an hour or two. I mixed up something to help her get her strength back, but if she isn't in too much pain, just give her a little whiskey." Lola handed the woman two dollars and she slipped it into her pocket. "She needs to stay in the bed for at least two weeks and for sure, no men for at least a month. By the looks of her insides she should give them up altogether."

Angel stood in the doorway and stepped aside as the woman

passed. "Is she going to be all right? She isn't going to die is she?" Angel asked.

"No, she won't die. Not this time anyway. You watch yourself, Missy, or you'll be the next one I call on," the woman said, pointing her finger in Angel's face.

Venus lay in bed for almost two weeks. At times she seemed incoherent so the girls took turns sitting with her. They put cold cloths on her fevered brow and fed her broth and tea laced with whiskey. When the fever finally broke, Venus sat up still pale and drawn and announced that she was hungry. Angel clapped her hands and smiled. She threw her arms around a surprised Venus. "Oh, I was so worried about you. I am so glad that you are better."

With Venus out of the working circle, the rest of the women worked hard to save their good customers. Several other houses had sprung up in the area and each man was now an important commodity. Angel refused to see any of the men that were customers of Venus. She preferred nice men with no aberrant behavior.

It was late on a Saturday afternoon. Angel had just serviced her last customer for the day. He was a small, shy man who preferred not to talk but get right down to business. His visits usually lasted only about fifteen minutes, which was fine with Angel. It kept her Tuesday afternoons free. Bored with staying in her room, Angel wandered down the hallway. Lola's door stood open. Angel stuck her head in. "Can I come in?" She asked.

Lola motioned for her to enter. Lola sat at her vanity, filing her nails.

Angel plopped down on the bed and rested her head in her hands. She was quiet for a few minutes. "Do you think God will forgive us for what we are doing, Miss Lola?" Angel asked.

"I have no idea about God. I try not to think on that subject," Lola replied.

"When you are too old to do this anymore, Miss Lola, what will you do with your life?"

"My goodness, why so many questions? Are you worried about something?"

"I know my mama would be real mad if she knew what I was doing. I know she would rather see me dead. She hated her own life and she never wanted me to follow in her footsteps. I promised her I wouldn't. It scares me sometimes. You know, maybe getting a disease or becoming pregnant. And I know that Ramona and Venus don't like me very much. I really have no one to talk to. I get lonely."

Lola sat down on the bed next to Angel. "Sometimes when I have a man with disgusting breath or one that heaves his weight upon me and takes an exceptionally long time to do his duty, I think that I should give it up right now. Then I wonder what I would do. Would I go to work in a factory or marry some bloke and father his brats while he is off with another woman? I don't want that for myself, Angel, but if you are bothered by what you are doing maybe you should quit," Lola said. "I know I shall never command respect from the so-called decent people in this community, but I had no respect from anyone when I was a poor textile worker either."

Angel sat up. "Maybe in a few years I'll think about quitting but right now I love looking in my chiffonier at all my pretty dresses and eating good food."

"Now, my dear, I need some rest," Lola said, yawning. "Tomorrow is another work day."

Ramona was the next to take to her bed. She contracted a bout of dysentery that lasted for over two weeks. The sickness left her so weak she was unable to work for almost a month.

When Ramona was finally out of bed and anxious to go back to work, she took a warm bath and prepared herself to meet her first customer in over a month.

Walking down the hallway toward her room, she stopped for a moment. The voice coming from Venus's room had a distinctive English accent, which she recognized. Putting her ear to the door, Ramona listened for a few moments. Venus was with Arthur, a gentle man who always left very good tips. Ramona beat on the door with both fists.

The door opened. "What? What is it you want? Are you trying to break the door down?" Venus said, standing in the threshold naked.

Ramona grabbed Venus by the hair and pulled her screaming into the hallway. "You bitch. How dare you take one of my regulars? You know I am the only one who sees Arthur. He was supposed to visit with me today." She yanked Venus' hair again.

Venus came up swinging, knocking Ramona against the wall, her silk robe slipping from her still damp body. "He wants to see me now. You haven't been around, remember? You were sitting in the privy that last time he came. And don't ever touch my hair again, you freakin' whore."

She turned and started back into the room. Ramona struggled to her feet and grabbed at Venus again. Within seconds both women were screaming, kicking and biting in a tumbling heap of skin and hair. Arthur, with his clothes in his hand, tried to squeeze past them but was tripped by a leg that also knocked him to the floor. The melee had garnered an audience. Angel, along with her gentleman caller, and Polly stood watching in amusement as the cat fight continued, with poor Arthur taking punches he didn't deserve.

When Lola heard the commotion she walked quietly from her own room and doused the women and Arthur with a pitcher of cold water. Sputtering and trying to get their wet hair out of their eyes, both women went to a neutral corner. Lola reached down and helped Arthur to his feet. "Please accept my apology for this distasteful outburst. Seems that both of my ladies enjoy your company. If you would like to come back tomorrow, there will be no charge."

"If you don't mind, Miss Lola, I think I'll pass," Arthur said, as he gathered his wet clothes off the floor and ran down the stairs.

With both women dressed and standing before Lola, they hung their heads waiting for their punishment.

"If I wanted gutter whores in my house I could find them by the barrels. I really thought you two had more class. I can see now that it took a while for it to come out, but I guess I was wrong. You both can pack your things and leave in the morning," Lola said quite calmly.

Venus let out a moan. "Oh, please, Lola. Don't fire me! Please. I am so sorry. She started it. She pulled me out of my room. I was only protecting myself," Venus said, pointing to Ramona.

Tears were running down Ramona's face. "I promise, I will never do it again. I was wrong. I'm sorry. Please give us another chance. I am begging you." Ramona dropped to her knees, her hands folded in front of her. "It's just that I haven't worked in almost six weeks and—"

"Get up! You look ridiculous. For the next week you will both give me every penny you make as retribution. You will be given one more chance and that is all. Do you understand?"

Venus and Ramona were beyond grateful answering in unison that it would never happen again.

Lola and the women remained in Pittsburgh until the early months of 1865. They had not planned on leaving but an unfortunate circumstance quickly changed their plans.

On a frigid January evening, under a steady snowfall, Polly lay in her bed looking at a picture book. The door opened and Robert Capp, a well-known financier in the Pittsburgh circle, and one of Venus's regulars, staggered into her room.

"Where is everybody?" he asked in a slurred voice.

Polly lifted her cumbersome body to a sitting position, pushing her box of chocolates under the cover. "They are with customers, Mr. Capp. I don't think you were expected here tonight. Did you have an appointment to see Venus? You are in the wrong room."

He swayed back and forth, leaning on the door to steady himself. "You'll do," he said. Robert Capp was not in the mood for small talk. Taking a long swill from the whiskey flask he pulled from his pocket, he began removing his clothing. As he approached the bed, he growled at Polly, "Turn over on your stomach."

"No, I don't think so," she replied, scooting as far back as she could in the bed. "I don't do that sort of thing. You need to see Venus."

"Turn over, bitch," he repeated as he got into the bed. He grabbed her arm and pinned it behind her back.

Polly let out a muffled scream as her head was pushed into the pillow. She struggled and kicked until she had pulled herself free of him. "I don't want to fight with you, Mr. Capp. Please let's, just have a little fun the right way."

Her words were no sooner spoken than his hand came up, catching her on the side of the face. The blow sent her reeling backward. Pretending to relax, she turned on her side. This time he hit her so hard she felt thunder go off in her head. Polly knew this was a fight she was not going to win without some help. Slipping her hand into the night table drawer, Polly's hand closed around a small, pearl handled pistol. "Get off of me!" she cried, pointing the pistol at him.

Mr. Capp let out a loud laugh and reached for the gun, his hand covering Polly's. She could feel her bones cracking as he squeezed her hand.

She didn't mean to do it. The gun went off and the bullet struck Robert Capp in the neck. A look of horror covered his face as he grabbed the wound, blood running through his fingers. In a flash, he slumped over on top of her.

Polly wriggled out from under the weight of his body and tottered down the hall. "Lola, come quick! I just killed a man!" She said as she pushed open the door to Lola's room.

Within minutes the room was filled with all five women staring down at the naked body.

Polly was crying as she told them what happened. Pointing to the red marks on her face she repeated, "I didn't mean to kill him. I should have just let him have his way. I didn't mean to do it. Now I'm gonna go to prison. They will probably hang me in the town square. Oh, my God! Oh my God!" Polly kept repeating.

"Hush," Lola said. "Now we must find a way to take care of this problem. Let me think a moment. You girls get him dressed. You are not going to jail over this bastard."

When Ramona rolled the body over, Venus let out a loud shriek. "Oh, my God. It's Mr. Capp." Venus moved toward Polly, "Stupid bitch. Why did you have to kill him?"

Polly put her hands over her eyes and began to sob. "I didn't mean to do it, but..."

"Robert Capp! Of all men to kill, you killed Robert Capp," Venus shrieked again. "He is president of the Federal Bank. We are in deep crap."

"That's enough!" Lola intervened. "We can't bring him back to life. We just need to find a way to get him out of this house as soon as possible."

Robert Capp's body was wrapped in a bed sheet. Polly watched as the four women carried him down the back staircase. They donned their capes and gloves and carried him to his coach. Venus hitched the horses to a second carriage in the stable and the two carriages pulled out onto the snowy street heading for the outskirts of town. Polly rocked back and forth in her seat, repeating over and over that it was an accident.

Pulling the corpse out of the coach, the women once again carried the heavy weight to the edge of a precipice of an abandoned strip mine. Unrolling the sheet, the body tumbled down the hill like a giant snowball, gathering speed as it continued downhill. It landed somewhere below the tree line. With their feet and hands frozen from the cold, they made the trip back to the house, leaving his coach blocks from their house.

As they warmed themselves in front of the fire, the silence was broken only by the sounds of wood crackling in the hearth, until Lola spoke. "I do believe it will be better if we consider leaving here soon. Mr. Capp was well known in this town. When his disappearance is noticed, there will be a lot of speculation. The law may assume he was accosted by thieves and killed or that he was kidnapped. Whatever they think, the investigation may eventually turn to us. I am sure that it was not a secret that he was a frequent visitor here. I don't believe his body will be discovered very soon. With all this snow it may be spring before they find him. We must start preparing to leave Pittsburgh, but not too hurriedly. We don't want to arouse anyone's suspicions. In the next few days start telling your customers that we are all anxious to return to our home in the South and may be leaving soon." Lola stopped and pointed to Polly, "And you, dear sister, will stay in your room. If anyone asks about you, I will tell them that you are not feeling well."

"There is a place on the coast of Mississippi called Lott's Point. One of my clients said it was a bustling town recovering quite well from the war. I think we shall go there," Lola said.

Part Five: Slave Women

What gives ya dah right tah makes me a slave— tah takes me away from my home and family and bring me tah a strange land? What gives you dah right tah lay wid my child agin her will? Your law may say it be right, but yah know your God would say you be doin' wrong.
Essie

Her name was Kayudante. She was a member of the Bonno-Mottie tribe living on the Gold Coast of Africa. Her tribe was usually a peaceable people that spent their days minding their livestock and tending to their gardens. An occasional flare-up between neighboring tribes could sometimes culminate in a war. Usually the conflicts were short-lived. Neither tribe wished to see their young men killed. Life and family were precious to them.

The children in the tribe were taught to respect their elders. Each family was a close-knit group looking out for the wellbeing of the whole. Women married young in Kayudante's village and then moved into the huts their new husbands had built for them so they could start their own families

The husband's duty was to protect his wife and children at any cost. The husband would hunt and fish while the women tended to the children and kept the home fires burning. Without new tribe members, their numbers would dwindle.

The Bonno-Mottie had few things they feared. They feared the storms that came in off the ocean, causing mudslides that covered entire villages. They feared the danger of wild animals, mostly the crocodiles that could pull them into the river without a warning. But most of all, they feared the white-skinned men who came from across the ocean in big boats. The men of the tribe would sit *around the fire at night and talk about the evil strangers who would gather up everyone and take them away, never to be seen again. It was a fear my grandmother never dreamed she would have to face.*

Chapter Forty

Kayudante was washing vegetables in the shallow water off the bank of the Gambia River. Humming to herself, she did not hear the men as they crept closer until it was too late for her to run. They had silently paddled their small boats up the river, using the dense undergrowth along the shoreline as cover. Without warning they came ashore and swiftly moved into her village. Chaos erupted as blasts from the fire sticks the men carried filled the air with dense, black smoke. Kayudante ran as fast as her legs would carry her toward her hut. Before she could reach the opening, a rope was put around her waist, jerking her to the ground. She was dragged along the rocky soil and then thrown into one of the long boats that was waiting at the shore. She could hear the shrieks coming from the other men and women as they were rounded up like animals and wrapped in ropes. She heard her own screams as she cried out for her father and mother. In the confusion, her pleas went unnoticed. No one heard her.

The light-skinned men spoke in a foreign tongue and carried long fire sticks and leather whips. Some of her people resisted the capture. They were bludgeoned to death or shot with the fire-sticks. Those who were too frightened to run became submissive to the angry men. They were tied together and taken to the boats. When there was no more room left in the boats, the men pushed the boats away from the shore with their captives.

As Kayudante's boat drifted away from her home, she looked back to see the ground littered with dead villagers. Some of the older women were trying to gather up the babies that were left behind. Kayudante was tethered to another woman from her village. They clung to each other, there heads bent low. Fear overwhelmed them both as they fell into a catatonic state.

For three days the cavalcade of boats traveled the hippopotamus- and crocodile-infested waters. At times the light-skinned men would fire their fire sticks to scare the hippos that crowded in the middle of the river, huge creatures that could turn a boat over with no more than a swish of their enormous girth. Everyone kept a keen eye out for the crocodiles that could surface at any time and snag someone out of a boat without warning.

Each night Kayudante and the other captives were herded together on the shore and forced to form a circle. They were given plantains and mangos to eat and were allowed to relieve themselves. The light-skinned men would stand guard around them as they collapsed into a restless sleep, exhausted from the day's long travel in the searing heat.

On the morning of the fourth day, the river widened and Kayudante could see the ocean on the horizon. She had only been to the ocean once in her life when she went with her father to dig for sea turtle eggs. Today, for the first time, she saw a ship just off the beach riding at anchor. Its large barnacle-covered hull pitched back and forth in the choppy water. There were more of the light-skinned men on the deck of the ship. When the paddleboats neared the ship, rope ladders were thrown overboard. Kayudante and the rest of her tribesmen were ordered to climb aboard. Two dark-skinned men opened a door that led to a narrow hatchway between the decks already crammed with captives. Kayudante and her people were led into the darkness and told to go down the narrow stairs. When it was her turn to step down, a nauseating stench hit her face and made her gasp. She stopped next to a dark-skinned man who was pushing people through the narrow door. Kayudante looked at him with pleading eyes but he did not seem to care about people who were the same color as himself. He prodded her in the back with a pointed stick. Along with the others, Kayudante was crammed into a space so small she could hardly move. Sitting side by side with the other women in the small space, she bent her head to keep from hitting the hard beams overhead.

Some of the younger men were chained to the wall with leg irons, while the older men and women were pushed onto wooden benches so miniscule that they were sitting one on top of another. The floor was slippery with excrement and urine that sloshed about as the boat heaved up and down in the choppy sea.

When the doors were closed the temperature began to rise until the heat was almost unbearable. Kayudante listened to the sounds. There were children crying as their mothers tried to keep them from falling from their arms. Wails and moans came from those who had been injured during the capture, and always the sounds of rattling chains and the crack of the leather whips. Everyone had the same question in their minds: Where were they going?

Each morning Kayudante and the others were brought to the deck of the ship and given their half-pint ration of water and a thin soup made from squash and chestnuts. She gobbled down her food, knowing there would not be another meal until that evening. At times the men would steal the women's food, leaving them nothing to eat until the next day. Humans who once cared for each other had been reduced to treating their peers no better than animals. The death of a chain mate meant more room for the others. Survival was the only instinct left to them.

On the third day, the slaves were taken to the main deck in small groups. The branding iron heating in the iron kettle smelled of burning flesh. One by one they were branded and sent back down the stairs with their skin blistered and bleeding.

At times when the sea was calm, the captives were allowed to pull buckets of water from the ocean and wash their bodies. The salt caked into their open sores and made their skin break open even more, yet even the pain from the open-wounds was better than the stench that made them ill. Sometimes, at the first opportunity, someone would break from the line and leap overboard to end their misery. The men on deck would place wagers to see how long it would take a shark to appear. The sharks followed the ships waiting for the next body to be thrown overboard.

The crew would look at the women as they came up the stairs, pulling one or two out of the line for their night's enjoyment. The women would be pushed down the stairs in the morning, dazed and bleeding.

On the twenty-eight day voyage, there were two storms that pitched and rolled the boat until everyone was almost comatose. There was no food or water given during the storms. The captives would put their hands up and try to catch the drops of rusty water that dripped from the grates covering the hatch. Each day the men from the ship would come into the hold and remove the bodies of those that had died from starvation or disease. Men, women, and little children who had succumbed to the overwhelming cruelty they had endured were carried up the stairs and tossed overboard, like trash, for the fish to eat. The blood brought a swarm of sharks, which followed the ship across the open sea.

Stripped of all human emotion, Kayudante managed to survive the arduous trip. She was fourteen years old and near death when she arrived on a new continent.

Just before coming into port in America, Kayudante and the others who were still alive were taken onto an island where they were given double rations of food to eat and pine tar ointment for their wounds. An emaciated slave covered in sores would not fetch a very handsome price. Each person was issued a set of clothing to put on before they boarded the boats again for the short trip to the mainland. Any hope that the next part of their journey would be more humane was quickly dashed.

Another prison awaited on shore for those who had survived the arduous journey. There were long, foul-smelling buildings with no windows and shackles on the wall for their hands and feet. Every day the white men would come into the buildings and line everyone up. They would look to see if anyone was sick or deformed or had bad teeth. Most of the buyers wanted those who were not slender of back and could handle arduous labor.

There was also an outdoor yard with no protection from the weather, where those who were unfit to sell were kept. Huddled on the ground, too weak to move, most of the slaves were beaten and died within a few days.

On the days when the slave market was open for sales, the men and women were taken out of the buildings and put on display. When it was Kayudante's turn, she was led to the auction block, where she was prodded and examined by white men dressed in strange clothes. They wore long pants and jackets. She stared out into the faces of the white men and women who had come to watch the selling of human flesh.

She and a few others from her tribe were sold to a plantation owner from Mississippi. His name was Mott Miller. While he rode in his padded coach, the slaves were crammed into wagons that creaked along the rutted roads for miles and miles, until they finally arrived at a tract of land just a few miles from Pass Christian, Mississippi. It was not far from a town called Lott's Point. Kayudante had no idea where she was and would only find out later. It made no difference to her. It was not her home.

Once at the Miller Plantation, Kayudante was clothed and then taken to a small wooden hut with a ceiling so low she could barely stand up. This would be her new home. She was housed with five other women. They were all unmarried and had no other family on the plantation. The next day she was put to work in the cotton fields. Those new arrivals who resisted felt the sting of the leather whip until they changed their minds – or died.

Her name was no longer Kayudante. After her age and cost was entered into Mr. Miller's slave ledger, her name was changed. She was now called Essie. Essie did what she was told. She had no other choice. She cried every night for her parents and siblings. She cried and cried. It did no good. She knew that she would never go home again. She would work and die in this foreign land where she now belonged to Mott Miller. Each day was like the day before, up before sunrise, work until dusk, eat a meager meal of rice and beans and then fall onto a thin pallet, exhausted. Sleep was the only thing that relieved the pain of living.

Just a few months after Essie's arrival, she was working in the field when one of the white overseers came up behind her. He was a dirty man with rotten teeth and a foul order that rolled off his body. He put his hand on her shoulder and motioned for Essie to follow him. He laid her down between the rows of cotton plants and pulled up her dress. Essie lay there, hoping to die as he moved inside her virgin body, tearing away at her flesh. When he was finished, he motioned for Essie to get up and go back to work. He walked away. Stunned, and still bleeding, Essie stumbled back to the field. She was too afraid to tell anyone what happened that day.

Three months later Essie knew that she was going to have a baby. When Master Miller was informed, he had her married her off to a slave named Marcus Woods. Essie was afraid of Marcus. They were from different tribes and did not speak the same language. At night, Essie would curl up in a ball in the corner of their cabin. When Marcus tried to touch her, she would scream and kick. He decided it was best to leave her alone.

When Essie went into labor, Marcus ran and fetched an old woman from the next cabin. The old woman stayed with Essie while she agonized in pain, giving birth to her daughter. She named her Kinya. Essie was grateful that Kinya did not have white skin when she was born. Sometimes in her dreams she imagined that her baby would look like the evil man that had raped her. Instead, Kinya was born the color of honey molasses, with soft, black hair. Marcus took care of Essie after she gave birth to Kinya. He was a kind man and in the years to follow Essie grew fond of him. Together they had three sons.

Just like all the other children in the slave camp, Kinya was put to work at the age of six. Her short childhood was over. Kinya pulled weeds in the cotton fields and carried water for the other slaves to drink.

At night while Kinya lay in her arms, Essie would sing songs that she had learned from her tribe in Africa. Essie had to sing softly in her native tongue. Slaves were only allowed to speak the white man's words and if they were caught talking to each other in their own language they were beaten. It broke Essie's heart to see her young child working so hard. There was nothing she could do to change it, but each night she prayed that she and Kinya would be able to leave this terrible place and return to her native land.

When Kinya was fifteen, Mrs. Miller sent for more slaves to work in the house. Kinya was plucked from the field and taken away from Essie and put to work in the washhouse. It was arduous work for Kinya. She and the other women would boil water in large tubs of water and scrub the clothes on a board using hard lye soap. Her hands were red and blistered when she returned to the cabin at night.

With little to do around the plantation, Mr. Miller began to take an interest in Kinya. He watched her as she hung up the laundry and swept off the porches while the clothes dried in the afternoon breeze. Her flimsy cotton dress, soaked with perspiration, clung to her body as she worked. Kinya's fine chiseled features and slender hips made her quite attractive, especially to Mott Miller, a man who slept apart from his wife and had no children to take up his time.

At one time, Mott Miller had been a kind and gentle person. After his marriage, his life changed. His wife was a harpy who screamed at him constantly. She took over the management of the house and most of their money. Mrs. Miller kept the house filled with her relatives, leaving little privacy for her husband.

Mott wanted children of his own, but after years passed and none were conceived, he moved out of the bedroom he shared with his wife to a place of peace. He was no longer happy. His solemn mood and brooding manner kept everyone at arm's length. Mott also had an eye for the young black women. His new quarry was Kinya.

Mott summoned Kinya to his house while his wife was away visiting relatives in Charlestown. Kinya knew what was about to happen. She had heard the other women talk and she had heard the story of her own conception from her mother. There was nothing she could do. Refusing the master would bring punishment not only to her but the rest of her family. When she told her mother that she had to go see Mr. Miller, Essie broke down and cried as Kinya was taken by wagon to the main house.

Marcus stood at the door of the cabin watching as his daughter stared back at him. With clenched fists he vowed that someday he would make sure that Mott Miller suffered as much as he and Essie were suffering at that moment.

Once at the house, Kinya was taken to the downstairs bathing chamber and told to cleanse herself. She was given a towel and a long robe to put on after her bath. Kinya soaked in the water hoping that perhaps Mr. Miller would forget about her. A knock on the door startled her and she bolted upright in the tub. After drying herself and donning the robe, she was led upstairs by one of the house servants. Kinya was made to lie on Mott's bed. He entered the room and disrobed without so much as a word to her. Kinya bit into her lip as she endured the first-time torture to her young body. After that day, it was her duty to visit him whenever he beckoned her. She was treated no better than his housedogs. The better she performed, the bigger piece of soda bread she was given to take home to her family. It was a small reward for the indecencies forced upon her.

And then the worst possible thing happened. Kinya was pregnant. She had prayed each month that it would not happen, but now a decision had to be made. Her baby would only be one-fourth African. That would mean the baby was sure to be light-skinned.

Some of the women in the slave quarters felt it better to let the baby die rather than be born with light skin. They prepared potions for Kinya to drink. Others boiled water for Kinya to sit in, causing her to blister as it scalded her body. Nothing worked.

She was still pregnant. When the rumor reached Mr. Miller that Kinya was pregnant, he seemed happy, a strange reaction for the owner of a plantation.

On one of his routine rides through the slave quarters, Essie Woods stopped Mr. Miller. She came along side his horse and looked up at him. There was no fear in her. She had to tell him was on her mind. "What gave ya dah right tah makes me a slave—tah takes me away from my home and family and bring me tah a strange land? What gives you dah right tah lay wid my child against her will? Your law may say it be right, but yah know yer God would be saying it be wrong."

Mr. Miller looked down at this Negro woman who was defying every rule made for her kind. He could have taken his foot and kicked her away or had her tied to a tree and beaten. Instead he just stared at her for a moment and rode on. He had no answer to her question.

Part Six: Changing Generations

What happens when you mix two bloods: Do they battle each other for dominance or flow together into submission? Is a Negro who has more white blood than black still considered a Negro?
Aden Woods

It is important that my story be told. I want you to know who I am, or better still what I am. It may change your opinion of me but I cannot continue to defend myself any longer. By telling you my story you may begin to understand the true nature of slavery. I will tell you about the side of the masters that is gentle and compassionate and those men who were a seething cesspool of humanity, caring little for the life of Negroes and using them for their own personal gain and pleasure.

Kayudante or Essie, as she was called in America was my grandmother. Kinya was my mother. My name is Aden Woods.

Chapter Forty One

I was born with skin of a white man. With light brown hair and gray eyes, I definitely did not have the look of a Negro child. I was a discard that needed to be removed from the Negro community. My mother held me after I was born and when the women came to take me to the woods to die, my mother refused to let go of me. She screamed and cried and they backed off, telling her she would be sorry. They said she had doomed her child to a life of misery.

My grandmother named me Aden. In her country it stood for warrior. She knew I would always be fighting a battle.

When Mr. Miller heard of my birth, he came to our cabin to see me. He stared down into the wooden rocker and then at my mother, who lay on her pallet. My mother was in a weakened condition after my birth. Mr. Miller had sweets and food for my family to share. My family attacked the food as if it were prey. My grandmother was convinced that Mr. Miller had an attraction to me, I was his firstborn son, or perhaps he had feelings for my mother. Whatever the reason, his meager generosity made our life a little more tolerable.

When I was old enough to play outside with the other children, Mr. Miller would sometimes ride his horse to the slave quarters. I could see him watching me and I would run inside and hide behind my grandmother.

As time passed, Mr. Miller once again began bedding my mother. My mother told my grandmother that it was different now. He treated her kindly and with tenderness. He often asked her questions about me and talked to her as if she were a real person.

My grandmother knew what was happening and she told Mr. Miller that it was time that my mother take a husband, but Mr. Miller seemed to balk at the idea of her consorting with anyone but him. He kept her as his concubine for the next three years.

My grandmother knew that the relationship between Mr. Miller and my mother was more than lust. She knew they cared for each other and she knew that it only meant danger. She feared that Mrs. Miller would have my mother killed and I would be sent away or she may also do harm to my grandparents.

When my mother discovered she was pregnant again, she was overwrought with grief. She knew that my life was not going to be easy and she did not want to bring another child into the world, fathered by a man who would never claim his children. She was confused over her feelings for Mr. Miller. She felt as if she had betrayed her own heritage and was willingly giving in to the wishes of her master. So in the community of slaves, we were the outcasts, shared by both the white world, and the black. My mother was the master's whore and I was his almost-white bastard child.

My mother went to Mr. Miller and begged him to send us away to another plantation, a place where she could create a story to explain her light skinned children. She would say they had lost their color due to a disease passed on from her. Mr. Miller refused, saying he wanted her to stay close to him. He told her that he had very strong feelings for her. It meant nothing to Kinya. She would always be his slave and he, her master. She fell into his arms in tears. He held her close and told her there was nothing either one could do. He told her that he would stay away from her and that she was not to come to the house ever again. She would go back to working in the field. Mr. Miller said it would be better for all concerned. But my mother did not share his opinion.

Mr. Miller stood fast to his words. My mother was put back to work in the fields and she was not called to the house ever again. A few weeks later while she was working in the field and I played nearby, my mother stopped working. She dropped her cotton sack and she took me by the hand. She headed toward the river. A slave working in the field watched her as she walked by. He wondered what she was doing. It was only when she disappeared beyond the rim of trees that lined the river the man knew something was wrong. He took off running toward her, but she was already in the water, holding me in her arms. The water cascaded down the slippery rocks and swirled around her legs like foaming hands beckoning her to come further. The worker dove into the river and swam toward her. Just as he reached her, my mother began to slip beneath the water, still holding me close to her. The man reached out, his hand caught my shirt and pulled me from my mother's arms. He scooped me up just as she disappeared beneath the surface. He called to her and furiously searched the water but could not find any sign of my mother.

Kinya was gone. The women who had gathered on the bank of the river wailed. One of the women took me home to my grandmother and told her what had happened. My grandmother dropped to her knees and cried. She came to me and held me close for a long time. I had escaped death twice, once at the time of my birth and again on that day. The Almighty had plans for me.

When Mr. Miller heard of my mother's death, he came to our cabin. He told my grandmother how sorry he was. My grandmother glared at Mr. Miller with hate in her eyes, but kept a tight lip lest she say something that would cause herself more pain than she already felt at that moment. Mr. Miller told my grandparents that she need not worry, no harm would come to our family. He moved my grandmother from the field to the kitchen of the main house. She knew it was his way of trying to say he was sorry, but nothing could erase the disgust that my grandmother felt for him. He had taken her only daughter from her and now he wanted her grandson.

For the next six years I was allowed to stay with my grandmother as she worked in the kitchen. I learned to peel potatoes and shuck corn. I hulled the peas and swept the floor and churned the butter. I would listen to the women as they went about their duties. They talked about the Master. They said he drank a lot and seemed depressed most of the time.

Mrs. Miller entertained quite often. She knew it was a constant irritation to her husband, but she did not care. His way of getting even with her was to call me from the kitchen and parade me around the room like a prize boar.

I was a curiosity to some of the guests with my almost-white skin and gray eyes. The women would stare at me and the men would snicker. A dalliance with another woman was one thing, but most of the wives were abhorred to think that their husbands did indeed bed black women.

At first everyone was curious as to why Mr. Miller was so bold as to produce the evidence that he had bedded a black woman and then flaunt me before his friends. He knew it was a topic even the men rarely talked about in open conversation. It was not a subject discussed in public, yet each plantation owner knew that the slave quarters could be used as his private bordello if he wished.

Mott Miller had a different agenda. Since he and his wife had no children, I was proof that it was his wife who was barren and he was quite capable of producing children. Or maybe it was true that he had loved my mother and wanted me to be close to him. Sometimes when he was drinking heavily he would have me sit on his lap in the dining room. Mrs. Miller would become livid. I could see the rage and embarrassment in her eyes.

After one of Mrs. Miller's dinner parties that turned into a disaster, she finally had enough. She could no longer stand the sight of me in her house. The house servants said she screamed at her husband that I had to be removed from the plantation or she was going to kick him out of the house and file for divorce. He still refused and so without his knowledge, she made arrangements for me to be sent away. I was to go to Charlestown and live with her cousin and his wife. My grandparents could not go. Mrs. Miller knew that separating us would be painful because we loved each other dearly.

I was twelve years old when I left the Miller plantation. My grandparents stood in front of me as I waited for the wagon that was taking me to Charlestown to circle round to the front of the house. She bent down and held both my hands in hers. "Ya lissen ta me, Aden Woods. Ya are who ya are. Ya be dah grandson of Kayudante from Africa. Ya be a proud black boy and don ya be fergettin' that. I be seein ya agin. Ya be strong. Ya hear? Ya be strong and don let dem white folks get da best of ya. Mammy loves ya." She hugged me so tightly I could hardly breath and then gently pushed me away. I tried not to cry, but as she walked toward the house and into the arms of Marcus, the tears ran down my face. I wanted to call to her and run back into her arms, but she was already at the door.

Two weeks after I left the plantation, Mr. Miller suffered an unfortunate happening. After a night of heavy drinking he had gone to the privy to relieve himself. On the way back to the house in the early light of dawn, a shot rang out and Mott Miller fell to the ground. No one knew who shot him, but the blast was strong enough to shatter his spine and put him in a paralyzed state for the rest of his life. He was confined to his bed or a wheeling chair. Since the slaves were forbidden to own or carry firearms, the consensus was that it was a hunter who had injured him. No one saw Marcus Woods returning from the far field with a shovel. What had he buried?

Chapter Forty-Two

William and Susan Bolt lived in Battery Square in Charlestown. The wealth of the home was evident just by the address alone. Mr. Bolt was a barrister and had done quite well in his business. Mrs. Bolt had come into the marriage with a large dowry, including the three-story mansion her parents had given her as a wedding gift.

William was a fair, but stern man, who seemed to smile very little, while Susan was a gentle person with sad eyes. Perhaps this was because even with such a comfortable lifestyle, their almost-perfect existence was flawed. After giving birth to only one child, Susan was no longer able to have more children. Their only son, Will, was born with severe health problems.

As a newborn, Will had quite a bit of difficulty breathing, coupled with the fact that he was very small and his hands were clenched into fists that could not be opened. As he grew, his spine curved and his undeveloped legs could not support him. He was confined to a wheeling chair. He constantly caught colds and influenza, which the doctors said were caused by his under-developed lung condition.

Mr. Bolt had spoiled Will beyond any reason. He doted on him constantly and granted his every whim. It was Susan who wanted Will to be treated like other children. There was nothing at all wrong with Will's mind, but William Bolt said his son was special and would always be treated in that manner. He silently blamed Susan for Will's condition.

With his father's approval of his bad behavior, Will took extreme pleasure in making everyone in the house miserable. He was so spoiled by his father that when he did not get his way immediately, he would scream and utter profanities at whoever was in earshot and urinate all over himself. At ten years of age, he was nothing short of a complete hellion.

When Susan Bolt attempted to control him during one of his

tantrums, Will slapped her in the face and called her names. At the point of breaking, Susan pleaded with her husband to find someone who could handle Will. Mrs. Bolt was ready to send him away to a private institution, but Mr. Bolt would not hear of it. When Susan knew she could not win that argument, she suggested that Will be allowed to have an educational tutor. Mr. Bolt reminded her that they had tried that in the past and Will refused to pay attention, always putting his head down on his tray and covering his ears with his hands. She said that perhaps with the help of a companion to make it easier for him to write and turn the pages he would be more cooperative. Something had to be done for him. He was out of control.

Susan Bolt thought perhaps a care tender closer to her son's age would be better than another adult. Will had chased off every one that was assigned to him. When Susan received a post from her cousin, Mrs. Miller, about her desperate need to sell a slave boy, Susan Bolt agreed to buy him.

When I arrived at the Bolt house in Charlestown, Mr. Bolt took me into his library and sat me down in a big leather chair. He explained to me that it would be my duty to take care of Will twenty-four hours a day. I was to be his constant companion. I was to help him eat, bathe, go to the bathroom and be with him at all times. A pallet of blankets was placed next to Will's bed. That is where I was to sleep each night in case Will needed me.

Susan Bolt was anxious about the first meeting between Aden and Will. She knew that her husband would watch every move to see if once again he would have to endure the wrath of his son as he vehemently ostracized a new attendant.

Dressed in brown pants and a white shirt, my toes pinched in my first pair of shoes. I was led down the long, upstairs hallway into an open conservatory. Standing quietly, I waited until Will turned in his chair to face me. Will's eyes narrowed. "What is this?" he asked. "You told me he was a colored boy. This boy is not a Negro. What are you?" he spewed at me.

I waited motionless, my hands folded as Susan Bolt gently explained to her son that I was indeed considered a Negro, since colored blood coursed through my veins and she had officially purchased him.

"You don't look colored to me, except for maybe your hair. It's rather wavy," Will mused. "What is your name, boy?" he asked.

"Aden Woods," I mumbled.

I seemed like quite a curiosity to Will. Instead of his usual tantrum, he delighted in the notion to turn this boy standing in front of him into a quivering mess by the end of the week.

From the very beginning my relationship with Will was strained. He called me names, hit me, and kicked me when I was close to his chair. I had to sit next to him when he ate, helping him cut up his meat and spoon soup into his mouth, which he often spit on me. He would kick and scream while I bathed him and combed his hair. I was only two years older than Will, but his frail body was no match for me. At times I wanted to hold his head under the water and teach him a lesson.

Whenever Will complained and it was brought to the attention of his father, I was called to the study. Mr. Bolt admonished me, saying that I was never to speak to Will unless I was directly addressed. I was an invisible part of Will's life. I was to be completely obedient to Will, catering to his every whim. And so even when Will spit in my face for not moving fast enough, I said nothing. I cleaned up the messes Will made when he ate. Sometimes just to make a bigger mess for me to clean up he would open his mouth and spit out the food, while pretending to be choking. I knew he wanted me to panic, but I didn't. I just silently cleaned up the mess. Maybe the look in my eyes told him I did not care if he choked to death.

It was only at night when I lay on the pallet next to the high bed that I had time to think about my life. I missed my grandmother terribly, but I remembered her words to me. "Be strong," and I would try again. Even though I hated Will, I would never show it. With my head shoved into my pallet I cried silently.

A month after I arrived, I was told to dress Will and wheel him into the upstairs study. It was a beautiful room and would soon become my favorite room in the house. There were massive windows that curved around two walls letting in the morning sun. Bookshelves that reached as high as the ornate ceiling held ledges of leather-bound volumes. A large mahogany desk was positioned in the front of a long library table that faced an oversized chalkboard.

A gentleman I had never seen before was standing in front of the desk. He was poised in a formidable position with a large pointer stick in one hand, tapping it on the desk. He looked at his watch. "You are four minutes late. That is unacceptable.

Class will begin each day at precisely nine o'clock."

No one had told me that Will was beginning his studies today. Mrs. Bolt felt that Will was quite capable of learning and that he should not remain illiterate for the rest of his life. It was the one argument she had won with her husband. He agreed that teaching Will to read and write would be good for him.

Will let out a loud laugh. "It will begin when I get here. That is, if I even decide to come to your stupid class."

The man strode across the room and knelt down, his face even with Will. "I have been told that you are quite difficult. I can be difficult, too. You see, I am on contract. I will start my class at nine whether you are here or not. I am being paid by the month. So if you decide you do not want to come, just let me know. This room has enough books in it to keep me busy for quite some time. 'Tis a pity that at your age, you cannot even read."

"I could read if I wanted to!" Will screamed.

"Show me." The tutor grabbed a book from the shelf and slammed it down on the desk. Folding his arms over his chest, he glared at Will.

"You don't talk to me like that. I will call my father. He will have you thrown out of this house immediately," Will said, his voice shaky.

"Yes, that is fine with me. I understand the next stop for you is an institution for mentally retarded people. That should be a joyous existence compared to learning how to read and write and perhaps even having a future of sorts."

Will was stunned. He had met his match. This man whose name was John Glassman was a formidable adversary.

"Roll me to the table," Will barked at me.

Mr. Glassman motioned to a chair nearby, "You. Sit there, next to Will. What is your name?"

"Aden Woods," I whispered

"Don't mumble, boy. Speak up" he said in a tone of authority.

"Aden Woods," I repeated. This time quite loudly. Mr. Glassman smiled.

Mr. Glassman was a fascinating man. With his precise British accent he had a way of speaking that made me hang on his every word. Maybe he really wasn't as good as I imagined, but for someone who had never even held a book in his hand, I was in awe of him.

Will complained and whined. He told Mr. Glassman he was unable to do letters with his deformed hand. Mr. Glassman said that nothing was impossible. He wrapped Will's gnarled fingers around a fat pencil and had me hold his hand closed. Will would then move his hand to form the letters. Each day we practiced until finally, with some difficulty, Will could make letters on the paper.

After a few lessons, Will no longer balked about going to class. Although he would not admit it to anyone, for the first time in his life Will began to realize that his brain was not as impaired as his body. He had been told for so long that he was unable to do anything on his own, that he had believed it. He was now eager to learn, yet his attention span was short and he often laid his head on the back of his chair and dozed off while Mr. Glassman spoke.

Will and I learned history and geography from a man who seemed to make it come to life for us. Will was indeed learning, much to the relief of his parents, and so was I. I hung on Mr. Glassman's every word as he talked about far away places that seemed impossible for me to believe existed. His lessons on Africa were particularly interesting to me. I wanted to learn all there was about my heritage.

Mr. Glassman refused to let Will chastise me when he was in his presence. Although when we were not in class, Will's treatment of me had not changed. He still delighted in remarks and actions that classified me as subhuman. Sometimes when he ran over my feet with his wheeling chair or bit my hand when he was not happy with something I had done for him, he would laugh and wait for my reaction. My outer skin was becoming hardened to his attacks, but inside I was boiling. I wanted to reach out and choke his spindly little neck and throw him on the floor so he could crawl around on his useless legs like a lowly insect. I kept myself calm by remembering my grandmother's words and the fact that I was getting a first-class education, something unheard of for black slave children.

Susan Bolt sometimes came to my aid when Will was being particularly cruel. She would help me clean up the messes Will made and every now and then chastise Will for his behavior. This seemed to add to Will's displeasure. He did not want to believe that his mother could even care one small bit for this strange colored boy who never talked. Will was so partial to his father, his mother's presence annoyed him. He was quick to report to his father each time his mother reprimanded him.

By the time the second winter raised its frigid head in Charlestown, Will and I had been attending class for almost sixteen months. Susan Bolt decided it would be nice for Will to get away for a few weeks. She planned a trip to visit his grandparents in Columbia, South Carolina. She also decided to leave me behind. She knew that I needed a rest from the constant torment of her son.

I was so very happy to see them leave. It was indeed pleasant not to have Will in the house. It was not only me, but also the whole staff seemed to be in much better moods. They no longer had to listen to his screams or worry about things being broken or thrown to the ground.

A few days after the Bolt's departure, bored and with nothing to do, I wandered down the upstairs hallway and looked into the library. Mr. Glassman was sitting at his desk reading. Peering over his reading speckles, he motioned for me to enter. "Come sit with me, Aden. I would enjoy your company," he said.

I moved slowly into the room and settled myself in the chair I occupied during class. Mr. Glassman got up and sat on the corner of his desk, looking at me. I remember his questions quite well.

"You know how to read, don't you Aden? I see your lips moving when Will is reading aloud."

I was afraid to answer. I did not know what to say to him.

"Come now, Aden. I will not tell anyone that you can read or write, for that matter. I see the attention that you pay during my sessions with Will and I do believe that you are learning more than him." Handing me a sheet of paper he said, "Here, write your name on this."

I picked up the pencil and proudly wrote my name in large letters.

"Very good. Your handwriting is quite legible." He handed me a book that he had been reading. "Read a few sentences for me."

I looked at the words and then opened my mouth. I handed the book back to Mr. Glassman, "Negroes are not allowed to be schooled," I said quietly.

"I am not your master, Aden. Read for me," Mr. Glassman said sternly.

My voice shook as I read aloud for the first time in my life. After a few sentences, he put his hand on the page of the book. "I can see you know the words, Aden, but your pronunciation of them is all wrong. If you are going to read English you must also learn to speak English. The language you are speaking is unacceptable by my standards. You must pronounce every word as it is written. From now on you will have two languages, Negro, which you will use for everyone else, and proper English, for when you are in my presence." Mr. Glassman put his hand on my head. "This will be quite an interesting experiment, Aden. The Bolts put you in this room thinking you were unable to learn. Perhaps keeping your race substandard is the only way they can avoid feeling completely immoral for keeping your kind as slaves. Although I dare say that you look completely Caucasian to me. I am sure if the rest of the county finds out your kind are quite capable of learning, it would throw them completely off balance. Let's you and I take their challenge, Aden and turn you into the brightest student I have ever had." He paused for a moment, perhaps waiting for my reaction, which I was too stunned to give.

"I really do understand your plight, Aden. In my country we do not own slaves, but you can be one just the same." Mr. Glassman walked to the window and leaned against the sill. He looked out over the courtyard. "You see, I was born a slave of sort: a slave to ignorance. My father was a coal miner, just like the three generations before him; he earned a living by climbing into the bowels of the earth and releasing coal into carts. He made pennies a day for the backbreaking work that got us nowhere. I followed in his footsteps. Marrying a girl from our village, I too, became a miner. Then the Devil came to our village."

He pointed his finger at me. "Learn this lesson, Aden. If you are given something by the devil he will surely take something else from you. On the day he arrived he set fire to the mineshafts, which blew huge holes in the earth. The whole village was consumed in flames, including my small home. I was twenty years old, Aden. I lost my wife and young son on that day. I lay in the hospital for months as the doctors tended to the burns that covered my body. When I was well enough to leave, the Devil gave me a check as compensation for my loss. Unlike the rest of the miners who were injured, I did not rebuild my house or climb down in another shaft. I used the money to get an education."

Mr. Glassman turned around to face me. "I know you are wondering why I am telling you this story. It is because education is a powerful tool. Illiteracy keeps you in the dark forever. Now I have the money to come and go as I please. I command a good salary to teach the insolent children of rich patrons. I should at least see some benefit from my knowledge. Sometimes I see a glimmer of hope in a particular student, but what I see in you is more than that. I see a sponge that is ready to absorb anything I put before it. You should at least reap benefits from being held captive at such a young age. I shall keep your secret."

I was overwhelmed with the idea that Mr. Glassman was not going to tell the Bolts. I would learn the King's English and when I grew up, I would run away and become a real person.

In the next two weeks while the Bolts were away from Charlestown, Mr. Glassman and I met every morning for a tutoring session that sometimes lasted all day. My enthusiasm for learning more than compensated Mr. Glassman for his time. He began to open up a whole new world for me, a world that I never knew existed. Together we looked at books on Europe and Asia, and Mr. Glassman showed me where my grandmother had lived before she became a slave. I submerged myself in the map books of Africa, running my hand over the smooth paper and memorizing the images.

On a particularly gloomy day when the light in the room was not good, Mr. Glassman brought a leather-bound case from his room and placed it on the table. "We cannot study all the time, Aden. We must make some time for enjoyment. I am going to teach you how to play a game. It is called chess. I have been dying to find myself a competent adversary."

I pulled back in my chair, staring at the carved pieces Mr. Glassman placed on the wooden board. They looked more like a work of art than a game.

"Go on, pick them up, Aden," Mr. Glassman said. "I will tell you the name of these fellows."

Although I could never win, I was quite a rival for Mr. Glassman. Our delight in the concentration of the game gave us both two weeks of enjoyment.

It was a sad day when the carriages arrived at the door,

bringing the Bolt family home. Returning to my humble Negro attitude was hard. Bowing and scraping, I was once again the illiterate slave who tended to Will.

Chapter Forty-Three

As the years passed, Will's health began to deteriorate. He was prone to seizures that wracked his body and left him weak for days. He had trouble swallowing his food and primarily ate broth and drank tea.

On occasion when he was well enough and wanted to attend the tutoring sessions, Mr. Glassman made sure that Will's chair was positioned in such a way that no one entering the door could tell if he were awake or asleep. He slept quite often, giving me more time to hone my own skills. With Will's failing health, I knew my time in the Bolt house was growing short.

Age and deterioration of his body had not improved Will's temper. His constant haranguing of the staff, especially me, kept the Bolt house in perpetual turmoil. He knocked trays from the server's hands with his elbows and with one sweep of his crippled arm sent the dinner dishes crashing to the floor. Even with my constant help and patience, Will seem to be spiraling more and more out of control. I was almost to the point of running away.

One day when Mr. Bolt was out of town on business, Mrs. Bolt invited me into the dining room and I sat quietly next to Will at the dinner table. I tried to feed him as usual, but tonight Will slammed his mouth shut and continued making guttural sounds. When I reached to the floor to retrieve Will's napkin that had fallen from his lap, he raised his leg and kicked me in the mouth. Seeing black spots before my eyes, I fell backwards, blood running down my lip.

"Enough!" Mrs. Bolt screamed. "Someone come here and take Will from this room, now!" I stood up, but Mrs. Bolt, turned to me and said, "Sit down, Aden." I immediately did so. One of the dining room servers hurried in and pushed Will into the parlor.

"You bitch, you stupid bitch of a mother. I want my dinner. Wait 'til my father hears of this. Where is my father!" Will yelled as he was ushered out of the room.

"You can eat his dinner, Aden," Mrs. Bolt said. "It is a shame to waste good food."

It was an awkward moment for me, but also tempting since the dinner was roast lamb, which I had never tasted. "Well, go on, eat it before it gets cold," she said. I eagerly followed her orders.

As I ate, Mrs. Bolt sipped her tea. The outburst from Will had quelled her appetite. "You are a very brave boy, Aden. I do not know how you put up with Will's outbursts. Someday I hope it will all change for you. Perhaps when Will is gone," she said with tears filling her eyes.

When I had finished my meal, I retrieved Will from the parlor. His usual string of profanity flowed from his mouth as I positioned him on the lift. Using the pulley to raise the chair to the second floor, I had a sudden impulse to let go of the ropes and let Will and the chair fall to the floor.

Once in his bedchamber, I had to wrestle him to his bed, all the while being bitten and scratched. As he continued to fight me, I had enough of his rage. I sat upon him, holding Will's hands behind his head. Will spat at me, barely missing my face.

"You listen to me, Will Bolt, you spit on me or kick me one more time and I am going to knock your head clean off your shoulders. Better still, I will put a pillow over your face and smother you until you stop breathing. Your parents will think you died in your sleep."

Will's eyes widened. He could not believe what he was hearing. I had forgotten myself and was speaking in perfect English with not even so much as a slur. Besides no one had ever challenged Will before. Except for his mother's outburst when Will had pushed her to the limit, he was never challenged.

Will began to wiggle under my hold. He screwed up his face and began to cry. "I want my mother. You are being so mean to me."

"I will get her for you, Will. But just remember, if you want to stay in one piece, you will stop persecuting me. Otherwise, I will find a way to do away with you." I pushed down harder on Will. "Do you understand me? If something happens to you they will never blame me. I'll just hang my head and pretend to be the good little slave boy. Now I will go get your mother so you can cry in her arms like the spoiled baby you are."

As I started toward the door, Will screamed, "No! I am not a baby and where have you learned to speak like that? Coloreds don't talk like that."

I couldn't help smirking. "Maybe I am not a Negro. Maybe I am some kind of demon from Africa who came here to take you away and drag you into the depths of the earth. Maybe I am some kind of creature who has fooled your whole family into believing I am real."

"Don't say that! You're scaring me," Will said. "You learned all that from Mr. Glassman. I bet you know as much as me, don't you?"

"I know more than you, Will. But you can never prove it. Just keep treating me badly and your parents will hire some bony-fingered woman to prod at you while she takes care of your toilet needs or worse yet, they will send you to an institution for invalids and you will be at the mercy of everyone there. And they will never come to see you. Stop being so disrespectful to your mother. She loves you and doesn't deserve your wrath. You should be grateful that you have a mother who loves you. Do you understand me?" Will nodded and I released him from my grip.

I had no idea that after I had taken Will from the dining room, Susan Bolt felt guilty for not letting Will have his dinner. Carrying a tray to his room, she had stopped just a few feet short of the doorway where she heard the entire conversation. Turning around, she took the tray downstairs and asked one of the servants to take it upstairs. She never mentioned the incident to me.

In the ensuing months, Will gained a new respect for me. I was not sure if it was because he was afraid of me now or that I was more brazen than any other black person Will had ever met. Although he had little conversation with me, Will ceased his assaults against me. At times, when he was annoyed, he would shout out, but a frown from me usually made his rage subside. Perhaps it was because Will's health was failing. His seizures were increasing in intensity and frequency with each passing month. Mr. Bolt said it was ridiculous to continue with Will's education, which meant Mr. Glassman would be leaving.

On the day of his departure, Mr. Glassman took me aside. "I have enjoyed these last four years and I hope the knowledge you now have will give you a better life, Aden Woods. Here, I want you to have this," he said, handing me the leather-bound case containing the chest set." He bent down and hugged me. The first hug I had gotten since I left my grandmother's house and the first present I had ever received in my whole life.

When Will was near his twentieth birthday he could no longer sit in his chair, and was confined to bed. His bones had become so brittle that even moving him from place to place would surely cause them to fracture. The long days of tedium made him restless.

One morning while I was straightening his bed cover, Will put his arm on top of my hand. "I want you to read to me, Aden. I cannot lie in this bed and stare at the ceiling all day. I do believe I am going mad. I need something to occupy my time."

"How can I do that? Your parents will surely find out. I will be punished and probably sent away."

"My father is gone from the house most every day and my mother rarely comes to my room. I will request that the door be closed to prevent a draft. You can sit with your back to the door and if anyone comes, I will let you know. I know that I cannot order you to do this, but please, Aden. I love to hear stories about pirates and big ships. There are plenty of books on those subjects in the library."

Will had said please to me. Never had Will used that word or tone. I could not refuse. Besides, I was anxious to read again. Choosing several books from the library, I carefully slipped them under my shirt and took them to Will's bedchamber. Will was not choosey. He wanted to hear them all.

We engrossed ourselves in the books. Sometimes I would pretend to be a pirate from the book. Changing my voice to a growl as I read the words made Will smile. On most days Will would doze off and on several times, but I just kept on reading, choosing other books that I preferred until he was once again awake.

In a moment of empathy for Will, I pulled out the chessboard Mr. Glassman had given me and taught Will to play chess. Unable to move his own pieces, he would point to them and I would move them around the board. Even with a deteriorating body, Will's mind was still sharp.

On a rainy October day, as Will lay with his eyes closed, I sat nearby reading to him as usual. There was something wrong. Usually I could hear the raspy sounds of Will's breathing. The room was very still. I slowly got up from my chair and went to

Will's bedside. Putting my hand on his shoulder, I lightly shook him and called his name. There was no response. In a panic, I ran from the room, calling to Mrs. Bolt. When Susan arrived in the room she rushed to Will's bedside and laid her head on his chest. She took Will's face in her hands and gently moved his head back and forth.

"Oh, God, no!" she screamed. "Have someone go for the doctor, right away, Aden! Will is barely breathing."

It was a long trip and it took too long for the doctor to arrive. Will was already dead when he got to the house hours later. Going through the formalities, the doctor put the stethoscope on Will's chest. Will's skin had taken on an ashen color and his body was becoming slightly rigid. The doctor stood up and addressed Mrs. Bolt. "I am so sorry. Your son must have passed away in his sleep. As I told you many times before his heart was very weak and it would be very difficult for him to live in that condition very long. Please accept my sincere sympathy for your loss."

After a week- long visitation, Will was buried in the family plot next to his grandparents. The sight of Will lying in the casket, dressed in his white Sunday suit kept me out of the parlor. I still had unsettled emotions about Will. We certainly were never really friends, but we did spend ten years together. Except for the last few months, when I read to him or we played chess, we were still master and slave.

After the funeral, still wearing her funeral dress, Susan Bolt sat in the chair next to Will's bed. The linens had been removed and replaced with a black coverlet. Tears ran down her face as she mourned her son. I stood at the door for a moment, hoping to retrieve a book that I had left under the bed table. When I saw Mrs. Bolt, I tried to get away quickly, but she saw me.

"Come in Aden. I was just sitting here wondering what I could have done to make my son's life happier. He was such an angry young man."

"Ya couldn't do nothin', Mizz Bolt. That be da way of da Lord. He be born wid too many problems. Ya waz a good mother ta him."

"Thank you, Aden. I needed to hear that from someone. I want to tell you how much I appreciate everything you did for him and please, you can speak to me in any voice that is comfortable for you. I know your secret, Aden."

I bowed my head. "How long have you known?"

"For quite some time now. I will not tell anyone, but you must be careful."

Somehow I knew this might be the only time I would ever find Mrs. Bolt in this vulnerable position. I knelt down in front of her. "Please, Mrs. Bolt, let me go. Please. Let me go free. I do not wish to be sent back to the fields. Please. Just give me my papers and let me be gone."

She was totally taken off guard. "Oh, Aden, I have no say in that manner. My husband takes care of all of the dealings with the servants."

"Then just tell your husband I ran off. I have served you well." pleaded with her.

"I will see what I can do. You sleep here tonight on your pallet. If I have any luck, I will come to you with good news." She left me still kneeling on the floor like a good little slave.

Unable to sleep, I sat in a chair next to the window. I wondered where I would be sent to next. Maybe Mrs. Bolt would want to keep me here and make me a house slave. I doubted she would be happy having me serve her, knowing my secret. I would probably have to do field work. Either way, my life would be worse than before I came to this house. I now knew the education I had been given was more precious to me than I could imagine. To put it all aside and go back to being a subservient human being was more than I could bear.

Just before dawn, I heard someone walking in the halls. Anticipating that it might be Mrs. Bolt, I opened the door slightly. Pushing it all the way open, Mr. Bolt stepped inside the room. I stepped backward, steeling myself for whatever would happen next.

"My wife has told me everything. I had no idea how badly Will treated you and for that I am sorry. I have something for you," Mr. Bolt said. He handed me a parchment envelope. "These are your signed papers along with a small stipend that may help you get to wherever it is you want to go. It is without regret that I do this. No one in their right mind could have put up with Will as long as you without at least once smacking him or cursing. You are a kind young man. You may leave whenever you see fit. No one in this house, except for Mrs. Bolt and myself are to know the reason we have set you free. Use your education well, Aden." He turned and left the room.

I stood in the dark. My hands were shaking. In my fingers I

held my freedom. Opening the envelope I read the paper that was written in rich calligraphy. The words said that I, Aden Woods, was now a freed man and no longer in the bondage of William and Susan Bolt. I fingered the five, one- dollar bills that Mr. Bolt had given me. It was real money and for the first time in my life it belonged to me.

After a sleepless night, I put my one change of clothes and the chess set on my pallet and tied it together with a piece of string. I decided I would wait until all of the guests who had come for the funeral were eating breakfast before slipping out of the house. I wondered if I would be missed.

I am now a free man.

Chapter Forty-Four

Walking, walking down the back stairs, walking through the courtyard and out the back gate. Walking down the carriage path and onto the street in front of the house. Men, women, and children walking past him. His heart hammered in his chest. At any moment he expected someone to tap him on the shoulder and ask him where he thought he was going. Standing on the corner, he felt the touch of someone behind him. Turning slowly, a man in a day coat moved around him. Perhaps the man was sent by Mr. Bolt to retrieve him and take me back to the house.

"Excuse me, could I please get by?" the man asked.

Aden stuttered, "Of course." The man walked past him and crossed the street.

He walked for hours, leaving the city behind. He walked on the sandy roads that ran parallel to the ocean. He walked until his legs were weak and his feet sore from the sand. He hadn't eaten all day and his stomach growled in discontent. Aden stopped at a roadside stand. An old Negro man stood behind a makeshift cart laden with fresh fruit and vegetables. Picking up two apples, Aden handed the man one of his dollars.

The man held out his change bucket. Aden knew the man could not make change and expected a person to be honest enough to take only what was due them. The bucket contained a few nickels and a dime.

"How much are the apples?" Aden asked.

"They be two for a nickel," the man replied.

Aden put the dollar in the bucket and took out the forty-five cents in coins. "That should be about right. Thank you," Aden said as he bit into one of the apples.

The old man stared at the dollar in the bottom of the bucket. "Ya needs ta pick out more things ta eat. Ya give me too much money."

Aden picked up two carrots. "Now we're even." He stood in

front of the elderly man, whose weathered face showed years of hard work. "You a freedman?" Aden asked.

A toothless grin covered the man's face. "Yes suh, I be a freedman fah ovah four yars now. Me and dah family, we lives over dar." He pointed to a tumbled-down shanty a few hundred yards beyond the fence. "We gots three acres and dis house from my Massa when he died. Yes sah, I be free and I gots papers tah prove it."

Even after four years it was still present in this man's voice, the fear that someone was going to drag him off to another slave market. Aden had been a freedman for less than one day.

When nightfall came, Aden left the road and climbed down the sloping bank to a grassy meadow. He laid his jacket in the crook of a cypress tree. Lying down, he looked up at the sky and for the first time in many years was so overwhelmed that his body wracked with sobs. "I'm going to find you, grandmother. I'm going to see you again," he said out loud. "I am a free man. I am a free man."

Aden roamed the banks of Charlestown and Pleasantville for several days. He had no direction and really didn't care. He was a free man. Spending less than fifty cents for a large bag of stale biscuits and dried cheese, he decided it might be time to look for work and a place to live.

Arriving at Hob Caw Point on a Monday morning, Aden sat on the rail fence and watched men working on a tall ship secured to crossed timbers. Jumping down from the fence, Aden walked through the shipyard until he heard a man barking orders at a group of men who tugged on ropes hoisting a huge beam up to the bowel of the ship. Aden walked up behind the man and stood quietly until the beam was in place. The man turned and stared at him. "What ya want, why ya walking up behind me?"

"I'm looking for work," Aden said.

"You work on ships before?"

"No, but I am a quick learner." The man eyed this tan-colored man with perfect English and clean hands.

"Where ya from?" the man asked, believing that this man was not looking for a hard labor job.

Without hesitation Aden replied, "New York."

"You read?" was the man's next question.

"Yes, I do, and I can write and also do numbers," Aden replied with pride.

"Go up there to the office. See Mr. Jennings. He's in charge. Tell em I sent ya up to talk to him."

Tom Jennings leaned over a wooden table covered with thin sheets of paper. He looked up when Aden entered. "What do you need?"

After a few questions, Tom Jennings decided he would put Aden to work in the storage room counting nails and other hardware that was used on the ships. Aden's job was to note numbers of nails purchased in his logbook before they were loaded onto carts and taken out to the shipyard. Tom Jennings did not trust most of his suppliers.

The yard workers were a good bunch of men. They knew that they were making top-dollar for laborers and most put in more than a fair day's work. There was little time to talk on the job. The sound of hammers driving nails rang from dawn to dusk.

No one Aden encountered in the yard asked him any questions about himself or what he was doing in Hob Caw. All they wanted was someone who could make sure that they were given the supplies they needed each day to do their job and a worker who didn't waste time. Bent nails had to be put into another barrel and returned to Aden. When he was finished with his paperwork for the day, he would sit with his hammer and metal plate straightening the nails. His hands throbbed from the many blows that missed the nails and landed on his fingers. It was a menial job, but Tom Jennings agreed to pay Aden two dollars a week and let him sleep on the floor of the office.

After seven months, the pile of wooden planks and beams that once littered the ground were now put together into a magnificent sailing ship. It gleamed in the sunlight from the twenty coats of varnish that covered its hull. Once the ship was completed, Aden noticed that there were fewer and fewer men reporting each day for work. Besides counting nails, Aden was given the task of making out the payroll drafts, a job Tom Jennings hated.

Sitting in the cramped office that was also his home, Aden was greeted by Tom Jennings. Tom walked over to the small stove that spewed out heat as well as smoke. "Well Aden, looks like the ship will be ready to roll to the shore in about four days. The owners will be here tomorrow to inspect it. She's a beauty."

"Then I suppose you will begin building another one?" Aden questioned.

"Wish that were to be true, but the owner of the yard is calling it quits. He is selling all his plans and prints to a company in New Orleans. It is too expensive to build ships here. Takes too long to get them into open waters. You and me are going to be without work. I'm thinking about going down to New Orleans. I thought maybe you would want to come along. There is a lot of your kind down there."

Aden's back stiffened. "What do you mean, my kind?"

"You know, men who travel around quite a bit. New Orleans is like a big stew pot with all kinds of flavors in it. People come and a lot of them stay. It's a pretty wild place, Aden. There are lots of loose women, spicy food, and good music. I'm ready for all three."

A huge sigh escaped from Aden's throat. Would this feeling of being inferior never pass? "Yes, Tom, I think I would enjoy going to New Orleans with you."

Chapter Forty-Five

New Orleans was like nothing Aden had ever imagined. Although he had read books about the city he was overwhelmed with the mélange of people in one small space called the French Quarter. Overcrowded apartment buildings spewed their waste matter through pipes into the gutters of the streets; fishmongers flailed their arms to keep hordes of seabirds away from their stands and music filtered into the streets from littered hallways.

Aden also realized that New Orleans was a starting point for many slaves that were brought straight from Africa, yet freed black men also congregated here in a durable culture of Spanish, French, and American. Aden would stand on the docks and watch the ships coming into the ports, unloading masses of German and Irish immigrants who had managed to survive long journeys across the treacherous ocean. This was not true for many of the slaves on the ships that anchored off the coast.

The one thought that never left Aden's mind was his desire to find his grandmother. It would almost be impossible to buy her freedom from the Millers until he had saved up enough money to make them a decent offer. He had gone to the post office several days after arriving in New Orleans and sent off a letter to the Millers inquiring about the health of his grandmother and a hope that they would tell her that he was well and anxious to see her. Months later it was returned to him unopened.

Aden and Tom rented rooms in a boarding house just blocks from Canal Street. Tom had no idea that Aden had never slept in a real bed before he came to New Orleans.

Aden enjoyed having someone to talk to even though it was sometimes difficult. He had to think before he spoke, especially when Tom asked him questions about his past. Tom was not one to pry, so short answers from Aden kept his curiosity at bay. Aden told Tom he had left home after receiving a formal education and had been on his own ever since.

Tom decided that he and Aden should enjoy a few days off before they got serious about looking for work. Sitting in a crowded brewing house on the waterfront, Tom tapped his finger on the scarred table. "I'm telling you, Aden there is nothing like shipbuilding. You look at the plans and at first it all seems so confusing, but one by one the timbers create a magnificent structure that can sail across the ocean. My father was a builder, too. We always wanted to have our own yard, but we could never afford it. I'm going to look around for a job at one of the yards here. How about you?"

"I'm not sure, Tom. I really do need to find a job. If you hear of anything let me know."

Fitting into the life in New Orleans was much easier than Aden imagined. He discovered the people called Creoles that seemed to be a mixture of races. Some were French and American, others Spanish, and still others were a mixture of black and white. Instead of hiding or being ashamed of their heritage, they banded together to form their own language and lifestyle: no one was excluded. Aden liked listening to their music and eating the wonderful food they made. They used the sea as their market and created gumbos and burgoos made of shrimp and fish. He felt comfortable around these people who seemed to be happy just being who they were. It was through their eyes that he began to feel that he was not subhuman or a cultural mishap caused by slavery. He had just as much right to walk the streets as any of the rich slave owners who cared nothing for his kind. Being here gave Aden a renewed sense of strength and increased his tenacity to prove himselg.

Finding work in an open-air market, Aden spent his days loading fresh fruit and vegetables into bins. He loved the smell of the variety of food that he had never seen or tasted until he moved to New Orleans. Filling his bags with food, he would walk the four blocks to his boarding house. He would nod and smile at the people along the way that were getting more and more familiar to him. After his second paycheck, Aden found a used book store where he could purchase wonderful books for five or ten cents each. It was a paradise to him. Even though Tom came by often and beckoned Aden to come with him on a night of drinking, Aden would rather stay home and read the night away.

One night Tom knocked on Aden's door and rattled off a proposal for a business venture. Aden was interested in his offer. Tom had secured a loan from the bank to build a ship equivalent to those that were being built in England and on the east coast of America. He would build a sleek ship that could speed across the ocean in half the time as the bulky mast ships. She would be longer in length and with sweeping lines. She would be crowned with yards and yards of white canvas reaching high from her lofty spires. This ship would carry cargo and entice travelers to book passage on her.

Tom wanted Aden to be part of his team. He knew that with Aden's education he would be an asset. "I'm telling you Aden, with your brains and my know-how, we can make this project work. There is a lot of cheap labor in this town. We can make it work, Aden — I know we can."

Even though he was saving the money to free his grandmother, Aden knew that at the pace he was going it would take years. If Tom was right, he could free her a lot sooner. Aden related to Tom that he had two hundred dollars he would like to invest in the project. Tom was overwhelmed. They shook hands and the Jennings Shipbuilding Company was created.

Chapter Forty-Six

It was September 1860. Aden had just celebrated his thirtieth birthday. He and Tom had been in business together for almost seven years. In that same month the Jennings Shipbuilding Company was building the largest number of ships on the southern coast and were in the process of building three more merchant ships for a corporation in England. It was a prosperous business for them both.

Aden loved his work and was now able to read blueprints with ease and calculate measurements so accurately that Tom was amazed. Aden's only disappointment was that his search for his grandmother had turned up nothing. With enough money to purchase her freedom, Aden had sent a personal courier to Lott's Point. When the courier returned his news was not good. The Miller plantation had been sold five years ago. All of the slaves were reassigned to other plantations. The name Essie Woods did not appear on any of the sale sheets. It was possible that she had already died and had been buried on the property. Aden's last hope of ever seeing her again was dashed.

By the end of 1860 the talk of war had been circulating throughout the private sector of New Orleans and was all that anyone talked about. Tom and Aden were anxious to get their ships built and on their way. With three half-completed ships, it was crucial that they finished the job quickly.

Each dinner they attended at the Canal Street Men's Club was flooded with the topic of conflict between the states and the secession of the southern states. Their years in business together had produced a cohesive partnership. They survived those first few years of total poverty and remained dedicated to their goal. It had paid off for them both, but now they knew it was time to change their strategy.

When their business was prosperous Tom had married a woman named Amanda, whose parents were proud to have him in their family. He was, after all, a successful businessman. Tom and Amanda had two children and lived in the Garden District of New Orleans.

Aden, who was still single, lived in a townhouse with a private courtyard just a few blocks away. He had a library filled with books and two servants that he paid well. Now, with the impending change in economy and a war on the horizon, time was of the essence. In order to save a few hours travel time each day, Tom and Aden decided to find lodgings closer to the shipyard so that they could keep a close watch on the workers.

Tom took a room above an alehouse just minutes from the shipyard, returning home every other week to see his family. Aden wanted something a little quieter. Searching the streets for a few days, he came upon a small restaurant with a "Rooms to Let" sign in the window. As he stepped inside the door, the tinkling bell overhead was interrupted by a loud voice.

"Whoever you are, you best not be walking on my wet floors."

Aden stepped back into the threshold and stood there for a minute, trying to decide which way to turn. It was then that a woman came down the steps wiping her hands on her soiled apron.

Her name was Maggie Greene and she was the proprietor of the building.

"What can I do for you?" she asked.

"I was inquiring about the rooms," he replied, wondering how such a loud voice had come from this very petite woman.

"Two rooms, two fire places, but sparsely furnished.

Two dollars a month and not a penny less. Three dollars if you want your laundry done," she said.

Aden smiled to himself. She was a woman of few words. "That will be fine. I would like to move in as soon as possible. Are the rooms ready?" he asked.

"Follow me and see for yourself," she said as she started toward the stairs. "You can walk on the floor now. It is dry."

Maggie was right. The rooms had little furniture, but there was a nice bed with a horsehair mattress and good light from the windows. Aden paid her two dollars in advance and moved in the next day.

The rooms suited his needs. Moving his clothing and books into the apartment was all that was necessary for Aden. Maggie's restaurant on the first floor would accommodate him quite well.

Aden ate his meals in the restaurant every day. Drinking a hot cup of coffee and eating homemade biscuits and gravy was a satisfying meal for him in the morning. He looked forward to the evenings also. Maggie was a wonderful cook. Aden watched her as she moved between the tables, filling the coffee mugs and wiping crumbs from the tables. Nodding to those who seemed to be regular patrons was the only greeting she gave. Her words were few, "More coffee?" "Ready for dessert?" "Here is your bill." She gave no one an opening to talk to her. Aden was included in her circle of few words. When he gave an occasional compliment to her on the food, she would answer with a quiet, "Thank you."

The January weather brought cold temperatures and freezing rain to New Orleans, something that rarely happened. Aden and Tom took turns staying at the yard until it was too dark to work. Tonight it was Aden's turn. Returning to his rooms after ten, he slowly climbed the stairs and put his key in the lock. He was chilled to the bone and looked forward to basking in front of the hearth as soon as he could get a fire going. Opening the door, Aden was greeted by warm air. Someone had made a fire in the hearth. Letting out a sigh, he flopped down in the chair in front of the grate and removed his shoes. He didn't know who had taken the liberty of entering his apartment without his permission, but whoever it was, tonight he would thank them. He didn't have to wait very long. Coming out of his bedchamber dressed in a nightdress was Maggie Greene. She jumped when she saw Aden.

"By God, you gave me a scare. What are you doing here?" she asked.

"I seem to remember that I live here. Is that still correct?" he answered.

"Yes, but I thought you were staying at your work. It was after nine and you were not home. The flue on my chimney is clogged with soot and I cannot make a fire in my rooms until I have it cleaned. Wouldn't want to burn up all your lovely things. I was cold. Let me get my clothes and I will be out of your way." She had just said more words than he had heard out of her for a month.

"No, please, you need a warm place to sleep. You take the bed and I will make a pallet here on the floor. It is no use for you to sleep in the cold." Aden was not sure if what he was suggesting was proper.

"You come share the bed with me and then I will stay," Maggie said.

Aden was startled by her suggestion. "I really don't think that would be a good idea, Maggie. I mean..."

"Oh swish. We are both adults. Now come lay with me," she said, taking his hand. "Put a pillow between us and you turn your back to me."

In the morning when Maggie should have been in the restaurant making biscuits and Aden should have been in the restaurant eating them, they were still entwined in each other's arms. Sometime during the night, Maggie had moved into the circle of his arms and he could feel her breasts against his chest. He tried to lie still so he did not wake her, but he could feel his own body beginning to pulsate as her legs wrapped around his. Maggie was not asleep. In the darkness his lips found hers as her hands moved down the hollow of his stomach. "You got a nice body, Aden Woods," she whispered. "I want all of it."

A beam of morning sun shining across the bed awakened Aden. It was after seven. Shielding his eyes from the glare, he quickly sat up. Maggie rolled over, her naked breasts resting on his back. "Oh Lordy, look at the time! I am going to be boiled in oil if I don't open the restaurant. Quick, Aden, find my bloomers." As Maggie jumped out of the bed and, for the first time, Aden got a quick look at the woman he had spent the night with. Her hair, usually worn in a bun on top of her head, hung almost to her waist. She was a tiny woman, not more than five feet tall, but the night before, Aden could have sworn she was as tall as him.

"Maggie, wait. I will go downstairs and tell your customers that the flue is clogged in the kitchen and you will be up and running by supper," Aden said, as she scrambled around the room, still looking for her shoes.

"And you, what about your job? Can you just lay in when you want to?" she asked.

"I'm the boss, I sure can," he said, laughing."

"Well then, good. Go downstairs and tell my angry patrons a big, fat lie and then come back up here to me."

With little fanfare or questions, Maggie began to spend every night with Aden. To her it seemed quite natural. She was a widow. Her husband was shot when a jealous man caught

Maggie's husband with his wife. She had no interest in marrying again and did not want children, but at twenty-eight she was not ready to be celibate. "I am choosey Aden," she said. "I am very self-sufficient and have no need for a man to be in my life every moment of the day. There has only been a handful since the old bugger died, but when I see someone that appeals to me, I usually make the first move. So don't get any ideas about being my man or getting married. That is not in my plans."

Aden smiled at her. "You are something else, Maggie Greene. I have never met anyone like you."

"And I doubt that you ever will," she replied.

Aden decided to keep his relationship with Maggie to himself. It would be very hard to explain to Tom who she was and why they only spent the nights together. They really had no other kind of connection, but Maggie was special to him. Aden was in a very strange situation, but one he truly enjoyed.

With the building of three ships in full swing, Tom was still concerned that they were running out of time to complete them. It was already March and the work was going slowly. The worker's cold hands were stiff and they shivered as they climbed the rope ladders. The same questions were asked every day: What would happen if President Lincoln actually declared war? Would they be able to finish the ships? The contracts for the ships were for a considerable amount of money and Tom knew he could lose everything if he could not complete them.

"I have everyone I can find working day and night, Aden," Tom said as they sat together in Tom's office. "There is still a lot of work to be done. I am thinking it might be a good idea to buy some slaves. We can always sell them when the work is done."

Aden quickly stood up, "If you want to buy slaves, I will agree to that. But when the work on the ships is finished we will give them their freedom."

"You must be touched, Aden. That would be ridiculous. There are very few left to buy and at seven-or-eight hundred dollars a head we would lose too much money if we just let them walk."

"How do you figure, Tom? You are not going to have to pay them and they work twice as hard as most of the men in the yard. You can take the difference from my share of the profit."

Tom leaned back in his chair. "I don't have the time or the energy to ask you why you are so adamant about this. I will send someone tomorrow to buy ten or twelve strong men. And you,

Mr. Woods, are going to give me half the money for them if I am committed to releasing them in less than a year."

That evening while Tom dined with his wife, he told her about Aden's reaction to his suggestion. "I don't know why, Amanda, but every time the subject of slaves comes up, Aden gets very defensive."

"He is from New York, Tom. Perhaps he is not aware of how slaves are treated. Whatever it is, I would just leave it alone. You two have such a good working relationship it would be sad to see something so silly as the subject of coloreds come between you," Amanda replied.

"There are other things also that puzzle me about Aden. Whenever I invite him to dine with us, he always begs off. I have attempted to introduce him to several really nice ladies and he refuses to meet with them. Do you think he is peculiar, Amanda?"

"Perhaps he is, Tom, but I find him to be good company and very polite. I also have no doubt that he is a very intelligent person. Now would not be a good time to question him about his private life. You both have too much at stake."

"You are right. He is all of those things. I am lucky to have him for a partner. With everything going on right now, I surely wouldn't want to cause any problems."

The news that someone from the shipyards was coming to buy slaves sent a scurry through the marketplace. The owners were in a panic to get rid of their stock of unsold slaves. If war did come it would be the slaveholders' duty to dispose of the slaves in one way or another.

Aden convinced Tom that it would be more beneficial for the shipyard foreman to pick out the slaves, since he was in charge of the manual labor force. Tom insisted that Aden go along with a man named Frank to make sure all the transactions were handled properly. After they arrived at the meetinghouse, Aden waited in the wagon for a few minutes. Aden knew that the sights and smells of the slave market would linger with him for days after the visit. It was one of the worst places he could imagine.

Sitting in the front seat of the wagon offered him a good view of the proceedings.

After the purchase of twelve slaves, Aden descended from the wagon to stretch his legs. Walking past the long row of holding quarters, a wire fence, topped with barbs, stopped him. As he turned to move past the fence he saw a small boy sitting in the corner of the slave pen. Aden decided to move closer. Walking near the enclosure, he bent down and put his hand on the wire. The boy drew his mud-caked legs close to his body and buried his head in his hands.

"Don't be afraid. I'm not going to hurt you," Aden said.

The sight of muddy boots in his vision caused Aden to raise his head. One of the handlers, his whip hanging from his belt, looked down at him. "You need something, Mister? These slaves in here ain't for sale. They're stragglers."

Aden knew the term quite well. A straggler was a slave that was either too sick or too old for anyone to want. "Why is this boy in here?" Aden asked, standing up.

The man shrugged. "Had a storm on the way here from Baton Rouge. The wagon turned over in the mud. Lost about seven slaves. His momma was one of them. Damn shame. Lost a lot of money that day."

"So, what happens to him now?" Aden asked.

"Guess he'll be put in a cluster. We group a bunch of them together. You can get 'em for a good price. Get rid of a lot of garbage that way."

As the man turned to leave, Aden called to him. "I want to buy the boy!"

The man turned. "Fifty dollars and he is yours."

"I'll give you thirty and you will be lucky to get that."

"Deal. Come 'round to the counter. I'll give you a bill of sale. Want me to get him washed up?"

"No! Just get him out of there," Aden said.

The handler reached down and pulled the boy up by one arm. "Get up, boy. This man is taking you with him."

The look of terror on the child's face was almost enough to make Aden leap over the fence and grab him. Instead, Aden waited until he paid the invoice and took the small scrap of paper that declared that Aden Woods now owned one Negro boy, approximately seven or eight years old. Could it be any simpler?

"What ya got there?" Frank said, loading the last of the men into the wagon. "He's a little young to carry timber, ain't he?" Frank let out a howl of laughter.

"Don't worry about him. You just drive this wagon back to the shipyard." The tone in Aden's voice was enough to let Frank know that he shouldn't ask anymore questions.

At the shipyard, the Negro men who had been bought were taken to the wooden barracks where they would live when they were not working. As each one was shown to a cot, Aden stepped inside the door. "I want you twelve men to know that as soon as the three ships we are building are finished you will be given your papers and you will be free to leave. The harder you work, the faster the ships will be done. I will give each of you five dollars when you leave here as free men." He was proud of his speech and the smiles that he received in return.

Tom Jennings was standing at his office window when the wagon arrived. He also saw the small boy that Aden had with him. Curious as to what was going on, he waited until Aden returned from getting the new workers settled. As Aden strode across the yard, the boy walked close behind him. Tom greeted Aden. "Looks like you got a good crop of strong men, Aden. Maybe we'll get those ships in the water sooner than I thought." Looking behind Aden, he asked, "Whose is this? Does he belong to one of the men?"

"No, I bought him. Right now I just want to get him home, get him cleaned up, and fed. He smells really bad. His momma got killed and he was in the holding pen."

Tom's brow furrowed. "Ah, then what, Aden? I mean, is that all you are going to do with that boy?" He put up his hands. "Don't get me wrong, Aden, what you do with him is your business. You bought him, he's yours. I was just wondering if you are—"

Aden finished his sentence. "Queer? Is that what you are asking me, Tom? Do you think I am some sort of a sexual deviant that would buy a small boy for my own pleasure? Are you more worried that your business partner has odd tastes rather than what is going to happen to this child? What would you say if you knew your partner was a Negro?" Aden blurted out, before he realized what he had actually said.

Tom was stunned. "I have no idea what you are ranting about, Aden. I wasn't suggesting any such thing. I think this conversation is over."

"You bet it is," Aden replied. "And if I did not have to attend to this half-starved, terrorized child, I would take the time to beat you to a pulp."

Furious from his conversation with Tom Jennings, Aden did not realize that he had frightened the child even more. By the time they reached his house, the boy was sobbing loudly and had urinated all over his already-filthy pants.

Filling the metal tub with warm water, Aden stripped the remains of the boy's clothes from his body and put him in the tub. Still sobbing, when he was submerged in the water, the boy screamed even louder.

Aden was still upset from his argument with Tom and lost his temper. "Be quiet. I am just trying to get the dirt off of you." It wasn't until the water turned a muddy, red color that Aden knew the real reason why he was now screaming. The boy's body was covered in a mass of cuts and sores. His groin was red and swollen. Strings that had come loose from his pants were wrapped around his penis.

"Oh, good Lord," Aden moaned. "I'm so sorry! This may hurt a bit, but we have to get you cleaned up." Pulling the rotted material away from his body, Aden could see the relief in the little boy's eyes.

Aden continued to talk to him in a soft voice as he washed the bugs from his head and the grit from his ears. Raising him out of the water, Aden wrapped him in a blanket and set him on the sofa in front of the fire. "You stay right here. I am going to the kitchen to get you something to eat. Now I mean it. Don't move."

Aden cut a thick slice off the bread loaf and lathered it with butter. He poured a large glass of milk from the pitcher in the window box, and carried both up the stairs. The room was quiet. With the glow of the fire shining on his face, the little boy lay on his side fast asleep. Aden put the tray on the side table and sat down next to him. He could see his eyes moving behind his closed eyes. Occasionally his mouth would twitch.

What have I done? I have bought a child. Look at him. He is so frightened and alone. I have bought a child. I have taken on a responsibility I am not sure I can handle, but to walk away from him today was like walking away from myself. Morning will come and I will feed him, and then what? He remembered his grandmother's words. "You be strong, boy. Help others, it be your duty." *Lord, if you can hear me now, I need help.*

Aden left a note on his door for Maggie. He said he was not feeling very good and had already gone to bed. He needed more time to decide what to do with his new ward.

In the morning, Aden awoke in a bent position from sleeping on the end of the settee. The boy sat on the other end, staring at him. The bread—now slightly stale—and the warm milk still remained on the tray.

"Good morning. I brought that food up last night for you, but you were already asleep." Before Aden could say he would go downstairs and get more, the child picked up the bread and began taking large bites out of it. Aden watched as he finished the bread and milk in record time and then licked his fingers for the last taste.

"Do you want more?" Aden asked. "If you do, you will have to answer me. Not just shake your head."

"Yes suh," he answered. "I be wantin' more."

Drawing out the details of how he got to New Orleans was difficult. Plying him with food made the boy open up to Aden. Slowly he related his story. His name was Lukas. He and his mother worked on a plantation in Baton Rouge. It was a terrible place with evil overseers who beat them often. They were fed only once a day. His mother was happy when they were told they were being sold. She told Lukas that maybe they would go to someone nice and have a better life. When the wagon turned over in the storm he never saw her again. He was put in the holding pen and had been there for over two weeks. He had to fight for the few scraps of food that was fed to them in large tin pans. If he cried for his mother, the overseer would beat him.

"I wants my momma," he said as he finished his story. "I miss her." Tears fell onto his naked chest. Aden pulled him close to him. "Don't cry, Lukas. Your mother is in a better place now. I am going to take care of you."

Lukas wiped his eyes. "Who I be tah you?"

"You will be my friend."

Aden explained to Lukas that he had to go to work, but that he would have someone bring him more food and bring something for him to wear. No amount of cajoling could convince Lukas that he could not go with Aden. Aden could tell he was extremely frightened to be left alone in this strange place. At the last moment, Aden conceded. Taking Lucas's hand, Aden reassured him as the two of them left for the shipyard. On the way to the yard, they stopped at the dry goods store to buy clothes for Lukas. Aden had no idea what was in store for him when Tom once again saw him with the boy.

Just minutes after arriving, Lukas asked what he was supposed to do. Even at his young age he was used to working. Aden decided that giving him menial tasks was better than having Lukas be his constant shadow. Lukas was given a bucket and told to pick up all the nails and pieces of hardware that had fallen to the ground. With a large grin on his face, Lukas accepted the job willingly. Tom Jennings said nothing at all to Aden about the boy. The day was used for business.

After a full day's work, Aden and Lukas returned to the boarding house expecting a warm meal and a good night's sleep. Lukas was still anxious, asking Aden if he was going to be with him in the morning. Aden assured him that he would.

Aden sat down at his usual table in Maggie's restaurant and positioned Lukas across from him. He was not aware of the stares from the customers who had arrived for the supper hour. Maggie came out of the kitchen door carrying a tray. After serving the patrons at a front table, she quickly walked over to Aden. "What is this colored boy doing sitting with you?" she asked.

"He is sitting with me because we just returned from work and we are both very hungry." Aden smiled at her.

"He can't stay here, Aden. I don't serve coloreds. Have him go 'round to the back door and I will have the cook give him something to eat."

"Never mind," Aden said, realizing his mistake. "We will just go upstairs and eat our dinner in our room."

As Aden and Lukas both stood up, Maggie stepped in front of him. "He cannot go upstairs. I do not have coloreds staying in my house. What is the matter with you, Aden? Now take him 'round back. I will feed him and he can sleep in the shed." This time, Maggie seemed irritated, but not quite as much as Aden.

"Come Lukas, we will go back to the shipyard and sleep in the office. We'll buy dinner on the way. I will talk to you tomorrow, Maggie," Aden said, leaving her standing in the restaurant with customers staring at her.

"If I be too much trouble, Massa Ada, ya kin jest leave me in dah shed and go back to yer home."

"No!" Aden said in a loud voice, not realizing he had scared Lukas. "If you are not welcome in the restaurants or boarding rooms, neither am I. We will make our own way."

Finding an open soup kitchen, Aden bought a pail of beef soup and half a loaf of bread. Taking Lukas by the hand, they walked back to the shipyard and into the small office. Aden lit a fire in the buck stove and covered Lukas with a blanket. Sitting together as the room warmed, they ate their soup in silence. Aden fixed a pallet on the floor and Lukas laid down. He yawned and within minutes closed his eyes. Aden sat in the office chair, his feet propped up on the desk. He had to stop trying to make his own set of rules. He knew too well where blacks were allowed and where they weren't. His defiance would only bring harm to Lukas and himself. Closing his eyes, he could feel Lukas staring at him. "I thought you were asleep," Aden said.

"I be causin ya a bag of trouble, ain't I, Massa Aden?"

"No, Lukas, it is not you. It is the society we live in that is causing us both trouble. You get some sleep."

In the morning, Aden told Lukas to stay at the yard while he fetched them some breakfast. Entering the restaurant, he nodded to Maggie and walked into the hallway. She followed.

"I'm sorry about yesterday, Maggie. I should have known better than to bring that boy in here. He is my responsibility now, so we are going to stay at the shipyard. I'll be back later today to pick up my belongings."

"Please, Aden, stay with me. We can find someplace for the boy. I don't want you to leave," Maggie said, tears filling her eyes.

"If it was at all possible I would, Maggie. But I cannot turn my back on him. I made him a promise and I am going to keep it." He touched her cheek. "I am going to miss you."

"Fine! You go take care of your little niggah boy. I thought you were different, Aden." She turned and went back into the restaurant.

When Aden returned that evening for his possessions, they were packed and left in the front hallway. Maggie was nowhere around.

Tom Jennings had acknowledged Lukas's presence with no questions asked. He knew he had said enough. He had heard from some of the workers that Aden was seeing a woman who owned a boarding house. Even though that gave Tom some degree of relief, he still could not figure out why Aden wanted to strap himself with a child, especially one of a different color. With his constant smile and cheerful nature, Lukas became a fixture in the shipyard. He learned all the men's names and would wave to them as he passed them, his bucket filled with metal. Even Tom could not help warming to this child. And now he found that Aden and Lukas were living at the shipyard. It was all very confusing to him.

As the weather grew colder, Lukas spent more time inside the small office. When he had nothing to do, Aden would hand him pencil and paper and tell him to practice writing his name. When Lukas was finally able to write his own name, Aden danced around the room. Lukas laughed, knowing how pleased he had made Aden. Tom thought it was totally useless to teach Lukas to write and speak proper words. When would Lukas ever have a chance to use his knowledge?

Aden realized he was meeting the challenge of being in charge of another human being. On a stormy night, when the sky lit up from streaks of lightning crashing to the ground and thunder shook the walls, screams from Lukas brought Aden to his side. Lukas coiled in fear, remembering a night like this one that took his mother from him. Holding on to the front of Aden's nightshirt, he begged Aden never to leave him.

"I be 'fraid, so 'fraid. You gonna go away like my momma did and I be all alone agin."

Aden pried Lukas' fingers loose from his shirt and put his arms around the boy. "You don't have to worry, Lukas. I will never leave you unless we both decide that is what needs to happen. You are stuck with me, and I with you."

In the spring of 1861 war was declared on the southern states, while two uncompleted ships rested on racks in the Jennings shipyard. An immediate blockade on the shipping lanes by the North had halted the flow of supplies to complete the ships. Most of the men working there had left to join the confederate army. Without the materials and the men, the work in the shipyard came to a halt.

"We are losing money, Aden. With only one of the ships finished we are losing money everyday. We can't afford to spend any more money on the two that are not completed. The war is on our doorsteps. We should cut our losses and close down the yard."

"I agree with you, Tom. It is time to move on," Aden said.

When the Jennings Shipyard closed, the skeletons of the two remaining ships were left behind.

Tom decided he wanted to take his wife and children further north. "I'm sorry, Aden, but Amanda is scared and she wants to leave. It is only a matter of time before this city is sealed off from the rest of the state and everyone here is in danger. We must take what resources we have available to us and make sure we invest them wisely. I have no confidence in our new currency." Tom continued, "There is not near as much money left as I thought possible, the last few months have caused quite a strain on our budget. I will deposit the money in a bank of your choice." Aden chose a financial institution in New York.

Tom shook Aden's hand for the last time. "It's been good doing business with you. I hope there are no hard feelings between us."

"No hard feelings, Tom."

"What are you going to do now, Aden?" Tom asked.

"I've given it a lot of thought, and I have decided to leave the country for awhile. There are a group of Polynesian Islands that sound like someplace Lukas and I might enjoy. I think we will go there for now."

"Good luck to you, Aden, and to Lukas, too," Tom said.

After several days of packing and settling his affairs, Aden was ready to leave New Orleans. He had one more stop to make. Leaving Lukas in the carriage, Aden entered Maggie's boarding house and rang the bell at the front counter. She was surprised to see him. "I have missed you, Aden. I still wondered what I did to turn you away?"

"I really don't know how to explain it to you, Maggie. Most of it was left over from my past and I have finally decided to give in to it. I wish I knew an easy way to tell you the whole story. I am leaving, Maggie. Lukas and I are going to New York and from there on to an island called Tahiti."

"I wish you well. If you ever come back to New Orleans, please come and see me." She raised herself up on her tiptoes and softly kissed him. "Goodbye, Aden," she said and then ran from the room. In May of 1862, the city of New Orleans surrendered and was in the hands of the northern troops.

Chapter Forty-Seven

When Aden and Lukas left New York Harbor on a passenger ship, Lukas was touted as Aden's personal cabin boy to keep everyone from asking questions. Lukas did not care. Unable to gain his sea legs, he lay in his bunk, and moaned that he was surely going to die. When choppy waters and storms hit, Aden held a bucket, while Lukas tossed up all the food he had eaten.

Twenty-seven days later when the ship pulled into the calm waters along the shore of Tahiti, Lukas, now ten pounds thinner, was so happy to see land that he wanted to dive into the water and swim for shore. He told Aden that he would never again walk on anything but solid ground.

The island natives greeted Aden and Lucas with some degree of caution. Once it was clear what Aden's intentions were, the brown-skinned people wearing little more than small pieces of bright-colored cloth welcomed him. Aden and Lukas chose a village called Hiannoati on one of the smaller islands. They were given shelter in a hut made of woven grasses and bamboo poles.

At first, Lukas was afraid of everything. He found the noises of the birds and animals to be frightening, along with the storms that came out of nowhere and sent bolts of lightening streaking across the skies. As he watched the giant waves pound the beaches, Lukas was afraid that the island would be washed out to sea. Aden had all but decided that he had made a mistake bringing Lukas to the islands and wondered how he would ever get him on a ship to go home, when Lukas made the announcement that he never wanted to leave Tahiti. Lukas was making friends with some of the island children and for the first time in his life he ran free across the beach with no one chasing him.

In the days that followed, Aden listened to the laughter

coming from the little boy who just a short time ago had no future. He watched as Lukas learned to snorkel, using a hollow reed as a breathing tube. He learned to throw javelins with ease. Aden also watched as the young boy shed his clothes for a small cloth to cover his lower body. He smiled as Lukas used his toes to shimmy up a coconut tree. His new son was happy and seeing him happy gave Aden a sense of contentment.

Aden also flourished in this land where the color of a man's skin mattered little to the natives. Tahiti was giving him a renewed sense of himself.

Helping the natives build double-hulled outriggers and flat boats gave Aden an inner peace that he had never felt while pretending to be a white man in the south. He began to shed the image of his outer skin that had imprisoned him for so many years. He listened while the men of the village talked of their fishing voyages and diving for black pearls. They would chant old tribal songs and laugh together. Aden was soon included in their practical jokes, which was the signal that he had been accepted as one of them. At night, when the sun filled the entire horizon, Aden and the men would sit around a fire pit and drink Hinano. Aden soon learned that after more than three cups full you could not remember your name the next day or who was the young Tahitian woman lying next to you. Throwing on her sarong, she would giggle, making you wish you could remember the night before.

The missionaries had set up communities on the islands and everyone was welcome. They were kind and gentle people that enrolled the children in schools. Lukas had no interest in learning, although Aden was persistent that he attend school. Taking Lukas by the hand, Aden led him into the open-air structure lined with tables and chairs. Lukas hung his head when the teacher asked his name. "His name is Lukas," Aden said. "He is being quite stubborn today. He would rather play than come here."

"I quite understand," she replied. "I assume you are his father. Is that correct?"

Without hesitation, Aden answered, "Yes, he is my son. His name is Lukas Woods."

Lukas looked up at Aden and a broad, toothy grin covered his face. "I think I will go to school, now," Lukas answered in the proper English that Aden insisted he used.

In the months that followed, Lukas's renewed body strength and the fading emotional scars allowed him to live a free life in Tahiti. He no longer feared retribution from Aden for the mistakes he made. Lukas knew that Aden would not strike him or treat him unkindly. He had formed a bond with this light-skinned man that he never knew was possible.

With the word "son" now attached to his name, Lukas prodded Aden for answers. "Why," was his favorite word? " Why did you buy me that day? Why did you bring me to Tahiti and why do you let me call you father?"

Aden decided he would try his best to answer Lukas. The explanation was not simple. Sitting in front of their hut, roasting tilapia filets on a skewer, Aden began his story in short sentences and plain words that Lukas would understand.

"My grandmother's name was Kayudante and she was born in Africa." When he had finished, he breathed a sigh of relief.

"So, what are you telling me?" Lukas asked.

"Well, according to the law of the southern states, I am still considered a Negro. Of course, there are those called mulattoes. They are half-black and half-white, but are still treated as Negroes. But I am only one-fourth black, so I am really more white than black."

Lukas shook his head. "I am real confused now. Tell me one thing. Are you still gonna be my father?"

Aden grinned. "Yes, I am. As long as you go to school and learn to speak proper English, I will be your father."

Lukas threw his arms around Aden's neck. "Dats, I mean, that is all that matters."

Chapter Forty-Eight

Aden and Lukas had been living in Tahiti for five years when the news came that the War Between the States had ended six months earlier and President Lincoln had emancipated the slaves.

Aden had become restless. Like the ebb of the ocean, something was pulling him away from the islands and back to America. He wasn't sure what it was. Maybe he just wanted to walk on American soil as a free black man rather than someone who had denied his own heritage most of his life. He wanted to find his grandmother's grave and put up a proper marker, with her real name on it, Kayudante, not Essie Woods and he needed to settle all the financial affairs that he had left behind.

From the few conversations they had about returning to America, Aden knew that Lukas was not happy about leaving Tahiti. He was now fourteen and except for his birthright, he considered himself Tahitian. He had even been given a coming of age induction ceremony by the chieftains of the tribe.

When Aden finally told Lukas about what he wanted to do, Lukas nodded in approval. "If that is important to you, father, then I think you should go. You may find the peace you are looking for there. I will wait here for your return. This is my home. I really don't want to leave unless you insist."

"You are wise beyond your years, Lukas. I was afraid to tell you."

"How could I ever deny you anything? You have given me life and it belongs to you."

Aden grinned. "Now, don't go getting too Tahitian on me. It is *your* life. Your mother gave it to you and I just kept the fire going until you were old enough to start it yourself. When I return, we should make plans for your future. You will probably be ready to further your studies. Maybe we can arrange for schooling in England."

"I really don't want to leave here, Aden." Lukas said. He reverted to using Aden, rather than father, whenever he was unhappy with a situation.

"But what can you do here the rest of your life? You are going to be an educated black man. Men like you will be needed to help the Negroes in America find a new life," Aden said.

"Who knows what I will do. I might become a missionary or maybe a teacher here on the islands. I might just decide to build boats and make fishing my livelihood. Or, if it suits me, I will sit in a coconut tree all day doing nothing. Isn't that what being free means? That is what you have taught me," Lukas said, watching his father for a reaction.

"You're right, Lukas. It is your life. Now I must find someone to care for you while I am gone." He put his arm around his son and walked with him to the beach.

Two weeks later, when the ship sailed into the bay, Aden waited on the dock with a small traveling bag. "Now remember, I will be gone no longer than two years. I will write to you often. That is a promise."

"I will miss you terribly, father, and I know you will keep your word." Lukas kept his arms around Aden until it was time to leave.

Chapter Forty-Nine

Aden departed from the ship in the New York harbor. Sporting a deeper tan and lighter hair, bleached from the hot Tahitian sun, Aden retrieved his luggage and headed for the nearest hotel. He was sea weary and extremely sleep deprived. Settling into the Broadview, where he rented a room for the week, Aden collapsed from exhaustion onto the bed. In the morning, he went to the Republic Financial Institution and requested that he be given all his funds in small denominations, the money he had earned during his years working with Tom Jennings.

Surprised at his request, the bank officer took some time gathering the money together. Aden left the bank with thirty-two thousand dollars in a brown, leather satchel. It was much more than he expected. He then boarded a train heading south. Traveling as far as Kentucky. He had to make the rest of his overland trip by coach. The railroad tracks were just beginning to be repaired. During the war they had been ripped up by the northern troops. Aden was in no hurry, not knowing what he would find when he finally arrived in Mississippi.

Watching from the coach window, Aden was shocked at the devastation he saw along the roads. He was not aware that there was such hatred between brothers of the same color. Leaving a path of ruin and destruction must have been the mission of the armies who invaded the south. Destroyed homes, graves turned out of the ground, and barren fields for miles and miles were distinct evidence of that hate. His decision not to fight in that war was now reaffirmed. On either side he would have been an outcast. He suddenly missed his island and his son. He wondered if coming back to America had been a mistake.

When he arrived in Mississippi in the spring of 1866, Aden bought a horse in Biloxi and headed for the Miller Plantation. Three days later his stomach was in knots and his thoughts in turmoil as he entered the gates to what was left of the Miller House. He had never wanted to see or think of this place. Now, as he looked upon the ghostly shapes of blackened timbers that leaned against each other for support, he wondered if Mr. Miller was still alive. As his horse picked his way along the path, overgrown with thick weeds and creeping vine, purple hyacinths poked their heads up as if this were just another ordinary spring. What remained of the plantation seemed desolate. It would be doubtful to find anyone living here.

Rolling a blanket out on the ground under an acacia tree in the front yard, Aden opened his backpack and pulled out his flint. After starting a small fire in a circle of stones, he settled himself down to ponder his next move. He knew that Mrs. Miller had moved some years ago and the slaves were all displaced. He wondered if it would be possible to find his grandmother's grave. She was the kind and gentle woman who kept him safe after his mother drowned. He remembered how she would hold him close every night and made sure he was warm, even though she slept without a blanket. His grandmother took chances everyday when she stole food from the kitchen to make sure he had enough to eat. After all these years, his heart still ached for her.

Aden awoke with a start in the morning. Looking up from his blanket, he stared into the eyes of an old black man, who carried a heavy stick in his hand.

"What ya be doin' here?" the man asked.

Aden sat up, rubbing his eyes. "Right now, I am trying to wake up. Am I trespassing?" he asked.

"You be kin to the Taylors?" the old man asked.

"No. I have no idea who the Taylors are. I'm just passing through. I was tired and just happened to pick this place to stop." He pointed to the horse tethered to the far side of the tree. "I got some good chicory coffee in my bag and some soda bread. Give me a minute to start the fire and we can have some."

The man's face broke into a broad grin. "Chicory? I ain't had no chicory in yars." He bent down and began repositioning the partially burnt logs.

Aden poured water from his canteen into a small pot he retrieved from his backpack and added the coffee. He nodded to the man. "Have a seat. I'm harmless."

"It be takin' me a while tah squat. I gots old bones." Putting the stick he had been carrying into the fire, the old man sat down on the ground, hugging his knees. "Smell dat. Dat be a good smell. I loves coffee."

"I lied to you," Aden said. "I wasn't here by accident. I lived here when I was small. I came back because I am looking for my grandmother. She lived here too."

"Don't recall any whites other than da Millers and da Taylors dat lived here. I be here most my life. I be called Ben. I was da shoe man in the livery."

Aden grinned. "I remember you, Ben. You worked in the stable. I was just a little kid then. My name is Aden Woods. My grandmother was Essie Woods."

Ben slapped his knees. "Lawdy be, Aden Woods! You be da little off-color boy. I do 'member ya. Ya be gon a long time. Why ya back here? Essie she be gone. Essie, she moved on wid dah others when Mizz Miller selled dah place to dah Taylors. Yeh, I sho missed dem all, but dey keep me here. Dey had lots of horses, dem Taylors. When dah war comes, dey leave real quick. Me and somes of dah others, we jest stayed. We jest too old to go anywheres else."

"Ben, do you have any idea where my grandmother was sent to?"

Ben slowly shook his head. "It happened real fast. One day dey be here, de next dey are gone. Dem big wagons comes and takes dem away."

"I think I will be here for a few days, Ben. Can you talk to the others? Maybe someone will remember something that can help me out."

Ben stood up. "Be real nice of you, sharen' dat coffee. You kin come wid me, and talk to dem yerself," Ben said, motioning toward the river.

"Whatever happened to Mr. Miller?" Aden asked.

"Dat ole man, he just sit in dat chair for yars and den one day he shot himself right in da head. Sure was a mess."

After putting everything into the backpack, Ben climbed behind Aden on the horse. Ben gave Aden directions as they cut through the woods behind the remains of the house. On the bank of the river a small group of men and women had set up a makeshift camp. Clothes hung on lines strung between the trees, wood had been nailed together to form the rough shelter that housed them.

When Aden arrived with Ben, several of the women

disappeared inside the shelters, waiting for whatever fate was in store for them. They had learned to be cautious of every stranger.

Ben raised his hand and called out to them, "It be okay. Dis here be Aden Wood, dah grandson of Essie Wood. He ain't here to cause truble."

There were thirteen in all, five older men, five women, a young pregnant girl and two small children. Weary faces and bent bodies were all that remained of the people who were left behind. Yet his arrival seemed to make them happy. Some of the women hugged Aden as though he had come to save them. Pouring the last of the chicory into a kettle of water, he sat with them and shared his food. A soda biscuit brought tears to their eyes.

Their story was the same as so many other slaves who were now free. After being set free from the plantation owners, they had no money, no place to go, and no way to get there. Left behind to fend on their own, they were prey to anyone who wanted to steal what little they had. Ben's group had stayed on the land owned by the Taylors for two years after they had left. They lived in their old slave quarters, patching together a few rooms to make life a bit more comfortable. The men fished and trapped game and the women tended to the garden. Life was not easy, but they were free. They had no idea how costly their freedom would be.

After the war, the soldiers came once again. They destroyed everything on the property, including the meager homes of the Negroes. The soldiers took their cooking pots, blankets and their shoes. They were left with nothing once again, yet they survived.

Sitting around the fire that evening, Ben expressed his concern for his band of stragglers. "We barely made it lass yar. Dis yar may take us all. We got no warm clothes or much food ta speaks of. We ain't welcome nowhar. We be chased off diffrent property three times. So we had tah settle for dis spot. Reckon somebody be gonna come and chase us from here too, or do us all in."

Aden stayed for three days hoping that someone would remember one shred of information that would help him in his quest. It was Hobart that came to his rescue. As Aden packed his things into his saddlebags preparing to leave, Hobart said he recalled that the man who drove the wagons and took the slaves away was named Moses Brickel. "I be tryin' tah 'member all dis time. Dat be dat bastard, Moses Brickel. He be a slave mover. He come and takes dah people from place ta place. Dat day when Mizz Miller sold off dah rest of her slaves, he come wid his wagons. He needed three, but only gots two. He pushed dem poor people into dem wagons 'til dey hardly had room ta sit. Your grandma was one of dem dat went dat day. I be sorry ta say dat yer grandpa, Marcus, passed yars back. Essie she be all alone 'til she met Keel Backer. He took care of her and deh got married. I be thinkin' maybe her name on dat list is Backer, not Woods."

A glimmer of hope returned to Aden. She could still be alive.

As he prepared to leave, the small cluster of people watched him. "I will make a promise to you. After I find my grandmother I will come back and get you. All of you. We will find a place for you to live. It may take a while, but if I return to this spot and you are still here, I will keep my word."

One of the older women came forward and kissed his hands. "Thank you. We be waitin' right here. May da good Lord make yer trip fast and safe."

Another month passed before Aden located Moses Brickel who was now living in Pascagoula, Mississippi. Moses had stopped his overland transport business when the war started and was now running a ferry across the Singing River. Locating him was not that difficult. Moses had a reputation that seemed to follow him wherever he traveled. He had more enemies than friends.

Aden hoped there was a slim chance that Moses Brickel had a good memory. As it turned out for the right price, the rotund Moses could remember almost anything.

Moses Brickel agreed to meet with Aden at a local tavern. Moses leaned forward as the two met, looking into Aden's eyes. "Don't think I kin recall you, but maybe you give me a few hints and I might bring it back." He spat his wad of chewing tobacco on to the floor.

"It's not me I want you to remember, Mr. Brickel. I am trying to locate a woman named Essie Backer. She was a slave that lived on the Miller Plantation on the far side of Biloxi. I understand that when Mrs. Miller sold the place she hired you to transport the slaves to their new locations. Essie was part of the kitchen staff. She would have been around fifty years old at that time."

Moses took a big gulp of his beer, wiping the foam off his mouth with the back of his hand. "Now, you ain't serious are you? That was over ten, maybe twelve years ago. I ain't got that good of a memory."

"Did you keep any records?"

"Course not. Keeping records only gets you in trouble."

Aden put a five-dollar bill on the table. "I want you to think real hard, Mr. Brickle."

Moses scratched his head. Pulling out a soiled pad of paper and a stub of a pencil, he began to put dates and marks on the pad. "I tried to make about four runs a year. Depending on the weather, you see. You say I had two wagons full of niggahs on that trip? Hmm...only did a couple of runs like that. I had to be in New Orleans in the spring of fifty-nine, so it was before that time. Hmm, let me see. Pass Christian... ain't that up near Lott's Point? Yeah, sure it is." He answered his own question. "I never cottoned to taking big groups of niggahs. I was always afraid they would run off and then I wouldn't get paid. Worse, you could get your throat slit by one of them gollywobs. When I took more than one wagon I had to hire extra guards. Why you so interested in this woman?"

Aden laid another five on the table without answering his question.

"Yeah, I remember now. I took two-wagons full from Mrs. Miller to a house called Myrtle Gardens in Gulf Port. Yeah, I remember. I remember because that old lady, Miller, she tried to short me. We had a big argument. I betcha half them coloreds are no longer in Gulf Port. Hell, after the war, they spread out all over. Got em coming down here right and left."

Aden got up and left the table while Moses was still talking. He wasn't interested in any more rhetoric from this illiterate bastard who made his living destroying people's lives.

Chapter Fifty

Myrtle Gardens was the home of Royal Herbert. The structure was a large white mansion that took up almost an entire block in Gulf Port. It had escaped the wrath of the war with minimal damage. The house had a familiar air to it, reminding Aden of the home where he lived in Charlestown. Aden had rented a carriage before going to Myrtle Gardens. He did not want to arrive with all of his belongings packed in bundles and tied to the horse. He was nervous. He had no idea what to expect since all of the slaves had been set free. The idea that his grandmother was alive or even still living at Myrtle Gardens was one of wishful thinking.

Walking up a path lined with red, crepe myrtles, Aden took a deep breath. He spotted an older man trimming shrubbery in the side lawn. Jumping over the runner of flowers, Aden approached him. "Excuse me, but I was wondering if I could ask you a question?"

"What ya need?" the man asked.

"I wanted to know if you know a woman named Essie Woods... or it may be Essie Backer. I was told that she lived here once."

A broad grin covered the man's face. "My sweet Essie, yes, she sure be here. She be in dah kitchen right now."

The words echoed in Aden's ears. The man said she was here. She was in the kitchen. He must have heard wrong. "Her name is Essie," Aden repeated.

"Yes suh, I be hearin' ya the furst time. Essie be in dah kitchen."

"Can you take me to her? It is very important," Aden said in a shaky voice.

The man pointed to a walkway that circled around to the back of the house. Aden felt as if he was walking in slow motion, each footstep thundering in his ears. He entered the stone outdoor kitchen building.

With her back to the door, a small woman stood at the kitchen table coring apples. Her hair was the color of spun silver and her hands were twisted from years of hard work. She must have sensed someone's presence. Turning around slowly, she stared at him.

"Grandmother," Aden said. "It's me, Aden."

The knife clattered to the floor; as the old woman almost dropped to her knees. Aden reached her before her legs buckled. Burying her head in his chest, she did not speak.

"Grandmother, let me look at you. It has been so long," Aden said, now holding her at arms length. He looked into her lined face and stroked her hair. "I cannot believe I found you."

"Aden, it be you! I kin tell. Dis be a mircle. I be prayin' to dah Lawd all des yars that ya still be alive. And here ya is. Let me look at you. Ya be a handsome man, my Aden." She hugged him again.

"Can we go somewhere and talk?" he asked.

Sitting under a shade tree, Aden began to talk. How do you catch up on twenty-two lost years? How can you explain all that has happened? How do you explain to your grandmother, a direct descendant from Africa, that you have now been accepted into the white man's world and that you have hidden your Negro heritage for many years?

"I have so much to tell you," Aden said. "But, first let me ask you some questions. Who is this man that calls you his sweet Essie?"

Essie gave a shy grin. "He be my husband, Aden. His name be Keel and he be a real good man. We be together for ovah ten yars now. Marcus, he died when I still be at Mizz Millers. When I come here, I met Keel. He takes real good care of me."

"How do they treat you here, grandmother?"

"I'd be fine. Massa Herbert, he be a real nice man, but my age is startin' to catch up. It be real hard for me sometime. I get it in dah back. Dem pots kin be real heavy. Keel, he be having some feet problem. Massa Royal he takes good care of us, but we jest be getting old, Aden." Essie paused for a moment, "You talk reel diffant now, ya been to school?"

"Yes, I have." He began to tell his grandmother what had happened to him. "When I left you, I was sad for many years and then..."

She listened quietly, sometimes nodding, but all the while holding on to him. He told her about his years with Will and how he became a free man. Somehow it was impossible to tell her about his years living in the white world. He wanted to, but looking into the weathered face of his grandmother, he knew telling that her truth would break her heart. He simply told her that Mr. and Mrs. Bolt had allowed him to be educated and after they freed him he went to work in the shipbuilding industry and had managed to make a lot of money. He told her she now had a great-grandson and someday he hoped they would meet.

"So, now that I am here, I would like to take you and Keel with me. I have some people I have to relocate. I promised I would come back for them. They are a small group of freed men, still living near Pass Christian. Maybe you can all decide what you would like to do. I want to buy you a house and a rocking chair and take care of you. No more cooking for you, grandmother. We will hire someone to take care of it."

Essie let out a loud laugh. "I swear Aden, dat don't even sound real, but me and Keel, we be too old to go on some place new. My heart it be thumpin in my chest and my eyes are real bad. Massa Herbert's doctor, he check me ovah and he be saying my heart is real bad. He tells me tah take it easy all dah time."

"Then I will stay with you. I am never going to leave your side again." He was leaving loose ends everywhere, his son in Tahiti and Ben with his group somewhere near Pass Christian, but right now, his grandmother was the most important person in his life.

Just eight short weeks after Aden arrived at Myrtle Gardens, Essie took a turn for the worse. The rattle in her chest was audible across the room. Taking deep breaths would send her into fits of coughing. Aden was able to locate a doctor who gave him medication for Essie. Keel administered the dosage, but after a few days Essie refused to take it. "Ain't no need fer ya ta be pushin dat into me. I gonna be gone real soon."

Aden stayed by her bed day and night watching her fading away. On her last day, she took his hand and rubbed it on her cheek. "Ain't no call fer ya tah be sad. Ya being here makes my passin' easy. Jest take me outside and let me feel dah sunshine on my face one more time." Essie died later that afternoon.

Aden cried that day for the first time in many years. He helped Keel dig the grave inside the rim of the Herbert cemetery. Carrying the wooden coffin containing her small body up the hill was effortless. Aden covered her grave with wildflowers he had gathered that morning and then he cried. This little woman from Africa was put to rest in the country that had taken her freedom, her daughter, and her grandson from her. He hoped she would rest in peace.

Chapter Fifty-One

Aden bought a wagon and two horses in Gulf Port. Once he had loaded it with supplies, he started the long trip to Pass Christian. He tried to convince Keel to come with him to no avail. Keel said he wanted to stay behind and keep the weeds away from Essie's grave.

Aden worried about making the trip down the narrow roads that were fraught with danger. The weather had turned cold and rainy. He hoped that it would help keep the marauders away from the muddy roads pocked with holes that could cripple a horse with one misstep.

When Aden arrived at the last camp where he saw Ben and his group, the collection of ex-slaves were nowhere to be found. Remnants of fire pits still remained, but the trampled ground was barren. He walked down to the river but saw no signs of anyone living in the area.

"Dammit!" he said to himself. Getting back into the wagon, he veered onto the road. He hadn't gone more than a few miles when he spotted someone darting into the bushes.

Aden stopped the wagon and stood up on the seat. Cupping his hands around his mouth, he yelled, "Ben? Ben, can you hear me?" He waited a moment, and then Ben emerged from the thicket. Ben waved his hands over his head. Aden let out a sigh of relief realizing the chance he had taken. It could have been a group of renegades waiting to ambush him.

"Over here, Mistah Aden! We be over here!" Before Aden could reach Ben, the road was filled with the people that he had met before. They smiled and waved and some cried out loud, "Praise the Lawd, he come back for us."

"We be watchin' for ya. We had ta move agin. It be getting too dangerous by dat river. We found a cave. We has been safe here, for now, anyways. Come sit by dah fire, Aden."

Since Aden had left, Ben's clan had acquired eight new

people, a young man and woman with six small children that they found hungry and afraid on the road. "They be in bad shape," Ben said. "Real bad shape. We ain't got much, but I ain't gonna watch dem chillin starve."

Aden unloaded the blankets and food he had bought in Biloxi and carried it into the camp built at the edge of the cave. Even though they were hungry and cold, everyone waited their turn in line to receive their rations. Wrapping the blankets around their children, the women huddled together under the covers, thankful for the warmth. Cans of beans were opened and overflowed into the only pot left in camp. A man named Hobart spread a paper on the ground and laid out the cheese and apples Aden had brought with him. "It be plain crazy, Aden. First dey shoots us if we runs off, now dey shoot us if we try to come back. It makes no sense at all."

After everyone had eaten and the children were put to bed, the adults gathered around the fire waiting to hear what Aden had to say.

Ben stood up and bowed his head. "We want ta thank ya, Mr. Aden. You said ya be coming back for us and ya did. Ya kept yer promise. Ain't enough words to thank ya for yer kindness."

Aden wondered how he had suddenly become in charge of this group of homeless people. He remembered the overwhelming feeling he had just taking care of Lukas. Now he had twenty-one people in his charge.

"Tomorrow we'll leave this place," Aden said. "We'll find somewhere to buy more provisions and a place to stop for the winter. We must stay together. The roads are dangerous. The women will travel in the wagon and those men that are able, will walk along side. The wagon will hold ten." He could see the look of fear in their eyes at the prospect of traveling on the open road, but it had to be done. Winter was closing in on them.

That evening as Aden lay on a pallet, Ben came over and sat next to him. "Ya savin' des people, it be a kind thing. Ya barely know dem. Ya be a good man, Aden Woods."

"Don't make me out to be a hero, Ben. I'm not. This all happened by accident and I just wanted to do the decent thing. Let's pray that it all turns out for the best. I was gone so long that I worried you might have given up on me."

"Ya be our only hope, Massa Aden, and ya done us proud."

Three days and two long nights spent traveling brought the

group safely to the ocean's boundary and a town called Lott's Point. The strong winds from the impending storm had moved into the Point and the rain would soon follow. Aden thought it best if everyone waited on the edge of town while he made sure that there were no marauders or renegades waiting on the road to ambush them.

Two wide streets cornered around a meeting square that comprised the center of the town. Stores and liveries stood side by side in what seemed to be a thriving community. The town seemed to be recovering nicely from the war and looked to be quite peaceful. With a sigh of relief, Aden dismounted his horse in front of August Lott's General Merchandise Store.

Aden walked up to the counter and asked to speak to the proprietor. The young man working behind the counter disappeared into a small office and returned with an older man wearing an ill-fitting hairpiece. Adjusting his glasses, the man peered over the top of them. "Yes, I am the owner of this store. What can I do for you?"

Aden extended his hand, which the man did not acknowledge. "My name is Aden Woods and I am escorting a group of people through your town and they are in dire need of supplies. They need clothing, shoes, food, tools, bedding, and much more. Would you be able to accommodate them?"

August Lott's eyes narrowed. "Who are these people and where are they?"

"They are waiting just outside of town for me," Aden replied.

"So, what is the big secret? You some kind of minister?" August inquired.

"No. These are colored folks and they need help."

August slapped his hand down on the counter. "I knew it. I knew you were up to something. I don't serve niggahs in this store and we don't need any more niggahs in this town. So you take yourself and them right on down the road."

"I have money to pay for everything they need. If you want to turn away a large sum of money, that is your prerogative, but I assure you, I intended to spend quite a bit." Aden turned to leave.

August came out from behind the counter and caught up with Aden. Tapping him on the shoulder, he said, "Now I am not above helping people if they really need it bad. Since business is not the best right now, I will allow them to buy from me this one time. I warn you though if they so much as take one thing that is not paid for I will have the sheriff after you. He does not take kindly to thieves or coloreds." August looked at his watch. "I'll be closing in thirty minutes. You come back then. Come 'round back and I'll open the door for you."

It was almost dark when Aden and the others descended on August Lott's store. To most of them, it was their first time in a real store. They wandered around in amazement, taking in everything. August's voice boomed across the room. "Don't be touching anything you are not going to buy. Keep your hands to yourself."

While Ben's wife, Dulcie, helped the other women find sweaters and shoes, Aden and Ben piled the counter high with supplies. Clearing the shelves of tea, coffee, sugar, and flour, they packed the bags on their shoulders and carried them outside. As August added up each item, the men carried hammers, saws, and buckets of nails to the wagon. With each person carrying a small bag of sweets, August yelled for Aden. "Look, this bill is getting very high! I need to see some money before you take another thing from my store."

Aden reached into his pocket and produced a roll of bills. "I think we still have a ways to go."

The trip to August Lott's store was an overwhelming experience for everyone and as the children sat in the wagon sucking on their first candy stick, Aden paid the bill. He owed August Lott almost two hundred dollars, which he carefully counted out and laid on the counter. "I do believe that takes care of everything. Thank you, Mr. Lott," Aden said, as August scooped up the money and recounted it.

Aden realized that his next task would be even more difficult. Cold sheets of rain had begun to fall and Calla, the young pregnant girl, was complaining of cramps in her stomach. One of the women said she was probably getting ready to deliver. They had to find somewhere to spend the night. Less than a mile out of town, Aden saw lamps shining in the windows of a large house. With the men following behind, Aden pulled the wagon into the driveway. He hoped that whoever lived here would be hospitable enough to let them spend the night in the sheds.

Leaving the wagon in the driveway, Aden walked onto the porch. He raised the heavy brass doorknocker and let it drop. A small black woman who opened the door frowned at him. "You need be goin' tah the back. You men ain't suppose tah use this door. Besides what ya doin' out in this weather?"

"Excuse me. I was not expected. I am here to ask the owner of the property if it would be possible for my fellow travelers and I to stay in your stable tonight. You see it is getting ready to storm and I have women and children with me," Aden said, pointing to the wagon.

The woman stepped out onto the porch, shivering from the cold air. "Lawdy be. You need tah get dem little ones out of dah weather. Ya go on back. Dey be a few lanterns back der. I'll tell the Mizzes dah ya be back der. Now go on."

"Thank you, thank you very much. May I inquire as to the name of this place?"

"It be called Magnolia. It be the home of Hallie Simmons," Nona said.

And now the rest of the story

Part Seven: Magnolia

They reached their destination after completing the trip from Vine Manor to Magnolia. Hallie, Mary, Lydia, Jasper, Nona, Asia, and the young black girl found in the field had faced the perils of an uncharted journey and arrived safely, but sadly without James.

After getting down from the wagon twice to remove tree limbs from the road, Jasper pulled the horses to a stop in front of the house. A glimmer of moonlight kept his footsteps steady as he shuffled along the porch and opened the door. Stepping into the foyer, Jasper struck a match to the lantern he carried, the yellow glow from the flame shown through the window. One by one, the weary travelers left the wagon and moved their fatigued bodies up the stairs and into the house called Magnolia.

Chapter Fifty-Two

Mary helped her mother climb down from the wagon while Lydia and Nona attended to Mandy. "Lawdy, we has a roof ovah our heads," Nona said. "Let's rest our bones. We kin talk in dah morn'."

Placing pallets on the floor of the parlor, everyone settled in. It was Mary who broke the silence. "I am going to say a prayer to the Lord for our safety." She gathered her skirt around her and knelt down. "Dear Lord, thank you for bringing us to Magnolia without harm. Thank you for letting us find Mandy alive and thank you for keeping us out of harm's way. And please Lord, welcome our dear father into your arms. I know he is in heaven with you, now. Please take care of him. We miss him terribly. Amen."

"Mary stop!" Hallie screamed. "Why don't you tell the Lord how much I hate him right now for what he has done to our family? He has taken away my husband and left us with nothing but ruin and sadness for no good reason. Ask him why he let thousands of men die in a senseless war. Why don't you thank him for that, Mary?" Hallie spewed.

"Dear Lord, if you are still listening, please forgive my mother. She is suffering so much grief, but she doesn't mean a word she said. Amen. There, mother, that should take care of your blasphemy," Mary said, getting up from her kneeling position.

The room was silent except for the quiet breathing and slight snoring of those suffering from days spent in the wagon with only fear and sadness as companions. After Hallie's outburst, no one wanted to speak.

As everyone drifted off, Hallie stared into the darkness, wondering why she was here. She wanted to die. She wanted to close her eyes and never wake up. Magnolia would just be another reminder of the times she spent with James. This was a house that was always filled with love and laughter. They had spent their honeymoon here, falling deeper in love. When the children were small, they would come to Magnolia for the summer. The four of them had water fights in the summer kitchen and tried to see who could sing the loudest when Hallie played the piano. Jasper would catch fresh seafood and they would all sit around the fire on the beach and eat shrimp and Nona's fried okra and cornbread. At night she would lay in her husband's arms while the cool breezes from the ocean wafted into their upstairs bedroom window.

Now she must endure each day alone since he had been stolen from her life. That didn't even seem possible. Everything she knew to be real and true was over. She had waited five long years for her life to return to normal and now she was a widow with two children and all she wanted to do was die.

Sometime during the night, her mind gave way to blessed sleep, which gave her a few hours of peace. She woke in the morning to an unfamiliar smell. Nona came into the parlor with a grin covering her creased face. "Get up, I gots a surprise for all of ya. Lookee here. I gots fried batter bread, fresh from dah fire. Ya all come and git it." Nona set the wooden plank covered with thin crisp cakes in the middle of the floor. Asia scrambled across the floor and picked up one of the brown-edged biscuits. "Lawd, Lawd, Nona ya be a savior. I be starving." He flipped the cake from hand to hand, trying to quickly cool it.

"Whar ya be getting the flour and grease for dem cakes?" Jasper asked, anticipating the taste of something other than stale biscuits.

"I gots up real early. I be diggin around in dah kitchen and der it was, a half sack of flour. Somebody plumb fergit it," Nona said. "And den I find a covered pot stuffed plumb full of lard. It be a blessin'." *Should she tell them that she spent the last hour picking weevils from the bag and pushing away the sticky clumps that had turned mossy green or that the lard she found was already a dark shade of brown? Surely the hot fire had killed anything that was living in the bag or breeding in the lard.*

"What does the house look like, Nona?" Lydia asked as she munched on her cake. "Is it very bad?"

"Not near as bad as I spected. Dar is somes furniture left and da walls ain't too bad. Jasper be gonna checkin' dah rest afta we done eatin'."

After finishing half her cake, Hallie slowly rose from where she had been sitting in the corner of the room. Brushing off her dress, she carefully stepped over those still sitting on the floor and entered the foyer. Looking up the stairs, she wondered if she had enough strength to make it to the second floor. Hallie's fingers closed around the banister as she slowly crept up each step. The sun shone through the casement window at the far end of the hallway, throwing rays of light onto the soiled carpet. Ghostly squares outlined on the tapestry wallpaper were a reminder of the portraits that once hung on the walls. Running her hand along the wainscot, Hallie hesitated before entering the room she once shared with James. The Coventry bed that James had made especially for the room still remained. Its massive frame attached to the ceiling must have been too cumbersome for anyone to consider moving. Holding onto the bedpost, Hallie's body shook as a flood of painful memories coursed through her body. Even though the fine eider mattresses had been removed, Hallie crawled onto the wooden bed boards and lay down.

Later that morning, Jasper's report gave a new ray of hope to Lydia and Mary. "Da roof, it be real sound and da house, too. We still gots all but a few of da winnows. Da house needs paintin real bad cause it's got a bad case of da green mold, but dat ain't no problem. Sums of da shutters be gone and course we gots to clear out all da weeds and brush before we can git close enuf to da house ta fix it." He smiled a toothless grin, happy to report something good for a change.

"That is so good to hear," Mary said. "We will have to go to town today and get some supplies and then decide what we should do next."

"When Mandy gets betta, we be startin' on the cleanin'," Nona added, eagerly. "Yes, we be cleanin' real good and start cookin' in da kitchen agin."

No one had noticed that Hallie was standing in the doorway. "And what do you plan on using for money?" Hallie asked. "I have twenty-seven dollars to my name. Do any of you have money?"

It was Jasper who answered her. Hallie's question about money jogged his memory. "You jest wait right dar, Mizz Hallie. I be right back." Jasper trotted out of the room and was only gone for a few minutes. He returned carrying the burlap bag that had made the trip from Vine Manor under his feet in the wagon. Dumping the contents from the clay encrusted bag on the floor, a muddy jar rolled out.

"Oh my goodness! Mother look!" Mary shouted, as she rubbed the dirt away from the glass jar. "Look! It's filled with money. I think they are gold coins!" She wrestled with the cumbersome lid until she was able to pry it off. Mary was right. The jar was filled with gold dollars. "There must be thousands of dollars in here," she added.

"Yer daddy, he be fillin' dem jars all dah time. Each time we goes ta da cave he put coins in da jar. Den right before he left for da war, we buried dem jars in da back of da cave. He told me dat I should remember dem if he didn't come home. I don forgot about dat bag until we almost left Vine Manor wid'out it. Lawd, I sure be glad I remembered," Jasper said as he gathered up the muddy bag and took it outside.

"Did James leave us a letter?" Hallie asked. Mary shook her head. "No, mother, that is all that is in this jar." Hallie turned and left the room not waiting to hear about how much money was in the jar, nor caring.

With Lydia sitting beside her in the wagon, Mary watched the changing landscape as Jasper guided the horses down the road to Lott's Point. New houses and stores replaced the remains left by the war and the rutted roads had been repaired. Mary was not sure if the streets had narrowed or if it was the crowd of people and carriages that made it seem so. She remembered them to be much wider. A cluster of shops had sprung up on Main Street, and the harbor was crowded with ships bearing marks of many different countries. Life had returned to Lott's Point with only one purpose in mind: money. The carpetbaggers and investors from the north and other countries had swooped down on the south like a hawk on the trail of an injured rabbit. Making impossible deals was their strong suit. Southerners with empty pockets sold off the last of their possessions for pennies on the dollar. The once rich plantation owners were getting poorer and the new intruders from the north were getting richer, along with August Lott, who seemed to be in control of the entire circus.

As Lydia and Mary entered the store, Hilda Lott stood at her position behind the mahogany counter that controlled the flow of traffic through one of the most complete general stores west of the Mississippi. Hilda could watch both ends of the store without turning her head and could sense a stolen candy cane in a child's pocket before it had time to turn sticky. She and August stocked their store with everything from the smallest embroidery needle to an iron harvester, which took two men to lift. They were shrewd businesspeople who had sold out of both the front and back doors during the war to make sure they kept their business from suffering.

A visit to the Lott's General Store was a bittersweet experience for most. Small children stared at porcelain dolls that they could never touch as their mothers ran their hand over the bolts of smooth, green silk. Whether it was the smell of oiled rawhide or the pungent aroma of white oleander talcum, August Lott had a way of tempting you into a purchase you could not afford.

August and Hilda Lott were best friends to all that entered their store until it came to anything to do with money and then even Beelzebub ran for cover. On this day they would have the first of many dealings with the Simmons women.

"I do declare! I just can't believe my eyes," Hilda Lott gasped as Mary and Lydia came down the aisle. " It is the Simmons girls. Look at the both of you, all grown up and right here in my store." Coming from behind the counter her flapping arms wrapped around Lydia and Mary. "When did you get here? Where are your parents? August, come quick! You won't believe who is here," she shouted without taking a breath.

August Lott stepped down from his caged loft, where he was working on his books, and removed his glasses. He forced a smile. "Mary Elizabeth and Lydia, how good to see you. And your parents, how are they? When did you arrive in Lott's Point?"

"We arrived here last night. I'm sorry to say that my father has been killed, but my mother is at Magnolia," Lydia answered.

Hilda put both her hands on her face. "Terrible, just terrible. Your poor mother, you tell her how sorry we are to hear such sad news." August stood behind Hilda, shaking his head. "How did it happen?"

"Well, you see, he had come home and—" Lydia said.

Mary interrupted Lydia's sentence. "It was the war, that dreadful war. He died from the wounds he received in battle." Mary took Lydia's arm, "Come now, we need to shop." After too much talk to suit Mary, she was finally able to tell August the reason for her visit to the store. "We need supplies, Mr. Lott. We will need all kinds of things, but today I just want to get some food and cooking supplies. We will have to compile a complete list and come again another time."

Mary filed through the aisles, picking up items and placing them on the counter. Hilda wrote each purchase on a piece of paper and put them in a box. When Lydia laid a blue cotton dress in front of her, Hilda smiled. "Please, Lydia, this is not a dress for you. I have some much nicer ones in the back of the store. I have to keep them away from dirty fingers."

"Oh, it's not for me. It's for Mandy. She has nothing to wear."

"And who is Mandy?" Hilda asked.

"She is this girl we found in the field and—" Before she could finish her sentence, Mary once again moved in front of her.

"She is one of our servants, Mrs. Lott. She tore her dress on the way here."

"I see, Mary, and how many of them are with you at Magnolia?" Hilda inquired.

"We have four Negro servants with us. Is that a problem, Mrs. Lott?"

"Of course not, dear. It is just that we are trying to keep the Negro presence in Lott's Point to a minimum. I'm sure you understand. They are quite belligerent and unruly now that they are free." Hilda returned to Mary's purchases.

While Hilda added up the totals, Mary addressed August. "I have a letter here I wish to send to the Dugan Storage Facility in Ohio. I would like to see if they would ship our things to us as soon as possible. It would make our life a lot easier."

August scanned the document. "Of course, Mary. I'll take care of it today. I suppose that means that your family is planning on staying for a while. I thought perhaps your mother would like to rid herself of the burden of Magnolia. Once again, I am sorry for your loss. Your total for today is eighty-two dollars."

Mary produced five gold pieces from her purse and laid them on the counter. August scooped them up and placed them on his register. "Very good choice, using gold, Mary. Very good." He handed her eighteen dollars in change. As the girls left the store, August opened his cash drawer and stared at the gold pieces. He wondered where they came from and how many they had. He should have known that once again the Vine family would not be ready to sell Magnolia.

Once the wagon was loaded, Mary and Lydia climbed aboard. "Mary Elizabeth Simmons, can you tell me why you interrupted me—not once but twice—when I was trying to talk to Mr. Lott? That was very rude."

"Mr. Lott need not know our business, Lydia. If mother wishes him to know, she can tell him. It is not our place. You know that Grandfather Vine was never particularly fond of Mr. Lott. He told father to be wary of him. Keep your thoughts to yourself, Lydia. It will make things easier to deal with," Mary said sharply.

Chapter Fifty-Three

With each new day of sunshine and nourishing food the inhabitants of Magnolia began to shed their armor. While Jasper and Asia worked to clear the yard, the women spent their days cleaning the inside of the house. Mandy had fully recovered from her ordeal and much to the dismay of Nona, Mandy was a constant chatterbox. At times Nona would have to tell her to hush. Even Lydia, who hated menial work, was not averse to cleaning walls and floors. Everyone seemed eager to have their life back in some semblance of order, everyone except Hallie. Aside from attending to her personal needs or getting a bite of food, she spent her days lying in bed. No matter how much they tried, Mary and Lydia could not console her.

Today it was Nona's turn. Hallie walked into the kitchen and picked up an apple off of the table. Sitting down at the table, she began to nibble on the peel. "Well, Lawdy be, look whose come down tah join us," Nona said, wiping her hands on a cloth. "Ya gots tah settle dis thing with yerself, Mizz Hallie. Dem girls need ya. Ya be keepin' tah yerself too long."

"Leave me alone, Nona. I am not in the mood for one of your lectures. Can't you see I am still grieving?"

"Yes'em, I kin, but ya can grieve jest as well wid a scrub brush in yer hand."

"Stop it! I hate you Nona. I just want to die."

"Thad be fine by me. I'll jest get a bucket of water and ya kin end it right now. Would that be suitin' ya?" Nona said.

"Oh, Nona, you know my head won't fit in a bucket,"

Nona covered her mouth to keep from laughing. "Dat be my Mizz Hallie." She put her arms around Hallie. "We is gonna make it, baby girl. One way or tuther we is gonna honor Massa James memory and make him proud."

"I hope so, Nona. I surely hope so."

The following week, Hallie received a messenger from August

Lott saying that he needed to see her on an urgent matter. Accompanied by Mary, Hallie made her first trip into Lott's Point without her husband by her side.

Hilda greeted Hallie with the same enthusiasm that her girls had met with the week before. The Lotts expressed their grief over the loss of James and once more Hilda pried as to how it had happened, and once more Mary diverted her attention. "I do believe you said you wanted to see my mother on an urgent matter. We don't wish to keep you from your business."

"Yes, of course," August replied. "Please come up to my office." Mary and Hallie followed him up the narrow step. "Now, Hallie I hate to distress you at a time like this, but there are certain business matters that I am trying to clear. This is a matter I would have been discussing with your husband if he were still alive. One of my duties as County Clerk is to collect the back taxes on the properties in this area." Rifling through a stack of papers, August produced a large document and laid it in front of Hallie. "Many of the property owners in this area were unable to pay their taxes during the war and we fully understood, but now the government is anxious to collect the monies due. The taxes on Magnolia have not been paid for over five years. I am afraid you owe a considerable sum. The amount is right here," he said, pointing to the bold print that jumped off the page. $2210.11 was the amount. "The taxes are very much past due and must be paid quickly, Mrs. Simmons."

"Oh, my goodness, I had no idea. James always took care of these matters. I am afraid I am a little short right now, Mr. Lott. My husband was in charge of all our assets. We also need to settle on the property at Vine Manor. I am expecting our possessions to arrive from the storage company in Ohio any day. I am sure there are quite a lot of things that we won't be able to use at Magnolia that we can sell to raise the money."

August stared at her while she was talking. He remembered the young girl with sparkling eyes and a quick smile that he admired. She had lost the bloom of her youth. It had been replaced with a more mature look, but she was still a beautiful woman. "Not to worry, Hallie. I can give you at least a month to settle this bill. You know I have always been interested in the property at Magnolia. If you ever wish to sell, I would be glad to take it off your hands."

Mary rose from her chair. "It seems very strange to me, Mr.

Lott, that my father didn't pay the taxes. In one of his letters to my mother he told her he had paid the taxes on Vine Manor. I wonder why he wouldn't have paid both. He was very meticulous in his business matters," Mary said.

August's jaw tightened. "I do not know, Mary. All I know is they are due and I am responsible for collecting them. I will be more than happy to buy Magnolia and pay the taxes. With the profit from the sale I am sure your family could find accommodations that would be less expensive and easier to care for."

Hallie stood up. "Thank you, but I cannot sell my home. Thank you, August, for allowing us time to pay the bill. I assure you it will be soon."

Hallie stepped outside of the store and put on her gloves. "Why did you question him, Mary? That was somewhat embarrassing."

"Because I do not trust him, mother. I never have. Mr. Lott overcharges for his merchandise. And how is it he kept his store stocked when everyone else is suffering? I do believe he would sell his own family for money. I hate the way he always brings up the fact that he wants to buy our house. Perhaps he thinks if we are out of money, we will strike a deal with him."

Hallie put her hand on Mary's cheek. "You are so much like your grandfather. I'm glad for that."

Chapter Fifty-Four

When the wagons filled with their belongings arrived from Ohio it was like Christmas for the Simmons family. There were oohs and aahs as each item was unpacked. Nona found her copper pots, which she held to her chest and when Lydia opened her box of lace gloves, she screamed with delight. There were tears when the family pictures were opened and Hallie once again looked into the face of her beloved husband. It was Mary who seemed the most intense. She scanned the drawers of her father's desk as it was put into the library. She leafed through stacks of books before they were put on the shelves. When she found the deeds to Magnolia and Vine Manor in a leather bound case she was excited. Dumping the contents on the floor, she searched frantically but did not find what she was looking for. Where was her father's investment portfolio? He was much too meticulous to have overlooked giving his family some clue as to where he had invested his money.

When Hallie announced that they needed to sell some of the items, Lydia let out a shriek. "No! These are our things. Please, mother, don't sell them."

"I don't intend to sell them all, Lydia, but we must sell enough to pay our tax bill if we want to keep our home. Besides, we need a proper carriage and another horse. Until our finances are repaired we have to have money to live on."

After some deliberation, Hallie decided to part with the heavy wool rugs that looked out of place in Magnolia. She also put aside a set of gold-rimmed china, service for thirty, which she decided she did not need. Those items alone should more than pay the tax bill. With some of their possessions once again loaded into the buckboard, Hallie and Mary headed for Lott's Point.

As August Lott scrutinized each item in the wagon he made notations on a pad of paper. "Well, Mrs. Simmons, you do have some lovely things that should fetch a good price in my store. I am willing to give you one-thousand dollars for the lot."

"Surely, August, you must be kidding. One of the Aubusson rugs is worth that much alone. I was expecting a great deal more," Hallie replied.

"Well, now, you know, I have to make a profit, too. That is what we call business, Mrs. Simmons." The irritation was evident in August's voice. He was not used to being challenged, especially not by a woman.

"Then I think we shall take our business elsewhere. Thank you for your time," Hallie said as she climbed back into the wagon and instructed Jasper to move the horses forward. August was left standing on the sidewalk, empty-handed.

"Where are we going, mother?" Mary asked. "There isn't another store in this direction."

"I know that, Mary. We are going to the docks." Mary's only answer was a surprised look.

It was an uncommon scene to see two women with open parasols in a buckboard riding down the road to the crowded piers. "There, Jasper, over there. Stop the wagon," Hallie said. Standing up, Hallie waved her hand over her head to the men unloading cargo from a Greek Steamer. "I have some lovely items for sale, if you are interested. All in good condition and at good prices," she called out. Two of the men standing on the bridge of the ship looked at each other in surprise. Before long she had attracted a crowd and within an hour she had sold everything in the wagon for three times as much as August Lott had offered her.

"My goodness, mother, I can't believe what just happened. I am awed at your tenacity. You have done the impossible again. Where did you find the strength to do what you just did?"

"It was because of you, Mary, that we made it safely to Magnolia. We could have all been killed if it hadn't been for your quick thinking. Lydia helped to save Mandy's life and since we have been at Magnolia all of you have worked very hard. It is time for me to take charge of my family again and repay them for everything they have done. Let us go back to town and give August his money and be done with him."

"We now know where to buy and sell wares a lot cheaper," Mary said as she held the stack of money on her lap. Next time we need to bring cloths to cover our faces. I smell like a fish monger."

The second trip to Lott's general store left Mary and Hallie laughing. August was not at all happy when he found out what they had done as he stamped their tax bill, *paid in full*. The news had spread quickly through the main streets of Lott's Point about the two women selling wares at the pier. Before they were out of town, several people approached Hallie and Mary wanting to know if they had anything else to sell.

When the money from the jar was depleted, Hallie pulled out the steel box that held the remainder of the funds from the sale at the pier. She could not believe how quickly the money seemed to be funneling out of the house. A new carriage and horse took a large amount, along with clothing and additional furniture purchases for the house.

Calling Mary and Lydia into the parlor, Hallie made an announcement. "I have met with Mr. Fells at the Barrister's Office and he has agreed to arrange for the sale of the property at Vine Manor. We must do it quickly since the government is confiscating property that they consider abandoned and there are also squatters living on many of the plantations. I know we will only receive a pittance for the acreage but I suppose that is better than nothing. Since we have been unable to find your father's financial records, we must deal with the problems at hand. I am considering renting out the rooms on the third floor for additional funds. It would surely help to have a steady income," Hallie said, looking at the faces of her daughters.

"Are we poor again, mother?" Lydia asked.

"No dear. As long as have food and a roof over our head, we will be fine. But right now we are using up all of our available funds with no prospect of any more coming in for quite a while. It would just be nice to have a cushion to rely on," Hallie replied.

"I agree," said Mary. "It would be the most sensible thing to do. There are six bedrooms up there that are just standing vacant. We might as well put them to good use."

"But, what will the people in town think of us if we become landlords in our own home?" Lydia asked in a pouting manner.

Hallie responded, "I cannot worry about that right now, Lydia. I must worry about keeping a roof over our head and food on the table. If that makes us seem poor, so be it."

Hallie was uncomfortable with the conversation and the idea of taking in borders, but she knew too well that her funds were depleting rapidly and that her bills were mounting. Perhaps the suggestion wasn't really that unreasonable. Everyone in the south had suffered from the war and no one seemed surprised at the changes taking place in the lives of those that once were society's elite. She had heard from some of the shopkeepers in town that the boarding houses were filled to capacity and there was a dire need for housing.

Although Magnolia had three floors and many rooms, it was still considered a small house next to the grandeur of the antebellum home that once stood at Vine Manor, the house that she had burned to the ground. The third floor of Magnolia was once used as living quarters for the house slaves that took care of the inside of the house and a day room for the children. Now those rooms stood empty. It would probably take most of the money that remained to properly furnish the rooms suitably enough for renters. And so with renewed energy, everyone in the house channeled their efforts into the third floor.

Within a month the rooms were complete. Jasper had whitewashed the walls and put clear glass in the windows. Nona and Hallie cleaned the wooden floors and polished them to a satin gloss. Mary hung new curtains and painted the washstands. It was arduous work, but by the time the furniture was in place and Nona had dressed the beds in the handmade quilts brought from Vine Manor, the rooms looked respectable and inviting.

Hallie waited anxiously for a response to the advertisements she had placed in the weekly newspaper published by August Lott. She had sent Asia to pick up a copy of the paper. She rifled through each page, looking for her advertisement. It was not to be found. Calling on Jasper to bring the wagon round, Hallie gathered her purse and the paper and headed for town.

August Lott was expecting her. When Hallie arrived at the store he pretended to ignore her until she called out his name. "Mr. Lott, excuse me, may I see you a minute?"

August slowly rose from his desk and descended the five steps into the store. "I placed an advertisement in your paper two weeks ago. It was supposed to come out in today's paper. I cannot find it," Hallie said.

"That is because I did not run it, Mrs. Simmons. I owe you ten cents for the cost of the advertisement."

"And why was that, Mr. Lott? You must know how important

it is to me."

"I suffered quite a bit of embarrassment after you made your announcement on the pier that I was overcharging my customers. Along with the fact that Mary practically accused me of double-billing you for your taxes on Magnolia, I was put in a very precarious position. I do not like to be made a fool of, Mrs. Simmons."

"Then I assume it will do me no good to ask for your forgiveness and to please run the ad next week."

"None whatsoever. I was hoping that the relationship between you and I would have been better than the one I had with your father. You see, Mrs. Simmons, I had fully intended on buying Magnolia for myself when your father stepped in and bought it out from under me. It was a bitter pill to swallow, since Evan was considered an outsider. We in Lott's Point like to keep to our kind. It is my newspaper and I can choose what I wish to publish."

"So for that, I am being punished? Is it your wish to see me completely in poverty so that you can come to Magnolia and offer me a pittance for my property? Well I will burn it to the ground before I give it to the likes of you!" Hallie whirled around and left August standing at the counter.

Chapter Fifty-Five

One week later on a sultry afternoon, a large, ornate barouche appeared in the driveway of Magnolia. Within minutes, five women exited the carriage and stood in the driveway. Before they could make their way to the porch, Hallie and Mary were peeking out from behind the parlor curtains in anticipation.

"Who do you suppose they are, mother? They look like theater people to me. Look at their clothes," Mary whispered. "They are wearing satin gowns and long gloves. It is much too warm for such clothes."

"Be still, Mary, they may hear us. Nona, quick, answer the door," Hallie whispered.

Nona answered the door before the brass knocker had time to drop.

"Yes, I am inquiring about the rooms you have to let. Is the proprietor of this property available?" the lady in the green dress asked.

Nona stepped aside and escorted her into the parlor while the rest of the women remained in the yard, cooling themselves with ornate fans.

Nona rounded the corner into the library and was met head on by Hallie and Mary. "I swear, ya done scare't the life out a me. Dat lady be in da parlor."

Hallie smoothed the front of her dress and tucked an errant curl back behind her ear. Pasting a smile on her face she entered the parlor. "Hello, I am Hallie Simmons. How can I be of service?"

The woman smiled. "I have come about the rooms you have to rent. My name is Lola Passion."

"I have six rooms on the third floor. They really are very plain. I hadn't really thought about accommodations for ladies. I supposed I would get inquires from gentlemen doing business in this area. Oh, but please, don't be offended. I am really new at this sort of thing." Hallie knew she was almost babbling, but she could not stop herself. "I will provide two meals a day in addition to your room. Linens will be changed every ten days and your rooms will be cleaned whenever you think it is necessary." She stopped and took a deep breath.

Lola smiled at Hallie. "Very nice, but now I need to tell you our needs. There are five of us. We all need our own room. We will take care of cleaning our own rooms and I wonder if you would mind if we added our own personal touches to our rooms?"

"May I inquire as to the line of work that brings you to Lott's Point?" Hallie asked.

Lola smiled. "We are in the entertainment business. Let's not mince words, Mrs. Simmons. I was wondering how you felt about gentlemen callers? Would that be of a concern to you?" Lola asked.

Hallie was taken by surprise at Lola's question. "Oh my, I hadn't even considered that. I suppose it would be all right. You could let us know when you are expecting guests and I would make this parlor available for you. We also have a small ballroom at the end of the hall. And we have a piano," Hallie answered.

"Suppose we wanted to entertain guests in our rooms...would that be a problem?"

Hallie looked pale. "Would you excuse me for a moment. I'll be right back." As she stepped into the hallway, an arm reached out to grab her and pulled her into the library. Nona and Mary had been listening at the door.

"Mizz Hallie, dem women, dey be prostitutes. Dey lookin' for a place tah do business. Ya jest send dem packin' right now."

"Oh, please, Mary and Nona, go back in there with me. I can't do this alone."

Before she took a step Nona had bounded across the hallway and threw open the door. Standing with her arms crossed over her chest, she waited for Hallie to enter.

"As much as I am desperate to rent out my rooms, I really don't feel like it would be a good idea for me to rent them to you. It's a respectable home and we wish to keep it that way."

"I do quite understand, Mrs. Simmons, and I applaud your tenacity. Too bad that it doesn't pay the bills. We are not prostitutes if that is what you are thinking. We are courtesans,"

Lola said with some conviction. "We entertain gentlemen for a fee, but our agenda is not always of an intimate nature. We give comfort and counseling to many misunderstood men who would otherwise take their aggression out on their poor families. We are neat and fastidious in regards to our own hygiene."

"Ya be whores," Nona stated standing her ground.

"Nona! Please," Hallie said, glaring at Nona. "I just don't know, Miss Passion. It all seems so.... I don't even know the word."

"Well, let me finish by saying that our callers would enter by the staircase at the back of the house. They would come only to the third floor and leave the same way. They would never intrude on your private lives. I am willing to pay you double what you were asking for rent. It is more than you will get from anyone else. Times are harsh right now, Mrs. Simmons."

"Nona, go invite the other ladies onto the porch and take them some lemonade. We have a spring that gives us very cold water," she interjected. "I need a few minutes to think about this," Hallie said, knowing that she was rambling again.

"Suppose I give you a whole day to think about it. My ladies and I are staying at Miss Annabelle's until tomorrow. She will only allow us to stay there for one night. I will call on you again after lunch," Lola said as she neared the door. She stopped for a moment and moved closer to Hallie. "I understand your plight, Mrs. Simmons and I would never want to cause you any harm, but this is a very good opportunity for you to make a good deal of money. Believe me, I have been in your position before. It is not good when your life falls on hard times."

Sitting in the kitchen, her hand on her head, Hallie pondered the situation. "I just don't know what to do. She is willing to pay twice the rent for five rooms: that would be over seventy dollars a week."

"We could always try it for a month, mother and if it didn't work, we could ask them to leave. That would give us time to hear back on the property at Vine Manor," Mary said.

"Really, Mary, women like them living in our house. That is appalling," Lydia added.

Mary stepped in front of Lydia. "Fine. Does digging turnips from the garden suit you better, Lydia?"

"Well, I fer one, ain't waitin' on no nasty women," Nona said adamantly.

Hallie stood up. " I have made my decision. We will let them live here for one month."

By the next afternoon, two wagons and the same barouche arrived in the driveway of Magnolia. Followed by her ladies, Lola Passion lifted her dress and walked up the front steps to her new home.

Hallie, Mary, and Lydia stood like soldiers at attention and waited in the parlor until the women entered. Lola made the introductions. "Of course, you know me, I am Lola Passion and this is my sister Polly." Lola pointed to a rotund woman with painted cheeks and a red dress that resembled a circus tent. Polly smiled and extended her hand. "So happy to meet ye."

Hallie detected an accent that she did not hear in Lola's voice even though they were sisters.

Lola continued. "This is Ramona," she said, pointing to a raven-haired woman, "and next to her is Venus." Putting her arm around the shoulder of a girl that appeared to be no more than a child, Lola added, "And this is Angel."

"Oh, yes, I forgot my manners," Hallie said. "These are my daughters, Mary and Lydia."

"Now, if you could show us to our rooms, we would really like to rest. It has been an exhausting week. Traveling, you know, wears a person out." She wanted to clear up why they were exhausted.

"Of course, follow me." Walking up the two long flights of steps, Hallie suddenly felt that perhaps she had made a terrible mistake.

"I'll leave you to rest. I will have Nona bring up fresh water for the pitchers and perhaps some lemonade. Is there anything else I can do for you now?" Hallie asked.

"I think that will be all, but let me pay you two weeks rent in advance." Opening her small-jeweled purse, Lola retrieved a gold money clip stretched to the limit and counted out the bills onto the bed. I believe this is the right amount. You can recount it if you like."

"Thank you," Hallie said, putting the money in her pocket.

After Hallie left the room, Ramona sat down on the bed. "Look at this place! You really expect us to live here? It's as bare as a baby's butt. Look, there's just a bed, dresser, and a washstand. Looks like some of the cheap hotels we stayed in.

Surely we can find better lodgings than this."

"And the town," Venus added. "It is so small we won't be able to shop there after the residents find out who we are. At least in Pittsburgh we could leave the house every now and then. I am not going to lay on my back all night and be a prisoner in this place."

"I thought the owner was very nice," Angel said.

"Oh, I'm so glad for that!" Ramona said mocking her.

Lola was irritated with the reaction from the girls. "Look," she said, "I told you when we left Pittsburgh that we are going to have to keep a low profile for a while. The incident with Mr. Capp will take a while to blow over. You are all going to have to be patient and make the best of it. When our things arrive it will make the rooms homier. If anyone wants to leave, be my guest. See how long you'll make it out there alone." Polly hung her head, knowing that she was the cause of everyone's anger.

Except for a clash between Ramona and Venus over the room with the windows facing east, the rest of the week was spent adjusting to life in a boarding house.

It took August Lott only a few days to find out what was going on at Magnolia and only a couple more days for Hallie to be the scandal of Lott's Point. The gossip was cruel and vicious, fueled by constant admonition by the congregation at Lott's Point Baptist Church, of which August Lott was a deacon. Hallie was now referred to as the Madam of Magnolia, a title August penned for her, a woman living in sin and leading her daughters down the road of debauchery. August had taken the task of removing such reprehensible behavior from his town as his personal vendetta. He was sure he could have her and her brothel removed from his town within weeks. Little did he know that law enforcement has a way of turning their backs on pleasure palaces when they are paid handsomely and given free services. The investigation could last for months at best.

Chapter Fifty-Six

The first few weeks after the women moved into the house were difficult for everyone. When the first coaches began to arrive and pull around to the rear of the house, everyone would gather at the windows and peek out from behind the curtains to catch a glimpse of who was coming to visit. When Hallie recognized Mr. Glass, the owner of the tack shop, she was shocked. "He is a married man! What is he doing here?" But Hallie knew that one of the conditions of the women living here was that all residents must keep a vow of silence. That included Mandy and Asia, who had no idea what a vow of silence was. They only knew that Nona had threatened them with the broom if they so much as uttered a word to anyone about the men coming to the house.

Except for an occasional burst of laughter, the sounds from the third floor were not at all what Hallie had expected. She was afraid that with the girls sleeping on the second floor the noise from overhead would keep them awake. Even though she listened quite earnestly, her new boarders never disturbed them. Hallie had imposed a strict rule that all gentlemen must be out of the house by eight o'clock. Lola had agreed, saying the girls needed a good night's sleep.

Hallie had given up the dining room for her roomers and along with everyone else she ate in the kitchen. Twice a day the dining room table was set for five. The food was put on the sideboard and the door was then closed. Mary would pull the bell cord to signal that the meal was ready. When the ladies were finished they would open the door before going back upstairs. Nona likened it to feeding stray cats on the back steps. "Put out da food, it be eaten, and den dey disappeared, leavin' a mess for me ta clean up."

When the occasion arose for the women to come downstairs to sit in the garden or leave in their coach, they were greeted with cool nods or a curt hello. Hallie had instructed Lydia and Mary to keep their distance and not to engage the women in conversation. It was only when Lola appeared at the parlor door one evening that the tension finally seemed to be lifted.

Hallie sat at the writing desk, working on her household ledgers, while Lydia and Mary were reading. The gentle knock on the open door caused all three to look up simultaneously.

"Excuse me, Mrs. Simmons, but I wonder if I might have a word with you," Lola said.

"Yes, of course," Hallie said. "Do you wish for my daughters to leave the room?"

"Oh, no. In fact, I would like them to stay. I have heard the rumors. I understand that Mr. Lott is waging a campaign against you. I am sorry if we have brought you undue harm."

"My battle with Mr. Lott started long before you came to live here, Miss Passion."

"Please, call me Lola. I just wanted to let you know that I would be more than happy to take care of the situation with Mr. Lott and ease your worry about him. I think I could quiet him for a while," Lola said. "And now I wonder if perhaps you and your daughters would like to dine with us some evening?"

"Thank you, Miss Passion, I mean Lola, but I'm not sure about dinner," Hallie mumbled.

It was Lydia who spoke up. "We don't know what to say to you or the other women. It would be awkward. What would we talk about?"

"Well, for starters, we could talk about the weather, or fashion, or even gardening. Ramona enjoys working in the garden and my sister, Polly, loves to talk about food, as you might be able to tell, but I understand. Have a good evening." Lola turned and left the room.

"Were we rude to her, mother?" Lydia asked.

"I am not sure. I don't know what it takes to insult them. I do suppose they have feelings."

Lola never really seemed to care what other women thought of her, but for some reason the Simmons women were different. Lola had never lived in a house with women who did not participate in the same activity as her. It seemed odd to be treated as an outsider. It was difficult for her to understand that the Simmons women did not respect her and thought of her as only a source of income. Were they any different from her? They were selling off their pride and good name for money just as she always had, only they did it standing up. She envied the close relationship between Hallie and her daughters. That was something she never had in her life. Maybe there was something she could do to prove her loyalty to them and make their life a little easier. She would think of a way.

The next morning, dressed in her blue silk dress with the low-cut décolletage, Lola sprinkled herself with lavender water. She drove her carriage into town and tied the horse to the hitching post in front of Lott's store. The bell over the door signaled her arrival. August Lott looked up from the paper he was reading and grimaced as she came toward him.

Smiling, Lola walked up and down the aisle making sure no one else was in the store. Picking up a pair of white lace gloves, she laid them on the counter. "I would like to purchase these."

"Those are two dollars," August Lott growled.

"That's fine," she replied. She stared at him for a moment. "I was wondering, Mr. Lott, if you and I could talk business? My friends and I are accustomed to certain items that we cannot find in this town. Would there be any way you could order these things for us? I have a list." Lola bent over the counter, revealing a long line of cleavage, and laid a paper in front of August. Leaning in close she said, "Now you see here, we cannot find a good grade of chocolate or brandy in Lott's Point. We also are fond of French perfume. Very expensive perfume." Lola was aware of what she was doing. August was staring straight into her bosom. Tiny beads of sweat crossed his forehead. Lola ran her fingers across his knuckles. "You have very nice hands. Has anyone ever told you that?" She slowly lifted her head, her long black eyelashes closing slightly.

"You stop that! I know what you're trying to do. You're trying to drum up business for your bawdy house. I ain't buyin' what you're sellin'," August snarled, pulling his hand away.

"My goodness, Mr. Lott. I do not have to solicit business. I have more than enough gentlemen who are always anxious to see me. I just enjoy talking to someone who is intelligent once in a while. I understand you are quite educated?"

"I don't know who told you that, but I am very smart. That is how I got where I am and I tend to stay that way. Now about your order, I think we can do business."

Lola ran her tongue over her lips, pulling her arms close into her chest. Her breast bulged against the tight material. "I know you are a busy man, Mr. Lott. If you would like to come by Magnolia around nine tonight, I can show you samples of what I want and perhaps we can make up an order. There would be no charge for my time. I am a very discreet person, Mr. Lott, and I could give you a sizeable order. I know you would be happy with what I have to show you. I would never reveal our business dealings to anyone. Now, if you decide to come tonight, just pull your carriage around to the back and come up the stairs to the third floor. My room is the first door on the right." Before August could say another word, she started toward the door. He stood there for a minute before he was able to move. She turned back to him and smiled. "I assure you, you won't be disappointed."

Arriving home, Lola found Hallie in the kitchen preparing lunch. "Mrs. Simmons, I am having a rather late-night guest. He will be arriving around nine o'clock. If you would like to look out your window, you might be interested to see who it is."

"And why is that?" Hallie asked.

"Just trust me on this one. I think it may surprise you."

Hallie, along with Mary and Lydia, took up their post at the bedroom window just after eight. Lola had piqued their curiosity. In the cover of darkness, the three women took turns looking out the window. When the sound of hooves broke the silence of the night, three heads peered over the sill. "Oh, good Lord!" Hallie whispered. "Can you believe it?" Mary and Lydia both giggled as they watched August Lott descend from his carriage and quickly rush up the back stairs.

In the morning, still dressed in her robe, Lola entered the kitchen. "Were you able to see who my guest was last night, Mrs. Simmons?" she asked. Hallie slowly nodded her head. "Good, then I don't suppose you have to worry about that little weasel causing you any more trouble. I think it would be just fine for you to shop in his store. And, by the way..." Lola said as she reached into her robe pocket and laid two items on the table: a gold money clip with the initials *AL* engraved on it and a handkerchief with the same initials embroidered in one corner. "You might want to keep these someplace safe. It would be pretty hard for Mr. Lott to explain how these things ended up at Magnolia."

Hallie gasped at the sight of the items lying before her. Lola yawned. "I have to get some rest. I had a boring night and a busy day ahead of me."

Chapter Fifty-Seven

Hallie Simmons tipped her parasol and smiled at the two men sitting on the bench in front of the barbershop. They grinned and nodded at her. She knew what they were thinking, but it had long ceased to matter to her. She walked to the hitching post and stepped inside her waiting carriage to make the short ride home from Main Street to Magnolia.

Once at home, Jasper opened the carriage door for her. Juggling her parcels, she gingerly stepped over a tree branch lying on the path. She would have to talk to Asia. This was totally unacceptable. It was his duty to keep the grounds manicured and uncluttered at all times even though Hallie knew it was an arduous task for a sixteen-year-old boy. Hallie adjusted her packages and opened the door. Venus was sitting in the parlor reading a magazine in her camisole and first petticoat. "Get dressed," Hallie snapped. "How many times have I told you not to come downstairs in your undergarments?"

Venus shrugged and slowly walked up the winding staircase to the third floor of the house. In the kitchen, Hallie dropped her bags on the table. Nona was standing at the stove stirring stew in a large black pot.

"Nona, I bought some cheese and cold meats. It is too hot for you to be cooking. I'm going upstairs to change my clothes and lie down. I have a miserable headache," Hallie said as she left the steamy room. At the end of the corridor on the second floor she stepped inside her own private quarters. She took off her hat and placed it in the box on the dressing table. She sat down on the small velvet chair and looked into the mirror. She sighed as she tried to rub the pain away from her head.

The last of her hopes for a better life for her children had been dashed against the rocks of disparity. A letter had finally arrived from Natchez the prior week. Her anticipation of a large settlement on Vine Manor had not materialized. The formal letter from the State Property Settlement Office stated that part of her property had been parceled out to displaced veterans from the war, while another portion had been given to the freed slaves, since the county clerk was under the impression that the property had been abandoned and no one knew where the family had moved. After taxes and legal fees, the remaining amount was only four thousand dollars. It was an insult to her that she was given only a pittance for a property that was once one of the richest plantations in Mississippi. She knew she had to accept the check or she would be given nothing. The government had succeeded in taking away her last hope of returning to a normal life. Even with the few dollars Hallie was able to save each week, she had no legacy for her girls.

While Mary still had hopes of continuing her education, Lydia had almost given up completely. With no dowry and no cotillions to attend plus the defamed name given to her by August Lott, she could not look forward to a bright future. Hallie tried to assure Lydia that the business going on in the house was only a temporary condition. Lydia did not believe her.

Hallie rubbed her forehead again. Her temples were throbbing. Unable to find her medication in her room, she slowly walked downstairs to retrieve her headache powder.

Hallie stepped aside as Mandy passed her carrying a tray covered with a white napkin. "I swear dat man is gonna eat us out of dah house. Dis be my second trip up to Polly's room with food," she said, groaning under the weight of the silver tray.

"Just be sure you keep track of what you are taking to them. Polly can add it to his bill. We aren't furnishing room and board for gentlemen callers," Hallie said, sharply.

Once back in her room, Hallie poured the headache powder into a glass of water and quickly drank it. She shivered at the acrid taste of the medicine. As she lay across her bed, she could hear music coming from the room overhead. Ramona must be entertaining Mr. Russell. He loved to play lively music on his banjo while he had his encounters with the voluptuous Ramona. Hallie knew them all. She knew all the names of the traveling salesmen who visited once or twice a month. She knew the wealthy men from Wells Fargo who passed through on their way to the banks and of course, the regulars, the men from town who came in secrecy.

The irony was that most of the men in town who now called

Hallie the Madam of Magnolia Hill knew that she was not a loose woman. There were times when Hallie had been approached by some of the men. Her answer was always adamant, "No!" Hallie would never consider doing what Lola and the others did for a living. She had daughters and their lives were hard enough living with their mother being called a madam. Being a prostitute would be unthinkable.

What would James think of her if he saw her now? Would he turn away in disgust or would he applaud her for making the best of a bad situation. She had loved him with every fiber of her being. After all this time, she still found time to grieve for him. Her mind running over that fateful time again and again, she drifted off to sleep.

Hallie awoke to the sound of the shutters pounding against the clapboard. An almost chilling breeze wafted into the room. She struggled with the shutters until she was able to pull them shut. A bad storm was brewing; she must make sure everyone was safe. Lola and the other women, frightened by the sound of the whistling wind, had descended into the parlor along with Nona and Mandy. Lydia and Mary hurried through the house closing windows and securing all the shutters. Jasper and Asia had gone to the stable to make sure the horses were in their stalls.

"Is it a hurricane?" Angel asked. "I ain't ever been in a hurricane. Is there someplace safe we can hide?"

"I think we will all be fine if we just stay here," Hallie said, as the wind's shrill sound echoed in the hallways. Although it was only five o'clock, Nona lit the lanterns and placed them on the tables. Scurrying into the kitchen, she returned with the cold meats and cheese Hallie had brought home.

"I suppose we can at least enjoy our dinner until the storms passes," Hallie said. It was then that they heard someone knocking at the door. Nona struggled to her feet and shuffled into the foyer. "Who be out in weather like dis?" she grumbled. Opening the door, Nona was greeted by a man whose clothes were soaked from the rain. She spoke to him for a few minutes and then returned to the parlor.

"Who was at the door?" Hallie asked.

"It be some travelers caught in dah storm. I telled them it be all right for dem ta go to dah stables 'til it passes."

"Why didn't you invite them in, Nona?" Hallie asked.

"Lawdy, no. It be a lotta people. A white man and a lots of colored folks. Dey be okay in dah stables. It be dry down dar."

Hallie's attention was diverted by the sizzle of lightning and clashes of thunder that shook the room. It was going to be a long night.

Sometime near morning the storm ended and everyone dispersed to their rooms. Hallie waited until it was light enough to see without a lantern. She went to the kitchen and put logs into the fire and stoked the hardwood under the cast-iron oven chamber. Donning her apron she began to mix flour and eggs for biscuits. A slight knock on the door distracted her as she kneaded the mixture on the table. "Come in, please," she called, her hands covered in dough. Hallie looked up to see a man standing in the doorway with his hat in his hand.

"Please excuse the early intrusion, but I was wondering if Mrs. Simmons is available?"

Hallie wiped her hands on a towel. "I am Mrs. Simmons. May I help you?"

He smiled and extended his hand. "My name is Aden Woods. My friends and I spent the night in your stables. That was quite a storm. I was wondering if you would mind if we got some water from your spring?"

"Of course, help yourself. That would not be a problem. Do you have food?"

"Yes ma'am we do. Thank you for letting us spend the night." He paused for a moment. "When I was coming across your yard I noticed that quite a few shingles blew off the house during the storm. We would be glad to fix them to repay your kindness," Aden said.

After breakfast, Nona and Jasper, curious about the overnight guests, slipped out of the house and walked down to the stables. Women and children sitting around on the floor greeted them with stares until Nona unveiled the basket of fresh strawberries and a small sack of sugar she had brought with her. Nona noticed that the stalls had been swept clean and made into makeshift sleeping chambers. The children had been bathed in the water from the spring and wrapped in blankets, while their clothes dried on lines hung between the rails. Nona could smell fresh chicory coffee and bacon frying on the open fire. Introducing themselves to everyone, it was Aden who stepped forward. He shook Jasper's hand. Within minutes, Nona and

Jasper were welcomed. They exchanged stories and Nona convinced Ben and the others that Hallie was a good and kind woman. Aden sat in the background listening as Nona told the group about the death of James and how they ended up in Magnolia. "I be tellin' you sumthin', dat Mizz Hallie, she be one special lady and ya be glad ya ended up here for dah night. Most folks around here would have chased ya off."

"It be jest a night," Ben said. "We gots a lots'o nights. Lots'o nights wid no place to go."

Jasper helped Nona to her feet. "I be seeing about dat for you. Me and Jasper need ta talk wid Mizz Hallie," Nona said. Even though Jasper once again tried to convince Nona to mind her business, he knew that as soon as she reached the house she would find Hallie. Jasper was right.

"I be tellin' you, Mizz Hallie, des people need somewhere ta stay for a while. Dey be tired ta dah bone. Dey gots a girl ready ta have a baby and dem youngins all gots runny noses. Dem old ones kin hardly walk and dey be livin' scared for months now," Nona said. Hallie listened as she sat on the porch peeling carrots.

"What do you want me to do, Nona? I can hardly handle what I have now. If you are suggesting that I take care of these people, you know that it is impossible. I have more than I can deal with already."

"Dey don need takin' care of Mizz Hallie, dey jest need a place ta stay for a bit. Dah stables be jest fine," Nona said in a pleading voice.

Hallie sighed. How could she refuse Nona's plea? Nona and Jasper had stayed by her side through all these years. Even now, as freed slaves, they were still not earning money of their own. She could not afford to pay them. Nona had raised her from a small child. She would honor her wish. "Tell them they can stay for a while if they want," Hallie said. "I can't help them much, but we will do the best we can." Hallie looked up to see Aden coming across the yard.

"Mrs. Simmons, when I was up on the roof I also noticed that some of the stones are coming loose on your chimneys. They really need to be repaired. They are about to crumble."

"Mr. Woods," she replied curtly, "I appreciate your keen eye, but there are a lot of things around here that need fixing. I simply do not have the man power or the finances to get them done."

"I'm sorry. I suppose it is none of my business, but I do have a proposition for you that might benefit us both. The people I am with need a place to stay awhile and you need help. In exchange for letting us stay here, we would be glad to help. The men can work on the chimneys and fix your rock walls and I know the women would love to help out in the kitchen and in the house. Think about it," he said.

Before he had taken three steps away, Hallie said, "I thought about it. You have a deal, Mr. Woods."

Nona looked at her in sheer surprise. "Ya be sure, Mizz Hallie?"

"I know, Nona. I want to keep you that way."

When Mary and Lydia found out what Hallie had done and realized that for the first time in months they would not have to spend each day cleaning and cooking, they were thrilled.

"I haven't read a book in over a month," Mary said. "Having help in the house is going to be sheer luxury."

"I plan to sleep at least 'til seven every day and maybe the cracks on my hands from the lye soap will clear up," Lydia added.

The next day everyone was aroused by the sound of pounding on the roof. With yells and groans from the women on the third floor, Hallie realized that Aden and the other men had begun working just as the sun came up.

"What in heaven's name is all that noise? What is going on?" Mary asked as she met her mother in the hallway.

"I'm sorry, Mary. It is those men from the stable. I knew they were going to fix the roof, but I had no idea they were going to be here so early. Well since we are up, we might as well fix the women a decent breakfast. I am sure they are not going to be in very good moods today."

While Mary tended the fire, Hallie carried two buckets out to the well. Turning the handle on the crank she lowered the pail into the deep well and filled it with cool water.

"Here, let me help you," Aden said, as he strode across the yard. "Those buckets are heavy. I suppose we woke everyone in your house this morning. I am sorry for that, but we wanted to finish before the noonday sun hits the roof. I was going to knock on the door and tell you we were starting, but either way, I would have awakened you."

"We have some unhappy boarders in the house right now. I have to make sure I feed them well this morning," Hallie said as Aden picked up the pails and headed toward the kitchen. "You're welcome to join us."

"Thank you for the invitation. I will hold you to it, but not today. I promised you I would fix your roof."

"Thank you for bringing the water in for me," Hallie said, smiling. "And for fixing my roof."

"You're quite welcome, Mrs. Simmons," Aden said, as he turned to leave.

"Who is that?" Mary asked, with Lydia looking over her shoulder. They both had been watching from the window.

"He is quite handsome, mother," Lydia added.

"That is Mr. Woods. He is the man who brought the Negroes to the house during the storm."

"What do you know about him, mother?" Mary asked. "And why is he with those colored folks?"

"I don't know. Maybe I am being naïve,but right now I don't care. Getting some of the house repairs done and help around the house may give me a moment's peace. I just hope he is a good man like Nona said," Hallie replied.

Chapter Fifty-Eight

It was a busy week with quite a few of the traveling customers in town. The train had pulled into the station the night before and today most of the men would be making their way out to Magnolia.

Mary and Jasper were sent to town to purchase coffee and to pick up the mail at Mr. Lott's store. They were told to hurry. Hallie always liked Jasper to be available to fill water buckets and keep the kitchen fire going when the house was full of gentlemen callers.

When Jasper returned, Hallie picked up the letters and newspapers from the table in the foyer and began separating them into stacks. Hallie could not understand why Lola still paid for the weekly newspaper from Pittsburgh since she had already told Hallie that she really had no ties to that town.

After Mandy delivered the paper to Lola's room, Lola began to peruse each page of the Pittsburgh Times carefully. It had been ritual for Lola since coming to Magnolia. She always looked for some mention of the death of Robert Capp. Today she did not have to search very far. On the front page of a two-week old paper was a picture of Robert Capp along with an article about him. She read it over several times. The article stated that a hunter discovered decomposed remains at the bottom of a ravine. A ring, still present on the skeletal right hand, identified the body to be that of Robert Capp. The newspaper piece also affirmed that before his death, Mr. Capp had been under investigation by his financial institution for embezzlement. He had taken large sums of money from his company to pay off gambling debts. It was assumed that the pressure had become too much and Mr. Capp had taken his own life or perhaps he was killed by someone he owed money. The cause of death could not be determined since predatory animals had carried some of the remains. No mention was made of his habit of visiting brothels.

The police in Pittsburgh were suspending the investigation since they had no leads on the case. Lola let out a sigh of relief. She should tell the rest of the women that they no longer were suspects in Mr. Capp's death. If she did, would they want to pack up and leave Magnolia right away? Lola decided to keep the information to herself. She liked living at Magnolia and did not want to leave at this time. She would wait a while longer to tell them. Lola folded the newspaper in half and tucked it under her mattress for safekeeping. The sound of voices in the hallway signaled the arrival of the day's customers.

The first gentleman to arrive that morning was a man name Clarence Dart, who would only see Polly. Pulling his horse to a halt at the back entrance to the house, Mr. Dart hurried up the steps.

"Come in, Mr. Dart, the door is open," Polly said when Mr. Dart knocked on her door. He bowed to her and today she knew he wanted to pretend that she was a queen and he was a king. She knew all his games. "Not today, Mr. Dart," she said. "It's too hot. Let's just get down to business." Polly pulled her petticoat from her body and waited for him to join her on the bed.

"I've been looking forward to this for a month," he said nervously, fidgeting with his hat. He began removing his clothes, folding them neatly and putting them on the chair. "I even wrote some new words for you to say. Can't we just pretend a bit?"

"No! No games today. Just get over here and do your business."

Fifteen minutes later, Mr. Dart was dressed. He put some money on the dresser and left. Polly got up and reached for the money. Spying only a silver dollar, she dashed to the window. Mr. Dart was heading towards his horse and carriage. "Come back here you little son of a bitch. Come back up here and give me the rest of my money!"

Mr. Dart looked up just as Polly hurled the silver dollar out the window, hitting him on the head. Mr. Dart let out a yelp, while Polly continued to scream obscenities at him.

Hallie ran from the house when she heard the commotion. "What is going on out here?" she asked. The commotion had also brought Lola from the parlor into the yard.

Polly watched as Lola talked to Mr. Dart, who stood rubbing his head. He pointed up at the window and shook his head, but Polly could not hear what they were talking about. "Is the little weasel going to give me my money?" she yelled as a naked breast dangled out the window.

Lola raised her hands. "Get inside."

Minutes later, Lola was in Polly's room. "Just what in the world do you think you're doing causing such a scene? Mr. Dart was unhappy with his visit. He said you have terrible body odor and you are not meeting his needs. That is why he didn't pay your regular fee. From now on he wants to see Ramona."

"Over my dead body! He's my regular. Give me my dollar," she said, putting out her hand.

"I gave it back to him and he will see Ramona when he comes next time. We can't afford to lose customers like him or let him tell others that our ladies are fat and smell bad. You must bathe more regularly, Polly," Lola said.

Hallie had no idea that Aden and a few of the children were standing in the yard and they had watched the whole scene unfold. Descending the steps, she groaned as she saw Aden. "Yes, Mr. Woods, is there something I can help you with?"

Aden seemed embarrassed. "Ah, we came to ask a favor. Would you mind if the boys put some traps under the causeway to catch lobsters and crabs?"

"No, that would be fine," Hallie, replied. She was unaware that above her head, Polly was once again hanging over the balcony, until she saw everyone looking up at her.

Polly called out to a small boy, who wore a rag tied around his face. "What is wrong with your face, boy?" she asked, loudly.

The boy shyly looked up, aware that Polly's breasts were resting on the railing. "I gots a toothache. I gots a real bad tooth," the boy replied.

"Well, go into town and have the dentist pull it. That's pretty simple," Polly said.

"No ma'am," he replied. "Dat toothman, he don see coloreds," the boy rubbed his hand over his face.

"Oh bull cocky. You wait right there." Polly returned a few minutes later with an envelope. "Here, catch," she said, tossing the envelope to the boy. "You go back in town and you tell Mr. Pope to pull your tooth. Give him this envelope. He'll pull it." She waddled back into her room.

"I suppose we should be going," Aden said. "It seems like you have enough on your hands right now, Mrs. Simmons."

Hallie smiled, knowing that she could burst into tears from

the embarrassment. "Whatever gave you that idea, Mr. Woods? I'm sorry you had to witness the bad behavior from my boarders. They seem to have no manners at all today."

Hallie entered the house and called for Nona. As Nona rounded the corner, Hallie grabbed her hand and pulled her into the parlor. Hallie's curiosity about Aden and the people who were now living in her barn was more than she could stand. She knew that Nona had become close with some of the women while they worked with her in the kitchen.

"Nona, please, tell me what Mr. Woods' position is? I mean, if he doesn't own these Negroes, why is he looking after them? Why is he working alongside them fixing my house? Surely, men as articulate as he don't have to do this kind of work."

"Cause he be a kind and decent man. You want tah know more, ya ask him."

Hallie knew it was not her place to ask Aden, but she would send someone who had a way of asking questions that did not offend.

Later that afternoon, it was Mary who took a pitcher of lemonade and glasses out to the balcony where Aden was now busy putting mortar between the loose stones on the pillars. "I thought you might be thirsty. My name is Mary Simmons. I don't believe we have ever been properly introduced."

"I'm glad to meet you, Mary Simmons. My name is Aden Woods." He wiped his brow with a handkerchief he took from his pocket. "Lemonade sounds good right now." Aden pulled a chair out for Mary and then sat down at the table across from her.

"The work you are doing here is quite wonderful, Mr. Woods. I can't tell you how happy my mother is to have some of these heavy tasks taken off her hands," Mary said, as she carefully poured the lemonade. "And my sister and I are thrilled with all the extra help in the house."

Aden smiled. "Actually, I hadn't realized how much I missed working with my hands. It is satisfying to see a project completed. And, of course, this is a small price to pay for your mother's kindness."

"I suppose you know we are all curious about you and the others. Is there a story behind your unexpected visit to our house, Mr. Woods?" Mary asked.

"I would prefer you call me Aden and I will call you Mary if that is all right with you."

"Yes, of course, Aden," she replied.

Aden took a long drink from his glass and set it on the table. "I was a ship builder before the war. I went to live in the South Seas for a few years, but I returned from Tahiti to find my grandmother. We had been separated for years. That is when I encountered Ben and the others living by a river. They had nowhere to go and no way to get there. Everything they owned had either been taken or destroyed by the roadmen. I couldn't leave them there to be beaten or killed by the likes of those that have taken over the south since the war ended. They have served their masters well and now they have been cast into the wind to fend for themselves. They do not know where to begin. Freedom is not an easy thing for them."

"That is quite kind of you, Aden. I don't know many men who would do the same for a band of Negroes."

"And what about you, Mary? Tell me about yourself." It seemed he was anxious to change the subject.

He had caught Mary off guard. Her words just came tumbling out.

"There are times when I feel like my life hasn't even started and other times I feel like I have lived two lifetimes. I had always wanted to be a teacher. The war and then the death of my father changed all that." She looked down at her lap.

"Don't give up your dream so easily, Mary. You are still young enough to do anything you desire. It just takes a lot of determination. Right now, I have six little children living at the stable who are bored and getting into mischief because they have nothing to keep them busy. They would love to have someone read to them or tell them stories," Aden said.

"Oh, I have picture books, some slate and chalk that I can give you so the children will have something to do," Mary said in an animated voice. "I brought them home with me when we came from St. Louis after the war."

"I have a better idea, Mary. Why don't you bring it down to the stable and give it to them yourself. That is, if you are not adverse to socializing with coloreds."

"No, I have no problem with that."

"Good, then come by tomorrow morning and I will introduce you to them." Aden stood up and took the last drink from his glass. "Thank you for the lemonade. It was quite good."

Mary picked up the tray and headed for the door. She

stopped and turned to Aden. "By the way, Aden, did you find your grandmother?"

"Yes, I did," he answered.

Chapter Fifty-Nine

After a very nervous first visit to the stables, armed with everything she could find to amuse the children, Mary looked forward to each morning. From the very first book she read to the children, they were mesmerized. Sitting in a circle in the meadow, they stared at the pictures in the book, while Mary told them the story. It wasn't long before a five-year old boy was sitting in her lap to catch a better view. After reading the book, the children laughed as they held the chalk in their hands for the first time and made marks on the slate. When Mary wiped it clean they were amazed. Her heart went out to these children who were so thirsty for knowledge that they cried when she had to leave. Although Ben repeated over and over to Aden that it wasn't natural for a white woman to be teaching the children, he refused to stop the sessions.

Hallie was also concerned, but couldn't bring herself to say anything to Mary. Mary was happy, really happy, for the first time in a very long time. There was no way Hallie could put an end to Mary's makeshift school. Besides, Aden and the others would be moving on soon enough. At least that was the plan.

Aden had other ideas. As he looked out the door of the stable each morning, he was met by a feeling of peace. The meadow was bursting with wildflowers and berries. Just over the ridge was the ocean. A few hundred feet beyond a grove of trees was the river. This was a beautiful spot for a settlement. He envisioned six or seven cabins made out of beech wood nestled together. Gardens could be planted in the fertile soil and an abundance of fresh and ocean fish would be available all year round. It would be a place where Ben and his family could raise their children without the constant threat of danger. If only he could convince Hallie of his plan. Splashing water on his face from the bucket placed on a tree stump, Aden decided that he had to talk to her soon. Everyone was getting much too comfortable at Magnolia.

After a few weeks had passed and everything in the house was running smoothly, Hallie began to enjoy her free time. Today she took her book and meandered into the garden. With the additional help, Jasper and Asia had time to once again turn the garden into a place of beauty: topiary boxwoods and stone paths lined with azaleas formed a backdrop for the pond filled with shimmering Koi and water lilies.

Settling on a wrought-iron bench, Hallie opened her book. She had only read a few pages when she was interrupted.

"I am sorry for the intrusion, Mrs. Simmons, but I was wondering if I might have a word with you?" Aden said, as he approached the bench.

"Of course," Hallie said as she closed her book and slid over on the bench to make room for him to sit down.

"I am not going to hedge. I will just come right out and ask you. I was wondering if you would contemplate selling off the lower meadow to me? I would like to build a settlement."

"Oh, my goodness, I could never do that. I mean, this is all I have left."

"Thank you, Mrs. Simmons, I quite understand." Aden stood up.

"No! I don't think you do. Please sit down." Perhaps it was because she couldn't believe how her life had evolved or maybe she just wanted to tell him about her life so he wouldn't judge her, or was it a need to talk to another adult who wasn't her child or a servant? Whatever the reason, Hallie spent the next hour talking. One hour talking, pouring out the story of her life with her father and James and what happened during and after the war. She talked about her daughters and their time in St. Louis and all the rage and sadness and disappointment they had endured trying to make a new life. She never gave him a chance to interrupt. She would stop only long enough to take a breath and then began again. "And so you see, having the women here pays the bills, but also this arrangement takes away a little more of who I really am every day. Each time I hear someone walking up those back steps, I cringe. I want to chase them away with my broom, but I know I can't. And then you came, and I just threw my hands up and said, "Why not let them stay here, too. I cannot sell you the land, Aden. You can stay as long as you like, you can build houses and barns and whatever you want, but

Magnolia and all its property will always belong to the Simmons family."

"Please don't think of me as forward, but if you would like the women to leave, I have some money that I would be more than happy to give you. I would hate to see you get arrested for sending someone backwards down the steps after you have clobbered them with a broom." Aden grinned.

The small squeak that escaped from Hallie was the beginning of laughter. "Oh, my goodness, I cannot believe I said that, but truly. I cannot take your money. I know you must think that renting the rooms to the ladies is wrong. Everyone else does. We are looked upon as lepers whenever we are in town. I suppose when I arrived here I was still agonizing over the death of my husband and I was worried about supporting my daughters. I should have worried more about what effect having loose women living in our house would have on them."

Aden was relieved that the tension had lifted, "This is a strange turn of events for you, but I am glad that you can at least laugh about it. I think Mary will be fine. I have only met Lydia a few times. I really don't know her very well. And as far as you are concerned, Mrs. Simmons, I am not one to judge people. I have made enough mistakes of my own. I will talk to Ben about your offer to stay on for a while. I know that they will all be very happy. They love it here. We have a new baby in the group now. Her name is Joy. I hope sometime soon you will come and visit us."

"I was wondering, Mr. Woods, are you comfortable living in the stable? I do have an extra room off the summer kitchen. You are welcome to stay there," Hallie remarked.

"No, I am just fine. I know it may seem strange to you, Mrs. Simmons, that I want to stay in the stable with the Negroes, but they feel safer when I am nearby. I should go now. I have taken up enough of your time." As he stood, she smiled at him and watched as he walked away.

As he waded through the tall weeds in the field, Aden thought about Hallie. For some reason he was attracted to her. There had been other women more eye-catching than she that he had passed on by, but Hallie had a way of making him want to stay by her side. The curls she had inherited from her mother framed her round face and she always seemed to have the glow of the sun on her cheeks. At times he just wanted to reach over and tuck those curls inside her bonnet and touch her soft skin. He liked the way her face animated when she talked about something she was committed to. He even liked the shell of thin armor that protected her fragile emotional core. She had said several times that she was not a strong woman. He disagreed. She possessed more strength than she gave herself credit for. He would make sure he saw her again, and soon.

Chapter Sixty

"My goodness, don't you look lovely this morning," Mary said as her mother entered the dining room. "And where did you get that dress? I have never seen it before."

Hallie smoothed her hands over the folds of lace on the yellow dress. "Lola gave it to me. She said she bought it before she became a... well, you know. She never wore it when she was with one of her gentlemen, so I guess it was all right that I took it."

"Really, mother, it is just a dress. I don't believe it is tainted," Lydia interjected as she buttered her toast. "Where are you going?"

"I thought I might walk down by the gate. Nona said there are some wild blueberries growing along the path. I am sure she could make us a lovely dessert if I gathered them for her."

"There are blueberries in the backfield, mother," Lydia added.

"The ones on the path are larger. I have to go. It will be getting warm soon." Hallie left quickly before Lydia could add that perhaps it was because Aden was working on the gateposts that she preferred those berries.

Lydia watched as her mother walked gracefully down the path. "Doesn't it seem like mother is spending a lot of time with Mr. Woods?" Lydia asked Mary.

"They enjoy each other's company. I have overheard mother and Aden talking about books they have read. I am sure she is lonely for some sort of adult companionship," Mary answered.

"Oh, so now it's Aden. You must be on friendly terms with him, too. Why is it I am the only one who doesn't know him very well? And don't you think it is too soon for mother to be spending time with another gentlemen? After all, father hasn't been gone even a year."

"For goodness sakes, Lydia, you are making far too much out

of a few casual visits together. I am sure she has no romantic interest in Mr. Woods."

"Well, I just don't know. Everything around here is changing." Lydia threw her butter knife on the table. "With mother running off to talk to Aden and you leaving to teach the colored children, that leaves me here alone. Nona is in the kitchen laughing and talking with the other women and I have no one, not one person, male or female, to talk to. Even Asia and Mandy prefer to spend time with each other than with me. I see young people in town walking together, but they turn their heads when I come into view. I hate it here! I think I might go mad if my life doesn't change soon. I shall be an old woman before I know it."

"Talk to mother, Lydia. Perhaps she can arrange for you to spend time with the Handmakers," Mary said.

Lydia pushed her chair back and stood up. "Haven't you heard, Mary? We have been disowned by them, too."

Hallie walked slowly down the path, stopping every few feet to pick the succulent berries from the vines. She carefully reached between the stems, avoiding the thorns that protected their prize. Twice instead of putting them in the basket, she popped the berries into her mouth. That was the best part about picking berries.

Making sure that her movements toward the gate were not too obvious, she traversed back and forth across the road several times. Hallie had convinced herself that there was nothing wrong with spending time with someone who could provide her with a diversion from the mundane routine at Magnolia.

"Good morning," Aden said, standing up from behind the wall. He was without his shirt. Beads of perspiration trickled down the side of his face as he wiped his forehead with the back of his gloved hand. "Excuse my appearance. I didn't expect company." He reached for his shirt that was laying on the wall and pulled it over his head.

"Oh, no, I'm not company. I am just out picking berries," she said casually.

"I see that," he said, a grin crossing his face.

"Well, you get back to your task. I will see you later. Do stop by this evening for a piece of blueberry pie."

Aden was still smiling at her as she turned around and headed back home.

Once in the kitchen, Hallie set the basket on the table and poured the berries into a bowl. "Oh, my goodness, look at me," she said to herself as she passed the mirror on the hallway wall. Her mouth was covered in blue stains. Now she knew why Aden was grinning.

Later that morning, Lydia paced back and forth across the balcony. Nona and a few other women sat in a circle under the Acacia tree shucking corn. She could hear their constant chatter, but she could not make out what they were saying. Her mother had gone upstairs to rest and Mary was with the school children. Lydia was bored. She had to find something to do. At that moment Angel came through the French doors, a towel draped over her arm. Throwing her leg over the balcony wall, she jumped to the ground without even saying a word to Lydia. She was halfway across the yard before Lydia climbed over the wall and trotted after her. Almost out of breath, she called to Angel. "Where are you going, Angel? Can I come with you?" Lydia knew that she was never supposed to associate with the women, but today she did not care. She wanted someone to talk to.

Angel shrugged as Lydia caught up with her. "I'm going to the river to take a swim. You can come if you want to. I don't own the river." She continued on her walk with Lydia keeping two steps behind her. Angel climbed over the split rail fence that signaled the end of the property. She pushed back the vines and bramble that covered a small path leading to the tree-lined bank. For a moment the river took a rest as it flowed into a cove of azure blue water.

Without so much as a word, Angel laid her towel on a fallen tree branch and began to undress. Shedding all of her clothes, she gingerly stepped into the water and let out a sigh. Paddling away from the shore, she turned to Lydia. "Are you coming in? It is wonderful."

"Oh, no, I couldn't." Lydia sat down on a large smooth rock and watched as Angel played in the water. Beads of perspiration formed on Lydia's head as she swatted away buzzing insects. After another five minutes in the heat, the temptation of the cool water took over. Quickly removing her clothes, Lydia ran into the water. She could not stop giggling as the water lured her into its liquid respite. "I can't believe I am actually naked in the river," Lydia said, "but it feels wonderful."

"This is my favorite place to come to. I sneak away whenever

I can," Angel said, paddling closer to Lydia. "Sometimes when I have taken all I can stand of those nasty men, it feels good to wash away the day. Come over here, Lydia, there is a shallow spot. We can sit on the bottom and let the fish nibble on our toes."

They sat together for a few minutes. Lydia kicked her legs each time the minnows came near her. Angel broke the silence. "You and I are about the same age, Lydia. This is the first time we have ever been near each other. I guess it's because your mother doesn't want you around my kind. Is that right?"

Lydia shook her head. "You have to understand that she is just trying to protect Mary and me. It really isn't working. As far as everyone in town is concerned I am as guilty of sin as you."

"No need to explain it to me, Lydia, I am a sinner through and through," Angel said as she turned over in the water. "It was my momma's doings. If she hadn't been a whore, I probably could have done what I wanted to do. I wanted to be a dancer, a high-steppendancer in one of those stage shows in California." She kicked her legs, sending sprays of water over her head. "But now, I'll probably just die from some disease like all the others."

"Don't say that! We are both young. Who knows what will happen to us." Lydia paused for a moment and then quietly asked, "Can you tell me, about the others, I mean, what are they about?"

"Well, let's see," Angel mused. "Lola is all about money, Polly is all about food, and Ramona thinks she's something special.., and Venus is just plain nasty. That about sums it up. They ain't too deep. We just sleep, eat, please the men, and then do it all over again. Me, I'm saving my money and if I don't die before I have enough, I am going to California. And then—"

"Shhh, I hear someone coming." Lydia put her hand on Angel's arm. The sound of twigs breaking and a rustle from the bushes startled them both.

Lydia quickly paddled away from the shoreline and into deeper water. Pulling down a branch from an overhanging tree, she covered her face and remained still. A few seconds later, a lone horseman appeared on the edge of the river. Angel stayed in the shallow water.

He was young—not much older than they were. He wore a tan shirt and riding breeches, his black hair pulled back in a leather-lacing strap. He moved his horse close to the bank.

Lowering its head, the horse drew long sucking drinks of water. It was then that the rider caught sight of Angel lying in the water. "I'm sorry, I didn't realize anyone was here. My horse was in dire need of water."

Angel did not respond. She laid her head back and let her hair drift in the easy current. Bowing his head to avoid looking at her, he pulled on the reins of the horse, which reluctantly obeyed. Before he could turn around on the path, Angel stood up in the water. Walking toward him, the water lapped across her stomach and ran down her breasts from her wet hair. "You don't need to rush off. The water feels wonderful today. Are you in the mood for a swim?"

Without turning around he said in a loud voice, "I think not." Once on his horse, he quickly moved away.

Bursting into laughter, Angel fell back into the water. "You can come out now, Lydia. He has left. Did you see the look on his face? He was as red as a beet. I wish he had stayed. He was quite handsome."

"Angel! How could you! You stood right up naked in front of him. What would you have done if he had started undressing? And here I am hiding in the bushes. If my mother found out about this she would lock me in the house for the next five years."

"Oh, please, Lydia. I see men naked all the time and I am not ashamed of my body. It might have been fun to have a romp with someone just for the hell of it and not even worry about how much he was going to pay me."

Lydia scrambled up the bank and began quickly dressing, her clothes sticking to her wet body. "Well, he isn't going to see me naked, that is unless I want him to." Within minutes she was running down the path toward the fence, unaware that several yards away the young man sat quietly on his horse watching her. Once Lydia was over the fence and far enough away that he would not be seen, he pulled his horse into the clearing. He stopped for a moment, looking back at the path leading to the river where Angel still languished in the water. Turning his horse once again, he headed back toward town and up the hill to the red brick mansion that was the home of his relatives.

A breathless Lydia entered the house trying to get upstairs before anyone saw her. "Why yer hair be all wet and yer dress, too? Where ya been?" Nona asked as she came down the stairs carrying an armful of linens.

"I fell in the river," Lydia said, quickly passing by her.

Fifteen minutes later, Angel came into the kitchen where Nona was cooking.

"I s'pose ya fell into dah river, too?" Nona asked.

"Nope, I walked in," Angel answered, picking up an apple from the table.

Chapter Sixty-One

Three days had passed and no one had mentioned the incident at the river. Lydia breathed a sigh of relief, deciding it was probably safe to return to the swimming spot. This time she would not remove all of her clothes. She would swim in her pantaloons and camisole. Leaving the house with a towel wrapped tucked under her skirt, she was well out of sight before anyone noticed. Perspiration ran down her sides and her hair was matted to her face as she ducked under the hanging branches thick with moss. She couldn't wait to get into the cool water.

At the river's edge Lydia began to unbutton her shoes when the rustle of branches diverted her attention. Moments later a familiar horse and rider appeared on the bank. Dismounting from his horse, the young man came towards her. "I see you are going for another swim today," he said.

"What do you mean another swim? How do you know I have been here before?" she retorted, putting her hands on her hips. "Is this the only place on the river where you can let your horse drink?"

He grinned. "That tree you were hiding behind barely covered your nose. I assure you I did not mean to embarrass you and your friend by intruding on you. Actually, I don't believe your friend was offended at all."

"She is not my friend!" Lydia called out adamantly. "She is a boarder in my mother's house, but she is not my friend. I would never be so bold as she was. I would never stoop to such antics."

"Then I assume you are not going to swim today?" he asked.

"No! I am not. I was only going to dip my feet into the water. I don't even know your name. I am not accustomed to speaking to men to whom I have not been properly introduced."

"Stephen Ayers. My name is Stephen Ayers. And who may I ask do I have the pleasure of speaking with?"

"I am Lydia Vine Simmons." Picking up her shoes, she lingered for a moment. She didn't want to leave. "Why are you staring at me?" she asked. "You are making me feel uncomfortable."

"You must have torn your dress on the way here. A part of the material is hanging below your hem," he replied.

Reaching down, Lydia pulled the towel from under her dress. "Well fancy that. It must have gotten caught on my clothing when I was leaving the house."

"Yes, I suppose so," Stephen said, smiling. "Would have made a nice drying cloth after a swim."

"Oh hush," Lydia said, laughing. "It's just that the weather has been so uncomfortable and the house only cools off at night when the breeze comes in from the ocean. I would love to go to the beach, but I am not allowed. My mother says the hot sun and salt water will damage my skin. The water here felt so good the other day, but of course, I was going to swim in my clothes today." She knew she was rambling.

"Well, I am glad you finally decided to come back to the river. I have been here for the last three days hoping by chance that you might return. I wanted to apologize for my intrusion on your private time. By no means did I mean to offend you. Am I forgiven?"

Lydia smiled. "You are forgiven."

"I wish I had more time to spend with you today," Stephen said, "but I cannot linger. I am expected at the house for an early dinner. Will you be here tomorrow?" he asked. "It would be my pleasure to bring refreshments and perhaps we can have a civil conversation."

"I would like that," Lydia replied. "I will meet you here at two o'clock."

Stephen put his foot in the stirrup and hoisted himself onto his horse. "See you tomorrow."

Lydia waited until he was out of sight before she started running, her feet were barely touching the ground. She could not believe that he had waited three days for her and now he wanted to see her again. Perhaps she was too eager when she accepted his invitation for tomorrow. Maybe she should have said no, hoping he would insist. But what if he hadn't? She was too happy to think about anything except her meeting with Stephen tomorrow. Should she tell her mother or Mary? Of course not!

They would not approve and she knew it.

Reaching the backdoor, Lydia stepped into the kitchen, breathless. Nona caught her off guard. "Ya jest better be tellin' me what's goin on with ya. Dat be two days ya be comin' from dah river. What ya be doin' down dar? Is it sumthin' yer mother should know?"

"Oh, Nona, please. You must keep my secret. I have met someone. He is very special and I am going to meet with him tomorrow at two. Please don't say anything to mother or Mary."

"What kind a person be meetin' ya at dah river? Dat don seem right." Nona frowned.

"His name is Stephen Ayers and he is young and handsome and please, just give me one more day to see him," Lydia pleaded.

"I s'pose I could. But I be goin' with ya tomarra. And dats a fact."

Lydia knew better than to argue with Nona. "Fine, you come with me and see for yourself. Now I have to go find something suitable to wear." She raced out of the room and up the stairs. Nona put her hands on her hips and shook her head. "Dem youngins sho do drive a body crazy," she said aloud.

Morning could not come soon enough for Lydia. When she awoke the next day, she smiled to herself and counted down the hours. At ten, she took a bar of lavender soap and her robe and went to the bathing room on the second floor. Filling the porcelain tub with tepid water, she soaked and scrubbed until the bar had almost disappeared. The loud knocking on the door startled her. It was Polly who interrupted her. "How much longer are you going to be in there? I need to get water for my pitcher." Polly knocked again impatiently.

Lydia opened the door. "Can't you wait until I am finished or go downstairs and get water? I am taking a bath."

"How many baths do you take in one week? You can't be that dirty," Polly whined. "I'm gonna wait out here until you're done."

Lydia stood up and reached for her robe. "I need to keep myself clean. It wouldn't hurt if you took a bath once in a while. You smell," Lydia said as she nudged past Polly.

"Oh yeah, well you be telling your mother to get me a tub I can fit in and then I'll take a bath. That bloody tub is way too small for the likes of me," Polly yelled after her.

An hour later, Nona met Lydia on the side balcony and

together they casually strolled down the path until they were out
of sight of the house. Helping Nona over the fence was not easy,
but Lydia managed to keep her from falling on her face. Lydia
tried to remain calm as she pushed back the overhanging
branches for Nona. When she reached the clearing she stopped.
Stephen had spread a cloth on the bank and arranged daisy and
primroses around the border. He had laid out cheese and
biscuits and chocolate truffles, along with fresh strawberries.
His smile faded when he saw Nona.

"Stephen, this is so lovely. Thank you. This is Nona. She is
my companion today."

Nona bobbed her head. "I be gonna sit over dar and do my
sewing. Ya jest go on with what ya be doin'." She pointed her
finger at Stephen. "I be watchin' you."

"You look lovely today, Lydia," Stephen said as he took her
hand and helped her to get comfortable on the coverlet. Sitting
down across from her, he poured her a glass of berry wine. "I
hope this is to your liking."

An hour passed quickly as Lydia and Stephen talked. He was
from Richmond, Virginia. He was taking a break from his
studies before going to Harvard to study law. His father was also
a barrister.

Her story, of course, was much longer. She told him about
her opulent life at Vine Manor, the misery caused by the war
and her time spent in St. Louis. Her voice cracked as she related
the story of her father's death. She then told them about her life
at Magnolia. Leaving out the part about their illustrious
boarders.

"So you see, Stephen, it was never my mother's intention to
run a boarding house, it just happened. She wanted to make
sure she could provide for Mary and me. Please don't think less
of me. I am a good and pure person and will remain that way
until I meet someone who convinces me otherwise, fat chance
that will happen anytime soon. I have yet to have a gentleman
caller come to my house. It is very lonely for me at Magnolia."

"There is nothing wrong with trying to survive in the face of
adversity." He paused for a moment his fingers just inches away
from her hand. "I have very much enjoyed our visit today, Lydia.
I find your wit incomparable to most. If you do not think that I
am being too forward, I have a question I would like to ask you.
My relatives are having a reception in my honor. There will be

dinner and an evening of dance. I would like it very much if you would accompany me. I would love to be your first gentleman caller."

Lydia was stunned. On the bank of the river, sitting on the ground, she was being invited to her first formal evening with a proper escort.

"This is the embarrassing part," he replied. "It is tomorrow night. I know that is short notice, but I had no idea when I was going to see you again. I have been coming here for the last three days hoping you would appear. It would do me great honor if you would accept my humble invitation."

"I am flattered by your persistence and I should say no, that I do not know you well enough, but I am not going to. I would love to spend an evening with you, Stephen."

"Wonderful! I will be at your door at seven tomorrow evening."

Nona stood up and walked closer to Stephen. "Dat sho not proper. Her mammy is gonna have sumthin' to say about that. Ya better come ta dah house and ask her mammy before ya go on makin' plans." Nona picked up her sewing, the signal that it was time for Lydia and her to leave.

Lydia helped Stephen gather up the dishes. As they stood close to each other, putting the dishes in his satchel, he whispered to her, "You smell nice."

On the way back to the house, Nona did agree with Lydia that Stephen seemed like a proper gentleman, but she still wasn't sure how Hallie would react when Lydia gave her the news that she was invited out.

Hoping to catch her mother off guard, Lydia entered the house calling "Mother!" in a loud voice.

"For heaven sakes, Lydia, lower you voice! What is so important that you have to screech at me?" Hallie asked as she met Lydia in the hallway.

"I met a young man. His name is Stephen Ayers. He is visiting here from Virginia. He is just lovely, and he asked me to go with him to a reception tomorrow night. I know you are going to say no, but please, mother, this is so very important to me. Please say yes. Nona met him. She likes him. He is very proper, mother. Please say yes. I know he should come here and ask you, but he has so many commitments because he is only visiting Lott's Point for a short time. Please, please, mother, say yes!" By this time Lydia was breathless.

Hallie looked into the pleading eyes of her eighteen-year-old daughter and remembered the first time James asked her out and she had to confront her own father. It seemed like she used some of the same words. "Yes, Lydia, you may go, but I do wish to meet this young man when he comes to escort you."

Lydia couldn't believe what she was hearing. Her mother had said yes. Yes, yes, yes. She threw her arms around Hallie. "Oh, I love you, mother." Jumping back, she danced around the room. " I need a dress, a special dress! And my hair, I must fix my hair and pluck my brows." She was off before her mother could answer her request. Lydia was running down the hall calling to Mary and Nona. Hallie smiled to herself, knowing how Lydia must feel at this moment. Yet she wondered who this young man was and how they had met.

Mary's reaction was quite different. "Mother, please! I can't believe you are letting Lydia go off with someone you do not even know. This is all so unconventional and improper. You have no idea what his intentions are."

"What is proper about our life right now, Mary? Lydia is not a demure little lady. She knows how to handle herself and I do think she has some good sense. Let's hope so."

Lydia stood in front of her full-length mirror. She was dressed in a blue, water-silk dress. With her coiffed hair done up in curls and adorned with white flowers, she knew she was sure to catch a few stares at the reception. She turned to look at herself in the mirror. Catching sight of Angel standing in the doorway, she frowned. "Is there something you need, Angel?" she asked.

"No, I just wanted to see what you had chosen to wear. I suppose you wanted to keep your meetings with our young man a secret from me. Perhaps I shall wait downstairs with you and say hello to him when he arrives," she said, laughing.

"He is not *our* young man. He is mine and you stay away from him. You have embarrassed me quite enough."

Angel smirked. "We'll see about that. I suppose you told him that you live in a brothel?" She turned and left, still laughing to cover up the sadness she felt that it was not her getting ready for a proper evening with a handsome, young man. Angel's evening would be spent with old Mr. Smythe.

Lydia clenched her fist. She had to make sure Stephen did

not find out what really went on inside the closed doors of Magnolia, at least not tonight. Lydia waited by her bedroom window for Stephen's carriage to arrive. With the first sign of dust on the road, she retrieved her shawl from the bed, ran down the stairs and out the door. As the carriage pulled up in front of the house, Lydia stood on the porch waiting for it to come to a halt. Before Stephen had put one foot on the ground, she was down the stairs and at his side.

"My goodness, this is a surprise. I thought I was to meet your family," he said.

"I decided you can meet them when we return. My mother was not feeling well." Without hesitation, Stephen opened the carriage door and helped Lydia to her seat. He signaled to the driver and they circled the lawn just as Hallie and Mary made their appearance on the porch. "Well, she escaped before we met her gentleman. I suppose I should have expected that. I will deal with her when she arrives home."

In the carriage, Stephen leaned forward, looking into Lydia's eyes. "You look absolutely lovely tonight, Lydia," Stephen said. "You are a vision."

"Thank you. It is all for you, Stephen. It took me hours to get ready, so you best appreciate me tonight."

Stephen broke into laughter. "I do believe you are one of a kind, Lydia."

It was a short ride. Entering Lott's Point, the carriage continued down the main street and up a gentle slope to a red brick mansion that overlooked the town. The house was ablaze with candles and lanterns. White gloved servants greeted each carriage as it arrived. Lydia could hear the sound of chamber music through the open doors. Her face wore a full smile. She could not believe what was happening. It was all too exciting.

When the carriage door opened, Stephen took her hand. "I'm anxious for my relatives to meet you. I am sure they will be pleasantly surprised."

Stepping onto the marble porch, Lydia noticed the stares from some of the other women. She was glad she had worn her mother's cotillion dress. They must be admiring her. As they entered the doorway, Lydia let out a gasp. Her knees were weak at the shock of seeing August and Hilda Lott standing at the head of the reception line. When Hilda caught sight of Stephen and Lydia she put her hand to her mouth and grasped her husband's hand. August hurriedly stepped out of the line and took Stephen by the arm. He quickly ushered Stephen to the back of the hallway leaving Lydia with a blank stare on her face. "What in heaven's name are you doing with that girl? Get her out of here immediately!" he said in a hushed voice.

"Why, what is wrong?" Stephen asked, thoroughly confused.

"Just do as I say!" August growled. "How dare you make a fool of your aunt and me by bringing that trash into our home."

Stephen did not have to escort Lydia out of the house. She had already left. She ran across the lawn and hid behind a large oak tree. Lydia covered her face as tears streamed down her cheeks.

"Would someone please tell me what is going on?" Stephen asked when he caught up with her.

"Why was I so stupid? Was I so anxious to be with you that I did not even bother to ask you the name of your relatives? I am mortified to be here! If I had any idea that August Lott was your relative I would have never come with you. I detest him and he hates our entire family. He treats us with contempt. Please take me home, now!"

In the carriage, Lydia wept openly, her face turned toward the window. Stephen had no idea what to do. "Can we at least talk about this, Lydia?"

"No! There is nothing to say. Did you see the way everyone stared at me? I am not welcome in your circle, Stephen. It is all too complicated to explain."

When the carriage came to a stop in front of Magnolia, Lydia bolted out the door and ran into the house, leaving Stephen without any idea of what had really happened. Stephen heard a woman's voice calling his name as he prepared to leave.

Standing on the terrace, a shawl wrapped around her shoulders, Hallie Simmons beckoned to him. "Would it be possible if I could speak with you for a moment, Mr. Ayers?" she asked. Hallie had seen the carriage drive in and Lydia running from it. She knew immediately that something was wrong. Lydia had been gone less than an hour. She wanted to know what Stephen had done to her daughter.

"Yes, I am Stephen Ayers. I was your daughter's escort tonight. You must be her mother."

Hallie nodded. "I am. What happened tonight?" What have you done to my daughter? Lydia is completely distraught."

"I am quite puzzled and embarrassed by the whole thing. I take full responsibility for what occurred. It seems that there is some sort of rift between my uncle and your family. My uncle was quite rude to her tonight."

"And who, may I ask, is your uncle?"

His reply answered all her questions. Hallie sat down. "Oh, I can't imagine a more awkward situation for poor Lydia. She must have been so embarrassed. Of course, I don't expect your uncle could have been gracious enough not to shame her even more. I'm afraid any further contact between you and Lydia will be out of the question. I do hope you understand."

It was Mary who consoled Lydia as she lay across her bed sobbing. "I wish I could just die, Mary. I have never been so embarrassed. What am I to do? I am sure that Stephen will never want to see me again. That damn August will forbid it."

"Hush," Mary said. "You stay here. I will see what I can find out from mother." Going downstairs Mary stood in the shadows of the draperies and listened to the conversation between Stephen and her mother.

Mary stepped out onto the terrace when Hallie finished talking. "Did you happen to tell this young man about all the terrible things his dear uncle has done? Did you tell him that during the war August was loyal to both sides just to make a profit? Did you tell him that the taxes he has levied on the proprietors in this town are outrageous, just as the prices in his store? Oh yes, and he wanted this property so he hoped we couldn't pay the taxes that had already been paid."

"Mary! That is quite enough. We both have our burdens to bear. August has a right to be upset with me, as I have to be with him. It is neither Stephen's nor Lydia's fault that they are caught in the middle. August Lott is his kin and that is where his loyalty should lie, unless he feels otherwise and that is for him to decide. Our feelings about Mr. Lott are well founded, but that is not to be discussed any further! Please go to your room. We will talk later."

"I am thankful for your time, Mrs. Simmons. I cannot tell you how sorry I am that I have caused Lydia so much grief. I am fond of her and she does not deserve to be treated badly. Please tell her so for me." Stephen stood up. "I will now bid you goodnight."

Long after everyone was asleep, Hallie stayed on the terrace.

She felt empathy for this young man who had expected to have an enjoyable evening, but instead found himself in a damnable position. Had she done the right thing by telling Stephen about Magnolia? Maybe she should have just encouraged him to leave. Someone walking across the yard interrupted her thoughts. "Is that you, Hallie?" Aden asked softly. "What are you doing up so late?"

"I might ask you the same thing, Aden. Are you having difficulty sleeping, too?"

Aden joined her on the porch. "I was going to see if by chance there might still be a lantern on in the house. I need something to read, but I would rather talk to you."

"Well, I have another problem, Aden. You may want to get a book instead."

Hallie related the evening's events to Aden. He listened intently. "They are young and impetuous. I am sure the attraction between Stephen and Lydia has only been fueled by August's outburst. Of course, it also gives August another rung on his grudge ladder. It may cause some repercussions, even though I don't know what else he can do," Aden said. "I really wouldn't worry about August. I hear that love conquers all."

"Do you believe that, Aden?" she asked.

"I would really like to believe it is so," he replied.

Hallie looked at him in the dim light of the moon. He always seemed to soften her worries. "You are wise, Aden."

He smiled, "I'm not wise, Hallie, I just always try to accept the lesser of two evils. Seems it usually works out that way in most situations." They sat together in silence for a few minutes just enjoying being close to each other. Each wondered how the other felt in this moment, but neither one was brave enough to voice their thoughts. "I suppose I should get a book and let you go to bed. You must be exhausted." He helped her from her chair, his hand gently touching hers.

As he walked down the stairs, he paused and turned back to Hallie. "I suppose I could never fault Stephen for falling in love with Lydia. She is another Simmons woman that is extremely hard to resist."

August Lott was furious with Stephen when he arrived home and Hilda was beyond consoling for what she considered a complete breech of etiquette for her first formal dinner of the season. She could not believe that the topic of conversation by her guests was consumed with talk of what Stephen had done. Behind opened fans the women chattered about the sinful women and band of Negroes living at Magnolia, and Stephen bringing one of those people to this house,oh my.

"And you, young man, can pack your trunks and leave as soon as possible. I will not have anyone who associates with the likes of the Simmons women staying in my house," August roared.

"That will be my pleasure," Stephen replied. "If you think bringing Lydia here was a ploy to embarrass you, that is completely false. Before I talked to Mrs. Simmons I had no reason to think there was any explanation why a young woman in this town could be treated so badly by you. I will leave in the morning."

Stephen's demeanor left August and Hilda wondering what the inhabitants of Magnolia had said about them.

In the morning, Stephen left the Lott mansion and rented a room in Miss Betty's Boarding House. After settling in, he acquired a horse from the livery stable and rode straight to Magnolia. Today he would make his peace with Lydia. He had only one week left before he must leave for Harvard. He planned to spend it all with her if she would have him. Finally getting past Nona, he was allowed to speak to Lydia in the parlor for a few minutes. Nona would be right outside the door.

Lydia, eyes swollen from a night of crying, was shocked that Stephen had come back to see her. With a limp smile, she accepted his apology and his invitation for a walk, with Nona just a few steps behind them. "It is my fault, Stephen. I was so anxious to see you again that I never bothered to question you on important matters. I also never told you the whole truth about Magnolia so I owe you an apology just as well."

Stephen reached for her hand and put it to his lips. "Thank you, Lydia. I do believe we have come to a new beginning."

Standing in the midst of the garden, Stephen held Lydia's hand, "I never meant to hurt you, Lydia. I know that we have only known each other for a short time, but I do believe that is all it takes for some. I will do my best to make you realize that you are very special to me. There is only one week left before I must return to school, but I have moved out of my uncle's house so that I could spend what time remains with you."

A flood of tears started again as Lydia fell into his arms. "Did my mother tell you everything? The whole story?"

"Yes, she did and none of it changes how I feel about you." Pulling her close they heard Nona clearing her throat loudly, which was a signal for him to retreat.

Hallie knew that Stephen was persistent and would make another attempt to see Lydia. She did not realize it would be so soon. It was useless to try and keep Lydia and Stephen apart, so she insisted that they be chaperoned at all times. With Stephen having only one week left before he had to leave, Hallie knew they would be vulnerable to their passion. Each morning Stephen would arrive before breakfast and most days not leave Magnolia until the sun was setting. He became a fixture in the house and at times Nona had difficulty keeping up with them. Hallie and Mary had both warmed to him and found him quite charming. The magnetism between Stephen and Lydia was apparent to everyone. They were already deeply in love.

On the last day of Stephen's visit, Hallie allowed Lydia to go for an hour's walk with him alone. Holding hands they walked down the path and settled on a stone bench in the garden.

"You look so sad today, Lydia. You know I will be back as soon as I can and I will write you every day."

"I will miss you terribly," she whispered. Lydia bowed her head and looked down at her hands. "Angel said that I am probably no more than a summer dalliance for you and when you go up north you will forget all about me. She said when you meet those sophisticated women at college, I will seem like a southern bumpkin to you. Angel also said that when your parents found out what you did, and you know they will, they would forbid you to see me."

"I have no idea why Angel is saying those things. My parents have little to say about my life. My grandfather left me ample money when he died, so I have more than enough funds to live on my own. I would never toy with your feelings, Lydia. I am not that kind of person. Will you believe me?" he asked.

"I want to very much, Stephen. I just wish there was some way I could be sure." Stephen took her into his arms and placed his lips on hers. "Does that help to convince you or should I do it again?"

"Maybe just a little more convincing would help," Lydia replied. Hand in hand they continued on their walk.

Chapter Sixty-Two

With summer in full force, the heat and humidity caused the least little incident to rankle the nerves and raise the voices of those in the house. The women complained when there was no business and complained when there was too much business, saying they were just too hot. Ramona and Venus seemed to be in a constant squabble over men, while Lola decided she was taking a break from everything. She positioned herself on the back veranda, with a book in her hand and her feet propped on a stool. She wanted no part of the constant bickering.

Angel was now seeing more clients than Ramona and Venus, which did not sit well with them. She continued to carry a full load of customers and her stash of money was growing. Although she constantly worried about getting pregnant or contracting a disease, she continued to practice her trade. She had no idea what she would do if either happened. Angel was unhappy with the continual visits of one particular elderly gentleman, Mr. Smythe. He was by far the most generous of all her clients but he wanted to take up most of her time. He wore strong cologne to cover the mustiness of his clothes and his chipped teeth from years of smoking a pipe were yellowed and quite unappealing. When he presented her with a cameo pendant and a ruby necklace that belonged to his deceased wife, she could not bring herself to tell him that she wanted to end the relationship and prefer that he find someone else. He was enthralled with her and on each visit he asked her to become his wife. She would fend him off by saying she found him to be a very sweet person and a great lover, but that she was not ready for marriage. It did not deter him. He continued to return to see her.

It was Polly who suffered the most in the heat of summer. Her corpulent body made it impossible for her to stay cool. Lying in her bed, completely unclothed, she dabbed wet cloths over her body and then fanned herself. She was a sight to behold and not too many people wanted to behold it. Nona said the spectacle of the fat rolls on Polly's body made her want to stop eating forever. Consuming large amounts of pastries and candies seemed to ease Polly's pain for short periods of time.

Today she reached into her box of chocolates and found it empty. She had eaten the last of them the night before, telling herself she should do so before they melted from the heat. Groaning as she raised herself from the bed, Polly wrapped her silk robe around her and went out to the balcony. Looking down in the yard, she saw a couple of young Negroes pulling weeds from the flowerbeds. "Boy," she called. "Yoo-hoo, up here." Twelve-year-old Gabriel looked up at Polly.

"I need someone to go into town for me. I need something from the sweet shop. I will give you a nickel if you will go for me," Polly said.

Gabriel studied her for a moment, knowing that his mother would tell him that he could not go into town alone. It was much too dangerous. "Be all right if ah take mah brother wid me?"

Gabriel asked, trying to use some of the proper English that Miss Mary was teaching him.

"That's fine. I'll give him a nickel, too," Polly replied. "I will put the label from the box in the envelope with the money. You tell the lady at the counter that I want another box of the same chocolates. Do you know where the sweet shop is?" Polly asked.

"Yes em," he replied. He had more than once salivated over the array of truffles and candies displayed in the window.

Taking nine-year-old Boz by the hand, Gabriel clutched the envelope tightly. On the way to town the boys kicked stones and found long sticks to drag in the mud. It would have been much better if Gabriel would have taken the back road around town and come in behind the sweet shop instead of walking down Main Street. If he had taken the back way, he and Boz would not have been stopped outside of August Lott's store by a man named, Delbert Higgins, who worked for August Lott. Blocking Gabriel's way, Delbert put his hands on his hips. "Whatca doin' in town, boy? Where's the rest of yer kind?"

"I'm mindin' mah business," Gabriel said. Taking hold of Boz he tried to veer around Delbert.

"Don't run from me, boy," Delbert said, grabbing Gabriel by the back of the shirt. What you got in that envelope? Give it to me."

Gabriel held tight to the envelope, giving Delbert a swift kick in the shins. Delbert let out a howl. "Git in the store, you little bastard." Delbert opened the door to the general store and threw Gabriel inside.

"Run, Boz! You run on home!" Gabriel called out to Boz who was standing on the sidewalk too frightened to move.

Three hours later a wagon pulled into the gate of Magnolia. Boz jumped out the back and ran to Jasper, who was pulling water from the well. "Ya gots tah help mah brother, come wid me," he said, taking Jasper's hand. In the back of the wagon, Gabriel lay with a blood-soaked rag wrapped around his head. Streaks of dried blood covered his face and shirt and his eyes were swollen shut.

"Go to dah house! Git Mizz Hallie," Jasper yelled to Boz. "What happened?" Jasper asked the driver of the wagon who now helped him lift the limp body of Gabriel to the ground. "Don't know," the man said. "I found that other little boy sitting on the side of the road with this one laying on the ground. I just put him in the back and he told me to bring them here. I got to get. Hope he is okay," the man said, climbing back into the seat. The kind man wanted no part of this mess.

Hallie and Mary came running from the house. Mary knelt on the ground and pulled the rag away from Gabriel's head. "Oh, God, I can see down to his skull. He needs a doctor. Quickly! We need to get him inside." There was no need to hurry. Gabriel was dead.

When the news of the injured boy filtered into the stables, Gabriel's mother let out a scream and ran toward the house. She had been looking for her sons for over two hours. When she saw Gabriel lying on the floor in the summer kitchen, his body covered with a tablecloth, she fell to the ground and buried her head in his chest. "Mah baby, mah baby! What has dah done tah ya? Oh, Gabriel, who done dis?" she screamed.

It was little Boz who stepped forward. "It be dat Delbert man. He don hit Gabriel wid a fire poker and knocked him clean off his feet. We be mindin' our business, but Massa Lott, he took dah note and money. When Gabriel asked for it back, Massa Lott said he be keepin' it and for Gabriel to go home. I seed when Gabriel grabbed dah envelope and ran for dah door, Delbert got tween dem and dah door. Den Delbert he picked up a poker and hit Gabriel couply times on dah head. Gabriel come out of dah store all bloody. I be hidin' behind dah rain barrel. Dats how I seed it all through the winder. I put dat rag around his head. Dat man named Delbert, he threw Gabriel in dah wagon and drove tah the edge of town and dumped him on the road. I follered behind, 'cause I didn't want him ta seed me. I stayed wid Gabriel 'til dat other man comes by and picked us up. Gabriel he don say nothin'. He jest lay der."

Aden had come into the kitchen while Boz was telling his story, "What envelope, Boz? Where did you get it?" Aden asked.

"Gabriel don got it from dat fat lady upstairs. She wanted sweets. She be goin' to give us a nickel if we went ta town and gets it."

The wailing and sobbing in the room was now at a shrieking pitch as the rest of the women came to the summer kitchen. After a few minutes, Aden picked up Gabriel's body and carried it toward the stables with a mourning procession, including Mary, in tow. Hallie knew that she should stay behind. Her knees were weak and she was shaking. The sight of Gabriel's blood-soaked body instantly brought an image of James into her mind. She knew how Gabriel's mother must feel. She would give the poor woman time to grieve in private.

That evening, Hallie, Mary, Lydia, and Aden gathered in the parlor. The sounds of Negro spirituals could be heard through the open windows as Gabriel was prepared for burial. A body would not last long in the July heat. The burial had to be done quickly.

"What about Polly?" Mary said. "This is all her fault. If she had not sent Gabriel to town, he would still be alive. He was such a bright child. I had high hopes for him," Mary said, wiping her eyes.

"It may be her fault indirectly, Mary, but that bastard had no right to do what he did," Aden said. "I think it is time someone let August Lott and his men know that they cannot continue to do whatever they feel like doing. I will be the one to deal with him."

Hallie pleaded, "No! Please, no more violence. We lost one child tonight. Harming August will only cause more bloodshed. That is what he wants. He wants us to come after him so that he has a reason to injure or kill even more of us. He would make sure the whole town was on his side. If we do nothing, he has no reason for revenge. I know of people like him. Eventually August will meet his match."

Aden would not be moved, "I have no intention of harming that scoundrel August, but I am going to have a talk with Delbert." Aden turned toward Jasper, "Go find Ben and Hobart for me."

Ben and Hobart were eager to go with Aden, some of the others offered too, but Aden said two were enough. They left Magnolia under the cover of a moonless night and returned near dawn.

In the early hours of morning, while mist still hung over the open field, an outline of figures slowly marched toward the edge of the meadow. The procession included Hallie, Mary, and Lydia, along with the other five women. Hallie had roused them from their beds, insisting that everyone—and she meant everyone—was going to Gabriel's funeral. Polly eschewed the idea, saying that she felt so guilty she did not know if it would be proper for her to be there. Hallie would not accept her excuse and when the eight women showed up at the funeral site, they garnered surprised looks from everyone, including Aden.

After the prayers and the last hymn was sung, the coffin was lowered into the newly dug grave and covered with soft earth. Gabriel's mother threw herself on the mound of dirt and wailed. The others walked away, leaving her there until she was able to pick herself up and walk back to the stables. It was their way of letting a mother gather enough strength to let go of her eldest son. Laying Gabriel to rest was difficult enough, but now those who had believed they were somewhat safe in their new home once again felt the strain of an uncertain future.

When Delbert did not show up for work the following day, August cursed under his breath and sent one of the stock boys to look for him. The boy returned, saying that Delbert's clothes and personal belongings had been removed from his room at the boarding house. August surmised that Delbert left town, fearing retribution from the Negroes. It was just as well.

Two months later a badly decomposed body was found in the underbrush on the bank of the river two miles down stream from Lott's Point. To avoid traveling the five miles to the sheriff's office to report the body, the two farmers who found it buried the remains in their field.

Chapter Sixty-Three

Hallie sat at the long table with an array of silver pieces spread out before her. "No school today?" Hallie asked a Mary as she came through the dining room.

"None of the children showed up. I waited for fifteen minutes, but they never came. I supposed they are still sad about Gabriel's death. I miss him, too. He was my helper. He used to arrange my supplies and keep the children quiet. Gabriel was a good student." Mary picked up a bowl and polishing cloth and began cleaning the rim. "I went to the stables to see if they were there, but Hobart said that most of them had gone to the river to swim. Mother, you should see the stable. Ben and the others have separated the walls and made living quarters for each family. They have a kitchen and washroom at one end and an area where they all gather in the evening. I was quite impressed. The floors are swept clean and all of the beds have coverlets on them. Except for the noise from the children, it is a good temporary place to live for now."

"Where does Aden stay?" Hallie asked, rubbing her cloth across a silver knife.

"I didn't ask that question, mother. But yesterday Aden told me that he thought the children would learn more if they had a schoolhouse and desks. He told me that even some of the adults would like to learn to read and write but they don't really feel comfortable sitting on blankets in the field. Aden said that he and the others could build a one-room school house in a couple of weeks if it was all right with you."

"This is the first I have heard of it, Mary. That must mean they are planning on staying here for a while. Yes, tell Aden that I have no objection to his plan."

Within days a space had been cleared in the field behind the stables. Trees were cut and the timbers trimmed for the walls of the building. With Aden's knowledge of shipbuilding, the planks for the floor were cut with a fine saw and notched together.

As the building was being erected, the older men worked on making desks and benches while the women sewed blue curtains for the windows. When the last of the shingles were nailed on the roof and the front door put on its hinges, Aden brought two large boxes from the stable. He had made a trip to Pass Christian and purchased school supplies and readers. Mary danced around the room and clapped her hands. She was now Miss Mary, teacher at the Woods schoolhouse.

Aden stood next to Hallie as they watched the children and adults enter the school for their first day of education. "This is a very special day, Hallie. Your daughter has taken on a task that few would have the nerve to do. Schools for colored children, Hallie, can you imagine that?" Hallie did not protest when he took her hand, "Come," he said, "Let's go see what a little tenacity has accomplished."

"It is you, Aden. You are the one that seems to propel everyone forward. You always seem to know what is best, while I still question every decision I make. And I am surely concerned about the school. Less than two years ago, the coloreds were forbidden to go to school. It seems too soon for Mary to take on such a large task. I fear for her safety."

It was Mary's enthusiasm that kept Hallie from expressing her fears. "You should see those children, mother! They are so excited when I write a letter on the chalkboard and they know what it is. And the idea that they can add simple numbers is so impressive. I can hardly wait until they can actually read," Mary said, returning from her first day in the new schoolhouse.

Lydia did not share her enthusiasm. When questioned whether she would want to come and teach a few classes, Lydia's answer was adamant, "No!" Lydia spent most of her time writing letters to Stephen or cutting out patterns for her trousseau that she planned to wear after her wedding. Today when Mary entered Lydia's sitting room, Lydia was sitting amidst yards of cream-colored satin. Mary sat down next to her. "My school is so wonderful. I just love it. I can't believe you haven't come down to see it."

"You are wasting your time, Mary, teaching coloreds to read and write. What do you suppose they will do with that knowledge? Buy property or own a business? I think not. It is all nonsense, Mary."

"And what are you doing? Making dresses you may never wear. Especially that one," Mary said, pointing to the layers of satin draped over Lydia's lap.

"I will too wear it! I am going to sew beads on it until Stephen asks me to marry him. And if it gets too heavy I will just be pulled down the aisle in a wagon!"

"In that case, Lydia, I hope he asks you real soon."

The news that Hallie now had a schoolhouse on her property where coloreds were learning to read and write was met with much displeasure by the white population in Lott's Point. How dare that harlot, Hallie Simmons, stir up another controversy? Hadn't she embarrassed the town enough already? Someone needed to put a stop to such going-ons. August Lott appointed himself champion for the cause. He would deal with Hallie and her school. It was time for him to end this nonsense going on under his nose.

When some of the blacks that lived in town expressed an interest in the school, their employers swiftly quelled their enthusiasm. Any servant or workman sending his children to the school at Magnolia would be promptly fired and suffer repercussions, at August Lott's counsel, of course.

Chapter Sixty-Four

Lola was the first of many to tell Hallie that August Lott was raising his ugly head and convincing the townspeople that it was time to put an end to all of the unsavory actions going on at Magnolia. It was difficult to go against him— many of the people did not wish to get involved, but there were others who were ready to do whatever August asked of them.

"I would be careful, Hallie. If you think he was in a dither when we came, or when his nephew, Stephen broke his allegiance to the Lott family, you should hear what he is saying now. The school for the coloreds has really riled him," Lola said. "I have another question. Do you have time to talk?" Lola asked, lighting a cigarette. "I was wondering if you knew that Aden is planning on leaving soon."

"What? Who told you that? He has not mentioned it to me. Are you sure, Lola?"

"Well, I was talking to Nona and she said that he would be returning to Tahiti some time before winter. You may want to talk to Nona, but I wouldn't want her to know that I told you."

"Why are you telling me this, Lola?" Hallie asked. "Is this what you *really* came to talk about?"

"I like you, Hallie. I have seen the look in your face when he comes around. It may not be love, but it is pretty close to it. Don't be a fool, Hallie. If you care for him, then tell him."

"There is nothing between us. I could never do that. My husband—"

Lola interrupted her. "Your husband is dead, Hallie and you are alive. When someone leaves, life has a way of filling that void. It keeps all of women from going crazy. Stop wishing for things that will never happen. Look at your life the way it is right now. If you're feeling guilty because you care about someone other than James, you're wasting your time. I gave up guilt a long time ago. Aden is down on the beach collecting clams. Go talk to him, but fix your hair and take off your apron before you go."

"I am not going down to the beach! If Aden Woods plans to leave here, he can come and tell me himself, and that is final!" Hallie said.

"Don't wait too long," Lola said, leaving the room.

Taking off her apron, Hallie stomped up the stairs to her room. She picked up her hairbrush and ran it through her hair. She had a mind to go down to that beach and tell Aden Woods exactly what she thought of him. How could he just go off and leave without telling her? She would go down to the shore and have a few words with him. Maybe it was just idle gossip. She could ask Nona, but why should I bother her with something so trivial? She would find out for herself.

Hallie hurried down the front path, crossed the road and stepped into the soft sand at the top of the dunes. Finding an opening between the sea oats, Hallie ducked her head and slid down the incline. Shielding her eyes from the sun with her hand, she scoured the beach. She watched as a single wide-winged tern searched the shoreline. Driven to this spot by an innate instinct, the tern silently plunged into the water, surfacing with a small fish in its mouth.

Holding up the edges of her dress, Hallie walked toward the rocks where she and James hunted for clams. They had a contest to see who could find the most. With her small hands she was able to reach between the crevasses of the rocks; she always won.

Aden was standing on those same rocks, his pants rolled up and his shirt lying on the beach. He bent over the shallow pools and turned over the stones. Standing up with two shells in his hand, he saw Hallie coming near him.

"Well, hello. This is a surprise. What brings you to the beach and without a bonnet?"

"You! Aden Woods, if you are going to leave here you could have at least had the decency to tell me, rather than let me find out from Lola. When were you planning on telling me? Never? Were you just going to leave without even saying goodbye?"

Aden ran his hand through his hair. "Whoa, just a minute, Hallie. For one thing I have not finalized my plans to leave and I would never go away without letting you know first. I think someone is carrying tales."

"Are you telling me the truth?" she asked.

"Yes," he answered.

Hallie sat down on the rock. "I am so embarrassed. I am going to strangle Lola when I see her. Why did I even think she would tell me the truth? Please accept my apology for yelling at you."

Aden stepped out of the water and sat down next to her. "You're forgiven." Her hair had become tousled from the wind and swept across her face. He slowly removed a few strands from her cheek. Running his hand across the back of her neck, he slowly pulled her close to him. She did not stir. With his head bent, his lips found hers. Her hand came up to his chest, to his bare, warm chest. Aden parted her lips and played with the tip of her tongue. She sighed slightly, tilting her head. After a moment, she slowly pulled back, looking into his face. "It's too soon, Aden. We should not do this," yet she did not move far away from him.

"I have something I want to say to you, Hallie. I have been wanting to say it for months."

Hallie put her fingers on his lips. "Don't say it, Aden. If you say it I will have to answer you and I don't think I am ready to do that. James has been gone just a little over a year."

"I will wait," he said. They started down the beach, Aden carrying his bucket half-full of clams. Hidden behind the rising dune, Aden once more took Hallie into his arms. "I have waited so long to hold you, Hallie." He kissed her once more.

Returning to the house, Hallie walked through the foyer and onto the back veranda. Lola sat with Ramona, both fanning themselves to stave off the heat. "Thank you, Lola," Hallie said and quickly left. "What was that all about?" Ramona asked. "She's in love," Lola replied. Ramona yawned. "Too bad."

After a light dinner and a cool bath, Hallie dressed in a simple, white summer dress. Her petticoats and corselet were put aside for cooler days. She went into the library and scanned the shelves for a book to read. She was restless. Her emotions were running high. Once on the porch, she sat down on the swing and opened her book. It did not take long for her to lose interest in the words. Hallie wandered out to the railing and stared up at the night sky.

A streak of lightening lit up the southern sky and the wind began to pick up. The smell of blessed, cooling rain was in the air. Pulling the French doors closed behind her, Hallie turned down the flame on the lamp. A light tap on the door startled her. Aden stood with his nose pressed against the glass.

"For heaven sakes, what are you doing out this late?" she asked.

"I haven't any oil for my lamp. I was wondering if I might borrow some. It didn't start raining until I was half way across the field," he said, shaking the droplets of water from his hat.

"I'm sure we have extra in the summer kitchen," Hallie said, picking up the lamp and going into the hallway.

Hallie's hand shook as she poured oil into an empty can. "Here, let me do that," Aden said reaching around her.

He was standing so close she could feel his breath on her neck. If she turned, she would be in his arms. She could see the outline of his face in the window as the lightning illuminated the room. "I just needed to be near you one more time," he whispered and pulled her near to him.

He caressed her body as though she were made of fragile glass. Each stroke of his hand sending signals to parts of her body that had been untouched for over two years. His kisses softened her taunt breasts and caused sensations in her stomach. "I love you, Hallie." She did not answer.

The sudden red glare visible through the open window caught his eye. He wavered for a moment before he realized that it was a fire. "Oh, my God, something is on fire!" he yelled releasing her from his arms. "Stay here, Hallie. I'll be back."

As Aden ran into the field Ben and Hobart met him. "No need tah hurry. It be dah schoolhouse. It be too late. It don be burnin' tah dah ground and I don' spect it was an accident. Twern't for dah rain I speck dah stables would have caught fire, too," Ben said.

Aden walked around to the back of the stables and looked at the smoldering pile of charred timbers. The smell of burning wood permeated the air and occasionally sparks flew upward from the debris. Except for the stone chimney, nothing remained. Aden headed back toward the house. Mary stood on the porch, wrapped in a blanket, tears running down her face. "It's gone, isn't it?" she asked, already knowing the answer. "I know it was August Lott's men who did this. Why can't he just leave us alone?"

Inside the house, Aden assured everyone that no one was

hurt in the fire. Huddled inside the stable the children were crying from the loss of their beloved school.

Chapter Sixty-Five

Hallie sat at the kitchen table drinking lukewarm tea. The sun had just risen above the horizon. She hadn't slept well. Aden returned with the news that the school had been burned down, and then left again before she had time to talk to him about their time together the night before. Anxious to talk to him, she also knew that the day had to be started and breakfast made. She wondered where the women from the stable were. When the door to the kitchen opened, it was not the women, coming to work, but Ben and Hobart who entered.

"We need tah talk wid ya, Mizz Hallie," Ben said, nervously. "Dat fire last night done scare't us all real bad. Since Gabriel been kill't, most of us been worrisome. Somes of dah others are packing up dar stuff. Dey don want tah stay here no more. Dey done asked Aden to take dem to New Orlans. Aden, he said he would, but somes of us older folks, we been talkin' bout the move and it jest gonna be too hard on us. We's wants tah stay here. I'd jest be my wife, Mandy, Hobart and me. Wes be wonderin' if dat be okay wid ya? We won't cause ya no trouble."

Hallie was caught off-guard. "The others are leaving! I need to talk to Aden. Where is he?"

"He be down at dah stables," Ben replied.

"Take me to him," Hallie said. For the first time since Ben and the others arrived on her property, Hallie followed Ben and Hobart to the stables. It was a place she had never cared to visit. Two wagons were pulled closed to the door, packed high with barrels and boxes.

Hallie lowered her head as she entered the door and waited while her eyes adjusted to the dim light. Walking down the narrow corridor between the open stalls, her mind flashed back to the time when her prize riding horses were kept here. She found Aden sitting at a long wooden table at the end of the corridor. Aden seemed surprised at Hallie's presence in the stable.

"Ben said that most of the people are leaving and you are escorting them. Is that true?" she asked.

"Yes, it's true, Hallie. I was going to come tell you as soon as we finished the details on our route plan. They don't want to stay here any longer. A few of the people have relatives living in New Orleans and they want to go there. They are very upset and scared and want to leave right away."

She had only one question. "Are you coming back, Aden?"

"Yes, of course. It will take me a couple of weeks to get them settled and then I will come back." His eyes confirmed his promise to her causing, the unsettled feeling that was holding her captive to disappear.

"Let me walk you back to the house," Aden said, taking her arm.

Just as they began to talk about their night together, they were once again interrupted. Asia and Mandy were waiting for Hallie in the yard.

Asia seemed nervous. He hung his head, not looking at Hallie. "I guess dey be no need to hem around, I jest come right out and say it," he said. "Me and Mandy, we wants tah go wid dah others to New Orlans. Mandy she be so thankful dat ya saved her, but now we be scare't tah stay here." Mandy stared at the ground, not saying a word.

"Me and Mandy, we be real close now. We likes each other lots. But, Mandy she be real scare't after what happened to her by dem men. Please, Mizz Hallie, let us go," Asia murmured.

"I will miss you both, but you are free to go wherever you want. I am not your master. If you want to start a new life somewhere else, I understand. You two have been through enough in your shorts lives."

A grin crossed Asia's face as he took Mandy by the hand. "Thank ya, Mizz Hallie, thank ya kindly."

Mandy stepped forward. "I be nevah fergettin' what ya people did fer me. Ya saved mah life and when I has my first girl youngin, I gonna name her Hallie."

As they walked away, Hallie turned to Aden. "Is everyone's leaving only about Gabriel and the school fire, or is there something you are not telling me?" she asked.

"Someone threw a black doll made of corn shucks into the stables last night after the fire. It had a noose around its neck and blood all over it. It was probably just chicken blood, but they took that as a warning that the fire was not the end of the violence and they fear one of them may be next. They are scared and I don't blame them, but I hate the idea that they have to move again. I thought this was going to be a nice place for them to settle. August Lott has a strangle hold on this town and he is not going to let up until he runs you and everyone else on the property out of town. I better leave. I have a long trip ahead of me. When I return, we will spend more time together." He mouthed the words, "I love you."

Mary was distraught with the loss of her school and students. She cried for days, saying her life was over. She now had nothing to live for even though Lydia assured her that she had to stay alive long enough to be the maid of honor in her wedding.

Chapter Sixty-Six

"Where are you going?" Angel asked Lydia, as she headed out the door. "You want to go to the river?"

"I don't have time today. I am going into town to post a letter. I don't think it would be a good idea for you and I to be seen together."

Angel hung back for a moment. "You're right. Can I at least walk to the carriage house with you?"

"What is the matter with you today? Why are you so anxious to get out of the house? Don't you have men to see?" Lydia asked, sarcastically.

"No, my afternoon is free. Lola is arguing with Polly. Venus and Ramona are planning something that doesn't include me. They told me to go away. I have nothing to do."

"I have plenty to do, but I have to get this letter off to Stephen. I haven't heard from him in over two months. I don't understand why he is not answering my letters." Lydia said.

"Maybe he is busy with school or—"

Lydia interrupted her. "I know what you are going to say, that he is busy with someone else. Well, I don't for one second believe that. He loves me and someday soon we are going to be married."

"That wasn't what I was going to say to you, Lydia. Maybe he is busy making plans for you to join him," Angel's voice softened. "I'm thinking about getting married, too."

"You! Who in heavens name are you going to marry? I didn't even know you had a suitor."

"Mr. Smythe has asked me to marry him. He says he loves me and he will take me anywhere I want to go. He said we could move away and he will even buy me a house." Angel ran her hand over the horse's mane. "I think I would like to live in New York."

"Mr. Smythe! He is an old man, Angel. Why would you even

consider marrying him?"

"He loves me, Lydia. And he will be good to me. Then when he dies, I will be a respectable, rich widow. I will have all his money and I can go anywhere I please."

"I am sorry, Angel, but I just could never marry a man I didn't love, especially one as old as Mr. Smythe. I would rather stay alone."

"That is easy for you to say. I have few options open for me. What am I going to do, Lydia? At least if I marry the old goat, I will have a chance at someday being something other than a whore. I don't want to die of some disease or from a bad pregnancy. I don't want to end up living over a saloon and being killed by some drunken sot. You tell me, what other choice do I have? For right now, this is our secret. You must promise me that you won't say anything to anyone in the house. "

Lydia touched Angel's arm, "I promise not to say a word. I'm sorry, Angel. I have been unkind to you. I was afraid that you would try to take Stephen away from me just to be mean.., and the temptation might be too great for him since I want to remain pure until I marry."

"That is a joke, Lydia. Your Stephen would never prefer the likes of me when he had you. Besides, if I am going to be a married woman soon I will be faithful to my husband, even though he is a far cry from your Stephen. Mr. Smythe's body is so wrinkled, he looks like he should be hung on the line to dry," Angel said, laughing.

Lydia suddenly felt a rush of empathy for Angel. "You are very pretty, Angel. Mr. Smythe will be lucky to have you. Now I must get to town to see if there is a letter from Stephen waiting for me."

Lydia had no idea that there were letters arriving daily from Stephen, but instead of being put into the post office box marked 'Simmons' in Lott's store, they were landing in the hands of August Lott. The letters she had written and taken to the post office were also never sent. They were stuffed inside a folder on the office desk.

A promise made to Stephen's parents that he would do his best to keep Lydia and Stephen apart was all the encouragement August needed. His jealously of the women living at Magnolia was almost more than he could bear.

After her conversation with Lydia, Angel decided it was time to take the offer of marriage from Mr. Smythe seriously. If she did not give him an answer soon he may stop coming to see her. Even though the thought of living with Mr. Smythe made Angel's skin crawl, she knew that this would be her one chance to escape from her profession. When he touched her with his gnarled fingers it was more like someone reaching for a biscuit. He always pinched her breasts and stomach. He was no longer able to complete his manly duty but insisted on continuing to try. Their sessions together were long and tedious. When he ate, food would escape from the corners of his mouth and land on his clothing. He had a bad case of flatulence, which compelled her to constantly spray her room with perfume. Yet he was a kind man. His wife had died many years earlier and he was alone and rich.

A few days later when Angel accepted Mr. Smythe's proposal, everyone in the house, except Lydia, was quite surprised. After a smiling Mr. Smythe left, Angel appeared at Lola's door to tell her that she would be leaving in the morning. Mr. Smythe wanted to move quickly to assure that Angel would not have time to change her mind. Her possessions would be picked up and sent to one of his homes in New York. After Angel said yes to him, he presented her with a very expensive engagement ring, which he carried with him on each visit to see her.

The next morning, dressed in a blue traveling suit, Angel said her goodbyes and rushed out the door to the coach that would take Mr. Smythe and her to Natchez where they would be married. If she had lingered for a minute more, she would have turned around and run back upstairs to her room.

"Can you believe it?" Venus said, watching the carriage pull away. "The little gutter snipe bagged herself a rich one. She deserves the old bastard. I hope he lives to be a hundred."

Chapter Sixty-Seven

"Polly, get up! You have got to get out of that bed and go downstairs and bathe. I cannot stand the smell of you for one more minute!" Lola screamed. "I am going to toss these bed linens in the waste bin and freshen your room. Now get up!"

"Don't scream at me, Lola. You know it hurts my feelings when you scream at me. My legs hurt. I can't walk down the steps. Just get me a basin and a cloth and I will wash here."

"No! I am warning you. If you don't get up I will have everyone in this house help me carry you down the stairs. I will be back in five minutes and you better be on your feet," Lola said, slamming the door behind her.

Polly sat up and pulled the blanket away from her body. She stared down at her swollen, purple legs that were pocked with sores, some of them seeping fluid. Polly had hidden the fact from Lola that she was suffering from some sort of awful condition, which was getting worse by the day. Terrible pains crossed her stomach when she tried to relieve herself and at times she could not urinate at all. If Lola knew that she was really sick she would send her to a hospital and Polly knew that she would never return to her sister. Polly had heard all the horror stories about hospitals and she wanted no part of them. But Lola was right; she stank...she stank something awful. How was she going to get down the stairs? Lifting her legs off the side of the bed, she looked down at the swollen mass of flesh hanging around her ankles. It was so painful to walk. Reaching for her robe, Polly pulled herself up and stood holding onto the bed. If she could make it into the hallway, perhaps she could sit down and scoot down the stairs, but then how was she going to get back up to her room? She had to do it for Lola. Her sister had been so good to her and after all these months of doing nothing and using Lola's money for extra food, the least she could do was take a bath.

Struggling across the room, her feet shuffling one small step at a time, she reached the door. She was out of breath and leaned against the wall. Her throat was dry and she was perspiring. After a few minutes she once again started into the hallway and toward the stairs. She was almost there.

Polly began to tremble as her legs gave way under her enormous weight. Teetering at the top of the stairs, she lost her balance. As she tried to right herself, her weight shifted onto the railing, each spindle breaking free like a row of dominoes toppling onto each other with Polly falling along right behind them. Reaching out, with nothing to grab but the air, Polly tumbled over the side of the stairs and landed with a loud thud on the marble floor of the foyer.

Lola was the first to arrive at Polly's side. Dropping the clean linens she had just fetched from the cupboard, she let out a piercing scream that echoed throughout the house.

Polly lay in a pool of her own blood, the wooden spindles strewn all about her body. Lola dropped to her knees and called to her, but Polly did not answer. The fall had crushed her skull and cracked the marble tile.

Lola covered her body with a sheet. "It's my fault. It is my entire fault. I told her she had to come downstairs and take a bath. If I wouldn't have insisted, she would still be alive," Lola sobbed. "I have killed my sister."

Ramona, who had been standing over Polly, backed away. "It wasn't your fault. It was an accident. My goodness, look at her legs! Whew, Lola, she really did need a bath."

It took Jasper and Ben until sundown to build a wooden coffin large enough to hold Polly's body and then the rest of the day to dig the hole for the grave. Lola said Polly would have liked to be buried in the field with the flowers and sunshine around her. Nona said Polly would rather have been buried in her pantry so she would be near her food.

Three days after Polly was buried, Ramona and Venus announced that they were leaving Magnolia. Since Polly had died, they were no longer concerned about any charges being brought against them for the death of Mr. Capp. They both had enough of living at Magnolia and planned to travel north. Lola was not surprised and wished them well, knowing that the volatile relationship between the two women would probably end before they reached their destination. Even though they hinted that she was welcome to come along, Lola declined. Her heart was still heavy with grief from the loss of her sister who had been her companion all of her life. She would stay behind at Magnolia until she decided what she wanted to do next. That decision would have to be discussed with Hallie.

The rooms on the third floor were officially closed to everyone. Lola's customers would have to find a new bedpost to hang their hats on. She was out of business.

The wind whipped around Hallie's legs as she tried to hang a bed linen on the line. She made several attempts before she had the pins in place. As she bent over to pick up another sheet, she saw someone coming. Throwing the cloth in the basket, Hallie began running across the yard. It was Aden. He was home.

Aden hopped the fence and caught her in his arms. "I have never been so glad to see someone in my life. I missed you, Hallie."

Still out of breath from the sprint, she kissed his cheek and hugged him tightly. "And I missed you, too. It has been almost a month."

He took her hand and they started back toward the yard. "I know it took a long time. We ran into bad weather, bad people, and illness. When we finally got to New Orleans, it wasn't at all as we expected. There is still a lot of unrest and we were not welcome in many of the places we stopped. I was finally able to locate some of their relatives living near the Bayou. For a time I thought that I might be bringing them all back here with me. I was anxious to get back. My only thought was of you," he said.

"Please come sit with me on the porch. So much has happened since you have been gone that I don't know where to start."

Hallie told Aden about Polly's fatal accident and that all the women were gone except Lola. Hallie continued by telling him that Mary spent her days helping with the chores and writing letters to women's institutes that she hoped would accept her as a student. Mary decided that she wanted to be a teacher.

Lydia was in complete despair, having received no word from Stephen and she refused to help around the house. Hallie could no longer afford to pay anyone to work for her. Jasper, Ben, and Hobart tended to the yard as best they could; Nona and Maddy helped in the house.

"They are all so old, Aden. They totter around here trying to help, but most times it takes them so long that I end up doing the chores myself. Nona can no longer handle the laundry or the steps, so she stays in the kitchen. All five of them are in bed by six o'clock every evening."

"I'm sorry I haven't been here for you, but don't worry, Hallie. Everything is going to be just fine. I am sure that both of your daughters are capable of handling their own affairs. I am more concerned about you. I think you need to rest for a few days. I have to unpack my things and freshen myself and then I will be back to be with you. This time not even a fire will make me leave." He kissed her softly and headed for the stable.

Chapter Sixty-Eight

Mary was eager to hear from at least one of the many colleges where she had applied. Her vigil kept her on a path to Lott's Store. Each day she would make a trip to the store to check the post office box for an incoming letter. Mary made her trips late in the afternoon when Hilda and August left the store for supper. Ruth Toth was in charge of the store for a few hours while they were away. Ruth did not harbor animosity against Mary or her family. She minded her business and did what she was told.

When Mary entered the store, Ruth's face broke into a broad grin. "A package came for you today, Mary. It's from New York."

"Oh, my goodness," Mary gasped, running across the store to the postal boxes. "It is not here, Ruth! Where is it?"

"It was too big to fit in the box. I put it on the desk in the office. I'll get it for you," she said rounding the counter. Mary was already half way up the stairs. "Never mind, I'll fetch it myself."

Mary picked up the envelope and stared at the return address. It was from the Potsdam Normal School for Women in Potsdam, New York. Sitting down in the office chair, she scanned the desk for a letter opener. It was then that her eyes landed on the address of a letter stuffed halfway into a brown folder. She recognized the handwriting. It belonged to Lydia. Peering into the envelope she pulled out three or four more letters. Putting them all back, she put the folder on top of her package and hurried down the stairs. "I found it, Mrs. Toth, Thank you. I will talk with you later."

Her heart thumped rapidly as she hugged both parcels to her chest, hoping to get away before August or Hilda spied her. Walking close to the building and out of sight of the windows, she dashed across the street and got into her carriage. Neither August nor Hilda were aware that she had been in the store until the next day when they discovered the folder containing Stephen and Lydia's letters was missing. Mrs. Toth gave them no clue as to where or how it had disappeared.

Mary's acceptance into the Potsdam school was overshadowed by Lydia's screaming. Opening the last letter that was sent to her by Stephen, she read a few lines. "He says that he is anguished that he has not heard from me and that he is afraid that I do not love him any more. His parents want him to go to Greece with them for the summer. Since he has not heard from me, he said he might go with them. Oh, my poor Stephen. He thinks I don't love him anymore! I am going to kill them both. I am going to get a gun and shoot August and then shoot Hilda. How dare they do this to me! After they are dead I shall have them thrown in jail for tampering with the mail. I hate those people!" Lydia stomped around the room until finally exhausted, she collapsed in a chair and sobbed.

Mary knelt next to her chair. "It will be all right, Lydia. You can write another letter to Stephen today and we can take it to Pass Christian to be mailed."

"Thank you, Mary," Lydia sniffled. "And I want to tell you how happy I am for you."

When Hallie told Aden what had happened he agreed to take the letter to Pass Christian. "I will go tomorrow and wait for the post wagon myself, so you better get busy writing a very good explanation. We will deal with the Lott's at a later time. Go...start writing," he said. "And you, Mary, please accept my congratulations."

After dinner, Nona made lemonade and brought it out to the terrace. Jasper sat on the steps whittling while Mary and Hallie sat quietly. "What is wrong, Mary?" Hallie asked. "You have been quiet all day. I thought you would be elated about your news."

"I am, mother, but the more I think about it, the less appealing it sounds. It is so far away and it will take two years for me to complete the course and then the expense of it all. I know our money situation and there is no way I can go to this school. We are going to be hard pressed for money this winter just to meet our living expenses."

"I know that, Mary. It saddens me to think that you have to pass up this opportunity. God, why is everything so hard?" Hallie asked, pacing back and forth across the porch.

"Is dat money from dem jars all gone, Mizz Hallie?" Jasper asked.

"Yes, long ago, Jasper."

Mary sat straight up in the chair. She had heard Jasper say, "Dem jars." They had only emptied one jar. "Jasper, did you say jars, like in more than one jar?" Mary asked. "We only had one jar filled with money. Is that what you meant. One jar?"

"Me and yer daddy, we buried two of dem jars in dat bag. I member dat rightly," Jasper replied.

"But when we dumped the bag on the floor in the house we only had one jar. The bag was all muddy and, Jasper, where did you put the bag the jar was in? Do you remember?" Mary asked.

"Yes ma'am, I be throwin' it behin' dat summer kitchen. Dats whar I put it."

As if a bolt of lightning had struck the porch, Mary and Hallie raced down the stairs and ran to the back of the house. The weeds had grown tall behind the stone house but Mary dove into like a rabbit with a fox on her trail. Crawling around on her hands and knees she moved stones and bits of broken pottery from the earth. "Nothing. There is nothing here, mother, not even a shred of burlap."

"Dats cause ya be lookin' in dah wrong place. It be ovah here," Jasper said, holding up the shreds of brown cloth.

Each time they were ready to give up the search, they dug a little deeper, unearthing more scraps of the bag. Covered in dirt, her hands bleeding from the sharp rocks, Mary let out a squeal as her hand closed around the top of the slender glass tube that had been sleeping in the yard for almost two years. "I found it! Oh my God, mother! I found it!"

"It is small. Maybe that is why we didn't see it," Mary said wiping off the side of their new treasure. We were so excited about the money, we completely forgot to check the bag for anything else."

Returning to the porch, Mary held the jar up to the lantern. "There is no money in this jar, only a few papers." She wiped her face with her muddy hand, "You open it, mother. I think it is a letter."

The wax seal had hardened onto the jar, making it impossible to peel off. In desperation, Hallie took the jar and dropped it on the floor. Amidst the shards of broken glass lay a roll of papers tied together with twine. Hallie slowly pushed the string off the papers, letting them unfurl like a morning flag.

Hallie sat down and smoothed out the first paper, leaving smudges of dirt on the edges. She cleared her voice. "It is a letter from James." She began to read to herself.

> *To my dearest wife, Hallie.*
>
> *This is a very difficult letter to write. If you are reading it, I have not returned to you from the war. How can you tell someone that you love with all your being that you will never see them again? I cannot write those words.*
>
> *Our life together was so incredible. I never dreamt that just waking up in the morning next to you could fill my heart with so much joy. I expected it to go on for many years, but it is not to be.*
>
> *Please don't be sad for too long. Sorrow will only diminish the special person you are. You have given me a lifetime of happiness and now you must try to find solace and comfort in your life without me. Perhaps you will say that the idea is totally impossible, but I say otherwise. You deserve to find someone who loves you as I did, if that is at all possible. This is what I want for you, my love. I give you my permission to be happy again, if only you will allow yourself.*
>
> *And to my daughters, Mary and Lydia, who have added so much to my life. Take care of your mother. Do not let the hate and anguish you are all feeling at this time destroy you. You are bright, intelligent young women who I know will succeed in whatever you endeavor. I love you both,*
>
> *I remain your loving husband and father,*
> *James Simmons*

Hallie dropped the letter to the floor and began to sob. Mary picked it up along with the other paper from the bottle. After reading the letter, she unrolled the yellowed parchment paper. It was a certificate of deposit from the French bank where her father sent his money before the war. "I do believe we are very wealthy, mother," she said, softly. Bittersweet emotions engulfed the two women, hidden behind a veil of tears that flowed down mud-stained faces.

They would have money once again. Money to send Mary to school, money to finish the repairs on the house, and money to keep them from worrying about their future. Somehow it did not seem so important at that moment.

Hallie read the letter over and over until she knew every word by heart. It was the unshakeable feeling in her body that troubled her. Each time she read the line, find someone to love you as I did, an image of Aden popped into her mind.

Chapter Sixty-Nine

With the letter written to the French Bank to reclaim Hallie's fortune, Mary prepared to leave for Potsdam. She was concerned about leaving her mother and Lydia behind, but she knew this would be her opportunity to ensure her future. Now that money was not an issue, it would be much easier for everyone. If only Lydia could pull herself together, Mary and Hallie would be much happier.

"I know this is awful for you, Lydia. Stephen meant so much to you and even if he did decide to go with his parents to Greece, he will have your letter waiting when he returns," Hallie said, trying to console her daughter. "You have got to get out of bed and start eating more. You're looking pale." Hallie pushed back the curtain and sat down next to her daughter's bed.

"You just don't understand, mother," Lydia moaned.

"I think I do. You have lost someone very dear to you. I understand."

"No, mother, you don't understand," Lydia said. She hesitated for a moment and then blurted out the words, "I'm pregnant."

Hallie jolted upright, "What did you say? Please tell me I heard wrong, please tell me you are not with child! How...I mean, when did this happen?"

"We slipped out at night after everyone was asleep. We didn't mean for it to happen, but our passion overwhelmed us. And now I am going to have a baby and I have no husband," Lydia sobbed.

Still stunned, Hallie asked, "Are you sure?"

Hallie reached across the bed and took her daughter into her arms. Lydia put her head on Hallie's chest and sobbed. "I am so sorry, mother. I have made another mess of things. I love Stephen so much."

In the New York Harbor, Stephen Ayers kissed his parents goodbye as they boarded a ship for Greece. The next morning he would be on his way to Mississippi. Lydia would have to tell him to his face that she did not love him.

Arriving at Magnolia before dawn, he lay down on the front porch and closed his weary eyes. When Nona came out to sweep the porch she poked him with her broom. "What ya be doin' out here? Ya git in dat house, dar be a girl wantin' tah see ya." She grinned as he got up and brushed off his pants. It was only a few seconds later that she heard the loud scream from the dining room. Lydia jumped from her chair and sent a plate of eggs sliding to the floor.

"I couldn't leave without knowing for sure what happened." Stephen said. "Why did you stop loving me, Lydia?" Stephen asked.

"Come Mary, I think these two need to be alone for a while," Hallie said. "I am so glad you are here, Stephen. You have no idea just how glad."

When Lydia told Stephen what August had done with the letters, he was livid, but the news that he was going to be a father took priority. They needed to make plans and quickly.

"At least you are not marrying a pauper, Stephen. I come with a handsome dowry," Lydia proclaimed proudly. "I am so sorry, Stephen. I do hope I have not complicated your life."

"I would take you and our unborn child with or without your money, Lydia. You are my love."

After much deliberation, Stephen and Lydia decided that they would be quickly married in another town and Lydia would return with him to Cambridge. He would tell his parents that they had been secretly married for months to cover up the recklessness of the pregnancy. His mother would be outraged if she knew the real truth. Even though it did not matter to him, Stephen knew that some of the pain would be eased knowing that Lydia was from a moneyed family. The idea that her mother ran a boarding house that catered to prostitutes would seem ridiculous and would be played down.

Hallie was losing both of her daughters within a few days. Seeing them both so happy kept her tears at bay, beside the fact that they were much too busy to dwell on emotions. Trunks had to be packed, clothing had to be prepared for storage.

"I really do love this pink shawl," Lydia said, picking the soft knit from the pile of clothing on Mary's bed. It would be nice to have when I can no longer fit into my jackets."

"Take it," Mary said. "There are gloves to match it. She rifled through her hatbox. "Has Lola decided what she is going to do, mother? Is she going to stay here?"

"I don't know. She is looking into some kind of business to buy. It really doesn't bother me right now. She is quiet and sometimes I enjoy her company," Hallie answered.

Mary frowned. "You are an odd pair. And what about Aden? I understand that he is going to be leaving soon. Is that true?"

"He hasn't said exactly when he has to leave. He has something to take care of that cannot be put off too long. We haven't had much time to talk in the past few days with all the activity going on around this house," Hallie replied.

"And what is he waiting for," Lydia said smiling. "He loves you, mother. When are you going to tell us that you love him, too? Now would be a good time since we are leaving." Lydia winked at Mary.

"If and when I make that decision you will be the first to know. Now let's finish the packing," Hallie said, changing the subject.

Suddenly the room was quiet, except for the rustle of paper being folded between the layers of dresses filling the trunks on the floor. Was it time for her to apologize to her daughters? Was it time to tell them she was sorry for the life she had chosen for them? Living those years in St. Louis during the war had showed them a life they never knew. They had learned to make their own living as well as their own beds. They had seen the death of their father and shared a wagon and frightful trip, with Mary in charge. Since they returned to Magnolia, they had endured the life of a servant. They had been ostracized by the community and witnessed the pain and suffering of others. They were no longer the wealthy, catered children of the Simmons family. They were both strong individuals with strong convictions about their future. Mary was leaving with confidence. She knew what she wanted and was going after it. Lydia was leaving with a man who loved her in spite of all the adversity that surrounded them. He was dedicated to her. No, she would not tell them she was sorry. She would send them off with all her love.

Lydia adjusted her hat and picked up her gloves. Mary rechecked her handbag to make sure she had everything she needed for the trip. "I am going to miss you terrible, Mary,"

Lydia said. "Who will be there to listen to my tantrums and solve my problems?"

Mary smiled. "You have Stephen now, Lydia. I am sure he will take very good care of you. I will miss you too, little sister. This will be our first time away from each other."

"What about you, Mary?" Lydia asked. "Do you think you will marry and have children?"

"I don't know. Right now I am so focused on going to school, I haven't really given it much thought. Perhaps it will come a little later for me. If not, I will expect you to give me lots of nieces and nephews to love." Mary could see the tears welling in Lydia's eyes. They threw their arms around each other.

As the last of the suitcases were put in the carriage for the trip to the train station, everyone stood outside waiting for someone to make the move to leave. It was Stephen who stepped forward. "Thank you, Mrs. Simmons, for allowing me to become a member of your family. I am sorry it wasn't under different circumstances but you must know how much I love your daughter. We will visit soon." He opened the door for Lydia. Holding onto her mother's hand she whispered, "I am so scared, mother. I wish you were coming with me."

Lydia dabbed at her red nose. "Can you believe it, Mary, me with a baby? I will think of you often." She kissed Mary's cheek. And turned back to her mother.

"You will be fine, Lydia. Stephen will take good care of you. Just remember that I love you very much." They fell into each other's arms and Lydia shuddered trying to hold back her tears. "Goodbye, mother. I love you," she said, and then bolted for the carriage.

It was difficult to say goodbye to Mary. Who would she talk with in the evening? Who would be the levelheaded person who helped her make decisions? Who would replace her dear Mary?

"I will write as soon as I get there, mother. After I am settled, I want you to come visit. Promise me you will. Take care of yourself." She too, quickly stepped into the carriage.

After her tears were spent, Hallie walked around the house engulfed by a feeling of loneliness she hadn't felt since James's death. It would be some time before she saw them again and she already missed them. They had been her lifelines and now she had been untied and set free like a kite with no tail. Which direction should she follow? Putting her shawl around her shoulders Hallie walked across the back yard, climbed over the fence and into the field of blue wildflowers. There was only one place to go in this direction.

"Aden," she called out, stepping into the dim light of the stable. "Aden, are you in here?"

"I'm here," he answered.

She pulled back the patchwork quilt that covered the door and stepped into his room. Aden sat up and laid his book on the bed.

"What is it, Hallie?" he asked.

"Oh, Aden, I am so lonely. My family has left me."

He reached out his hand, "Then come stay with me."

Hallie moved close to the bed. Aden's hand reached behind her head. Small, wet kisses landed on her delicate neck as he pulled her into his arms. She closed her eyes, her face resting on his chest; she could smell the scent of pine from the trees he had cut that day. Pulling back, her lips brushed his ears and he shivered. Hallie unlaced the front of her jumper and pulled it over her head before she lay down next to him. His hands searched her body. She could feel each callous and graze on his work-worn hands as he tenderly moved down her body. She pushed herself back, her head touching the wall as the rhythmic motion of their bodies covered them with waves of sensual pleasure.

With the girls no longer living in the house, Aden was invited into Hallie's bed almost every night, although he always left before morning. The unfamiliar feeling of their first night together had passed and the passion they felt for each other seemed natural. When their emotions were spent and they lay together wrapped in each others arm, Aden would profess his love to her, yet Hallie kept her feelings for him locked in her heart.

The words would not come. If she told Aden she loved him, then what of her love for James? Would that mean it no longer mattered?

Chapter Seventy

August Lott still was not happy. He had prided himself in the fact that he was able to rid the town of Lott's Point of all but one of the prostitutes and all of the Negroes that did not belong there. He did not like the idea that Hallie was still living at Magnolia. He was puzzled as to how she existed without her boarders. August had no idea about the transfer of funds to Hallie, since the money was put into a bank in Pass Christian. Just days after her daughters had left, he presented her with a proposal to buy her property, which she promptly refused. Hallie knew that August would never be satisfied until she was far out of his sight.

"I do believe it is time for you to finally put an end to this, Hallie," Lola said. "Until you put him in his place, which is out of this town he will always be a thorn in your side."

"And how do you propose I do that?" Hallie asked.

"I have a plan. First I need to know where I stand with you. You have made no mention of whether you want me to stay at Magnolia or leave. Is it possible that you and I could live under the same roof for a time and maybe go beyond just being civil to one another?"

"I think it is quite possible, Lola. I suppose in my *other* life, I would probably never believe we would have a conversation. We would have been on opposite ends of the gamut. I would like you to stay. I cannot consider living here alone right now, especially since Aden has to be gone awhile. I am sure there are certain subjects that you and I will never be comfortable talking about and I know you are aware of which ones I mean. Now what is your plan?" Hallie asked.

"I know I can do it, Hallie, but I would have to count on you for some financial support. I have saved quite a bit of money and so had Polly, but it is not enough for what I have in mind. We have to do something about August if we want to make Lott's

Point our home or simply move away, which is what he wants. It is your decision, Hallie."

Hallie vacillated about telling Aden what she and Lola were up to. She did not want him to get involved. She agreed to be Lola's silent investment partner.

Hiding behind the curtain in her carriage, Lola waited until the store was empty before she made her entrance. Once inside she turned the bolt on the door and flipped the hanging sign to "*closed.*" August looked up from the counter where he was stacking boxes. "What are you doing in my store? Get out!" he growled.

"We need to talk, August," Lola said.

"We have nothing to talk about. Mrs. Simmons already refused my offer, so for a little while longer, you still have a home. Don't get too comfortable."

"What would you say if I made you a counter offer? How much do you want for this store and all of its stock?"

August let out a loud roar of laughter. "You must be joking. Have you gone crazy? What makes you think I would ever sell this store and if I did, why would I sell it to the likes of you?"

Lola drew circles on the counter with her gloved hand. "Several reasons cross my mind. Mail tampering, false taxation documents, the unfortunate death of poor little Gabriel. We have a witness, you know, who saw what you did and oh, there are these things, too." Opening her hand, August stared down at his handkerchief and money clip.

"You bitch! I knew you took them. You little bitch, give them to me. I will have you thrown in jail for theft and blackmail." He reached out and Lola pulled back her hand.

"Then does that mean you will not sell me your store?" Lola asked, backing up. She could see the fury in his face and his clenched fist. She had seen that look before on the faces of men in her presence and knew it was time to put a safe distance between herself and him. "Then I see no other recourse than to build another general store on this street. One larger, with finer merchandise and oh, cheaper prices. We'll see how loyal your customers are. Perhaps doing business with a former madam may not seem too distasteful. You have held the people of this town captive long enough, August Lott. Oh, and if you plan to retaliate against me or Mrs. Simmons, you may want to know that I have letters in the hands of good friends that are to be sent to the proper authorities with proof of your actions. We have stood by and watched you get away with murder, but not any more. Good day, Mr. Lott." Lola held her breath until she reached the door, half expecting an object to come hurling across the room at her head.

Lola made sure that by the time she was ready to leave town that afternoon, that quite a few of the residents were aware of her plan to build a new general merchandising store in Lott's Point. Although the women in the restaurant pretended not to be listening, their ears were perked to the conversation between Lola and the waitress whom she had just given a dollar tip. There was also the same conversation at the tailor shop, the pharmacy and the outdoor market. By the time she boarded her carriage for Magnolia, Lola was sure that August Lott was in a complete state of rage.

Lola was right. August paced the floor of his store flailing his arms and cursing aloud. He wanted to put his hands around her neck and kill her. She had put him in a position that no one had ever been able to put him in before. He was a master at covering his tracks and cunning when it came to getting what he wanted. His dealings during the war could have had him hung for treason, but the right goods in the right hands made him a rich man. He knew which people were easily intimidated and those whose loyalty a few dollars could buy.

August stopped and rubbed his head. So, he couldn't have Magnolia. Why didn't he leave it alone? It was Evan Simmons that told him that he would never own Magnolia and that was a challenge he could not let go. Now he was backed into a corner. If Lola did build a store in town, would his customers shop there? He knew the answer. His prices were inflated and most of his merchandise inferior. Even if he did get the law involved and accuse her of theft, it was petty compared to what she claimed to know. A long legal battle could be costly. And then there was Hilda. If she left him, she would expect a good deal of his money for his dalliance with Lola.

When Hallie revealed to Aden what Lola had done, he was distressed. Confronting Lola, he asked, "Why in the world would you do something like that? August will surely raise his ugly head again."

"Since Polly died and the other women have left, I have had a good deal of time to think about what I wanted to do. I know for sure the one thing I don't want to do is go back into my former profession. I like it here, Aden. If August accepts my offer, I will be killing two birds with one stone. He will be gone and I will have a new business."

"And you really believe people will continue to shop at that store, knowing that you are the owner?" Aden asked.

"Let's face it, I will always be a source of gossip and curiosity. The women will stay close to their husbands, but even if they have to come into the store and buy something just to fulfill their inquisitiveness, they will come," Lola commented. "Besides I plan on supplying the women in this town with items that will be desirable to them."

Shaking his head, Aden added, "I still think it is a bad idea. I just hope you know what you are doing."

"What about you, Aden? How much longer are you going to live in the stables and pretend to be a handyman? I am sure you have better things to do with your life."

Aden's voice softened. "I have to stay, Lola, I am in love with Hallie. I have to stay until she tells me she loves me."

Chapter Seventy-One

The news in town that August and Hilda had decided to move to Memphis and that Lola had bought Lott's Point General Merchandise Store was not to be believed until the day the new signs were posted. The original store sign was removed and replaced with one that read, 'Lola's General Merchandise and Emporium,' and two others that said, 'Sale' and 'New Merchandise.'

No one suspected that most of the new merchandise had been in Lola's possession for some time—gifts from the men she serviced over the years. Even though the saddles and buckets of nails remained in the back of the store, ornate perfume bottles, lace fans and cameo brooches were among the articles displayed in velvet, window cases. Polly's porcelain doll collection was put on sale for a fraction of their cost and her once oversized clothing that had been stored away in trunks, was turned into yards of bright-colored, silk and lace.

With nothing much to do at home while Aden was busy with building cabins for Ben and Hobart, Hallie found herself spending her days at the store. Staying out of view, she worked in the backroom with Nona. They wrapped bars of lavender soap in blue ribbons and tied rose petals in netted bags from material once covering Lola's risqué lingerie.

The women of Lott's Point were overjoyed with the new merchandise and prices, although none of them had the courage to enter the store until Ruth Toth stomped down the wooden sidewalk brandishing her umbrella and made her way through the group of women at the front windows. "Make way," she said. "I want to take a closer look at these things." Standing in the doorway, she motioned to the crowd, "Well, are you coming in or not?"

The customers still found it quite strange to be buying products from Lola Passion. Lola was still met with a cool reception when she spoke to them. Putting their purchases on the counter they would pay for them and quickly leave.

Lola had a private laugh at the oohs and aahs over the merchandise in the cases. What would the women of Lott's Point do if they knew they were buying articles that were sometimes used for payment for her services over the years?

Within two weeks Lola had hired Ruth Toth to help in the store and an accountant to take care of the paperwork that she found daunting. It was now her job to walk around the store dressed in her finest dresses and peddle a completely different type of merchandise.

"I suppose we should be going home," Hallie said to Nona as she put the last of the apples she had shined into a wicker basket on the counter. I haven't seen Aden all day. I want to fix him a nice supper."

Nona did not answer her. "You don't seem to like Mr. Woods very much, do you Nona? I always get the feeling that when he is around, you prefer to be somewhere else," Hallie asked.

"He be yer choice, Mizz Hallie."

"You see! That is what I mean. You never give me a straight answer when it comes to Aden. What is it that bothers you about him?"

"Secrets be like a weed, dah longer ya let dem grown, dah biggah dey git, til ya can't see dah truth no more. Den ya kin tell yerself dat the truth don matter cuz dah weed don covers it all up."

"I have no idea what you are talking about, Nona."

"Ask Mistah Aden. Dats all I gots tah say."

Nona knew she had hit upon a subject she should just let lay, but she was tired of pretending what Aden was doing was okay with her. It was Ben who told Nona about Aden while she sat with the others under an acacia tree on a warm evening. Ben was talking about when he worked on the plantation with Essie Woods. When Nona questioned him about Essie's last name being the same as Aden's, Ben told her that Aden was Essie's grandson. He told Nona the whole story. When Nona asked why no one had ever said anything to Hallie, they all shook their heads and said it was none of their business. They said that Aden was planning on telling her. Even Jasper agreed that Nona should not say anything to Hallie for fear that Hallie would be very upset with Nona for keeping the secret.

When they returned home from the store, Hallie put on her apron and began to wash the vegetables that Jasper had brought in from the garden. Aden arrived a few minutes later. Passing behind Hallie, he touched her back. She smiled at him. They talked while they prepared dinner together. Nona stood at the stove, tending the pots, trying hard to keep silent.

She waited until after supper to face him. While Hallie was clearing the table, Nona escaped out the back door and caught up with Aden as he carried empty buckets across the yard toward the well.

"Mistah Woods, I be wonderin' if ya could give me a minute?" Nona asked politely.

Sending the bucket down into the well, Aden stopped for a moment. "Of course, Nona, what can I do for you?"

"Ya kin be telling Mizz Hallie dah truth. It hurts mah heart tah know ya bin keeping things from her, things she should know."

"Who told you?" he asked in a startled voice. She had caught him completely off guard. "Was it Ben?"

"Be no mind who tell'd me. Be yer mind dat ya be keepin' it a secret all dis time and nows ya have Mizz Hallie comin round to you. Taint fair, Mistah Woods, ya be a colored man and all."

"Nona, you don't understand. I am not—"

She interrupted him. "Ya kin say what ya like, but ya be a colored man. Yer granny, she be black, yer momma, she be half-black. Ya got Negro blood in ya and ya was a slave jest like me and Jasper. Difference bein, me and Jasper, we knows our place. Slave or not, we knows our place and it ain't in dah white world. I love Hallie, like she be my own, but she ain't, and so's I keep mah place. She be white and ya and me, we be black. Ya gots tah tell her, Mistah Woods. She be needin' tah know. Ain't fair ya be hurtin' mah baby girl."

Aden started to say something but Nona put up her hand. "No need tah say nothin' tah me. Ya be talkin' tah Mizz Hallie. I ain't doin' too good lately. I gots a hurtin' in my chest dat tells me mah time ain't long. I gots to make sure before I goes dat Mizz Hallie be alright wid the world." She turned and slowly walked away.

Aden laid his head on the side of the well. He had dreaded this moment, but he knew he would have to tell Hallie.

Hallie opened the back door. "Are you coming with the water,

Aden? I want to wash the dishes."

"Yes," he answered. "I'll be right there."

Visibly shaken by Nona's confrontation, Aden slowly walked across the yard. Hallie waved to him out the window and he forced a smile.

How would he tell her? Would he tell her while they lay in each other's arms or while they sat quietly on the porch swing? Could he tell her when they played on the beach together, holding hands and dodging the waves, or while they walked in the meadow gathering wildflowers? Would it be while they sat quietly across from each other reading...or never.

"There, all done," Hallie said, putting the last dish in the cupboard. "What shall we do now? Would you like to go for a walk? You have been awfully quiet since supper."

Aden slowly rose from his chair. "Yes, a walk would be nice. Let's go down to the stable. I have something I want to show you."

Hallie chattered on about her day at the store unaware that her world was soon to be torn apart. He silently prayed that she would understand. He sat down and reached under the bed. Pulling a brown leather satchel from beneath his cot, Aden took out a parcel wrapped in brown paper. He untied the string and slowly unwrapped a photograph. Putting the lamp close to it, he handed it to Hallie.

"What is this, a present?" she asked.

"No, Hallie, it is a part of my past, a part I think you should know about."

She stared at the blurred images on the metal plate. There was an old colored woman seated in a chair, with a younger girl standing behind her. The old woman held a small boy on her lap.

"I don't understand, Aden. Who are these people? Were they your slaves?" Hallie asked in a puzzled voice.

"Whenever Mr. Miller, the plantation owner, had the photographer come to his estate to take family pictures, he would sometimes let some of the coloreds get their pictures taken too. The woman standing is my mother. The woman sitting is my grandmother. They were slaves on the Miller Plantation."

Hallie stared into the photograph. Perhaps her eyes were playing tricks on her. "You mean *they* were slaves," she paused, "These are colored women, Aden. And the little boy?" she whispered.

"The little boy is me."

Hallie sat down on the cot, still staring at the faces.

"My grandmother was born in Africa. She was taken against her will by a white overseer and became pregnant. Fifteen years later, my mother was handed the same fate at the hands of Mr. Miller, a white man. He was my father."

Hallie laid the photograph on the cot. What was she hearing? Words danced in her head, slave, colored, grandmother. She was shaking, a sudden chill invading her body. She abruptly announced, "I need to go."

Aden put his hands up, "Hallie, please, let me explain."

"No! Not now. I need to go!" She rushed passed him and began running toward the house. At the fence, she stopped, her breath coming in short gasps. She could feel her legs giving way beneath her. Aden caught up with her. His arms reached out for her as she began to fall. Hallie pushed his hands away. "Why? Why now, after all this time? What else have you kept from me?" He reached out for her. "Don't touch me! Leave me be," she cried as she struggled toward the house.

Covered by the night, Nona sat on the porch rocking slowly in the chair Jasper had made. She cooled herself with a wicker fan. She waited until Hallie was almost up the steps before she called her name. "Mizz Hallie."

Hallie stopped in front of her. "You knew, didn't you? Oh, Nona, why didn't you tell me?"

"Twernt my place, baby girl."

Hallie dropped to her knees and put her arms around Nona. "Oh, Nona, what am I going to do?"

Nona stroked her hair. "It be a mighty big problem. Ya gots tah pray to dah Lord for some answers tah dis one."

Chapter Seventy-Two

Morning. The earth turns. The sun comes up knowing what it has to do today. Today the magnolia buds will open into scented flowers. The ocean's tide once again will rise and fall and Nona's corn will grow a few inches taller. To most, morning is a welcome sight. To Hallie this morning held no wonder for her. It was another day filled with questions and emotions that imprisoned her mind.

Aden had come to the house twice every day, begging to see her. Choking back his own tears, he faced Nona, her arms crossed, guarding the stairs to his forgiveness.

"Mizz Hallie, she don want tah be seein' ya. Jest go on now and give her time."

Aden would leave only to return later on with the same plea.

On the third day he did not come. It was Lola who came to her room. "Aden is leaving," Lola said. "He came to the store today and told me he has his train fare and ship reservations secured. He is leaving tomorrow. You have got to see him, Hallie. You cannot let that man leave here without at least giving him time to explain. You owe him that. The man loves you. It wasn't his fault that those damn men couldn't keep their hands off those poor, colored women. Look, Hallie, he is an educated man. What was he supposed to do, come shuffling in here, bowing and scraping? He did what he thought was best for him and he is being punished all over again and that is all I am going to say." Lola finished, stomping her foot.

"I will see him," Hallie said in a barely audible voice. "Tell him to come here this afternoon."

Standing outside the parlor door, Hallie leaned against the wall trying to steady herself. He was Aden, now a stranger to her and he was waiting to unburden his soul.

He stood when she entered. He took a step toward her and stopped. "Thank you for seeing me, Hallie. I can only start by saying that I never meant to hurt you. I never meant to fall in love with you, but it happened and I will never be sorry."

"Stop! Please, Aden, don't make this anymore difficult than it already is. I am here to listen to what you have to say." She sat down in a straight-back chair, her hands folded in her lap.

Aden leaned against the mantel. "My grandmother's name was Kayudante. She was born in Africa. She was fourteen when she was taken from her home and brought to America. Her name was changed to Essie Woods."

He told her everything about his life at the Millers and then about the time he spent with the Bolts. He told her about Will and Mr. Glassman and his eventual freedom. "I had no idea who I really was, but I wanted something better for myself. "

He continued, telling her about his years in the shipbuilding industry and what happened to change his life at the beginning of the war when he found Lukas. Aden could see the pained look on Hallie's face. For the first time she spoke. "So, you have a son. Where is he?"

"I took him to Tahiti. He is there now, waiting for me to come back. After I found my grandmother I fully intended to go back, but I had to take care of Ben and the others. That is when I met you. My plan was to get them settled and then go back to Tahiti, but you were the gravity that held me here. I wanted to tell you. Each time we were together I wanted to say the words, but I was afraid that you would turn your back on me, and I was right."

"I don't know who you are anymore, Aden," she said softly.

He quickly crossed the room and knelt down before her. "I am the man who loves you more than life itself. We were happy together and we can be that way again. I am the same man you laid with and shared your passion. Come with me, Hallie. Come to Tahiti with me."

"My life is here, Aden. My children are here and soon I will have a grandchild. I have a house filled with memories that I do not want to leave."

"Be honest with me, Hallie. Are those the real reasons you won't come with me?"

She could no longer be strong. Tears fell down her face. "I trusted you. I have given you my mind and body and now I have to rethink everything I knew to be true. I don't know how to do that, Aden."

"Let it fall into place, Hallie. Think about our life together.

Give yourself time to forgive me. Just tell me you love me and maybe there is still a chance for us."

She looked away.

"You still can't say it, can you, Hallie? You still cannot tell me you love me." Aden rubbed his hand across his brow. "I have done all I can. I have begged and bared my soul to you. I cannot change your mind if you do not want me. I am sorry for that, Hallie. We could have had a good life together. I am going to leave now. There is nothing more I can say or do to make you understand." He slowly stood up. "Good night, my sweet, Hallie."

Folding the last jacket, Aden placed it into his open satchel. He gathered his shaving utensils and placed them in his knapsack. Taking one more look around the room, he retrieved the photograph of his family from the night table. He sat down on the cot and stared into the faces of those who loved him and endured the grief of life, the same grief he felt at this moment. A tear rolled down his face and spattered onto the images. His fingers pressed into the brittle tin until it began to break into pieces and fall to the floor. He buckled the satchel and left the stables.

The room was dark, yet it was morning. She hadn't changed her clothes or removed the pins from her hair. She had simply laid across her bed and prayed that she would make it through the night with one burning question running through her mind. If on the very first day she had met him, the light-skinned, well-educated man of mixed color who was living in her stables, what would she have done if he had told her of his Negro heritage? She knew what her answer would have been.

Lola opened her door. "I brought you tea and a message. Aden is leaving in two hours. Right now he is standing at the fence waiting for you. He said to tell you he would wait until ten o'clock for you. It is going to rain, so if you're going to him you best do it soon."

"What does that mean...he is waiting by the fence?" Hallie asked, her voice hoarse from hours of crying.

"It means he hasn't given up. It means that he loves you and doesn't want to go away without you."

Hallie slowly walked to the window and looked out toward the stable. A few feet from the grove of magnolias Aden stood looking up toward the house.

"What would you do, Lola?"

"I'd write a letter to each of my daughters and tell them I will be back in the spring and then I would go find some happiness with someone who loves me. But that is me. Of course, you and I are very different. You have accepted me for who I am, Hallie. Can't you do the same for him? Think about it. I'm off to the store. If you're not here when I get back, I'll keep the house running."

"There is a difference, Lola. You never pretended to be anything but what you really were. You knew your place. You were honest with me from the beginning," Hallie said, without turning away from the window.

"Yes, Hallie, I knew my place and it was my choice. What choice did Aden have?" She did not wait for an answer.

Hallie couldn't leave her post. Just knowing she could see him gave her time. Time reminiscent of the beautiful hours she spent with him.

The thunder off in the distance signaled the coming rain. Still he waited, standing by the fence, looking toward her window. Did he know she was there?

It was almost nine. The clouds were low, filled with the tears they would soon release on the field. She drank the remnants of her cold tea. The quiet of the room was broken by the sound of rain hitting the roof. She walked to the window. The droplets were now sheeting on the glass. Rubbing her hand across the pane she looked for him. "Aden, where are you? I cannot see you." Her heart began to race. Had he already left and walked out of her life forever?

Hallie gathered her skirt and ran from the room, down the stairs and out the door. As the rain drenched her clothing and blurred her vision, she ran. She ran across the yard, toward the fence, toward Aden.

"Aden, where are you? Aden!" She wiped the water from her face. She couldn't see him. She had waited too long and he was no longer there.

"I'm here, Hallie," he said, stepping out from under the trees. "I'm here."

She fell into his arms. The warmth of his body took away the chill from the cold. His kisses covered her face. He looked into her face. "You're not coming with me, are you, Hallie?"

"No," she sobbed. The salt from her tears mixed with the rain and washed down her face. "I'm so sorry, but I can't come with you, but I had to see you one more time. I needed to tell you goodbye."

"I knew that you would not come with me, Hallie, but I prayed you would change your mind." He took her face into his hands. "Let me look at you. I want to remember every inch of your face. I want to close my eyes and have you with me." He kissed her damp cheeks and held her close. There was no more time. "I have to go. I will never forget you, Hallie. I will wait for you the rest of my life. Think of me often, Hallie." He released her from his arms. He picked up his satchel and began to walk away. "Goodbye, Hallie."

* * *

Hallie closed the iron gate of the cemetery and walked down the path to the church. She pulled her shawl over her head as she stepped inside the door. Her footsteps echoed on the marble aisle as she made her way to the front of the church. Sliding into the pew, she knelt down and bowed her head.

This church held many memories for Hallie. She squirmed in these pews when she was a child, restless through the long sermons on Sunday morning. She knelt in these pews through the funerals of her father, Rebecca Vine, and Paul Dunn. She walked down this aisle when she married James and stood in front of this same altar while both of her daughters were baptized. Now three years after James' death, she once again came to St. Stephens to give her husband a proper burial. Hallie had hired two men to locate the makeshift grave where he was buried. His remains were put into a wooden coffin and brought to the church.

The muffled sound of soft-soled shoes interrupted her thoughts. A gentle hand touched her shoulder. Hallie looked up into the face of Father Mendoza. "That was a very nice service. Thank you for officiating, Father," she said. "I have waited a long time to make sure that James had a proper place to spend his eternity."

"You're welcome, Hallie. May I sit?" he asked.

Hallie slid over on the wooden bench. "Of course. The war still haunts us, doesn't it, Father?" Hallie asked. "Will it ever go away?"

"Yes, I know. It is still with us every day, Hallie. I hope

someday we can forgive and find peace." He was quiet for a moment. "Tell me news of your family. How are the girls doing?"

"I have a grandchild now, Father. Lydia had a baby boy. His name is James. She and her husband Stephen will probably be moving after he graduates from law school. I am hoping it is closer to me. Mary is doing well. She has one more year to go with her schooling. She is planning on returning to Lott's Point and opening a school for girls when she graduates."

"And you, Hallie, how are you doing?" he asked.

"I keep busy. I still have the house to maintain, and I have my share in the store which is growing by the month." She looked down at her hands. " I lost both Nona and Jasper this past year. I miss them both so much. Nona had a bad heart and after she died Jasper just seemed to wither away." She was quiet for a moment.

"What are you not telling me?" Father Mendoza asked.

"Why do you say that, Father?" she asked.

"I suppose I have been in this profession long enough to be able to tell when someone is hurting inside. I know burying James was not easy, but I still feel you have something else on your mind."

A single tear rolled down her face. "When I lost James, I felt like my world had ended. But he was gone forever and I had to pick myself up and go on even though my heart was broken. My heart had just begun to heal when I met someone else, Father. He could never take James' place, but he is a wonderful man. He is kind and articulate. He has a vulnerable side, which he is not afraid to share. My feelings for him grew over time and I found myself falling in love with him. Just when I thought I could commit myself to him, I found out that he had been keeping secrets from me, very important secrets. You see, Father, he is one-quarter African. He was also a slave at one time. When he finally told me, I turned my back on him. I sent him away," Hallie said, softly.

"That is a difficult situation, Hallie. I can understand that finding this out must have been quite a shock to you," Father Mendoza said.

Hallie wiped her eyes. "He deceived me. He never told me about his heritage. That was wrong."

"My goodness, Hallie, can you imagine how difficult it is to awake every morning and feel ashamed of what you are? To have to hide the truth from everyone, even those you care about, and just so you can have a decent life. I am sure telling you the truth must have been the most difficult thing he ever had to do." Father Mendoza shook his head. He put his hand on Hallie's shoulder. "I cannot tell you what to do, Hallie. Any decision you make is one you will have to live with every day of your life, but find some other reason to discount this man, other than the ones you have given me. If he was worthy of your love once, you may want to dwell on the reasons why he was important to you."

"Thank you, Father," she said. She rose to leave. "I will think about it. I must go now, my driver is waiting." At the door to the church, Hallie looked down the long aisle. The sun was making a pattern on the white marble through the stained-glass window just above the crucifix. Beams of light radiated toward her as if someone was reaching out for her.

As Hallie stepped into the carriage she advised the driver that she had one more stop to make before going to the train station.

Inside a white building on Dell Street, Hallie took her place in line. When it was her turn she stepped up to the desk. "Yes, I would like to inquire about a steamship ticket to Tahiti."

The End

About the Author

Originally from St. Louis, Marlene makes her home in Kentucky now. A mother and grandmother, Marlene has a wide range of interests including watercolor and oil painting, yet writing has always been her passion. That comes through loud and clear in her wonderful novels!

These novels reflect a genuine sincerity with very strong characters to which her readers can relate. It took Marlene a long time to start writing, but now she can't stop. The stories just keep on coming.

Also from Marlene…

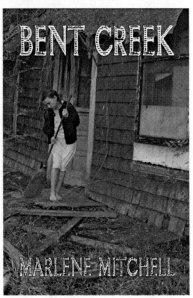

at www.blackwyrm.com

Also from Marlene...

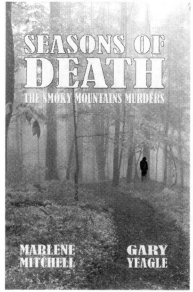

at www.blackwyrm.com

CPSIA information can be obtained at www.ICGtesting.com
Printed in the USA
LVOW131058311012

305244LV00003B/1/P